Bad Girl Magdalene

JONATHAN GASH

Allison & Busby Limited
13 Charlotte Mews
London W1T 4EJ
www.allisonandbusby.com

Hardcover published in Great Britain in 2007.
This paperback edition published in 2008.

A CIP catalogue record for this book is available
from the British Library.

10 9 8 7 6 5 4 3 2 1

ISBN 978-0-7490-7932-1

Typeset by Joseph Brown

The paper used for this Allison & Busby publication
has been produced from trees that have been legally
sourced from well-managed and credibly certified
forests.

Printed in the UK by
CPI Bookmarque, Croydon, CR0 4TD

JONATHAN GASH is the author of a number of crime novels. A qualified doctor specialising in tropical medicine, he is married with three daughters and four grandchildren. He lists his hobbies as antique collecting and his family.

Dedication

To my grandparents, Mr John and Mrs Mary Grant.

Thanks, Susan.

Chapter One

Magda decided to kill the priest in the Offertory.

No. That was wrong.

Kneeling there, Magda worked it out. Sister Paulina would never pass *that* for proper thinking.

Sister Paulina would say, 'Oh, praise the Lord! Six-One has woken up at last, but not *quite* sufficiently to provide us sinners with a *notion* of what she means!'

Then would come the most terrible phrase on God's sweet earth.

'*Miss* Six-One shall now explain *precisely*.' And in that terrible sing-song falsetto that set you stuttering until you broke down in tears, 'We...are...*wait...ing*!'

Magda felt tears start as the priest on the altar raised the chalice. She heard the altar-boy strike the gong and lowered her head, mouthing the Latin she did not understand. Then she tried, really did try, to get it right, because Sister Paulina was *wait...ing*.

'I vow to kill the priest,' she enunciated to herself slowly, making sure the words didn't come right out into the open where the other thirty-five, maybe forty, in the congregation would hear. 'I shall choose my time. Right now, I happen to be in St Saviour's Church, County Dublin, and the priest has just finished the Offertory in Holy Mass.'

She went over it, for clarity. 'I didn't mean I was going to kill Father Doran right here and now during the Offertory, no. I only decided during the Offertory that I am going to kill. And it is Father Doran up there who will do the dying when finally I get on with it.'

Right, she'd got it right! She felt so proud, kneeling there looking up at the altar while the priest did his sacred stuff. Sister Paulina would say to the rest of the class in St Joseph's in the Magdalenes, 'Finally Six-One has consented to tell us exactly what she meant! Applause, girls!'

And the rest of the class would clap and Magda would feel so proud at having got it right. Logic was Sister Paulina's god.

Magda had not meant she was going to kill him dead while he was doing the Offertory in Holy Mass, dear God, no. That would have been the most terrible sin. Sacrilege at least, she didn't wonder.

No, she would do it somewhere else, and not on consecrated ground like a church. Dear God! The very thought of killing a priest right here was beyond thinking. She would still need to work it out, how and where and that.

Father Doran came to the old folks' home where Magda worked. A chance right there! Given her by God as a kind of invitation, if she dared think about it.

Now here was a problem, though. Did you have to say Amen at the end of a decision like that? Like, 'I, who was Six-One at the Magdalenes, and am now Magda, vow to murder Father Doran,' and simply leave it there? Or was it right to say, so as not to offend God Almighty, 'I, Magdalene, vow to murder Father Doran. A...*men*'? With the Amen of course pronounced like Catholics always had to, Ayyyy...*men*, to show Heaven you were of the One True Faith and not a sinful Protestant, who would die for certain and fry in Hell for all eternity and bad cess to the lot of them. Protestants always said, English fashion, Ahhhh...men, and bad cess to *them* and all. She thought about it all through the Consecration, and finally thought, oh, well, God will know I'm honestly trying to say it properly, for He is listening hard to catch you out. Magda said a careful 'Ayyyy...*men*.'

There.

Done and dusted, as Mrs O'Hare said to Magda and the other cleaners at the St Cosmo Care Home for the Elderly when the sluice was straight about one o'clock.

Murder the priest, that same Father Doran as ever was, and then get on with being pure and holy like a good girl. She was sure it was that one and the same Father Doran, so the quicker she got on with her sworn solemn duty to murder him, the better.

Her own special Amen made it an oath, decent and truthful. Magda, loyal to the Faith, would carry it out. She didn't really know how, never having done anything like this, but a dutiful daughter of the Faith had to be faithful, or you went to Hell.

Now she had taken that mighty oath, Magda wondered about details. You would have to make it tidy like a hospital corner on a bed. (She was good at those.) You couldn't shirk an oath. God was up there witnessing. If it worked, then it would be a sign – *if* it worked. Then she would go to confession and see how little she could get away with telling the priest for it to be a true confession and not a false one, and be pure again.

Her only risk was dying before she got shriven, for then she would fry away for all eternity with them Protestants for company, and what was the use of that?

No. Do it quick, murder the priest, then rush to confession and she'd be white again after doing a bad black deed. The Magdalenes had taught her to stay a good girl. Whatever you did, don't be bad. Ever.

Ayyyy...*men*?

She went dutifully up to the altar rail for Holy Communion, and even looked up at Father Doran when he came along and gave her a Host by placing it gently on her tongue, the way she had been taught to receive the Body and Blood of Our Lord, and never to chew it (you went to Hell for all eternity) or to let bits of it to get stuck between your teeth (Hell, eternity again), and what if you then forgot what it was and spat it out (Hell, etc.).

She went back to the pew and knelt, and when her mouth was clear and the Host safely swallowed – she always peeled it from her palate using her tongue and then got it down in one, for safety from Hell – she waited for the *Ite, missa est* dismissal.

It being Sunday, she went home. Bernard would come about eleven o'clock, almost as soon as she got back, and do his shedding with her, and she would feel quite refreshed afterwards and pleased with life, and that she'd done right by everybody.

Six o'clock she would go on duty at the old folks' home. She'd work out how to go murdering the priest. It sounded simple, said quick.

* * *

You couldn't muck about with oaths. Hers was now sacred. She didn't really know why she'd not thought of it before. It made her feel quite proud, a sacred oath to herself.

But.

Lucy still kept falling to her death during every one of Magda's sleepless nights, over and over in the dark down the deep stairwell. Lord God Almighty, You know it, for You see everything. You were there. And the girl, Magda's friend, kept falling. Even when Bernard the Garda was doing his shedding in broad daylight in Magda's bed-sit, Lucy kept falling in the darkness of Magda's mind, even as Bernard was exploding in passion or whatever happened to a man when he spent. Night or day, Lucy kept on falling. You know it, Lord. And Father Doran must know it too. Except, does he remember how Lucy died? Does he remember who Lucy is? I do, Lord.

She walked from the church, crossing herself as she left. And I pray that afterwards, she thought nervously, wondering if she was being cheeky to God asking this outright, when the priest is buried and in his grave in the arms of Your tender mercies, Lord, please let Lucy stop falling and give her eternal rest in Heaven, and give her some lovely dinners with maybe even lamb chops, if it is Thy divine will, oh Lord.

I hope so. Please let the priest not suffer, but please let him know and understand why he had to get murdered. I think this quite essential, or he won't really understand and maybe it wouldn't count.

Maybe then Lucy will stop falling, she thought, and I shall be able to sleep.

Amen.

Chapter Two

The bed-sit took Magda by surprise every time she came back
to it.

This was her own place, where nobody else, *no body
else*, could go unless she said they could – and that was an
amazement. She had to wander round it every time, looking
at the walls as if fearing they would vanish and there she'd be,
back in the Magdalenes under prying eyes ready to punish her
for whatever she got blamed for.

Even now she walked slowly round, touching things. The
Baby Belling had frightened her at first. A cooker this small,
this personal, her very own that switched itself on whenever
she clicked its switch, that cooked whatever she put into its
miniature belly and slid onto its narrow grill? She felt sorry
for it. So servile. Then she thought, look, it's got its own place
where nobody can worry it. That made it her friend, and she
felt fond.

The wallpaper was ugly for sure, but its skewed roses and
deformed faded vine leaves soon became her ugliness, and it
too was an ally. The bed tilted in its springing, but that was

all right because it was hers. It let down from the wall and hid there during the day once Magda had folded its sheets away. Not her sheets, of course, and Mrs Shaughnessy checked them every week when Magda had to pay for old ones to be washed. The fridge was another friendship, devoted and yet busy. It kept mackerel best for Fridays, which was also sheet day.

Magda thought Mrs Shaughnessy guessed she couldn't count or read but the old lady never said anything about it. Magda felt truly happy there. It was like being a princess in her own tower.

Sure as God made Eire good and England bad, here came Bernard O'Fallon at eleven o'clock. She'd made him soda bread with thick Kerry Gold Irish butter that Bernard liked. She resented the price of things. Butter was a case in point. It cost more in Eire, she'd heard well-travelled folk say, than in England. Magda knew it was because the evil English made pure Irish butter cheap for Protestants and really dear in Eire. That was their way, always against Eire, whose farmers struggled might and main to make butter pure and wholesome, and there were the wicked English making fortunes for themselves. Everybody knew why, except Magda. She couldn't read or write so had to pretend in the supermarket and ask them to find things for her and take money for the shopping from her purse. She had to trust folk. Shamed because of her lack of the letters and the numbers and the counting, Magda longed for somebody else to take the blame. Sadly there was no one. It would have been grand to have had reading and numbers. Things were all the worse because she was truly wondrous about the meaning of words. She'd only to hear a word to use it right and get it exact every single time, her one saving grace. Her head must be like a whole dictionary inside, sure it must.

Bernard was splendid in his Garda Siobhana uniform. It thrilled her. She was ready for him and saw that he ate well. She did eggs for him mixed so no soft bits showed, and was glad to see him gulp it away good like a Christian. She watched him finish his tea, marvelling at the way God had made a man tender in the gullet so they couldn't swallow hot drinks like any decent woman could. Yet here was Bernard the Garda, the one male in the whole of Eire who could drink hot tea still a-bubble from the heat. The *only* man in Eire with a gullet like a woman. Would you think of it! Magda wondered at the ways of God. What had possessed Him to make one man with a throttle as leathery inside as a woman's? But God had purpose in His workings. His wonders were inscrutable.

After, she perched astride Bernard's legs, amazed at the bulk of the man, and helped him off with his uniform jacket. Judging when the man was ready caused her anxiety, especially at first. She'd had a hard time learning that, getting it so badly wrong she sometimes cried herself to sleep, even after he'd been doing it to her a good sixmonth. These were things the nuns never taught you at the Magdalenes. You had to learn it on your own, trial and error, which was a terrible way for people to have to get on. God, wasn't she nineteen years of age, if she could believe them Magdalene Sisters? Magda had no way of knowing if anything they taught you was true or not, not having the letters or numbers.

Another thing about…what it was a man did to a woman, though folk nowadays spoke that word even on TV plain as you like. It was impossible to pass a railway station stall without seeing naked people printed in different colours a hundred times. Her friend Theresa said it was the English who forced Eire into that bad way of thinking, for hadn't she the proof in the TV programmes shown scandalously every night on Irish TV, the RTE, sometimes even speaking the words aloud bold as brass? Theresa knew somebody who'd talked with somebody's wife's cousin who could prove that the English were determined to corrupt Eire like they were themselves, by buying up all the magazines and TV stations in the land to spread sin.

Her problem for now was being still while Bernard was doing it, and trying to think ahead and see if she could predict what he'd want in a minute, before or after he did his explosion, or whether he'd want her to get going. That was what he said, 'Get going, Magda.' She had then to start moving. A list of things put down in order would help, what you had to do, then if she could read it might ease her mind. The libraries should write it down for everybody, or the Dail in Dublin parliament, so the Taoiseach could say it was right and proper and get it stamped by the holy Imprimatur so people could learn it. Also, move how exactly? The first time he'd given her that gruff command, she was stricken in alarm, and even tried to ask it right out, 'How exactly, bonnie?' but he'd gripped her and shoved her forward and back, forward and back. She hadn't known until then that some men had kindness, whatever the degree of scald-resistant leatheriness of their gullets. Bernard had kindness. He'd shown her how to move when he said to. The relief of that!

He gave her money afterwards, sometimes, but it was nothing to do with her letting him do it, because they were friends. And he was upset quite often lately, which was new to her because she'd had no idea men ever got upset. It was the sort of thing you didn't think they bothered with, but Bernard was, more times than he let on. When it happened, he would have shiny eyes, like tears tried to escape. Now, a woman simply let go, which was good because it meant that the tears weren't wasted at all, just doing what God intended, to leak the sorrow there inside that caused them in the first place. That way – God had worked it out – the tears carried away the sorrow, at least enough of it to get you back on your feet so you could make do until something happened that made the day manageable.

No, Bernard rose from doing it to her, and when he went to wash or get himself smart in his Garda Siobhana uniform to go on duty, she noticed he'd washed his face and his eyes were dry and level again.

But for the moment, there she sat while he rocked and the pressure on her thighs was beyond belief, so bulky was he. She always wondered why God made a man so massive and the woman less. It was part of God's inscrutable design for mankind, the man heavy, the woman light. Sometimes, too, she started to feel heat, and even start to move with, against, with, against, Bernard's thrutchings and sometimes she too grunted, feeling urges she never would have believed. She told of them in confession, of course. Bernard also shouted when he did his explosion, threshing and his mouth open like a cavern and she had to cover his gaping gob with a hand to stifle his noise.

It was exhausting, but God had it planned all right, because what if they never even got tired and kept on and on, what would come of civilisation then with everybody staying at it all the time and never going to work? The wondrous works of God were unknowable, yes, but some of them weren't as inscrutable as all that, or where would we be? Bernard slept heavily after spending. She often wondered too at the stuff he spilt, what it looked like, what would it feel like between your fingers, did it have the colour and how many little creature things were inside it, that sort of thing.

She'd heard girls talking, once at the Magdalenes when she was in the laundry duty with her friend Lucy (the same one who kept falling every night since she died in the dark stairwell), who was always called by her number, Three-Two, because the nuns didn't say names much of girls who had no parents. One of the other girls said in a whisper, 'I saw it once. There's an English word for it, jism, didn't you know? It's sort of sticky cream.' It had been the talk of the whole place for days and days until they got overheard by one of the nuns and the whole place got docked the next meal.

Magda wished she'd not thought of that, for Bernard was starting to flail almost, maybe another ten or twelve pushes and he'd be done for this time, and she liked that bit because then she relaxed knowing she'd done her womanly duty. She then started to harbour secret feelings and they sometimes rose and even engulfed her so she too sort of jerked and grunted and even, sometimes but not often, flailed in a kind of lesser way that was surely sinful but fulfilling.

But today thoughts of Lucy made Magda stay meek and motionless while Bernard, who today mercifully stayed mute and didn't give his gruff command for her to do one of them quick turn-overs she had to sometimes do at the last minute, gave his loud groan (Magda's hand swiftly over his mouth for Mrs Shaughnessy on the landing) and flailed like a cable in a storm.

This time, he continued spending into her somewhat longer than usual, which Magda didn't mind because what your man did was of a pattern. He held her in a grip so punishing she could not get her breath going until he eased, and she was glad to inhale and work out how she felt. She knew Bernard was not being different, just vehement, so that was all right, staying within the tramlines of his carry-on. It did not mean new behaviour, no. That would worry her. Magda naturally wanted the creature to stay all of a sort, fixed in the things he did and said, however strange, and what on earth could be stranger than this that he kept doing every single time?

Magda often wondered how a man learnt this. She thought, I mean, it can't simply be that they tell each other what to do, can it? For that would get about, folk would hear and they'd get a right royal thrashing from the priests and the Gardai too, and questions would be asked in the Dail and the Taoiseach would go mental over the terrible state of morals in Eire, and it might even get into the holy papers.

No, Bernard stayed the same. It was just that Magda watched out for switches in his mood, for moods can be anything. If it meant he moved out of her ken, away from her understanding, then the mood was bad and dangerous – never mind how or why, it was definitely to be abhorred. If he stayed in his tramlines, then he was all right and she was safe in her mind. It was the way God made each and every one of us, even the sparrows. The Bible said that, so there you go.

This time, though, she felt his behaviour was a little changed. It wasn't just the long spillage he'd just come to an end of, no. It had something to do with the thinking in his brain, and that meant he might say it out or keep it to himself. In either case, it was nothing she'd done bad or wrong, just that he wasn't quite what she could now predict as safe and tramlined.

Fine, he had a wife, and had two children fathered of his very own, which was all right because marriage was immutable. People had to stay married for life, except where the English had their foot in the door to start everybody divorcing like mad, being Protestants and therefore evil by nature like Communists. No, nothing to do with her, just something in himself. Magda couldn't help wondering if it was to do with those occasional silent, no-crying tears he kept to himself that she was never to notice at all. That might cause Bernard's behaviour to change, which would never do because that would be her fault. He wouldn't leave, no, she was certain of that.

She never helped him to dress up in his fine gear afterwards. She often wondered about that because when he'd had his meal she usually, unless he was in a desperate hurry, had time to help him take off his jacket. But afterwards? No. Was it that he felt he had to be careful and show no sign so he'd not leave traces of Magda others might see? Something simple like that. He was going on duty and had to know where everything was – pen, watch, notebook, a set of forms and a small telephone thing he didn't want her ever to touch at all.

'You're a fine man, bonnie,' she told him. A man was an admirable thing despite his ferocities, which was probably why God made Himself male and left the other things to females or nuns.

He was checking himself in the mirror. 'I wish to God I was, Magda.'

'Oh, y'are, Bernard, a grand sight.'

'I wish all men were, Magda.'

And he sat down, which was a rare thing for Bernard to do after he'd done it and dressed, because usually he was out of the door with her listening on the landing for Mrs Shaughnessy, who had ears like a bat and a voice like a Liverpool ship's foghorn.

'Oh, all men are made—'

'Stop that.'

He said it in his Garda voice, which meant she was to say no more until this was over and done with. She knew it was that silent trouble come back again, best cleared up before he left.

'Sorry, bonnie.'

He stayed with his fingers linked, his arms on the rests of the wooden chair, his knees apart and staring into the fire, which she always made when she knew he was going to call. It was as important as feeding him, this fire, and warmth in her place while he did the thing. She had only seen him adopt that posture once before, when he had found somebody dead in a garret, though it was natural causes only and caused no real fuss at the Gardai station, where he had to fill in a stack of forms causing him trouble for days.

He said, eyes into the firelight, 'I passed a man today.'

'Ah.' Here it was, the threatened silence coming out.

'I knew him.'

'Did you now?'

'Yes.'

She knew to stay quiet, not busy herself about the place nor even take his hand like felt natural. He didn't offer more. Into her mind came the terrible sight of her friend Lucy. Falling into a dark stairwell was a fearsome thing only God could explain, if He could bother with Magda wanting to understand so terrible a death.

'I knew his name, once.'

'Ah.'

Magda felt resentment against educated folk. They could read, have whole sentences they might say at times like this so the man would be pleased. If she had the letters and the writing clear in her mind, her words would soothe the man and he would be made well, which only went to show how fine it was for girls who were made educated and how hard it was for those who weren't. Times like this she almost hated educated girls, trying to be better than God made them and mimicking the English.

'He was but a lad when I caught him.'

'You caught him,' she said, soothing away, the best voice she could manage.

After a time he said, 'He was on the town hall windows. Broke one.'

'Broke it, y'say.'

'Broke it. We took him in, me and Gallagher. You don't know Gallagher. He was from Ballybrack. Had two sisters and a brother who played in the hurling.'

'Ah, the hurling team.'

'Because he broke the window, they sent him to the Maltebior.'

'Ah, there.' She felt blank.

'The fishing school. It's in Sors.'

'Sors.' She'd heard tales of a terrible place by that name, a place of suffering children.

'He was a lad of seven, maybe eight, and he'd broken a window.'

Magda had never heard of it, thanks be to God from the way Bernard was staring, with firelight setting his gaze glinting like he was seeing some hellhound.

'He can't be more than twenty-one now, mebbe twenty-two. He's a broken man, Magda. He looks like to die.'

'God help the poor soul.'

'He walked stooped, hands in his pockets, like wanting to beg but hadn't a hope of getting a copper from any passing soul.'

'What a shame.' Magda could keep this up all day long, and night too if she had to, lacking anything else for the man.

'He didn't recognise me, thank God.'

'Ah, he didn't.'

'He didn't look, either. He just saw my uniform.'

'Ah, your uniform.'

'He shrank away, Magda. Crossed to the other side of the street. He looked hardly able to walk.'

'Poor man.'

'He'd drink taken. His trousers were stained, like he slept in his clothes. And looked a hundred years old.'

'God help the man.'

'Sure, Magda.' Bernard stood and straightened. 'God help the man, for sure as death we didn't. I didn't. The magistrates didn't. The Church didn't. And they didn't at Maltebior.'

Magda knew she should have asked (if he was different somehow or, maybe to the point, *she* was) why he didn't call after the disturbing man in that street who seemed to have been made such a wreck. She might have said, 'Oh, bonnie, why for goodness' sake did you not think to perhaps invite him round to your house for afternoon tea, or convey him to your club at St Stephens Green, perchance?' like they did in the grand TV stories she was addicted to and which she couldn't ever get enough of during the nights she stayed awake with her tiny TV set watching black-and-white reruns to stay awake so she needn't dream of Lucy forever falling. But Bernard would have thought she had taken leave of her senses, which she would have, to talk to him like that. And anyhow in those stories the gentlemen were always called Sir Willoughby Maltravers or something, and she would be Mistress Euterpe Devonish-Fanshaw with servants and carriages and all and visiting squires who left cards on silver trays carried by servants.

No, that kind of talk was not for her, nor for Bernard. Not because, she instinctively understood, we are Irish in Dublin, but because things come from the past in each of their lives.

Like, Magda knew, her friend Lucy, and you didn't have the right to say things out loud.

This explained the fault of Eire itself, the green sod where all that was natural and holy lay. Eire's great pretence was that dark events were in the past. If there was trouble with the Taoiseach's rivals in the Dail, then it was the fault of some famine long gone. Everybody knew that. The greater the traffic hazards, it was the fault of the English who'd left streets deliberately tangled so they always got in a stew round Trinity College and caused horrific road accidents. If an Irish horse lost in the Grand National, why, some royal duke in England had nobbled the poor beast so it fell at the last fence before the run-in, despite fervent prayers for its success at the Cathedral in Liverpool. Past events lurked. All were evil. Blame elsewhere had to be found, logic as ever was, in politics everybody could talk of safe and sound and know they would get agreed with.

She herself looked straight into the fire. Sometimes, if he wasn't sorrowing, she would take out a breast and put it to his mouth and he would chomp on it quite like a barn, poor lamb, and he would say nothing until afterwards when he'd give her a curt thanks and get up and check his appearance once more. Not vanity, understand, just checking.

He left soon after that, and Magda knew the trouble, whatever had caused it, was over and Bernard would be right as rain. She felt so relieved. People had tramlines to guide their behaviour, and that was that. Stay in them old tram rails, you went in the right direction and life stayed fine. She decided she might say a prayer for Bernard maybe about teatime, before she had to get ready to go to work at the St Cosmo Care Home. There was still time for a bath, though she hated washing man-scent off her. Its possession was a secret she carried about for the rest of the day, and she knew she wore that knowing smile that had the merit of irritating her friend Oonagh from Armagh, who was a little older than Magda but not half the experience, having been fostered out to an aunt when she was ten and raised like a good Christian. That had undoubted merit, but didn't get the chance to irritate and madden friends the way a more varied life could.

Chapter Three

The old folks home was called the St Cosmo Care Home for the Elderly. Magda had worked there, not since she'd left the Magdalenes, but as a result of meeting Faith. It was when Faith O'Banyon came looking for a job after failing the nursing course at the hospital. Magda had been cleaning the ladies' toilets and Faith had come in. It changed Magda's life.

Faith was irreverent. She'd been doing her hair after complaining about the state of the loos. It was one of the many extra jobs Magda did at the paper-packing firm where she was sent as an out-worker among the older girls at the Magdalenes, who'd all finished their schooling and had to go out to work from there.

'Who's supposed to do these loos out?' Faith demanded on that fateful day that changed Magda's whole life. The paper factory was noisy. Faith had to shout.

'Me,' Magda remembered bleating in a panic.

'There's no loo paper.'

'I'll get some!' Magda rushed to get the cupboard door open.

She straightened to find Faith standing watching her, cool as a cucumber.

'What's the matter with you, for God's sake?'

'Nothing! Please don't tell!'

But there was loo paper still in the loo Faith had just used, only not very much left on the roll.

'Look at the state of you, girl!'

Faith let Magda scurry past. Once inside the loo Magda didn't know what to do with the new roll, because there was still a bit on the old roll and there was never a place to put the new one.

'Only we're not allowed.' Magda was close to tears. This was bound to get back to the nuns, and Sister Philomena would have her walloped sure as God made everything.

'It doesn't matter.'

'They'll get angry. Please don't complain.'

'All right,' Faith said, though Magda didn't know she was Faith back then, her being a stranger and just calling in.

'Oh, thank you, thank you.'

Faith stayed still, observing Magda's dilemma over the toilet paper, and said, cool, 'Are you that scared?'

'No!' Magda's voice rose almost to a shriek. She glanced guiltily at the door and said in a whisper, 'No, no. I'm sorry for doing wrong.'

'What's your name?'

'Magda. Magdalene really.'

'Last name?'

'I have no last name. They say I'm Finnan, because I was taken in from somewhere by there.'

'Don't you know?'

'Not really. I was Six-One at school in the Magdalenes.'

'Six-One, Magda Finnan?'

'Yes.'

'You work here?'

'It's where I...' Magda's problem was words. That was why she longed to read but couldn't. She didn't want to tell this new worker from outside anything at all, from shame. All the time she was trying out new words, every moment of her time. But Faith's question needed answering. Where I belong? Where I live? Where I stay? Where I am? 'Here,' she finished lamely.

'Right.'

'Is it to tell on me?'

And Faith smiled. It was so lovely. 'No, Magda. Not to tell. I never tell. Just to remember your name, OK?'

'What for?'

Magda stared at this apparition, knowing she would be trying to recall every stitch the girl wore, every turn of the head, every bit of her features and how she walked and the things she said, the minute she'd gone. Magda was always like this, for whoever she saw might even be some relative, and she had had none right from the minute she was born and taken to the Magdalenes.

'Nothing at all, Magda Finnan. Just friendly.'

And Faith left. Magda was so baffled by the interlude that she actually went back into the loo Faith had used and stared at the place as if it had changed somehow, or thinking it might be different from all the other cubicles in the place. It was as clean as Magda could make it. She was always good at cleaning, always had been, had to be because of the domestic supervisor, Sister Philomena, who got reports back from the factory.

That was how Magda met Faith O'Banyon. And three weeks later a letter came from Sister Stephanie, supervisor of the St Cosmo Care Home for the Elderly, and on the recommendation of ex-Nurse Faith O'Banyon, who suddenly was transformed from stranger into long-lost cousin, Magda Finnan was changed from part-time paper-packer in paid employment to paid employee of the St Cosmo Care Home for the Elderly. It was to be on probationary trial. Magda had to get Faith to read it out to her, and tell her the address and how to get there.

The switch was an ordeal because Magda had no idea what was happening. At first she thought it was a punishment. She couldn't get the hang of the special instructions given her by Sister Superior when she went on trial. It was only when Faith explained she was to stay free and lodge in a nearby block of bed-sits, where she would have her own special place all to herself, that she stopped thinking of the change as a dream.

Two months later, when the probationary period had expired, Magda realised for the first time she was free.

Life changed for ever. She got registered as a legitimate employee and was paid, working a month in hand as Faith called it.

Faith was irreverent, and tried to get Magda to be the same. They kept up the falsehood of being cousins, but that business went by the board after a while and Faith told Magda to forget it, because it had only been a trick to spring Magda. Faith was full of slang words, 'spring' being one, meaning to cheat people and get away if you didn't like them. Faith left soon after, never to be seen again. 'Going to England,' she said. 'I've had enough of getting told off.' She said ta-ta, and went.

When she realised, Magda wept for three nights running, for she'd never had a relative all to herself before, and now she was back to being on her own without another living soul.

It was there, after a while, that she met Bernard.

* * *

It was terrible busy when Magda got on duty.

She had difficulty with her housemaid's cap. So much frill and every edge to be ironed, like the hems in petticoats that needed ironing really flat though never to be seen by mortal eye, of course, because if it wasn't ironed everything sagged and didn't lie true. Sister Stephanie – of whom Magda was mortal scared, she having once supervised the Magdalene Sisters of the Third Order Regular, where Magda had been worked and taught over in Sandyhills – always insisted on everybody being properly turned out, which only went to show rumours spoke true.

Other girls tried continually to get away with it and skimped on the ironing, only to be found out and given a hard time by Sister Stephanie. And one girl in particular, a Mrs MacLehose, who had five children, said in quiet asides to Magda, 'and no more of them children, thank God, knowing what I know now,' which was most terrible indeed and might surely send her down the chute to Hell when she died, God rest the poor screaming soul heading for eternal damnation. Worse, when discovered talking like this and Sister Stephanie standing there like the wrath of God with her hands tucked inside the folds of her sleeves about to deliver rebukes that would freeze the heart of Cromwell himself, Mrs MacLehose would sniff and say, 'Sister, I'm a busy woman and I've work to get on with, so if you've quite finished I can earn me merit with the Good Lord and mebbe store up some indulgences with Him, seeing I do my very best and me with my arthritis and all that comes from slaving for my children.' And, while the whole world froze in horror at such sledging right back into the very face of the staff supervisor nun, Mrs MacLehose would say, casual as you like, to somebody standing like Lot's Wife in the Bible (who turned into a block of salt when she looked back at Sodom and Gomorrah being crushed under fire raining down from Heaven), 'Would you pass that next pile, Magda, so I can get on instead of standing here all day dreaming.' And should Magda or whoever it was not move fast enough, she would give out a rebuke of her own, even in such a terrible plight: 'Well, girl? Will you help instead of standing there with your two arms the one length?' And that would set everybody scurrying and Sister Stephanie would march away with her lips set in that thin line that meant somebody soon was going to catch it. It was always somebody else, never Mrs Jenny MacLehose.

And that evening after dinner, Magda stole a tablet, to help herself kill the priest. Not that Father Doran doubtless had some good in him somewhere, for who could judge another person? It was written in the Good Book, if you could read, that you hadn't to judge somebody 'unless ye yourself be judged' or something that way on.

Once she got started, Magda stole the tablets slightly different every time because you couldn't be too careful. This was her way:

Old Mrs Borru had to take two little white tablets each day, and everybody in the whole wide world knew it was so, like some rule St Benedict himself had laid down. You heard old people always saying to each other through the livelong day, 'Is it time Elsie had her tablet now?' and somebody else would say, 'Elsie? No, not yet. That comes at eight o'clock after supper.' And somebody would add, 'She took this morning's one because I was there and that man we all like was reading the news.' And then everybody would go on about who liked the weatherman on RTE and who hated that girl who forever was showing off with her posturing and smiling so fetchingly in front of the TV weather map of rain over the Irish Sea and saying how the ferries from Stranraer were going to be delayed again. In fact, Magda too hated that weather girl, but there you go, because hate was a sin and you had to do penance for a venial sin, venial being only small, because the pretty weather girl really was horrid and thought too much of herself.

Back to the tablets. They were little and white and mortal strong and came in a little dark bottle. There was a theory that dark-bottle pills and potions stayed effective, that in transparent glass they degenerated and lost strength. Sister Stephanie said so.

That particular day, old Mrs Borru spilt the tablets, a few lying white and shining on the carpet. Magda had already hoovered.

'Goodness, Mrs Borru. You've dropped your tablets,' Magda said.

'What, my dear?'

The old lady could hardly see but spent her days watching RTE. Whatever was on did for her, even football and those endless snooker games and athletics. She even hummed along to any old music, even if it was from radio programmes in the next room. Sometimes she seemed deaf, other times she had hearing like a bat.

'Your tablets. I must call one of the nurses.'

Magda rushed to find Nurse Maynooth, who was on duty that particular day, but of course Murphy's Law struck and she was nowhere to be found, so it was Magda herself who scraped the tablets up and put them back in the bottle, all the time worrying herself stupid that they had no power in them now they'd been dirtied on the carpet, though she herself had vacuumed exactly that spot earlier. I mean, she argued with herself, what if the tablets lost their vigour from touching the Wilton pile? It might be so. And how like the English to make a fine carpet that had a secret power of sucking the tablets' force out instead of leaving them strong as ever.

'No need for that, dear.'

Mrs Borru hadn't the faintest notion who Magda was. She said the same thing to the removal men when they'd had to take away one of the old beds that kept falling through. Mrs Borru thought one of the men was her husband and tried telling him off to bring his van round to the side door and take the bed out through the kitchen, though of course the poor man didn't have a van at all and wasn't her husband.

'Will the tablets be all right still, Mrs Borru?'

'Leave off your worry, dear. It doesn't do, a girl young as you.'

Which was really kind of Mrs Borru. And maybe secretly she too was scared of the nurses or the nuns raising a fuss and telling her off. So that day Magda let the matter go, yet anxiously waited for the nurses or the nuns to come round counting everybody's tablets and, finding one or two missing, blame Magda saying she'd spilt them and had left Mrs Borru to take the blame.

She later told Sheilagh, who was almost as casual as Faith, because Sheilagh truly was going to be a nurse, trained and registered, when she got her exams, her father (a real live father) being an accountant with a head full of the numbers. And Sheilagh laughed.

'You are a hoot, Magda,' she said. 'Dear God in Heaven. Who has time to go counting tablets already in bottles with the pharmacy stamp already there on the side with all them initials and letters after their name?'

'What if there's one lost, though, Sheilagh?'

'Then it gets sucked up in your hoover machine, and gets thrown into the Pit of Despond.'

Magda didn't know what the Pit of Despond was, and wondered if she ought to search in the mounds of dust and rubbish to look for Mrs Borru's tablet. She learnt, asking Sister Stephanie as casual as you like about it, that it was a place like Hell that an English Protestant called Bunyan once wrote about and not to bother her head. Sister Stephanie was displeased with Sheilagh for mentioning that to Magda because many girls were impressionable. The upshot was, Magda was mighty relieved and thankful there would be no counting of tablets or speculating what if one tablet got itself missing.

Which set Magda wondering, because on the bottle there was said to be a stark warning that nobody, nobody, was to take the tablets except as prescribed by a doctor. They were poison. Sheilagh said warnings were on every medicine bottle, and that was what the letters meant.

Now, poison set Magda thinking of Lucy, and the murder she had to be doing fairly soon.

The one thing Magda remembered was, there was a time when Lucy hadn't fallen at all. They were both back there in St Joseph's at Sandyhills, in the Magdalenes, and it hadn't yet happened.

Part of Magda's sorrow and determination to kill Father Doran came from the feeling that, if God Almighty Himself, or maybe some fairy, like in those pantomimes at Christmas that Magda had seen on RTE TV (men actors dressed as old women and girls dressed as young men and swaggering and talking like they were saying poetry and everybody laughing and shouting back from the audience) offered Magda the chance of saving Lucy from falling by putting the clock back to those times when Magda and everybody was still back there in the Magdalenes, Magda knew she would kneel and say, 'Thanks, God, for the offer, but I could never go back there in a million years ever again, so ta, but no. I accept that Lucy would stop falling if You put the clock back, but I couldn't bear it. In fact, I'd be the one to start myself falling down the centre of a massive stairwell to certain death and burning for ever in Hellfire, sure as You made apples.'

So Magda was a murderess in her heart even before she recognised Father Doran saying Mass that day in St Saviour's Church, for she would never live her horrible childhood over again, not even in order to save Lucy dying over and over the long nights through. So it was right that she, Magdalene Finnan, if that was her name, should be punished by them terrible dreams.

And in the next spell of afternoon shift of duty at the St Cosmo, Magda pinched a tablet from the brown bottle and stored it in a paper tissue in her pinny pocket, as if it was no more than a paper handkerchief she intended to use for hygiene around the old folks, in case she sneezed.

She kept it wrapped for darkness in an old Bisto Gravy bottle, well washed and dried in the oven at the St Cosmo kitchen, so as not to wash out any of the poison power in the tablet. It stayed back in her bed-sit like it was simply an empty gravy bottle, and became a slowly growing store of poisonous white tablets over the weeks.

By the time she made sure it truly was Father Doran by going to sit at the front in St Saviour's, she had several tablets. Now she was certain. Tomorrow, she vowed to steal another one.

She became skilled at the art. She made sure she called Nurse Maynooth to see next time Mrs Borru spilt her tablet bottle over the side of her bed. It was during a TV Old Tyme Music Hall from Leeds in England, where they sang and all dressed up in old time clothes like in the time of Queen Victoria, bad cess to the country that was condemned to perpetual excommunication by the Holy Father himself. Magda pointed out to Nurse Maynooth that the old lady seemed to have fewer tablets than there had been this very morning.

Magda didn't tell it in confession, not all of it. She simply said she had been careless with the tablets of some old folk where she worked, though she made sure she hoovered everywhere 'after having a careful look under the beds and everywhere,' and the priest always gave her three Hail Marys and one Our Father for penance. That was as far as Magda ever got of a Saturday when she confessed about the gathering of poison tablets ready to kill Father Doran. Indeed, Magda had a sense of fair play so strong that she once went to Father Doran to confess that she had 'tried to make sure that the old people's tablets were always counted exactly right,' adding she wasn't sure for they sometimes spilt them.

He reassured her, which was really kind. Magda was careful, however, not to push her luck by going to him for confession every Saturday, no. She went instead to Father Culkin and even Father Duddy, who scared her stiff with his black swarthy hair and his loud voice, and whose black hair even seemed to grow down to his finger nails like a gorilla's.

'You'll turn to stone standing there, Magda,' Sister Francesca said crossly one day after Magda had stolen another tablet, successfully, she thought, until much later after she'd done the deed, 'when I want you to be scouring the kitchen swill out for the refuse collectors.'

'I'm sorry, Sister Francesca.'

'Then get on instead of being sorry and you won't need to,' Sister Francesca gave back, sharper than ever that day, though usually she never gave much blame around. 'There's one old lady worse than ever, and her husband's come in sicker than herself tonight.'

A grand opportunity came to take more than one poison tablet from another old folk's bottles three days later. It was easy. Magda pretended to count out the whole bottle of white tablets (though she couldn't be sure it was the same poison as the little white things she had a store of in the Bisto Gravy bottle back in her place) after a lady died. She counted the tablets, all three sorts, out with utmost care after Nurse Maynooth and Mrs Jenny MacLehose had been told by Sister Stephanie to clear out the bedside cupboard because they were about to perform the last offices and wash the body. She couldn't do the counting, of course, just pretended.

She left the small bottles, all three in a row, on the bedside locker, and Nurse Maynooth said well done and even Sister Stephanie said it was good to see one of the girls being so careful, as she took the bottles of tablets away.

And Magda saw her later washing the tablets, and one small bottle of sticky cough medicine from the stock cupboard, down the sluice sink without even counting any or measuring the sticky cough medicine, which was a grand relief because it meant Magda's prayers were being answered so far. This was wondrous because it meant that one or even two tablets from any of the old people's bottles would not be missed, most probably.

So Magda's store in her room hidden behind her one-grill Baby Belling cooker, went up gradually.

Lucy kept falling during the nightmare, and it was all Magda's fault because she was to blame.

She sometimes imagined that same questioning, with God saying, 'Magdalene Finnan, if that's your name, what if I, in My infinite mercy, allowed the clocks to go back to the time before Lucy fell to her death? How about it? What would you say? Yes or no?'

And Magda knew she would answer, 'No, thanks, Lord God. I couldn't bear to go back among the Magdalenes, not even for that.'

'You sure, Six-One?'

'Yes, Lord God. I'm so ashamed. I'm so sorry, Lord God, but I'm not up to much. Forgive me, I pray.'

'Then it's down to you that Lucy, your friend, keeps falling in that old nightmare. Just you remember that, OK?'

'Yes, Lord God,' Magda in this particular dream kept saying back, kneeling and keeping her head and eyes cast down so she didn't stare Him in the Face and see His agony at her backsliding nature.

It was all the more piteous when she kept remembering how God had died on the Cross for her sins, and here she was adding to things and making it all worse.

'Yes, Nurse Maynooth,' she said again to something, and got down to cleaning the sluice.

The priest came that evening to give Extreme Unction to a dead old folk, and the whole of the St Cosmo was deathly quiet. The old people were shut in and kept themselves quiet and sombre as if working out who was oldest and who was next.

The store of tablets, by innocent planning and meticulous taking of chances, grew until finally Magda had almost plenty of little white tablets, plus a few pinkish larger ones, and a variety of small coloured oval jobs. And she knew it would soon be time to judge when she was ready. In a way it was sad. In another way, it wasn't anything of the kind.

Chapter Four

The first time Magda did it with Bernard the Garda was the time he saw her back to her room in the girls' resident block the day an old man called Mr Brannigan died. He bled from his mouth and Magda had the awful task of cleaning up the mess. There was blood everywhere, and his sheets and blankets were soaked dark brown, very little of it looking like the red of her month and that the cowboys and Red Indians shed once they got shot in the chest in the westerns Magda loved on the night TV. Only once had she been to the Gem Cinema on Connaught Road down beyond the Blackrock bus stop, but it smelt musty and she was troubled by so many people.

Mr Brannigan had been a soldier, very brave some people were saying after he passed on, in the wars when he'd gone fighting. He had scars on his chest. Mrs Borru turned lucid for an hour or two after hearing of Mr Brannigan's death and smiled to herself and began to tell how, to Magda's horror and the scandal of God's ears should He be listening, which of course He would be, Mr Brannigan and she, Mrs Borru, had been kind to each other in the lantern hours when the place was asleep.

'When who was asleep?' Magda had asked.

'Everybody, silly girl.'

'Kind? What about?'

'Solace, silly. A man needs solace, whatever his years. It's what women are for, even in this place.'

'What place, Mrs Borru?'

'This place. Don't you listen? You'll do bad at school, cloth ears you have, never listening to a word anybody says.'

'Kind, eh?' Magda remembered saying that fateful day when Mr Brannigan died. 'That must have been nice.'

'It was,' Mrs Borru said, dreamy and smiling distantly at the far wall where the Sacred Heart was in a coloured effigy showing His Heart to the cruel sinful world to demonstrate how hurt it was when people were sinful. 'He liked my knickers off and on the floor by the draining board in the kitchen.'

Magda thought she misunderstood. 'Your what?'

'He was a one for breasts. He loved bosoms, did old Jim Brannigan. He was a gay old stick.'

'What?'

Magda finally began to understand and was struck with alarm hearing this.

'He was slow – being on them tablets they give old men whose blood pressure goes up. That and being old.' Mrs Borru frowned at the far wall and the holy effigy. 'Or is it down? Do you know?'

'Know what?' Magda said, almost shouting out the question, desperate for the next query from the old dear to be something innocent, like what was for tea and could she have Earl Grey or maybe the impossible Lady Grey tea instead. Or maybe asked for a buttered crumpet for a change, instead of the Battenberg they had on Thursdays.

'Them tablets. Though I heard Mrs O'Brien in that end ward, with the leg, has the same coloured tablet as Mr Brannigan, so maybe it doesn't count whether you are man or woman.'

'I don't know,' Magda yelped, frantic at what was coming out.

She had been sent to make sure Mrs Borru had been to the loo so she had to stay and find out. The commode hadn't even been moved since the morning, so there was no way to tell unless Magda went round the entire place – somebody said all sixty-five of them inmates, but Magda couldn't count so didn't know – asking if Mrs Borru had been to the loo today and been cleaned afterwards. She had to do her job right, or she might get sent back to kneeling and scrubbing and getting walloped at the Magdalenes amid those girls with the white faces where Lucy had done her first fall. Magda had only been a little girl back then, not nineteen.

'Mr Brannigan was a right lad.' Mrs Borru went back into her dreamy mode. 'The first time we did it, we did it right here in this bed. He said I was brilliant.'

'He said...' Magda tried faintly.

'He said my arse was sweet as a nut.'

'Your...'

'I think there's two sorts of men, don't you?'

'I don't know.'

'You'll learn, girl.'

'Two sorts?'

Magda tried not to ask the question but was drawn in despite herself. For some reason she thought of Chaucer, which she'd heard of when, unlettered as she was, she'd listened to the lettered girls in the Magdalenes talking after collecting the papers for the girls' exam. One girl had said, 'Just our luck, eh?'

and told Magda the notices said *On No Account Is Chaucer To Be Allowed*. Magda forever associated Chaucer, whoever or whatever he or it was, with evil thoughts, the sort you let in if you weren't determined when you woke suddenly in the nights. Sometimes, she couldn't sleep and wondered why she was this shape, and what God in His infinite wisdom thought He was playing at.

'There's the man who's mesmerised by bosoms. And there's the man who can't stop being mesmerised by legs and bottoms. Mr Brannigan was fascinated by breasts. You know what I think, girl?'

'No,' Magda said, thinking, but Mr Brannigan's barely yet cold with pennies on his eyes in the next room's third alcove with his dinner going cold on the bed table.

It was sinful to talk like this. In fact, Magda knew it was dire sin to even think these things, and probably even worse in the scale of everything to listen to this old bat rabbiting on about how she and Mr Brannigan, *requiescat in pace*, had done shameful and shameless things to each other in the candle hours right here in the St Cosmo Care Home for the Elderly.

'It's only the way men start off with you that's the main point.'

'Start off?'

'Start *you* off, I mean.'

'Start *me*?' Magda almost ran but felt transfixed.

'They all have to start by getting in you, is the truth. It's the way they are. Can't help themselves. You know what my Auntie Winnie used to tell me?'

'No.'

'She said, more than once, "It's for men to try, and women to deny." What d'you think of that?'

Magda almost repeated it but caught herself in time.

'She was a daft old biddie who knew no better. She had an unhappy life, did Auntie Winnie. Her husband ran off with a girl who worked the boats. I don't know what it means to this day.'

The old lady smiled at the Sacred Heart bold as brass, straight at the figure of Our Lord doing His suffering and everything on the wall.

'What what means?'

'You're not listening. Worked the boats. I've told you twice, her husband ran off with a girl who worked the boats.' And old Mrs Borru gave Magda an absolutely beatific smile. 'Doesn't it sound romantic? She *worked* the *boats*. It makes me think of the Far East in hot climes, like in those sailing poems we used to learn at school. We were made to stand up and recite Masefield and Wordsworth and Coleridge.'

'Poems?'

The old lady was rambling now, so perhaps it was becoming less sinful with each passing minute. Magda decided to stay, but was disappointed the talk had come down to poems when it had been horrid but fascinating.

'Coleridge.' Mrs Borru smiled. 'I loved the ones about romance. Coleridge was a strange stick, right enough, with more strings to his bow than a man ought.'

'Was he?' Magda knew nobody by that name in the St Cosmo.

'How does it go? *The red leaf, lust of its clan, dances as often as dance it can.* Isn't that lovely?'

'Lovely,' Magda said guardedly, ready to say a swift Glory Be in case it wasn't lovely at all but something truly foul.

'I thought of a red leaf trying to dance when it was going to fall, just like all the rest.'

'I see,' Magda said, who didn't.

'Red was the colour you were forbidden when I was a girl,' Mrs Borru said. 'You got your legs smacked good and hard if you were seen in red knickers, or petticoats, or a dress. I always longed for red shoes, after reading that Coleridge poem.'

'Did you get some?' Magda asked, drawn in deep now despite the wicked side to the talk.

'No, bless you. Different when I was married. It didn't matter then because my husband bought me some. We'd gone to England. We lived over a shop and I got cast-offs and seconds from their stock, and one was a red woollen dress that hugged my shape. I went mad in that. I danced as often as dance I could.' She giggled, a marvellously happy sound to Magda. She loved people to laugh, even old Mr Vennoshay whose teeth clacked when he had a good laugh if he'd forgotten his sticky stuff for his false plate.

'You danced?'

'I just told you. I danced for my husband in our flat and in our bedroom. Women forget they have a duty to their man, to please. That's how you stay together. They forget that these days. It's the way they get divorced.'

'Is it?'

'Don't you read the papers?'

'No,' Magda said truthfully, because she hadn't the lettering. Also, it seemed a tragic waste of money to go spending on newspapers with racing results and what the Taoiseach was on about in the Dail when everybody else talked of it all the time anyway.

'I'll miss Jim.' The old lady's eyes filled, to Magda's consternation.

'We all shall, Mrs Borru.'

'I'll miss him more than anybody, God's truth. It's comforting to have a man nearby, even though we're too old to even see each other. I always kept an ear out to listen after Jim, how he was getting on, even after he went to sleep for good.'

'A shame, God rest him.'

'Don't you just go saying that, girl. You mean it or don't go saying it at all, d'you hear?'

'Yes, Mrs Borru.'

'He wore me out sometimes. He would take his time getting to the spillage. We never made a mess in the beds, did we? You didn't notice any mess, did you, after we'd done it during the night?'

'No,' Magda said faintly. 'I didn't know.'

'We did it once in the summer house. It was mortal hot. Jim was like a mad thing. I was frightened, like being a girl again, scared some nun would come along and send us out to St Andrew's where the lunatic people all get sent when they've been up to no good.'

'A dreadful risk.' Magda imagined being sent to the mad house of St Andrew's.

'He had his thing out and I started on it like a crazy woman. It went everywhere, all over my clothes. You know what we did?'

'No?'

'I said I'd stumbled against the fountain, y'know, where the birds splash, that bird bath? It wasn't even filled, so I had to get a watering can from the gardener's and fill it in the little pool and carry water to the bird bath then we could pretend I'd stumbled and got myself wet.'

'I remember washing your dress, Mrs Borru.'

'I know. That's why I'm telling you.'

'I'd best get on, Mrs Borru.'

Suddenly the old dear's eyes took on a wicked glint.

'Here,' she said, lowering her voice. 'Are you the girl who pinches my tablets?'

'What?' Magda paled.

'You're the girl who pinches my tablets.'

'No. I mean…'

'Shhhhh,' Mrs Borru said, and closed her eyes smiling.

That was the day Magda cleaned up after poor Mr Brannigan, and got took home by Bernard after a new old man was brought in. Magda let Bernard do the thing to her. She was being compassionate to a kind man, which was what God intended, same as Mrs Borru to old Mr Brannigan. It was how Bernard began it regular, usually twice a week but sometimes more often unless he had duty when there was racing at the Fairyhouse or Leopardstown.

She was shaking, so shocked was she, when the new man, who was seventy-two and riddled with lice and fleas and Heaven-knows-what, had to be cleaned by the two-blanket method and sundry lotions poured on the festering sores that blotched his skin. The Garda Siobhana brought him because he was going for trial after a fight in Connelly Station.

That was how Sister Stephanie said the Gardai were to take Magda home afterwards, as a kindness, seeing she'd worked six hours extra without overtime money, because there was never that at the St Cosmo. And the Gardai were three hours over their own time, so Bernard said he'd come back on his way after signing off in the police station, which he did. And he ran Magda to her girls' resident block, and saw her up to her door, and when Mrs Shaughnessy saw it was the Gardai she sank back into her doorway further along the landing. Magda explained to the old toot that there had been things going on at the Home today which made it all right.

Then she made some tea and Bernard sat down, and Magda said she'd scramble some eggs and would Bernard be wanting some. He said yes that would be grand. And she was pleased because she had cleaned up in the sluice at the Home, so she was able to let him see her wash her hands before she buttered some bread while the eggs were doing. The bread was soda bread that was too friable for making sandwiches, like most of the old men wanted to eat their scrambled eggs, but she was glad when Bernard said it didn't matter one bit, and made thick sandwiches with two slices of soda bread on each side, larded with Kerry Gold and hang the cost.

She was glad too he liked brown sauce instead of the red tomato sauce, and that reminded her of the red dress that Mrs Borru said she'd worn while dancing for her husband and spouting the poetry about the red leaf dancing, the last of its clan. That made Magda feel she too had rights in certain things and smiled across at the eating man.

He was stout and thick, head and neck like a bull's, with hands that seemed too soft for most men. She felt embarrassed letting him see her bold as brass and natural as anything eating away, quite like they were man and wife, which was something beyond normal how de do. But still she had her eggs but didn't of course make butties from it, which wasn't quite proper. Ladies in the old TV pictures they showed during the night didn't eat like that.

And then he took hold of her waist when she passed to get fresh hot water for the teapot, it being sensible to offer the starving hard-worked man another cup before his long drive home. It wasn't as far as all that, though Howth seemed quite a distance if you thought, not quite as far as Killiney where she'd always hoped one day to live close by the little railway. She'd been there once, too far back ever to remember why and who with.

She was astonished to feel him underneath her – underneath, which was a terrible word when you thought about it, *under* where everything was, though designed by God in His infinite wisdom, and *neath* meaning *right* there where it all happened.

And he put his hands, which seemed larger by the minute, on her leg and felt the skin quite roughly through her skirt which made her dizzy. Then he pushed his hand beneath her skirt onto her legs and felt that she had no stockings on or tights – she hated tights because they were so expensive. Stockings were more of a problem in the morning to get them straight with all that twisting, and especially difficult when there was only a small mirror on the mantelshelf to see yourself in.

And he said, 'Is this all right?' and she said, 'Yes,' because why wasn't it if Mrs Borru and old Mr Jim Brannigan did it, the last time six weeks before when Mr Jim still had a few weeks to go before meeting his Maker? And she let Bernard do it, and was pleased feeling she had got away with something like murder.

And the girl Lucy fell, not just once but twice, while Magda was under Bernard's colossal weight. She groaned 'Jesus, Mary and Joseph' and tried to inhale. It was all right because he shifted just slightly enough for her to get her breathing going by one long inhalation, so she managed.

He took his time about finishing, and she waited like a dutiful wife should while he worked away and she thought, I'll have fine sets of bruises in the morning, that's for sure, but nobody will see them down there on the inside of my thighs. And they must be what Mrs MacLehose called her medals, when Magda had exclaimed once about the bruises on her upper arms, several blotched blue dabs, and Mrs MacLehose smiled while she said it and another girl laughed further along with the tea trolley when she overheard the exchange. And Magda had asked, what did that mean, what sort of medals? Both laughed and another girl, who was forty if she was a day, had giggled all the way through dishing out tea to the old folks. Everybody, whatever age, were girls to nuns, like the whole world was made up of Magdalenes to them.

So this is where the medals came from, which was a truly shocking thought, that everybody was doing it and getting the giggles when it was talked of.

Magda wondered, when Bernard began to snore, still his weight crushing her almost flat, why it was that all the females were called girls. Everywhere in Dublin it was girls, girls, never women or ladies. The girls in the Magdalenes were as old as forty-six, one was, and still she was a girl who did the clearing up in the commercial laundry they ran, steaming night and day between the great vats. And the little children, five and upwards, were also girls. And girls it stayed, even at the old folks home, all the helpers and workers called girls. Except for the nuns, and the nurses like Nurse Maynooth and Nurse Tully.

And how come Mrs Borru said nothing but 'Shhhh' when she'd asked Magda about stealing the poison tablets from her? And then the old lady had slept peaceful like a babe.

Magda didn't know how babes slept, never having seen one sleeping, not even when she was at the Magdalenes or after, but then she'd never had the chance. It must be brilliant, so lovely, to see one sleeping and know it was there just trusting in you staying awake and keeping watch to keep away wolves from the fold or other dangers, or in case it woke and wanted something.

She nursed Bernard then, and gave him a breast just as he started to wake up, which made him like her own bab, and that was how their pattern began, and she hoped it would stay for ever and ever Amen, even unto the consummation of the world. She now knew it wouldn't. A murder had to be got on with, or Lucy never would be able to stop falling to her death in that stairwell.

And Magda knew it would be her murdering of Father Doran that would give poor dead Lucy eternal rest, so it was a sworn Christian duty.

Chapter Five

Magda's first remembrance in Sandyhills, County Dublin, was suddenly being there and frightened. She learnt she was just coming up to five. From other girls who knew their birthdays, Magda knew she too must have a birthday, but didn't know when it was. She had cried, because everybody else had one. What hers was, she had no notion. Counting birthdays was a problem from then on, especially as they all laughed at her because she couldn't count or even learn her letters.

'I once weighed four stone two pounds,' a girl called Isabel said when Magda had been there so long that the snows had come round again.

Magda longed to weigh four stone two pounds too, but how did you get to know?

For a long time she asked other children how you found out, so badly wanting to weigh four stone two pounds that she prayed to Baby Jesus to make her that and not be different, and cried herself to sleep. She knew that, whatever her numbers turned out to be, they would never be four stone two because that would be too good to be true. After getting used to the idea that everyone in the whole place was different, her wish would be simply silly. There were good things, and there were bad things. Being four stone two would be a privilege, and not for her.

More than once, she got into trouble looking about for stones that might be the ones that decided who weighed what. She tried working out this stone thing. At first she thought, being small, that it was something to do with the way you breathed. Good breathing, as near to Jesus's method that you could manage, must give you this four-two mark. It was only when she started working in the kitchen for Mrs Rooney, scouring and fetching, that she learnt, and it gave her profound hope, that everything – *every* single *thing* – had a weight in it, so kind was God and so generous was Baby Jesus who'd heard her prayers and decided everything and everyone should weigh something. Maybe God's kindness would mean she'd be four stone two?

Magda lived in hopes. She no longer needed to cry herself to sleep at night because her weight was out there somewhere just waiting. It was nothing to do with breathing, because vegetables didn't breathe at all and they had weight, so good was Almighty God. Magda finally tried to do a deal with the Almighty. She would pray an extra prayer each night, a Hail Mary, because Mother Mary could wheedle when saints might not get very far. She would even settle for just four stone without the two.

Carrots didn't breathe. Magda, with an older girl called Lucy, learnt this and other essential facts of life by carrying in vegetables from the delivery at the postern gate at the end of the walled yard. A man, big and whistling and slamming things and yelling at other people unseen out there in the street – all doubtless as terrified as Magda, who waited in the doorway to come at a run when the delivery man had gone after knocking with his five thumps and starting up his motor and driving off – well he was the delivery man, same every Monday and Thursday. He had no name, and no nun ever came to check things because it was too early for nuns.

Magda and Lucy had to be there, waiting outside the kitchen door, by six o'clock when the nuns were being all holy and praying for the sins of the girls and other hard-line sinners – Sister Annuncion's words for the girls in Magda's class – in Holy Mass and the delivery man was due and Mrs Rooney hadn't yet come to open the kitchen door. Their job, sworn to 'loyal and holy duty' (Sister St Paul's oath they had to take when put on kitchen work) was to leave the baskets of vegetables and other provisions untouched ('unsullied' in Sister St Paul's punishing oath) but bring them under the shelter of the doorway. At six-fifteen Mrs Rooney would open it from inside and stand there with the same bark, 'Get them in here, then off with you.'

They would carry the baskets in, and then go back fast as legs could go, back to the toilets, trying to get chapped thighs and bottoms clean before hurrying to the gruel that was breakfast.

Each Monday and Thursday Magda and Lucy had a hard time telling the girls in whispers only and punishment by smacked legs to make you limp all day if you got caught talking, what they'd carried in when the little hatch by the postern gate was filled with heavy baskets and the delivery man's engine had taken him, whistling and shouting about racehorses, off up the road to wherever it was.

The other girls didn't believe them when they said they hadn't eaten any of the provisions.

In vain Lucy and Magda swore they hadn't stolen a single mouthful, and didn't even know what was inside the baskets, and in any case there was no chance of looking because the baskets were tacked with heavy canvas all the way round so nothing could go in or out. And Mrs Rooney saw the baskets lifted inside then sent them both off and didn't even let them stay and see what food had arrived or, to Magda's burning loss, what they weighed, because Mrs Rooney had a scales with big black weights marked in Imperial Pounds and Imperial Ounces, with crowns over those standy-out letters in the coal-black metal. So the weights were from English times, which meant maybe it was sinful to even want a weight of your own, possibly four stone two pounds if God was specially kind.

Still the other girls kept on accusing them of stealing. Lucy in particular always hotly denied stealing potatoes, which puzzled Magda because how did Lucy know there were potatoes in any basket? Magda had never even looked inside. She and Lucy had to take the empty baskets out after prayers before they went to sleep, putting them in a stack in the hatch so they could be lifted out by the delivery man next time he came. You had to do it that way or the man might see in and watch the nuns, which was a terrible crime that Sister St Paul said would deserve Hellfire for all eternity.

Magda asked Lucy, ready for rebuke, if that's what her question deserved, 'Lucy. How do you know there were potatoes in them baskets?'

'They smell of them.'

Magda was astonished at this. Weights, and now smells? Potatoes *smelt*?

'Do potatoes smell?' she asked with timidity.

'Course they do, daftie.'

'What of?'

'Potatoes, of course.'

'Does everything have a smell?'

'Course it does. Carrots smell of carrots. Potatoes smell of potatoes, lettuces of themselves.'

'Is it just them old vegetables?'

'No.'

Lucy looked round so as not to be heard by anyone. They were in the laundry where, having small-girl jobs, they had to drag the empty linen skips into the yard. When they were older they might be allowed to work inside where it was steamy but warm and in out of the cold and the rain. Once you got wet there was no drying you until you dried in class, and like as not got told off there for wetting the benches with your wet clothes. The nuns had a terrible suspicion that the girls who stained the benches with damp had peed in their knickers, and peeing in knickers was the most terrible insult to the Order and thereby to Almighty God, who 'detested filth in thought, word, and deed,' as Sister St Paul put it.

This nun did a lot of hunting for transgressors. Two girls were always at it, peeing their knickers and getting blamed for every drop even of rain that clung to garments and skirts and the thin shawls the girls were given. Magda did what many girls did when they were in the yard and it came on to rain. Instead of covering themselves with their shawls, they would press into the entrance archway, and wrap their shawl round their middle. That way, the shawl would get a good soaking from the rain but the skirt would stay dry as near as could be, depending on the downpour. That way, they could take the shawl off when called inside, and the skirt was almost dry. With astute arranging, it would not show dampness of rain on the bench. The shawl was put with the rest on the window sill for collection afterwards. Your hair got wet, sure, but wasn't that the price to be paid when avoiding Sister St Paul's clouts from suspicion of wetting the bench from a sinful pee?

'What else is there?'

The food was gruel, a runny oat water, with a bread every second day, butter Fridays and the same repeated. Lucy sometimes stole bits. The one time Magda tried stealing from somebody else on the same table they caught her and she got walloped first by the nun and then by two of the other girls and had her hair pulled so it bled. Lucy was fast, but never gave any she stole to Magda. Lucy kept it for herself and ate it on the way out if she could, which was only fair because Lucy was older.

'Meat,' Lucy whispered.

'Meat?'

'Yes. There's meat. Y'know, from sheeps and that. Cows, more like.'

Magda knew the older girls' lay teachers and the nuns had meat, for it set your mouth filling with wet spit. She vaguely remembered meat but didn't remember where from. It was hardish and floppy on a plate that had pictures on it – blue drawings of funny little people walking on a bridge over water with waves, also blue, and trees that stayed the same all the time and had branches shaped the same as the waves. Magda tried remembering more about the picture on the plate but couldn't. It was back from before she came to the Magdalenes. Two people in the picture had long frocks on, and an umbrella each. The huts they were walking to were stacked up almost on top of each other on to the edge of the plate. She often wondered how she knew about the blue-pictured plates. Somebody cut the greyish meat up for you and you could eat it with your fingers, or you could use a shiny pusher thing while somebody laughed and said about people being clever to learn that. And a deep slow chuckly sound, that went *huckle-huckle-huckle* and a scent Magda ever after associated with meat, though it came from a bottle she was allowed to play with on the floor. But that was then, and there was no such plate with pictures and things at the Magdalenes.

'Yes, daftie. It comes from the butchers.'

Magda wondered if she had once been in a butcher's house. Doubtless there would be meat there.

'When?'

'Wednesdays. Never Fridays.'

'Do we not bring it in the baskets?' Magda was disappointed.

'No, daftie. Meat's mortal heavy.'

'Is it?'

Magda admired Lucy for knowing so many things. She wanted to be like Lucy, really clever, and longed to see this heavy thing called meat. Maybe she could remember more things about pushers and plates and being on a carpet and playing with a bottle, if only she saw this meat.

'Course it is, daftie. It comes to the postern gate when we're in class.'

'Is it like a dog?'

Magda knew the delivery man had a dog, because he shouted it to guard. Magda knew what a dog was, remembered lying on a *carpet* with a *dog* that snored. She had heard one of the older girls telling her mates that she stood on a chair to see, when the nun was out of her class, and claimed she saw a delivery boy, the butcher's, delivering meat in boxes. 'Fish on Thursday for Fridays, see,' Lucy said, but she was only guessing. Lucy was good at being full of scorn. Magda suspected, but had no way of proving, that Lucy even thought and sometimes quietly spoke, her scorn about the nuns, which was sinful.

'Don't be stupid. A *dog* is a dog.'

'Is it heavy?'

'Course it is.'

Lucy nudged Magda, seeing the shadow go by the end of the corridor, which meant the boss nun was coming back so they'd have to stop talking and stand in 'an attitude of dutiful obedience and preparedness,' in Sister St Paul's sworn oath. This meant feet together, standing with hands folded and looking at the floor until spoken to when they would have to respond quickly and do as they were told.

'Time you shut up about it,' Lucy said. Lucy could get angry quick as wink.

'What?' Magda couldn't follow what Lucy meant.

'You're always on about how heavy's this and that.'

'Sorry, Lucy.'

'It's OK.' Lucy was jaunty, which thrilled Magda. It must be great to be jaunty, thinking all sorts of wild things Magda wouldn't even dare let into her head for fear of Hellfire.

She had the nerve to ask. Learning Lucy, her admired partner, was seven years old – whatever seven was – Magda asked how old she was, of that same Sister St Paul, and was told, after a cursory glance of appraisal, 'You're five, I'd say.'

'Five, Sister?'

'Five. How old were you when you came?'

'Please, Sister, nobody told me.'

'Five, then. What date did you arrive?'

'I don't know, Sister.'

'Then you're rising five. Do not ask again, understand?'

'Yes, Sister.'

So at rising five, Magda had an age and a definite date for it. To Magda, this was momentous, to stay unforgot for life. She asked another nun, Sister Annuncion, what saint's day it was in Religion and Doctrine, and got a point for asking such a holy thing. She was told it was the twenty-second of July, this being the feast day of St Mary Magdalene.

So then Magda knew that, thanks to God being kind, she was rising five that very day, and she had a birthday all her own, and it was the twenty-second of July, whatever those words meant. And rising five, she learnt from Lucy, meant the day following whatever this rising business was. So on that day she would become five. Nobody said anything when the next day came. Magda was disappointed, though nobody else ever seemed to have any birthdays to speak of, not even Lucy, who had developed a mortal bad cough.

Lucy couldn't worry much about birthdays, she told Magda. She said quite cheerily, 'I'll be dead soon because my cough spits blood. That's always bad. I'm going to the arms of Jesus, Mary and Joseph soon, and I'll have proper dinners and tea in white cups and saucers with coloured grapes drawn on them.' Other girls said that was a truly terrible way to talk because it meant you were ungrateful to being part of the Church Militant Here On Earth among the pagan foes, but Little Sally, who you had only to call by her number, One-One-Three, because she, like Magda and others, had been born out of wedlock, said it was an affliction and made your shit go black. It had happened to her mother, which was why she was in the care of the Magdalenes.

None of the other girls took any notice, because it was only Little Sally. If you were born out of wedlock it didn't matter who your mother was or what happened to her because she'd been bad and serve her right.

The nuns had special days, which were the anniversaries of when they'd come into the Order, but that was some extra thing, like what Magda finally learnt to scent as meat. This was a grey slab of food, and was for nuns and teachers but not the girls, being exactly as God said it was to be. They were nuns and teachers. Girls were girls, forever. God said so, and all was right with the world.

There was an event when she was growing up that happened to Magda, and it concerned one lad called Damien, who shagged, or tried to shag, Magda against the wall of the commercial paper-packing sweatshop where Magda, being fifteen and supernumerary to the Magdalene commercial laundry, was sent out to work.

There were other events that preceded her departure. She was given a stern lecture three times over by Sister Sophia about Living Out Among the Heathen. These were mostly the people of Dublin who Had Truck With England, not to mention Liverpool, which was somewhere even worse. Dublin City, Sister Sophia said darkly, making Magda solemnly repeat her stern warnings, was utterly given over to drinking and speaking bad words for no other reason than that they were all heaving with sin day and night.

Magda, though, didn't think the delivery man, her sole experience of the male gender until then, was wholly evil, for he whistled at his dog and called it affectionate names she didn't understand. Spalpeen was one, which might actually have been its name. Magda wanted to see the dog, but it vanished when Magda was about twelve, and instead a new dog called Tearaway came to be shouted at. It was never called Spalpeen, which was kind of the delivery man, Magda thought.

She imagined Tearaway to be a giant thing because she once heard it snuffling when she waited with blood-spitting Lucy under the rainy archway of the kitchen door with all those lovely scented foody smells. It was there under the arch that she imagined meat most of all.

'That must be a big bastard,' Lucy said, shocking Magda to the core.

'Lucy!' Magda cried. 'A word like that!'

'Why not?'

'It's wrong!'

'Why is it wrong?' Lucy said, truculent. 'We're mostly bastards.'

'We're not.'

'We are.'

'We're nothing of the kind!'

'We're mostly bastards. It's why we're here.'

'I'm not.' Magda wept at that.

'You are,' Lucy said with comfortable certainty.

By now Lucy was wheezing most of the time, though still slick when stealing bits of bread from other girls at meals. She would even steal a spoonful of gruel if you weren't quick enough to stop her, but the ensuing struggle, if you dared try to prevent her hands from getting at your dinner, sometimes caused spillages and you might get spotted by the invigilating nun and sent out of the refectory without finishing your food and you then went without.

'I'll die soon,' Lucy often said, having proved that Magda was a bastard like herself. Lucy was the thinnest in the class.

'No, you're not, Lucy.'

Magda didn't know why it was important to stop Lucy talking like this. She knew nothing about dying, though it was a happy business because the nuns said so, and in Religion and Doctrine they had to learn the Stations of the Cross by heart and the Canon Laws of the Church and other essentials for the Meaning Of Life. When you died you were in Heaven and that was the best you could hope for, especially illegitimates and orphans, who were lucky to get anywhere.

'Course I am. I'll get a special place in Heaven. You know the first thing I'll do?'

'No?'

'I'll take away all seventeen telephones the King has in his grand palace in London.'

Magda was awe-struck. 'Will you?'

'Serve him right. The Pope has only one telephone, but the King has seventeen. Who needs seventeen telephones?' Lucy spat blood, which was all right because it was raining and her spit swam away in the puddles outside the kitchen archway.

Magda had heard this before, because it was often preached as evidence of the sinfulness of the Protestants, who had tons of money they stole from Catholics down the ages, which was why the Pope was so poor and the Protestants could drink all day long and resort to sin. Lucy also knew about numbers.

'See, those of us who have names count as bastards, though we weren't born out of wedlock like One-One-Three. That gives us promotion when we die.'

'Ta, Lucy.'

Without Lucy's guidance Magda would have known none of these essentials, though that wasn't quite true. It was more that Lucy explained things for Magda so she could understand what the nuns were saying. Magda cried her heart out when Lucy, true to her prediction, died. She died one night, being found twisted and bloody in her blanket that was wet through from sweat. Except it wasn't that simple, because Magda knew what had happened, which was why she now had the duty of murdering Father Doran.

Magda felt really bad about things. She told herself she guessed, but wasn't sure and nobody ever explained, that Lucy had tried maybe to get out of bed to get some water, having sweated so heavily that even her pillow was damp and the blanket stuck to her with blood. She had pooed herself, her shit sticking black and smelly to the blanket and the brighter blood she had sicked or coughed – maybe both? – staining the blanket and her chin.

It was Seven-Eight, who secretly was Vera and claimed to know her surname – yet another lost element of identity Magda knew would prove another insuperable weight-age problem – who claimed to have found Lucy like that, though it wasn't true. It was about four in the morning, and the dorm was soon a silent parade of lights, torches, nuns flitting and bringing things and carrying canvas with two long sticks they had difficulty shoving inside the tough hemmed edges. They made Magda, still in the gloaming of the coming dawn, close her eyes tight and pray while Lucy went to her eternal rest, because it was a specially holy moment and one they all had to learn from to their lasting benefit throughout life.

Magda was fearful and betrayed Sister St Paul by pretending to herself that she was unable to cross her thumbs exactly right without opening her eyes just a crack to see as the nuns panted by carrying…carrying what looked like potatoes lumpy and long in the canvas thing. One nun actually told the other off, who held the flashlight to show the way to the door, because the older nun, whose name Magda didn't know, had forgotten to bring the brace-irons for the stretcher, whatever those were.

It looked like one long tube of canvas, and Magda tried to pray but the words didn't stick themselves together the way they should in any ordinary prayer.

And Magda cried that morning all through the *De Profundis*, feeling really sad even though Lucy was joyously wrecking the Protestant King's seventeen telephones from her special place in Heaven and happily feasting on meat and milk and honey and whatnot on the Right Hand of God. And Magda was smacked three times for keeping on weeping when she should have been dancing with joy at Lucy experiencing ineffable joy up there among all the saints. She chimed in with,

When my hair stiffening on my head shall forbode my approaching end...

Lord have mercy on us...

But who would wipe Lucy's chin, as Magda so often did in the night when Lucy whispered she was frightened her mouth blood would show on the sheets? Would those stealthy nuns, carrying her off in a thing like a sack because the old nun had forgotten the brace-irons, wipe her chin? And did they mop her clean? And wash her bottom and legs after all that black stuff came out of her bottom when she died? And did anybody remember to give Lucy a drink of water before she went to be buried? And where exactly was Lucy now? Magda badly wanted to go to see where Lucy was, so she could pray over the headstone and make things all right. She felt it was shameful, but maybe that's what happened to everybody when you died.

'Washed in the Blood of the Lamb,' Sister St Paul intoned during the Litany For The Dead, which probably explained all that blood and dark colour. Only One-One-Three, who was Sally, cried like Magda did that day, and got her legs smarting

too with Sister Annuncion's thick round ruler just like Magda
for wasting time in superfluous grieving.

Nothing else really happened in the Magdalenes, except
numerous disappointments, but they were like weather and
came every day in different guises, until Magda went to work
unpaid in the paper packers. The girls who reached the age to
live out were sent to families, if they could read and write and
were decent, or to a job under matronly supervision, returning
at evening to sleep in the Living Out Block under a nun's stern
monitoring.

There she met Damien, who didn't last long, except he
caused ructions within Magda that almost caused her to take
her own life, but she got lucky and managed not to, mostly
from fear.

Magda was sent to the Living Out Block, in another dormitory.
No school this time, just girls working. It was a revelation.

There, Magda heard so many new things that she was lost.
One strangeness was newspapers. People mixed willy-nilly in
the street with anybody. Churches were islands of familiarity
of sight, sound, incense scent. There was no King with his
seventeen telephones and hadn't been for many years, though
a Queen over the water doubtless had as many phones, and
Liverpool was a place where footballs teams caused serious
arguments in Dublin bars.

Damien strove to insert his fingers in her behind the paper
packing sheds and caused some blood but the month passed
and Magda was relieved she was not pregnant. She was told by
two other girls she'd had a narrow escape. A girl called Emily,
who had a last name and been raised in a different convent of
a different order because her auntie was one of the nuns there,

explained to Magda all about sex. It was astonishing, and made Magda shocked but thankful Jesus and his Mother Mary had escaped that terrible business. She associated sex, whatever it meant to mankind, with a struggling grappling turmoil behind some paper-packing shed where the foreman might come upon you and send you to prison or worse.

'Just think, Magda,' Emily warned. 'You might have had a baby and then what?'

'What?' Magda asked, stricken.

'The baby would go into the Magdalenes like you did, and then you'd be back there for life.'

'Would I?'

'Course you would. That's what they're for. Machinists most of them, or in laundries for life.'

The baby, though, would do what Magda had had to do – grow up there. Damien was uncaring about everything, and reputedly had several other episodes – though only two reached the dick, Emily explained blithely, because the lads are mortal scared of doing more than fingers in case they got forcibly married or punished by the courts. The girls were well known, and Magda was one of them, being pointed out by some of the other lads who were drivers and loaders of the baled papers the firm sent out at five o'clock of a working day.

Magda couldn't understand how the system of sex – snogging, mauling, getting as undressed as far as you could manage without letting anybody see what was actually going on, getting the lad to spill into some convenient paper or rag that was afterwards thrown away among the waste – had come to be when it was forbidden everywhere. Vaguely she eventually came to believe that it was possibly not all the fault of the English, who had, until she grew out of the convent, been wholly responsible for the persistence of sin everywhere. It was a mystery who kept sex going among the Faithful, though she knew she had a deal to do with its persistence, having started out early by having Christ crucified before she was even five.

She was eighteen when she recognised the priest she knew she had to murder. It was almost a relief, because it brought into her mind the understanding that there was a degree of finality to the problem of sinfulness and deaths of lovely people like Lucy.

And, more to the point, of Lucy as she kept falling, because that was the one event that Magda could not get rid of. In fact, she often wondered, after her sixteenth birthday, when she'd felt so full of herself that she'd allowed Damien to do his rutting and work his fingers into her so painfully, how it came to be that she had been so idle in thinking of this horror that she had waited so long before deciding that steps had to be taken.

The memory caused serious distress still, though she never spoke of it to anyone and, as far as she knew, while still in the Magdalenes nobody else ever mentioned it. It was as if it was some secret they had all agreed never to reveal in case the wrong people got hold of it and it might do damage to the entire system of life on earth and the Church in particular.

Magda never could get the hang of thoughts, because they sometimes proved wayward. It was only when she recognised Father Doran and knew instantly what she must do, that she felt a kind of release, like seeing a pathway she knew would, whatever the hardships and obstacles that might lie along the route, eventually resolve her state of mind. This was a self-indulgence, of course, something that no doubt would prove costly when she'd have to explain it in confession. Or, worse, when finally she was summoned to stand before the Throne of God for the terrible Last Judgement when all would be revealed and she would be made to explain – dear *God*! – every evil thing she had done and all her wrongs would be exposed before the Company of Saints and Mother Mary would stare accusingly down. It was selfish to want peace of mind. Was she not fit to carry the Cross of Christ by staying mute and attentive, in a state of obedient duty, as Sister St Paul had so often made her swear on the Holy Book? Not really, not after Lucy's death. Killing Father Doran, however, would straighten it all out, she hoped.

She went to work at the Cosmo Care Home, run by a compassionate Order of nuns, and there she developed and worked hard and for wages she actually kept herself. It was to be her life, she told herself. It might get her off part of the penances she was doubtless accumulating, to be paid back for the Final Judgement. She would need a deal of holy indulgences to expiate those sins, for she started a kind of regularity of sin that proved so hard to stop.

Poor Lucy, of course, kept falling in Magda's nightmares, but eventually there might be a way of helping the poor mite, and give her peace. It was *a worthy and wholesome thought to pray for the dead that they might be loosed from their sins*, Magda knew, because that's what the prayer said. That being so, wasn't it also a worthy and wholesome thought to think of doing something about Lucy to stop her from falling night after night in order to not only loose her from her sins, poor thing, but also give her eternal rest?

And let Magda sleep. But that was selfish.

Chapter Six

Magda set her mind on confession. The big question, in her mind ever since she recognised Father Doran at Mass, was what to confess.

'See,' she told Grace who worked in the sluice at the St Cosmo and was forever saying her Rosary, 'it's what you say to them, isn't it?'

'You've to tell them everything.'

'Every single thing?'

In Magda's mind, besides Lucy, there was the problem of the lad whose rough busy fingers made her bleed that time and set her worrying she was going to get pregnant so she'd be shunted back into the Magdalenes and the baby, her baby as never was, would never even set eyes on her, its very own mother. Glory be, what a way to live, all because of some lad gasping like a landed trout, though Magda had never seen a landed trout. She imagined having all kinds of telltale evidence about her from Damien trying it on, like maybe evidence on her one tubby-shape cut-down skirt that a simple girl called Margaret had given her – that is, *given*, truly a real gift, because

Margaret was going to live in a house where a proper family of real people lived, and they would buy – that is, buy, pay for in a shop – clothes for her. And Magda felt like a queen when she wore it, though it was too long but that was all right because long meant concealment, there being lads who looked and whistled and did things with their fingers in the air and grinned when they went past.

Grace was definitely holy, and could tell you things about the lives of the saints that would curl your hair. Like St Jerome, who was always condemning harlots about lipstick and putting powder on your face and hanging out of windows looking at street lads and soldiers but who was the cleverest saint in the whole of God's Church Militant, even counting St Augustine who had been a bad child and a worse lad and who wrote it all down to warn sinners.

'You go to Hellfire if you don't tell everything,' Grace warned.

She was a saint herself, with all the stinky stuff she had to sluice from the old people in the Care Home. One was especially foul – not his fault of course because he too was made in the image of God Almighty, but he was old as the hills and shat his bed. It was a lucky day when old Mr Liam MacIlwam didn't shit his bed and need the whole bedclothes changing.

Magda didn't mind helping in this terrible chore because it was like when Christ was crucified. The women and them saints who put Christ into His shroud and then put him into that old tomb of His, well, they must have polished Him up because that's what is the ineffable duty of women. So Magda said a prayer to Christ when she helped Grace to wash Mr MacIlwam's bedclothes, and it was the one that Sister St Union said was meant to tell you how to keep your soul clean and pure for the time when you and God would become one in Heaven, so you had to stay clean all the time, in thought, word and deed. And it was this:

Lavabo inter innocentes manus meas, et circumdabo aktare tuum, Domine, ut audiam vocem laudis.

Which meant, Magda had learnt by heart from listening to Lucy, who read the English out to her when they were allowed to share a Small Roman Missal at Holy Mass:

'With the pure in heart I will wash my hands clean, and take my place among them at thy altar, Lord.'

This was as far as she could get, because Magda could never get the hang of reading, which was the reason she still had something of a limp on her left leg, from nuns giving her a right whack with that old round ruler they often carried, though some were rounder and longer than the ones other nuns carried.

She dreamt of the time when, with maybe some friend from outside if ever she found one, she would get learnt her letters, but there they stood on that old page and never jumped into her brain like they did for Lucy. It was unfair, Magda would have thought, if she'd dared to think like that, that Lucy hadn't had the power to leave a will in writing, so the courts would see it through for her to get Lucy's great gift of reading. Then Magda would be able to read away like any old priest and any old nun and wouldn't be slow and simple, because that's how she learnt she was too stupid to read.

'There is a place in Heaven,' Sister Annuncion told her more than once, which was really kind.

'For me, Sister?'

'Of course for you, stupid girl. Who else?'

'Because I can't read like the others.'

Magda had just guessed she was rising nine, and had marked the day down as her birthday, so naturally she was interested. But this was when Lucy was still alive and hadn't been carried off by the White Spit, that the nuns called TB. It was strange that, because Lucy's spit was rusty, then bright red and even full of blood and nothing in it of grolly – as the girls called the phlegm that was thick and pussy yellow when you got a bad cough – and it should be called Red Spit, though what did a girl rising nine know if she couldn't even read? God rest Lucy, though.

Anyway, she was cleaning up old Mr Liam MacIlwam, who had shat himself again, when she saw he was wide awake. And looking at her. She was embarrassed, because the old man was always fast asleep when the nun – this particular day it was Sister Claire – did his last wash, which included his lower regions where nobody was allowed to see because there were men's things that women hadn't to see.

'What?' she said.

Sister Claire was gone down the ward to bring the clean sheet and the plastic under-sheet that was always put under the old folk in case they got shitty so the mattresses didn't get dirty.

Old Mr MacIlwam's eyes were wet. She stared at him with horror, in a panic wondering if this was the start of a stroke because that's what one old woman had done in the other ward, twisted up on her right side and pissed herself and shat in the bed then her eyes had run water like Mr MacIlwam's eyes were doing.

'I keep seeing Terry,' Mr MacIlwam said.

His voice was creaky like the dormitory door back in the Magdalenes. The only time Magda had heard it before was when he had suddenly tried to sing along and join in a hymn and the nun had told him to sing it silently because it would help the others if he kept quiet.

It had been *Sweet Heart of Jesus Fount of Love and Mercy*, the hymn, and Magda had heard Sister Claire tell Mr MacIlwam that and thought what a shame, because God might actually like that old scratchy voice. It might have reminded Jesus of some door in St Joseph's carpenter's shop in Galilee or wherever and brought a smile to His Face, though you never did hear of Jesus smiling in the Gospels. At least, Magda had never heard of it. But old Mr MacIlwam shut up as he was bound to do and stayed silent all through until the end of the hymn.

'Terry?'

Who was Terry? Magda wondered if she should run and bring Sister Claire from the laundry cupboards, where she could spend half an hour, always tutting and then going off to tell some other woman from the other side, where the healthy old folk were, that they ought to keep the cupboards tidier because it made difficulties for everybody else and had they no pride in being decent handmaidens of the Lord?

'Terry,' old Mr MacIlwam said in his cracked-door croak. 'You remember Terry.'

'Yes,' Magda bleated as quietly as she could so as not to get the old man in trouble, for conversation had Seeds of Iniquity when exchanged unlawfully. For this reason, Mary the Mother of Jesus never got a look-in in the Gospels, poor woman, because it might have given way to thoughts other than what was holy, because you never could tell. So said Sister Annuncion. One girl back in the Magdalenes got a good point for asking that question when it was Religion and Doctrine, and Magda wished she could read so she too could discover things like that in the Gospel and get a point.

A good point didn't give you anything, but the other girls in the same section of the class always treated you better for getting a good point, in case it gave something they might share if anything came of it.

'I keep seeing him falling.'

Magda almost swayed and fell in a faint at that. She even sank onto the edge of the bed, which made old Mr Liam MacIlwam look surprised because nobody had ever done that. Magda went dizzy too. Nobody else, surely, had the same terrible dream, of seeing the girl falling like she did. Also, Mr MacIlwam was a man, who could only have been in a boys' school, so how could he have seen the girl fall?

She had a sudden vision, Lucy's cardigan so close Magda could have touched her before she moved, and those words Magda could never remember but which were clear as day…

'Falling,' she repeated, frightened out of her wits.

'Falling down. In the cold.'

'In the cold.' Magda could have fallen down herself.

'In the schoolyard.'

'Schoolyard!' Magda repeated with relief, 'Schoolyard!'

'You remember it, don't you, Tom?'

'Yes,' Magda bleated, quietly now so as not to betray Tom, whoever Tom was and wherever he might be.

They might have been boys forbidden to watch Terry falling down in the schoolyard, and people said funny things in fright or when daydreaming. She knew that, having several times been caught out in the school or at work in the kitchen or in Holy Mass, even, suddenly saying something out loud that one of the other girls heard and repeated along the kneeling line so they started giggling and that's how you got found out and your legs made all chapped and red and blistered from round ruler whackings.

'It was the day after mitching.'

'Mitching.'

Running away from school when you were not allowed was mitching.

Mostly the girls who mitched were the ones who had families somewhere. They were girls to be envied, because at least they had families to run away to, but the ones that got treated worst and whacked more than most were the girls who had no families at all and who came from orphanages. And they included Magda, and were a Stigma on Holy Mother Church, being evidence of past sinfulness in their families and so deserved their fate.

'Tom.'

'Yes?' Magda said, being Tom for the whilst.

Old Mr MacIlwam beckoned like men beckoned, with a kind of tilt of the head. Magda had tried this, even in the mirror of the corridor where she had to clean the wooden things with Mansion Polish, which was a terrible sin because you looked in the mirror often enough and Satan himself would stare right back at you and that would be that. In the big rectangular mirror she tried the men's gesture, tilting her head so as to say come here, like the old inmates of the Care Home, but it didn't look right at all. Maybe it was something the men were all taught and maybe even born with. She wondered if Christ Himself had done it to his earthly father St Joseph, the carpenter, saying, 'Pass that hammer, St Joseph,' or some such, or maybe instead of saying, 'Here, St Joseph, come and see how I've made this television table' or whatever it was, simply jerking His head and saying, 'This here table, will it do?'

'I wanted to go instead with Tom when he mitched off.'

'You did?'

'Sure to God I did. Anything to be away from them old Christian Brothers.'

'Really?'

Magda prayed hard for Sister Claire to come back with the plastic undersheet but she could hear her clear as day down the end of the room telling somebody off ('Yes, Sister,' and 'No, Sister,' and 'I truly repent, Sister,') and going on and on when she should be coming back fast to save Magda the terrible responsibility of hearing all this from old Mr Liam MacIlwam.

'You never did, Tom, though, did you?'

'No,' Magda answered.

'I watched long after you'd gone in. I took the risk, and saw Terry fall. He was blue with cold.'

'Was he?'

'They stood the three lads in line, all three of them, in the cold all through the playtime.'

'Playtime.'

'You remember when we came out to get our dinner they were all three in a line there, lying in the cold and blue. I was frantic. I cried and those two lads from Canav started laughing and kicked me stupid.'

'Kicked you.'

'I bled like a stuck pig all afternoon.'

'All afternoon.'

Surely it wasn't sinful to say the words old Mr MacIlwam was telling her when she didn't even know what the story was about? Except she was so sad about Terry being left in the cold all morning and through the midday and then into the afternoon, stiff and blue in the cold on the floor out there.

'My arm got broke that time. Callum from the Frackrelett Industrial School. He was a transfer, from fighting back with one of the Brothers there. It healed bent wrong.'

Sure enough Mr MacIlwam's left arm stuck out at an angle that wasn't quite right, the elbow being at an odd shape with the wrist turned as if he was always reaching into his pocket or trying to lift something that was just that bit too heavy.

'The Christian Brothers said it was the judgement of the Lord for staring at Terry on the playground floor when I should have hurried into class when the bell rang.'

'It was really Callum from Frackrelett?' Magda, helping the old man along.

'You weren't there when they set on me. The whole class got punished.'

'What happened to Terry?' she asked, drawn in.

'Terry got better. The other lad, Six-Nine, was taken away.'

'Taken away where?'

'Taken away.' The head-beckon pulled her slightly closer. She could hear Sister Claire's voice in that tone of finality, 'Well, just you remember your solemn duty, all of you!' so there would be no more time for all this listening.

'The cold was mortal bad that day. The frost never went. The snow began about the last Angelus. The lads were covered in white, blue under the layer of snow, see?'

'Snow?'

'They didn't move. They all finally fell down. Brother Patrick did it.'

'Did what?'

'He was the one always did it. We said you never came back when you went to get punished by Brother Patrick.'

'Never came back? Terry never came back?'

'Course not. You remember. You were in the same team.'

'So I was,' Magda said, baffled.

'Six-Nine never came back. He went for good. Terry got better. The other lad I didn't know. He had a dad come for him in the end, with papers and everything. He wanted to be a singer, but there was no way to get his voice going. No song in him, see.'

'No song.'

'I always had a good voice.'

'You did, sure you did.'

The old man's eyes clouded and then ran more sad rain down his cheeks. Magda looked away.

'Where did he go?'

'Who? Six-Nine?'

'Yes, him.'

'They said he died.'

'Six-Nine died?'

'They always said – we said, we told each other – they got buried in Tooley Cemetery, but the graves were never marked. We didn't know if that was true or not.'

'Tooley?'

'Tooley Cemetery. How could we know? We never went out.'

'Well, you couldn't know.'

Sister Claire's footsteps sounded on the linoleum, closer and closer. When they went quiet for a beat of two steps, Magda would know she was coming within earshot because there was a piece of carpet tacked there on the linoleum for the nuns' feet to rest on.

'I blame myself, Tom.'

'It wasn't your fault.'

'See.' The head-beckon, and she bent closer still. 'If I had maybe tried to go with him, maybe he wouldn't have been killed like that.'

'Killed?'

'Maybe they'd have thought, them old Christian Brothers, that we were four, and that four was too many. Are you seeing my argument?'

'Yes. Would it have made a difference?'

'Honest? You think not, honest?'

'No. It wouldn't.'

The answer was that Six-Nine would have died anyway, poor lamb, stuck there in the cold playground until he fell and froze from cold and went blue so he had to be taken away to the Tooley Cemetery.

'Haven't you finished yet?'

Sister Claire came wafting in, and that was the end of the conversation. Magda was almost faint from relief at seeing the nun, and dutifully completed her tasks.

She asked permission to help Grace to wash old Mr Liam MacIlwam's bedsheets once she was free, and the nun said that was a Christian compliance to a worthy labour, and that she could.

Magda helped Grace with the washing in silence, and Grace asked what was the matter. Magda said nothing about old Mr MacIlwam's story of the boy Terry who fell down in the frosty playground from being kept standing there until night from mitching from the Christian Brothers. She did not know where the idea came from, her being hardly able to tell one formed alphabet letter from the next, but it took form and held in her mind.

Killed.

That was the word that took hold and somehow came to dominate the rest of her mind as she rinsed and then wrung the clothes out in the mangle with the heavy iron handle. She caught the sheets on the other side of the rollers in a bowl and hung out in the yard with those silly pegs with the chipped wooden ends that gypsies made from wood they stole from trees and even gate-posts along the roads, so it was rumoured.

Killed?

'Grace,' she said after a while, when she had returned from hanging out the washing. 'What do you tell the priest in confession?'

'You've to tell them everything, silly.'

'Do you?'

'Yes. You have to. It says everything.'

'Does it?'

Grace knew Magda could not read, in fact, had to be shown the page, even, and then helped by letting her pretend to follow where your finger had got to in the Ordinary of the Mass so it didn't look too bad if the nuns came along, scouring the girls with their eyes for any backsliding.

'I mean, every single thing? What about if you have done something like, well, if a lad says something to you?'

'If you didn't do anything with the lad, then you needn't say anything to the priest because you resisted temptation.'

'Then how do people get married?'

'They stay pure until they are married, see?'

'What if it's something they're going to do wrong?'

This was the bit that mattered to Magda, who was by then already well into her plan of storing up those small white tablets in a safe place so she could poison Father Doran, and the Lord

God would be pleased and maybe lift Lucy to eternal glory so she could stop falling. Then Magda could sleep the sleep of the just and her life would be one white cloud of holiness, even in this job.

'That's wrong.'

'Is it? Every single time?'

'Course it is.' Grace was scathing. 'You'd be able to say you were going to rob the railway station in Galway, like, and the old priest wouldn't be able to tell anybody because that's against God's law.'

'He couldn't tell?' Magda had heard this was so. No harm making sure.

'No. He'd go to Hellfire if he did, and that would be the end of him. It would be wrong.'

'Why?'

'Presumption,' Grace said. 'It's not allowed, otherwise there you'd be, robbing the station in Galway where all the tourists go, and then you'd get clean away.'

'It's wrong?'

'It's not allowed. You'd get spotted. God spots things like that.'

This was a new difficulty. Magda asked Grace if she could make a kind of confession without saying what she was going to do, but Grace grew suspicious and looked funny at Magda, so she shut up and said nothing more.

Killed, though.

She wondered how many more people in the world of Eire – the truly good Catholic world where God ruled and all was well in Heaven and Earth because of Ireland – kept seeing other friends falling down, and why. Until then she had somehow seen men, the whole lot of them, sinners that they were because look at Adam and Cain and that old Pontius Pilate and all them evil Jews who crucified God Almighty, the whole lot of them as almost all-powerful and able to do everything they wanted. Though she had, of course, heard of the lads in the Industrial Schools being punished, though some grown-ups said it wasn't so bad and they had to somehow keep order. Others said different but wouldn't talk, and Magda never knew any well enough to even ask. Still more stayed silent, which was a truly terrible thing, for a man had no right to stay so silent you didn't even know what was going on in his mind.

And maybe she knew now, after listening to old Mr Liam MacIlwam tell his terrible dream memory of the boy Six-Nine falling like his pal Terry in the school playground in that horrid old frost and snow, that maybe many people, who had once been children, kept dreaming and screaming silent in their minds.

In penance, she kept her pay packet unopened all the weekend, as punishment for herself for having imagined she was the only one to suffer from seeing anyone fall time after time, like Christ who was continually crucified every time some sinner sinned against Him.

And sometimes Magda remembered the name of the girl who kept falling, and on those nights she woke screaming in herself but stayed quiet and never uttered a sound. She had promised.

Some promises were hard to keep. This was one promise she would keep to her dying day, because she had promised Lucy, the falling girl, she would never say a word about it to another living person. She had never even said a word about it to the priest in confession, and he was standing in for God, wasn't he?

If she forced herself, she knew she might, just might, be able to speak it, but that would be a kind of betrayal. Lucy's name had to be kept away from her mouth. That way the secret could be kept even from God in the confessional of a Saturday.

Chapter Seven

Kev MacIlwam's mother told him he had to go. He didn't want to.

'It's your turn, Kevin.'

'I'm due in work on the hour, Mam.'

'That can wait. Table tennis isn't work. That old sports club.'

'Won't you be going to see him later on today?'

'Going this morning is you.'

'I think Teresa should go. It's time she went.'

'She's got Inter examinations and needs her time.'

'I need my time for practice. The championship's next week, and you know what they're like.'

'Teresa's got enough to do, Kev. Spend time arguing, there'll be no time for anything.'

'I went last week.'

'Once.'

Mam could get scathing when she'd got her mind set on anything and if she suspected Kev particularly of trying something on. This was the worst sin in Mam's vocabulary, people 'trying something on', which meant escaping duty. Times were changing too fast. They should stay the same. All right, things always do change, but it should be slower, give her time to adjust. Too many folk talked too often of money, getting something for nothing. Everybody was always trying it on.

'OK.'

Kevin had a motorbike, a small old Velocette, true, but still going despite being on the blink now and then. The other Gardai at the garage joked about his sole means of transport, and sometimes left bottles of strangely concocted fuels, daring him to use it for his bike. He'd had a scrap or two over them slipping the odd glug into the fuel tank. Well, it was dangerous, and they'd since stopped all that. He supported Manchester United over the water in Lancashire, and his mate stuck up for Liverpool, where his brother Jerome was a prison warder.

He grumbled some more, finished his breakfast, ignoring the cereal despite Mam's protests that it was all the goodness he was leaving behind and only eating fatty things that were bad for you.

She kept up the diatribe as he got his leathers on.

'You're a fiend for fat, which will rot your heart away clear when you're forty. You should eat the corn flakes.'

'It doesn't fill me.'

'You never try it.'

'Eggs and bacon's good. I only have sausages at dinner time.'

Mam knew that wasn't true but kept the family peace by arguing as if it were.

'It's in all the papers all the time about fat foods.'

'What's up with Grampa?'

'They said to come this morning. If it's anything, you phone and tell me after you've seen him.'

'OK.'

He said his so-longs, shouting up the stairs to Teresa, who still hadn't come down yet though the bus was due in ten minutes, when she'd come flying down in a rush and catch it by a whisker to the convent school at Sandyhills.

He drove to the Care Home to see old Grampa MacIlwam, grousing to himself about the lack of practice for the table tennis. He'd been chosen for the championship and took his selection seriously. He hoped to win a sizeable bet on himself – eight-to-one wasn't bad, and he'd got in early at Joe Reef's corner emporium. With his winnings, if he made it, he might have enough to pay for a trip over the water to the Cheltenham Gold Cup, where he knew of a certain winner that would break the French bastards who – with them two new training stables they'd got, all Mohammedan Arab money from Kuwait, the sods – were trying to muscle in and own everything. It wasn't right. He'd punish them in coin, if only he had half a chance by getting enough money together to lay a decent bet on when the racing came.

To do this, though, you really needed to be there, see the call-over before the Gold Cup, see the horses enter the parade ring as they stirred and walked, see the sweat on their flanks, get the crack around the stables. He had a second cousin in Aintree who'd give him the last word, and together they might actually make a killing. Money in rather than money out. He would have to give Eoin a chop, of course, maybe a sixth of the whole bet for the quiet mother, the word that would determine his final choice of horses in the sacred ring in Gloucester, which had seen so many past Irish champions, but he would try to talk Eoin down to accepting maybe as little as a tenth.

It was hardly fair, though, to interrupt his training at the sports club on his one day off from the garage at the Gardai because of Mam's dedication to her stupid duty.

He went to see Grampa MacIlwam. With luck he could be in and out in ten minutes, and be in Blackrock in double quick time. Mam wouldn't know how long he'd spent.

Magda went to confession.

It was Father O'Reardon. Of course, she thought in trepidation, it would be the one made her go almost silent. You couldn't change your position in the queue just when you heard the priest's voice – she could never read the name on the door, hung there by a nun before confessions started, because the letters always ran into each other and, in any case, the light in the church wasn't all that good.

Also, it was a shameful rejection of God to decide you wanted to go to this priest rather than that priest, because it only meant that, in your heart of hearts, you were unwilling to accept God's law. The priest was set there by Canon Law to sit in the place of God Himself. How could you reject the Almighty? 'Who,' Sister St Union would say, eyes raised and shining piously at the ceiling, with that half-smile Magda always found so disturbing, like the nun was secretly enjoying something hidden and really rather horrid, 'who among us sets herself up to be above the good Lord Himself, instead of humbly submitting to His decisions made for us in His ineffable mercy?' On a bad day she would go round the class, picking on girls and asking, 'Do you, Bridget? Do you, Five-Oh-Two? Do you, Six-One?' Six-One was Magda. This was especially bad because Magda could never speak out in class and it would be the old round ruler and the legs aching and getting all chapped again.

So she shuffled along, taking her turn and moving up slowly with reluctance towards the low door, to rise and go in after the one before came out.

Father O'Reardon put the fear of God in her. She thought he had hair down to his fingernails when he hadn't. They gave out Holy Communion just like the dainty fingers of Father Byrne, but she felt Father O'Reardon seethed with hatred and passionate denunciation of everything outside his dark confessional.

She went in and knelt. She heard him pray something in Latin. Well, she would say it as she always did, as she had had drummed into her.

'Pray Father give me your blessing for I have sinned. It is one week since my last confession.'

The fact was, she sometimes thought afterwards, and even before, that she had no real idea whether she had sinned or not. Well, that wasn't quite right because she always had, for hadn't she the mortal Original Sin on her soul, from having been born human? And inherited the stain of terrible sins that could only be washed clean by a pure and blameless life?

'Yes, my daughter?'

The low register made the confessional rumble. And now here it was, the terrible question of whether to tell him what she was going to do. Father Doran would visit the St Cosmo Care Home this afternoon, which was why she had come to make her confession this early before work.

'I have told three lies, Father, and was slow in my work when I should have been working in eager obedience.'

She paused.

Could she say, and I have stolen some tablets with malice in my mind towards one of the priests who come visiting the

Care Home, or not? Would he tell the Gardai and send them chasing after her in their marked motors? Would they put her in them handcuff things, to her shame and the shame of all the girls and nuns at the Magdalenes throughout the world and cause the horrible re-crucifixion of the Baby Jesus? She wasn't really sure, but she kept thinking maybe she had already done that several times over by stealing the tablets in the first place. The old lady Mrs Borru had spotted her, so the Gardai would be able to prove she'd stolen them, because if one old lady had known all along then they with their bottles and jars and computer things could tell it was herself in a trice.

'Yes. And?'

'I have deliberately shirked my duties at the…'

Longer pause this time, because this was skating near the edge of some terrible crack in the ice.

'Yes?'

She decided to risk it, and said, 'At the Care Home. That's where I work, you see, Father.'

Another pause, breathless this time, and she could feel her breathing trembling all the way across her.

'Yes?'

He was becoming impatient. This would not do. Once they got it into their head that the penitent was hiding something, they became like terriers, never letting up until they'd hunted their way down those tunnels into the mine and then cornered the rat of suspicion and worried it to death. She wondered for an instant how she had acquired that image, because she was still mystified by those extraordinary creatures called dogs that everybody else seemed to take for granted, just things that were there knocking about to no purpose or on a string while you went out for a walk. There was old Mrs Derrig, who was allowed to keep a small thing called a Yorkshire, a barkish animal like a small rug that chased about in the backyard until the groundsman put it into its kennel at various times. Mrs Derrig took it for a walk round Carrick Park, where it did its business on the grass, which Magda thought wasn't too good because what if poo dried up and became dust and blew into the old folks' food of a mealtime? Then it would mean the old folks, far from being looked after, were actually eating what they shouldn't be made to eat at all, but she couldn't say that and never broached the topic, not even with Grace. Grace said all animals were sweet, and God's creatures just like us.

'I have sometimes made mistakes, Father.'

'What kind of mistakes?'

'Serious ones, Father.'

No good beating about the bush, not now seeing she'd got so far with her story. It was now that she should come clean, like they had to on the late-night telly when she earned extra money by sitting up with some old person who was serious poorly and the nuns had to be elsewhere, praying for all the poor children so that the world would be a better place. When that happened, Magda sat in with the sick old person and switched the telly on, and if it was RTE, she'd maybe listen and watch with the sound turned almost down to nothing at all, and watch the fillums from America or even England, though she always said a Hail Mary in case, especially when it was from England because they were not Catholic like Americans were. There was a lot of gangsterism about the American pictures, often serious bad. In them pictures the baddies always had to come clean, as they said when they were strapped in a chair and the detectives shouted in their faces. A lot of detectives smoked, she noticed in American pictures, though only in old

English pictures, a rerun of one made a long time ago in black-and-white.

'What were they?'

'To do with tablets, Father.'

There. It was out. It was what he might make of it now. There was no going back, because a priest had to ask the nature of the sin, and what it meant as far as God was concerned, or there was no arrangement between God Almighty and the penitent. That was the Church's teaching.

It was the Canon Laws of Holy Mother Church, and was made by the Holy Father in Rome so as to keep the Catholic religion, the One True Faith, unsullied by the depredations of the sinful Protestant corruption that was, in Sister Annuncion's words, 'now extending its pernicious tentacles everywhere to erode our Faith.' Magda had learnt this by heart, nearly got a good point by asking Sister to repeat it so she had it off by heart, saying it over and over. She might not be able to read, could not sign her own name, but she had a good memory for the word spoken.

'What kind of tablets?'

This was it, the finality of her presence kneeling before the priest who was, for the moment, God, there through the grill. Apart from the lad in the paper-packing warehouse place, Magda had never been so close to a man except in confession and during Holy Communion when the priest put the Host in her mouth, and Bernard.

'Please Father, some little white tablets. I don't know.'

That was true. She felt relieved, striking a blow for truth and honesty against all those evil religions, from Jews to Mohammedans, from other Christians to Quakers, none of who ought to be allowed but were out there against the Catholics.

'You don't know?'

'Please Father, no. I tried to read the bottle but couldn't.'

'What did you do?'

'I...'

'Did you tell the sisters in charge?'

Here was a real problem. To say no would mean she had concealed the missing tablets. Magda tried hard to remember if she had said there was more than one missing or only one. Odd that she would have remembered instantly if it had been something she'd heard somebody else say, but trying to recall what she herself said was difficult.

'Please Father, no.'

'What did you do?'

'Please Father, I said to the lady who had the tablets. She has to take one every so often. She knows when.'

'You told her?'

Well, Magda thought, I might as well have told her, because after all when she asked me I didn't deny it, like when the cock crowed and St Peter tried so hard to say he was a friend of Jesus, but couldn't bring himself to say it out because they'd have been cross with him as well.

She felt for the moment like Peter, who would surely understand, and said, 'She asked me if she was missing a tablet.'

'What did you say?'

Pause, with anguish in her heart and soul, which was having a terrible time of it, and Magda was so close to admitting to God and revealing all, and betraying Heaven in its eternal strife against evil forces.

'Did you admit that you had been careless?'

'Yes!' Magda felt so happy. All was resolved for her, in that one phrase.

God had spoken out in favour of what she was about to do. She felt close to tears. Her voice choked when she said, 'Yes, Father. I let her know that I had lost the tablet.'

There in one sentence was all that St Peter had done and the cock had crowed and who was the worse off? Nobody, because the poor saint by the campfire on Good Friday Eve couldn't do anything to help Jesus anyway, could he?

'Tablet' was a bit of a sin, though, singular instead of plural, because Magda had her store of tablets, including the pink ones and one dusky brown thing that could have been anything or the same, she didn't know. There was no way of telling, short of reading all the bottles in the drugs cupboard to which the nun in charge alone held the keys.

And there was another sin in there, only words God would understand. 'Admit' was fine, though she had not told the old lady outright that she had stolen the tablets. She just cleared her throat and went on with what she was doing, followed by Mrs Borru's bright understanding old eyes. That was an admission, really, wasn't it?

'Please Father, yes, I did.'

'Good.' The priest leant forward, closer to the grille. 'You do understand that it is vitally important to Our Lord that you confess all the sins you have committed in the most honest way you can?'

'Yes, Father.'

'And that Our Lord is crucified over and over every single time you deny him, do you not?'

'Please Father, yes.'

'Then make a sincere act of contrition, and say a penance of three Hail Marys and three Our Fathers.'

She said her prayer and left with relief. In a way, she mourned more than anything the inability to read, because she could have read through the *Small Roman Missal*, and come to some arrangement about the coming murder.

But Lucy had to be stopped from falling, because it was so hard on her to keep suffering so, with her worn woollen cardigan with the cotton stitches over the three holes in the right shoulder where she had tried to darn it in Free Time when they were to pray after doing the nuns' knickers. Tuesday duty, they had to sit in a circle with the other girls and do 'subsidiary tasks to the benefit of the community', as they were called. That was the day, inevitably, Magda's hand often bled from the long needles. She got whacked with the round ruler for not handling the needles properly. She hated Tuesdays. One day, she thought, she would have her own knickers bought from a shop, maybe, but that would be cruel because all it meant was that some little mites like herself would be out there sewing away and making their little hands bleed just for grand pennies for others. That would be so hard. There was just no way round these things.

For the penance and the confession she had just made, though, Magda felt really proud. She had worked something out all by herself. It was perfect so far as it went because she hadn't yet murdered the priest. It would come up soon. She thought it would be a sign from God, if her tablets proved quite sufficient to the job in hand, and killed him there and then when he came to have his tea with Sister Stephanie in the Care Home. That would confirm that the Almighty had approved, and that she was doing right. What more could she do except tell the priest that she was going to kill Father Doran, who had been at the Magdalenes the night Lucy started her falling?

That awful sad day, Lucy had wept so bitterly, and then during the night. And, in her stitched and badly rucked cardigan, she had then fallen for the very first time in the dark stairwell and had been falling ever since. It might possibly end soon, if Magda played her cards right and poisoned the priest so he died on the spot at the nuns' tea party, which they held in their grand conservatory.

'Conservatory' always sounded to Magda like a kind of jam, but who knew? Maybe it was where they used to make jam in the olden days when the English were here instead of in Liverpool playing their football.

When she got to work, she reported as usual to the nun in charge, who today was Sister St Simeon, an elderly nun who had grown fatter, Grace said, from too much praying over the past year. She spent much of her time at a desk instead of doing what Sister St Jude did – rushing about checking whether the kitchen staff were weighing out the food proper and decent for the cooking of the day. Sister St Jude was much to be preferred over the stout wheezing older nun because she got things done and it was more in tune with what Grace and Magda knew was the right way for nuns to behave. Sometimes, you could hear Sister St Jude shouting in anger from the other end of the building, and that wasn't always pleasant, but you knew things were as they should be when she was in charge. This pair tended to swap duties, one taking the morning rota and the other the afternoon, with both sharing the evening when things were in a rush. Some sets of relatives sometimes visited their old folk regular.

This particular morning, though, Magda was worried, because when she got to the Care Home she saw that a man was astride a motorbike in the gateway of the drive, where there had been an old statue, doubtless those old English with their Protestant madnesses. He looked for all the world like he was about to zoom off on his filthy machine the way they sometimes did so you took your life in your hands crossing the Kilfoyne Road, where the traffic lights kept you guessing anyway.

When she got nearer she could see the man was not moving, just sitting in the nook the hedgerows made with the rose garden, where old Bert who, folk said though Magda was always too scared to ask, had been a soldier and fought in wars and who was the only paid gardener the Care Home could afford, dug and weeded and wheeled things away in his wheelbarrow to set fires near the yard with the barking dog.

There was nobody about when she began to walk, but now there was this man. She could see he was young and thought she recognised him. He sometimes visited old Mr Liam MacIlwam, the old man who kept shitting himself so he needed extra sheets.

Magda was always disturbed by men, almost as much as by the very thought of them, because when you got down to the reason there were men and women made by God in His image, it was truly strange. There was your man, with his thing that, she knew from her meagre experience, was a rubbery dangling thing from his belly down, made to do nothing else but to stick inside a woman so they could procreate and increase the human race according to The Scriptures. That was all right. But the feeling you got from contemplating this was profound. Magda had always been good hearing words and registering them. She knew at least as many words as anybody else she knew of, just from listening, though God alone knew how them words spilt their little inks onto the pages in the right shapes. Anybody except herself could read them out and all get them sounding the same. 'Profound' was a word made for serious things, like contemplating men, and their sticking business of their rubbery thing into some woman. It was truly strange. And she could not help wondering who'd first thought of doing… well, doing that to a woman. Adam, she supposed. Sure to God it was bound to be the man because rumour and gossip and the women domestics she overheard sometimes often laughed about things like that. Magda tried to shut her mind to them because it was sinful, probably, though they seemed not to think so. They thought it a hoot.

And here was this youngish man, though maybe a bit older than she herself, who, now she was freed of the Magdalenes, was getting on for at least nineteen, due to move up to that special number in July, which was about halfway towards Christmas, at a guess.

The trouble was, the young man looked like he'd been crying. Now, this was new.

Magda wondered why. Maybe he too saw sometimes in his sleep (or near-dozing before he really went off in bed) somebody falling? You could never tell, because 'nobody knows the hour' as Sister St Union kept telling the girls at the school. Lucy said it was the time you died, though how could nuns know if that was true or not? Magda told Lucy not to be so terrible, because nuns had things explained to them that ordinary people didn't. They were close to God and sure to get to Heaven unlike everybody else, except priests.

But here was this man who looked like he had been crying, though how could you tell? And it couldn't possibly be, because Magda had once seen him visiting Mr Liam MacIlwam wearing a belt badge of the Gardai, yet there he was with tears streaming down his face and dripping, actually dripping, off his chin onto the bulbous tin of his motorbike where the oil went, if Magda guessed right. And his filthy motorbike had a badge on it, too. Maybe it was a cold? You got colds from, she guessed, driving about like a maniac. Them great noisy gadgets sounded like the clap of doom haring up and down the Borro. And him presumably being Garda and all.

She ducked her head, intending to walk on by, shamed and ashamed by the spectacle, pretending she hadn't noticed the man looking like she'd never seen before. Crying was for women, not for men to sit astride motorbikes in the alcove of a gateway and looking like they'd been weeping.

She had almost succeeded when the man's voice followed her and she heard him say, 'You the bird as sees to Grampa?'

It was in a normal voice so maybe she'd seen wrong, like when something was going on bad at the Magdalenes and you weren't to see or even remember, and you hadn't to raise your head and look. You'd just to walk on by and forget what you'd seen. It didn't always work, like when Lucy kept falling, because how could you forget everything that happened the night when Lucy fell the first time and carried on doing it night after night and day after day still, when it was how many years ago? She kept her eyes down on that old shingle path Bert scraped with a rake, whistling some tuneless song, the old gardener liking his daft old tune.

'Yes,' she said, scared of getting told off indoors for talking to a man in the street, well nearly in the street, by the gateway.

'Half a sec.'

'I'm due in.'

'Give us a sec.'

'I'll get told off.'

'It's quarter to.'

'I know.'

A lie, though only venial and making her due for Purgatory sure as apples, yet wounding to God all the same. Still, it was either that or Sister St Union's tongue and extra work instead of a break. And what had forced this possibly weeping man on her but the events of the day? The only event that so far had happened was that she'd gone to confession. She could have been taking her time.

'You nurse Grampa MacIlwam, don't you?'

'Yes.'

That too was possibly another venial sin, because she was no nurse, not like real nurses who came in every second day and saw to the old folk, mostly those with horrid tubes in their bellies and that, not the ordinary oldies who were normally taken care of by girls like herself. This was proving a seriously contorted day and it had hardly started yet.

'Hang on a sec.' There was the sound of his boot – he wore chunky kinds of leather-looking boots to drive his stinking machine. She'd seen him at it once or twice, scaring all the birds in the garden and setting old Bert's dog crazy, wanting to bark twice as loud and go running after it.

She stopped. 'I can't stop,' she said, not turning round yet. 'I'm due in.'

There. That made it all right and maybe cancelled out her lie. Maybe she'd even rescued God from Heaven-knows-what torment caused by her previous untruth. Mrs Fogarty, a married woman about forty but in any case getting well on for senile, who cooked in the kitchen and supervised the food being prepared for the hundred or so inmates of the Care Home, said fibs caused no harm, here or Up Above. Magda thought that was a truly sinful thing to say because the Church knew best. Mrs Fogarty just said, 'Oh, well, you think what you like. You'll learn yourself different in God's good time, girl.' Grace, who overheard that, said she should tell Sister St Simeon and did, but nothing came of it, just the nun's lips grew sort of tight when she walked by Mrs Fogarty, who still made the most noise banging her old tins about the kitchen of a morning whatever people, even nuns, said, telling her to keep the noise down please.

Then he said something that really stopped her right there.

'Please,' he said.

He was ginger-haired, when she turned and looked at him. It was uncanny to be there in broad daylight, staring at somebody who was male, that word beyond which there was no other sense or meaning, just the word itself. He had shiny, blackish, leatherish tight clothes on, with those thick giant boots. He was propping up the bike by simply letting his legs stretch to the ground. She had the notion that he didn't even care whether the bike toppled or not, so casual he seemed. It was quite at odds with his great wet tears streaming down his face to his chin, setting the garments even blacker where they dripped onto him. She told herself, yes, it must only be one of them old colds and soon he'd start sneezing all over her to prove it.

'You see to Grampa MacIlwam, don't you? I know you do.'

'Yes.' She struggled with honesty a few moments. Maybe he saw her difficulty because he gave her time. She felt a bit of gratitude, though why? It was her difficulty, her time come to that, nothing to do with him and his old smelly bike. 'Sometimes, when he's...when the old gentleman's not been very well.' How could she describe the mess old Mr MacIlwam got into, to this man? God, how did married people get on with their terrible lavatory secrets revealed for each spouse to see? Jesus, the thought made her head swim.

'He says you're the one he talks to.'

'Me?'

'Yes. You talk to Grampa.'

'Me?'

Was she in trouble? Thoughts of Lucy falling raced through her mind, and Lucy's cardigan with the crudely inept stitching, nothing more than ordinary cotton all in the wrong colours, just before she fell. What a terrible sad state to go to meet your Maker in a rotten cardigan. And she'd no right to be chatting to this Garda man astride his bike in his leathers, with his blue eyes staring right the way through her like they shouldn't, because who knows what could happen if you kept this sort of thing up?

'He said so.'

'I only do what the nuns say, or the nurses on the days they come.'

'I knew it was you.'

'I only do what I'm told.' She almost shouted the words, then caught herself and said it gentler, 'As I'm told by the nuns. They know what I've to do, see. I'm not a nurse. They come eight o'clock to four in the afternoon.' Old Mr MacIlwam didn't have a tube in his belly yet. If he had, she'd have told this man to talk to the nurses and ask them what it was that worried him like that. He shouldn't be out here waiting for her nearly in the street.

She thought, why am I telling him this? She said again the bit about doing only what she was told.

'Give us a minute.'

'Minute?'

The last time she'd given a lad a few minutes she'd ended up scared witless that she was going to have a baby and bleeding so unexpectedly into her knickers. She'd made a Novena to the Virgin Mary for that, and told it all out in confession and had got a penance that she ought really to be still saying if she'd taken her time with it, fifteen Credos to start with and three Rosaries one after the other and no daytime meals for a week.

'What time do you get off?'

'Me? Six o'clock.'

He nodded, thinking. Magda turned to glance at the windows of the Care Home. Nobody showed there. They would all be getting ready for their breakfast, which she would carry round in the end block very soon if she could get away from this motorbike lad who was still dripping his great wet blobs.

It would be dark later, and sometimes she and Grace walked home down the Borro together for safety because of bad lads and shouting drunks or, as Mrs Fogarty cheerfully said in joke, in hopes of lepping onto some passing young feller-me-lad and shutting him up good and proper, which made Magda go red and set Grace praying.

'I'll be here.'

'No.' She almost shouted that, too. She turned and started away.

'I want your help with Grampa,' he said after her, his boots scuffing the gravel so she worried for an instant that he might be getting down off that bike and coming after her. 'Please.'

That word again made her pause. She looked back. 'What do you want me to do?'

'Help him. Promise?'

'Yes.' She was going to say of course, because that's what she did. Ever since she'd arrived at the Care Home she'd helped people. She thought she did it well.

'Do you catch the bus?'

'Sometimes.'

'I mean tonight.'

'Maybe.' Then, in panic because she'd the murder of Father Doran to plan this afternoon, when the priest came a-visiting the old people and the nuns, and he had his special tea with Sister Stephanie where they chuckled about, doubtless, holy things, she said, 'No, not tonight.'

It had to be worked out today, because it had taken her so long to get herself to this pitch of preparation. She knew she'd never kill anybody, much less Father Doran, if she didn't make a decent start and put a good foot under her.

'Why not?' He looked at her and her voice dried up, like her throat had suddenly got oldish.

'I dunno.'

'You working late tonight?'

'Yes!' She cried out the lie with relief.

'Tomorrow then? There's not a lot of time.'

Well, she'd no watch and you couldn't see the clock over the porch from this far away, and in any case she'd never been too good at numbers written, clocks included.

'Tomorrow?'

'Yes. I'll be at the end of the Borro waiting, OK? Tomorrow.'

'I don't know. What for?'

How could she explain she was going to work out how to kill Father Doran today? The man had already wept himself out from the look of him. He'd started his challenge of her with red face and a wet chin, and now looked pale as death.

'You must. Please, Magda.'

'Well...'

'Look out for Grampa, will you?'

'Course I will.'

Then he said it, the one thing that swayed her and made her vow to help him whatever the consequences.

'Don't tell the nuns or the others, whatever you do, will you?'

'Tell them what?' she asked quick, stricken.

'That I talked to you.'

'Me?' Stupid, stupid. Who was there, but the two of them?

'Or what I said about Grampa?'

'No,' she said, truthful now.

'Promise.' He wasn't asking. He was telling. Anyway, she thought, firming resolving to get herself moving, it was fine by her.

'Promise.'

She always kept promises, wherever she had made it and whoever it had been with, for promises excluded nuns, except the ones due to God, and that was a special arrangement called conscience. Even to Lucy she had kept her promise, though whether it should include confession or not she would never be sure. Once she finished killing the priest, that would be an end to it and Lucy would stop falling and the whole world would be at peace, Magda in there too with the rest of them, all like sleeping babes.

She hurried indoors, thinking, where did he say? End of the Borro, six o'clock tomorrow when she got off duty and the old folks were all settled for the evening. She went to work out her plan, wondering whether she ought to say a prayer for the poor priest.

The trouble was, she thought, Holy Mother Church never taught rules for things like this.

Chapter Eight

Father James Doran was the most presentable priest in the bishopric. He was sure of this, and easily found reasons.

For one, he kept his youthful form, and his cassock of fifteen years still fitted. His future position as monsignor was almost assured. No taint attached to his reputation or his record. He had acquired his B.Theol. degree, though not with honours, and kept in touch with his old tutors. The seminary asked him along to give seminars on the nature of priestly duties 'in the field', the title of the two-day stint he did every month for young priests there. He was warmly welcomed.

Ambition was not sinful, no. Ambition honestly applied, with considerations of conscience and a sufficiency of prayer on careers, was duty thoughtfully applied and sincerely executed. Father Doran's intention was, with the bishop's approval, to establish a series of diocesan lectures on the Changing Nature of Priestly Life, without any dangerous Shavian interpretations of post-John Paul II's suggested variations, which were seeping into the Church's established doctrine. He had spoken with the bishop on several occasions with the aim of setting in the prelate's mind the worthiness of appointing a special recruiting monsignor as an autonomous division. This would be a post of power – relatively, of course, but having influence. It would inevitably lead to greater things.

If the incumbent were successful, it would hallmark the appointee and without question lead to a bishop's mitre. The present bishop, a pleasant and affable man, was ailing and elderly, and besides, had seen too many harrowing lawsuits to be of much further use in rebuilding the solid reputation of the Church. More conviction could have left the Church unsullied. As things stood, however, there was no doubt in many people's minds that the Church was going through times of hardship, abused from all sides. London newspapers were proving their usual scurrilous selves, their pernicious influence extending across the Irish Sea into Dublin and the rest of Eire. The terrible, sad events in America's Boston had encouraged the hounds of the gutter press to come baying after the Church. In Doran's view, this was only par for the course. The Church had always been beset. Enemies were abetted from within by incompetence and weakness, well illustrated by the hopelessly inept lawyers and clergy of the diocese of Boston in Massachusetts, USA. That was the road to bankruptcy.

He sighed, waiting for his audience to assemble. They would consist of eleven nuns and the Sister Superior today. They always notified him two days beforehand, so he could tailor his talk to their understanding. There were doubts, sometimes, not a few expressed in ordinary converse about the tea table, some even surfacing these days outside the secrecy of the confessional, quite as if any and every subject was open to question. Outrageous, new, dangerous. There was one nun in particular, Sister Francesca, who seemed to harbour a faint uncomplicity, which might, if not nipped in the bud, burgeon into doubt itself.

Almost shuddering, Father Doran composed himself to form his thought sequence. There were various ways to do this. Charles Dickens, a scurrilous propagandist, was wont, he had read in a biography, to establish in his mind a circle, each sector dealing with a particular part of his theme. Dickens would then speak on each in turn, until the full circle of his talk was done. He would end with a reading. No wonder the man was so successful, though he had spoken, and written, a derogatory account of the Americans.

America. Father Doran always grew angry thinking of the gutter press. Its evil miasma had turned the noble diocese of Boston into a charnel house, a veritable pit of sinfulness. London's newspapers, of course, gloried in the discomfiture of Holy Mother Church, telling how the most sacred institution on earth, established by God Himself, had been somehow involved in paedophilia and the physical abuse of children entrusted to the Church's care. Typical that the English press should resent so, and delight in New England's discomfiture, for hadn't the original Boston, Lincolnshire, been named after the English St Botolph, as Botolphstown? Crimes detailed in the media were unnatural and impossible. Father Doran had heard the news reports on television. An abomination, of course, and utterly unbelievable. Who could do such a thing to innocent children? No. It could only be explained by the spread of false accusations. Moral laxity, the immorality of drugs and carnal expression of wanton profligacy extended all over the world.

One consequence was most distressing of all. Doran hoped to be sent to the United States on an exchange, perhaps for a sabbatical year, and then who knew? A complete transfer, with all the opportunities that might represent, could be on offer. Emigration, following brilliant clergymen of the past, to live successfully in the USA. The final destination was unknowable, but promising. Canada too had suffered, with the Christian Brothers falling prey to the media's malignity even there. And Australia. Who knew where else?

The nuns entered. He rose, composing his features into an expression of benevolence and pleasure. Eleven today, with the two senior nuns in the lead. Words were exchanged, all smiling. Father Doran always liked to create an impression of eager activity at this point, so he allowed them to sit and started immediately.

'I thank you as ever, Sisters, for the invitation to visit and to bore you, huff-huff, yet again with a few thoughts about the sacred duties we all concern ourselves with. I was just considering when you arrived how the social sphere – welfare, legalities, the Church's wider roles in the community – has come to overlap that of the exercise of piety within the Church...'

Magda heard them at it in there as she carried the trays to the hallway and laid them on the mahogany table one by one. When the talking finished, she and Philippa took the trays into the nuns' refectory. They had a separate tray to take in to the office where the two senior nuns would give Father Doran his tea before he started in his rounds and heard the confessions of the old folk, if they asked for him.

Philippa was a Magdalene who now lived with her auntie and an uncle near Moore Street Market. She said she'd been born in the Rotunda and got rescued from the machine shop in the Magdas when her brother became of age and walked, bold as you please, and signed for Philippa. The ungrateful girl still gnawed over the years her brother took coming with the papers, and took no notice when Magda, shocked at the girl's lack of gratitude, said, wasn't Dominic just a-growing like she was herself and unable to do a single thing on his little own?

'You should be grateful Dominic didn't do a wrong thing himself,' Magda said when she got to know Philippa well enough to say such a terrible thing to another Magdalene. Some could create. She'd seen some truly terrible fights, out here in the open, beyond any restraint of the other convents, when one person said such a thing about another. Though, strange to tell, Magdalenes never fought each other, just said things low down and into their bosoms so nobody would even hear what the ex-Magdalenes were saying or, especially, thinking, when they spoke of the past.

'It's true, Magda.'

'You still should not say such a thing.'

'I blame my uncle too.'

'You can't!'

Magda's head always reeled over Philippa's wickednesses, because who knew who put them into Philippa's brain to speak right out in the first place? Satan, maybe.

'I can to be sure, Magda.'

'He's a good man, Philippa.'

'Good to hisself more like. And to my aunties. And to Dominic.'

'And to you.'

When two Magdalenes talked, even out here now they were free and employed with honest wages and long stringy paper chits showing numbers of money at the end of the week, they always talked quieter than anybody else. The ladies who slammed about the kitchens were loud and raised their voices.

Not only that, they would hold their chin up and their register – that's what it was called, like a soprano had a higher register than an alto – was always high, as if they hardly cared who heard. Especially the married women, though they of course had husbands to stick up for them if anything came of what they said. It was then up to the husband to correct his wife according to the Scriptures and that.

'Your uncle gives you bed and board, Philippa!'

'Sure he does.'

'Then what's wrong with that?'

Magda thought that must be truly beautiful, a man arguing and laying the law down and not caring if he swore or whistled and the women wanting him to stay quiet. There he'd go, whistling or maybe singing away and looking at the football news and shouting the results over the wall to pals who would come with a bottle of the brown stuff to swill back and argue politics and all kinds of daft things you never heard of.

'He should have come for me sooner.'

'How could he?'

'He was my uncle, wasn't he?'

'Yes, course he was.'

'Then he should have let Dominic get me sooner. He could have. Dominic told me he'd asked him.'

'When did he tell you?'

Magda had a trial of conscience over this. At the time they were in the sluice and Philippa had decided to start smoking – the crime of *that* – and Magda didn't actually know how to ask something about Dominic, who she hadn't seen at all, ever. She thought the words 'your brother' far too intimate, because they implied all kinds of things that had gone on in the family between mother and father that you didn't mention, not properly. Also, were you allowed to speak out somebody's name just like that? It might mean you were taking terrible liberties, as if you had spoken to them without anybody else being present, like she had with that lad with his legs astride the motorbike earlier. No, even the short question was something of a risk. Perhaps all talk really was, if you went into it.

'Dominic?' (The dreadful ease with which Philippa said that, a man's name straight out, though of course he was her brother and all.) 'When he come for me.'

'What happened?'

Philippa had told her the story several times before, but Magda couldn't get enough of hearing it, word after word. It was quite beautiful, because there was Philippa in the machine shop, having trouble as usual threading the under-reel on that terrible old Singer sewing machine with the loose leather on the treadle that kept slipping so Philippa's legs were always going to cramp, and the broken needle the nuns were too mean to replace except at the end of every week, as if Friday was treat time when the girls would all be thrilled, even though Saturday was also a work day, five o'clock finish instead of six.

And they sent for her, a nun with a message to go immediately to the Mother Superior's office that very instant, and Philippa was so frightened she almost weed herself running up the corridor and thinking she was going to get a good old clouting for almost dropping off to sleep in Holy Mass that morning, and she'd knocked...

Magda could say the words with Philippa in her head, '... There was this man, a grown man, with Mother Superior. He was standing up, and he had a paper in his hand, and Mother Superior was saying he was my brother.'

'Then what?'

Magda was so thrilled at the tale. She kept seeing herself instead, in Philippa's place, and the nun taking the paper and saying, 'Magda, here is your brother and he has brought legal papers to have you released from our care. Now, I have serious admonitions to make before you can be handed over into your brother's charge.'

But it was Philippa who was telling the lovely story like some fairy tale they told on the RTE channels, which Magda loved to watch over and over when they did lessons for the little ones. The sad thing, sad for Magda, was it was Philippa who was in the story and not her.

'What happened then?'

'I said his name, Dominic. It was such a strange sound in my head, and kept saying itself round and round.'

'And you didn't know...'

'I didn't know I hadn't said a single word at all until the Mother Superior told me to say hello politely like a sister should, and thank him for bringing the legal papers from the law so I should leave.'

'And you were so scared,' Magda prompted, tears in her eyes every time it got to this bit, because Philippa did as she was bid and then simply flew to get her one other pair of knickers and her comb, which you weren't allowed to carry with you, and the prayer book that was always sent out with any girl who suddenly got a family or somebody to rescue them safe out of the Magdalenes.

'Terrified,' Philippa said, every time making it worse and worse, 'that my brother would have gone when I got back to the Mother Superior's office.'

'But he was still there!' Magda cried at this juncture, almost delirious each time Dominic was still waiting in that old Mother Superior's office, still standing like he was planted on that grand carpet with his precious paper that would get Philippa walking with her brother out of that old Magdalene machinery place.

'He was still there.' Philippa always entered into the story when she got to that bit, saying 'still...*there*' like he could have gone anywhere else on earth but no, there he was all right. And Magda, in her ecstasy and relief that Philippa was about to be saved yet again, so the story would still be true for ever and ever, cried it inwardly with her, 'Still...*there*!' And it was the very best feeling.

'I listened to the Mother Superior telling me about Christian duties and responsibilities and how I must conduct myself in the family I was going to live with from then on, and I hardly heard a single word because I was thinking, oh, please, God, let us go and let my brother here not say something like he'd come back to collect me next week or sometime that might never come.'

'But he didn't!' Magda knew her face was shining with rapture.

'No. He took hold of me, my actual hand, bold as brass, with the head nun right there, him looking right in my face, and smiled and told me—'

'He told you,' Magda always interrupted here, beside herself with impatience to get Philippa out of that corridor smelling of Mansion Polish and down those big wide stairs with the bannisters and out of that front door and crossing herself so she could leave with her brother and her brother saying...

'And Dominic said to me when we stepped onto the top step—'

'Put your arm through mine, Philly,' Magda said, out of breath at so much contact between a brother – a man, after all

– and a girl in full view of the world and especially the nuns, and Mother Superior probably itching to call a Novena to save their lost charge from perdition and the burning in Hellfire at such goings-on.

'And I'll tell you what was the strangest thing on God's earth,' Philippa said, remembering what had happened that fateful day. 'I'd no idea that my mother had a pet name for me before she died, but she had always called me Philly, God rest her soul.'

'Amen.'

'And ever since Dominic always calls me Philly. So do my aunties and my uncle, like I'd never ever been anyone else at all.'

'That's marvellous,' Magda breathed, relaxing with the utter relief of Philippa's tale, as Dominic with Philly on his arm walked bold as brass out of the gate to a car belonging to the Garda Siobhana parked at the kerb, where two of the Gardai were having a smoke.

'I kept thinking, will they send me back?'

'They couldn't, though,' Magda protested, anxious now at this bit and keen to defend Philippa from last-minute dangers. She explained for the sake of thoroughness, 'Because your brother had the papers, see?'

'Because he had the papers.'

'And nobody could touch you.'

'That's the truth, Magda. Thanks be to God.'

'Amen.' Magda had started asking, a routine as the story of Philippa's rescue reached its conclusion, 'Can the Magdalenes still come for me?'

'Now you're eighteen? I don't think so.'

'I'd run away.' Magda said it without conviction, because there was never a chance of anybody running away, not ever.

They always sent the Garda Siobhana after you and brought you back. Look at the story the old man Mr Liam MacIlwam told her, whose relative she was going to see tomorrow – if she dared turn up where he'd told her to be at six o'clock, him on his old motorbike and dripping tears on his chin.

'I keep asking Dominic to look at the papers and tell me if they're making new laws about me,' Philippa said, putting the fear of God into Magda who instantly felt faint.

'Can they do that?'

'Yes.'

'Will they?'

'To take us back? Not any more they won't. That's what Dominic tells me, but he never says it when my aunties are there or my uncle.'

'Why not?'

'They get mad.'

'With him?'

'Sure. Dominic says talking like that makes them feel bad, like they ought to have done something a lot earlier and didn't.'

'Why?'

'It's been in all the papers, Magda.'

'What has?'

'Bad things. At the industrial schools and that. The Magdalenes too, though we got away light, so they say now. Except they weren't there.'

'Who? What schools?'

'Ranter. Lots of others.'

'What happened?'

'I listen to the old ones here talking. Sometimes it's them who were there. Sometimes it's their friends. Sometimes it's their relatives. It's what happened.'

Magda knew the old folk talked when they should have been sleeping in the afternoon, but she never woke them or even went to them unless they called for her because the nuns were always off somewhere and the real nurses, who wore hospital badges to show they'd got trained proper, only ever said hush, hush, to them and said things were all right now. You could never tell with old people if what they saw was real and what they were thinking was from times past. Magda knew then it was the same with her and her friend Lucy, the falling girl.

'What things?' Magda was mad with herself for being so stupid she couldn't read. Otherwise she would have been able to read newspapers like Dominic. He was a clerk in the library and 'could look things up' any time of day or night, even while he was at work. This meant finding things out.

'Shhhh.' Philippa's warning came just in time to interrupt Magda's daydreaming, because the lecture was ending. Father Doran in there was chuckling and the nuns were tittering and the chairs scraping away and feet sounding on the boards. So it was time to carry the trays in.

Father Doran had been about on duty the evening of the night Lucy had fallen. Magda had seen him, but Father Doran had not seen her, thanks be to God.

'The tea trays, girls,' Sister St Jude said, cruising past with her long skirt swishing the floorboards.

'I hope it's Dundee cake today,' Father Doran said with a laugh as he emerged among the nuns.

'Oh, Father Doran!'

'I trust I shall be forgiven in Heaven!'

'Amen to that,' Sister Francesca said, but without a smile.

'Now, Sister Francesca,' Sister Winifred said in mock rebuke which set the nuns laughing. Magda noticed, but instantly averted her eyes so she would not earn a rebuke, that Sister Francesca did not smile with the rest and wondered if she had been told off. Though nuns could hardly be told off as if they were ordinary lay people, could they? They were nuns, after all.

Father Doran slapped his own hand in sham punishment.

'Take that, for going on too long about Infallibility. I knew I should have chosen a different subject!'

The nuns laughed, and this time Sister Francesca did permit herself a small smile, but tight like she had a kind of coming toothache that was causing her difficulty. She scanned the tea trays, her duty, and saw Magda was holding the one for the office where Sister St Jude would entertain Father Doran to tea for a half hour, and gave a curt nod.

'Dundee, I see, girls.'

'Yes, Sister.'

'Who baked it?'

'Please, Sister Francesca, Mrs Malahide did it last evening. She says it should be left a day or two more to get firmed up, but it was either that or Battenberg.'

'Then Mrs Malahide did right, girls. Please tell her thank you from us, will you?'

'Yes, Sister.'

'The tray now, and set the water boiling.'

'Yes, Sister.'

Philippa had the gift of seeming just the same the instant the nuns showed, but Magda knew she could not stay looking like she was innocent. Philippa could be talking all kinds of perdition, yet once the nuns were in sight her face composed itself into a diligence that would deceive an angel. It was remarkable. Magda was so envious of Philippa, not just because she had a real brother and real aunties and an uncle she lived with, but because she was untouchable and nobody could take her back into the Magdalenes, having a family.

Soon, though, she thought, as she picked up the tray and went slowly and carefully up to the office where Sister St Jude and Father Doran waited for their teas, she would have set Lucy free by killing this Father Doran, and that would free herself too and she could sleep like a Christian safe from dreams.

One terrible, possible horrendous, thing happened as she carried the tray slowly inside and laid it on the tray trolley within Sister St Jude's reach, as she and the priest sat facing and talking, and received a nod to leave.

Father Doran said, quite audibly, as Magda reached the door, 'Has that girl been here some time, Sister St Jude? I have a notion she was at one of the places I ministered to.'

'Magda? She was a Magdalene child, orphan and farmed out to work.'

'Ah. Maybe it was there I noticed her previously.'

'You remember her from somewhere?'

'Perhaps.' A sigh. 'There are so many.'

'Yes, and more is the pity, Father.'

'Indeed. The plight of the schools is my concern in this diocese, Sister.'

'Has Bishop MacGrath said anything more? Anything that may be divulged, I mean.'

'I blame the gutter press. They lack all sense or restraint or responsibility to children, Church or the state of Eire. Thankfully, though, they seem to have dropped it for the whilst.'

'Perhaps other things concern them.' Sister St Jude spoke with irony.

'Yes. Some scandal with a pop star, or some football outrage.'

Magda slowly let the door click. It was glass, though, and she knew the shape of any listener could be seen quite clearly if the light was on in the hall, which it almost invariably was even in daylight. She stood listening but to one side of the door.

'Magda?'

Sister Francesca's voice almost made Magda yelp. She stood back, startled and afraid. She stared at the nun, who was within a yard of where she had been eavesdropping.

'Sister?'

Sister Francesca beckoned Magda away to stand close to the vestibule.

'Were you deliberately listening to the priest's conversation with Sister St Jude?' And after a pause, 'I am waiting, Magda.'

'Please, Sister Francesca, Father Doran asked if he had seen me before.'

'He meant you in particular?'

'Yes, Sister.'

'And did he address you directly?'

'No, Sister.'

'To whom was he speaking, Magda?'

'To Sister St Jude.'

'Then by what right do you listen to the conversation of two people in authority over this establishment?'

'Please Sister, I know I was doing wrong, but I was frightened.'

'Frightened? Of what?'

'That Father Doran would send me back, Sister.'

'Back?' Sister Francesca inspected Magda as if for presenting to an audience. 'Back where? You were in the Magdalenes, weren't you?'

'Yes, Sister.'

'Where? Sandyhills, wasn't it?'

'Yes, Sister.'

'There is no possibility of that, not now or at any future time. That is the case.'

'Yes, Sister,' Magda said, who didn't quite believe it.

'You were an orphan?'

'Please, Sister, yes. I was Six-One.'

'And you are happy here?'

'Yes, Sister! Of course, Sister!' Magda's constant, if terrified, reply since she was rising five.

'Then do not commit an offence of that kind ever again, do you hear?'

'Yes, Sister.'

'Very well. I shall say no more about it. Go back to your duties.'

As Magda turned away with a mutter of thanks, the nun said, 'Magda? You did not meet Father Doran before, did you?'

'No, Sister. Not that I remember.'

'Did he attend your convent?'

'I don't know, Sister. I never saw him, no.'

'Very well.'

Magda was dismissed and hurried away. She felt Sister Francesca's eyes on her all the way to the bend of the corridor.

It had been a near thing. She wondered about Sister Francesca. How many of the lies Magda had just told her had she detected? Any? None?

Chapter Nine

Magda finally worked it out.

Killing a priest counted as murder, so you would have to be careful. Two more days, and she'd do it. The question was, how? Dundee cake, or the liquid he swigged when talking to old Mr Gorragher, who had no first name but who said he once worked in Sheriff Street on the north side of Dublin? He worked in a bar there.

Killing a priest was a serious matter, and she didn't want the ginger-headed Garda motorcycle lad to come round in his black leathers and boots arresting her with his sergeant and taking her to be hanged. Where would that leave Lucy? Forever falling into that terrible pit of suffering as she fell again night after night, and her bloodied head and matted hair spread across her pillow. And the nuns struggling to carry out the girl's body from the dormitory so ineptly because they'd forgotten something. Silly stupid women that they were, in spite of God backing them up. No man would ever be so forgetful when he had some serious lifting to do, no, he'd be whistling and maybe grunting a little then saying things like, 'This side down a bit, George, now go straight' while the other man, his mate, would say, 'Got it, Harry,' and they'd lift easy as wink with that incomprehensible, 'One, two...*six*' they called out to lift anything together. They'd remember the iron things to put across between the poles that slotted into the canvas stretcher. No, the nuns that horrible horrendous night forgot the iron so they couldn't lift it properly and they carried the dead girl from the dormitory in a canvas bundle like a carpet.

Old Mr Gorragher was a man who had been a soldier. She heard him talking to nobody when she hoovered round his bed and he was scratching, forever scratching at nothing on his head where several scars showed ugly puckering of the skin that had gone extraordinarily white, like it was trying to untangle something all knotted up within. She heard him the afternoon Father Doran came. That's what gave her the idea of changing her scheme of how to kill the priest and so stop poor Lucy falling.

'See, Alanna,' old Mr Gorragher suddenly chimed up, quite as if she had been chatting to him the best part of an hour when in fact she had only just come into his little alcove with her noisy vacuum cleaner, 'I thought the whole fucking army was terrible, seeing everybody was trying to kill everybody. That's what they say, Father.'

Alanna? Father? thought Magda, hoovering away round the old man's bed but saying nothing, just keeping on with her work because Sister Raphael had ears like a bat and would come swishing up in her old nun's gown complaining and asking what was wrong. Sister Raphael forbad any interruption in the cleaning, the business of housekeeping, the cooking and especially the machines – Jesus, the machines, they had to keep going night and day because otherwise it proved to Sister

Raphael that you'd 'caused serious expenses to be incurred by the Care Home that were quite unwarranted'. It meant it was your fault. A girl called Liz, whose mam was born in Mary's Lane back of Four Courts, where she kept telling everybody there was nothing but judges and lawyers as far as the eye could see, and who was so misshapen you had to be charitable about her legs, this girl called Liz left something cooking in the microwave – she knew how to work it – and Sister Raphael smelt the burning. There was merry Dickens to pay, and Liz was told she'd have to pay the money for the microwave oven, only a titchy thing, from her wages. Liz said that was unfair and said she'd get those old judges to write to Bishop MacGrath to complain that Liz was being oppressed and disadvantaged, words she had to explain to Magda, who overheard and was intrigued. She was intrigued because somehow Sister Raphael never said another Christian word about the microwave and Mr Bourne, who came to mend things, mended it and said it was good as new but was like to catch fire if used much longer.

That caused a right old barney for two days.

When old men started going on about what had happened in the past, they tended to use bad words Magda did not quite follow. She never tried to get to the bottom of such talk because Heaven alone knew what they might mean. So when Mr Gorragher started on about his wounds he had several more, one great long one in his belly because of some terrible fight in one of his old wars – and the swear words came, Magda just hoovered on, not listening. He was only talking to himself and not really to her at all.

'I learnt different.'

'Oh?' One of Magda's absent responses.

'Truth to tell, they were the dregs.'

'Dregs, eh?' Another of Magda's keep-going responses then she could get finished and clear herself for the next job with Sister Raphael and not get into trouble.

'Armies always are, see?'

'That's so, is it?'

'Sure 'tis. Gutter crew, they said we were, all for the King's shilling.'

And he sang a little bit of that song that started:

The wandthrin' one
Since time begun
Has yearned for native soil
And sorely grieves
The man who leaves
His homeland by the Foyle.

'Now you shush, Mr Gorragher, there's a good man.'

Magda said that because it wasn't really a very Christian song at all, but was probably one of them songs they sang in Northern Ireland, where the English drank themselves stupid on their strawy old beer and there were Union Jacks all over the place and the Red Hand of Ulster, which caused all the wickedness that haunted mankind ever since God had made the Garden of Eden. You didn't ought to sing some songs, that's all. Magda tried to stop him singing his song, but not caring much at all, while she vacuumed away round his bed and then the rest of his alcove.

The old man sang on:

To preach the word
Face battle's danger
Praise the Lord
And serve the stranger

Then came the awful uncomfortable part Magda never liked. It went:

And one by one
They took their bonds
And bad farewell to Erin...

The song left you hanging there and thinking, well, get on with it, did the soldiers ever come home or not?

'I used to sing that with a Lancashire lad who was a thief.'

'A thief, was he, Mr Gorragher?' Magda had heard it all before.

'Nimble as that little fairy thing that goes red at Christmas with Peter Pan on that old stage show.'

'Oh, I know that one all right, Mr Gorragher,' said Magda, though she didn't. 'At Christmas, isn't it?'

She left the hoover running, standing straight up so it wouldn't fall, so as to keep bat-eared Sister Raphael happy in her old office along the corridor, and started dusting round Mr Gorragher's few possessions – just a lick and a promise, as the cooks would say when they had to wipe down the kitchen surfaces for the inspecting nun to come and say they could all go and the day was ended.

'I took the grandchildren. Pantomime.'

'Ah, them things.'

'He never stole from me, or from lads in the company.'

'That's a good lad, then.'

'Not even from any other squaddie in our unit, though God knows we were hungry enough. The fighting started and the shells were bursting all over and round. Shit flying everywhere.'

'God help them poor boys.'

Magda wasn't sure whether she had heard this story before. She got mixed up with other tales the old men drifted into telling of a late afternoon when she had to side up and finish the cleaning. She knew soon Mr Gorragher would start telling how he and his mate stole some stores from the locals and sold them. Then he would offer her a drop of whisky, telling her it was ouzo or wine from Italy.

'Two boys bought it next to me and Lanky, standing there one minute then simply folded up like newspapers with blood all in their middles.'

'God rest the poor souls.'

He was in his afternoon chair, legs out on them raised things Magda could never lift, so the old man's feet would raise up to where they didn't get fat and start having big red sores.

'It was so peaceful.'

'With all them old guns and bombs? I'm coming round that side with the hoover. You'll have to let me swing your feet round, Mr Gorragher.'

'Best job I ever had. War isn't so bad. It's like a raffle.'

'Is it, now. Feet.'

'A million times better than in the Ranter.'

'Ranter. Is it, now.' Magda tried to make this bit without a question in case it got the old man started on how he'd been a little boy in the Ranter. She never liked this bit. 'Keep still.'

'War was the same for us all, officers and men up against it. The war took you in ones, twos, a few at a time, or a lot, or none of you and you were safe. Ranter wasn't.'

'Wasn't it.'

Still without a question, but what could she say? She couldn't pretend she wasn't there, the old hoover whirring away or she'd get in trouble with Sister Raphael, and what then?

'Ranter was hell. Blothey was there too. A Christian Brother slammed his head through the stair sticks and twisted him.

That's why he died. He wailed. He didn't scream, didn't Blothey. He just wailed. I'll remember it to the day I die.'

'God rest the poor boy.' Blothey was a new name. The last time Mr Gorragher had told this tale it had been a boy called, what, Dondie, was it?

'They made a picture for the television. I should have gone to them and told them. I heard they were asking for oldsters like me to come and tell them what happened. The priest said at St Gabriel the Archangel that telling things and making TV pictures about them was the devil's work. He said it would be destructive to the Faith.'

'You didn't go.'

'No.'

'Perhaps it's just as well, Mr Gorragher.'

'You think I should have, Jane?'

So she was Jane now. Two afternoons ago she'd been Elspeth. She knew neither, had never even seen Mr Gorragher have a visitor, except for Father Doran to swill some of the old man's dreadful poteen stuff.

'Least said soonest mended,' she said, coming under his outstuck feet.

'That's what everybody said in the parish. I don't know. I started to watch the fillum but couldn't go on with it. Blothey died soon after. He couldn't walk.'

'God rest him.'

'I wondered after, when the fighting ended and we came back and I got a medal, a real decoration, not just a dinner gong like they called the routine issue, why they didn't know Blothey died when the Christian Brother – Patrick, spelt the old way, not this new showy way – shoved his head through the staircase railings and twisted so he started wailing and died.'

'They didn't know.'

Magda said all these standard replies in a comforting kind of voice so it would ease the old man, who would often get agitated when he spoke of these things. There was a terrible story of a well and somebody shoved down there that was particularly frightening. Ding, dong, dell, like in some children's rhyme they sang on RTE. Odd, though, it was the food that got her most. She sometimes found herself weeping for no reason, because what was she crying for?

'Nobody knows unless you tell them.'

'Well, they wouldn't.'

'I should have gone to the lady who was making the fillums. She had real cameras and everything.'

Did Lucy keep on falling because Magda didn't tell anybody? Was that what he was saying? But she had never ever told anybody, except God and He knew anyway. The question was, if she went and told…told who, though? If she did, would Lucy then stop falling, all night long in Magda's dreams, just like that? Magda knew she wouldn't. Magda would have got herself out of trouble, a responsibility that she owed to Lucy, not herself, especially after what Magda had done the night Lucy died.

No, she had to rescue her dead friend without help from anybody. That's what the deal was. A deal with God Almighty, no less. A promise was a promise. In doing that, Magda would rescue herself from the pit of Hellfire.

'My hand was turned wrong at the wrist.'

And here old Mr Gorragher would always hold out his left hand like an offer. He would keep it there held out, though he was practically blind and couldn't see a thing any more, simply waiting for Magda or somebody to take hold of it.

'Go on, test it. There's a bone missing, see?'

And Magda had to press her fingers round the old man's wrist, feeling the bones, though what was there to feel in an old man's wrist? Except where there should have been a kind of a knob sticking out, there wasn't.

'The army took me in spite of that, and they said it wouldn't matter. I should be a driver, they said. But we were in uniform and learnt shooting and then we were off overseas. The fighting began and nobody worried any more about my old wrist being a bone short. I was taken prisoner just like the rest of the lads.'

He sounded so proud.

'No driving, then?'

'No driving. Me and Lanky went through the war together. We got taken up by a unit of the Duke of Wellington's, noisy load of sods they were. Me and Lanky got captured. They suddenly came one day. The enemy guards cleared off. We were taken back. Know what?'

Magda had finished her cleaning and started winding up the flex.

'No. What?' though she already knew. There were only slight variations in the story. Some others did vary, though. The old ladies were the most consistent, never varied a single phrase or a word out of true, like a poem learnt in school.

'They kitted us all up. We had hardly a stitch left from the prisoner-of-war camp. We went through some Yanks, a whole battalion. They stood watching us march through, just silent, rows of them. They looked like giants and fat and tall. They hardly spoke a word, but one said, "Jeez, Tommy, you alive under that thar skin?" And his mate said, "Never seed anybody that thin in ma laaaf, man." I didn't even know them Yanks spoke English like us till then.'

'Then you came home.' Magda wanted it all over and done, old Mr Gorragher getting to the terrible bits like he had to come back full circle before he'd let anybody go.

'We got examined then back to the teeth arms. I was made a rifleman again, and we landed on the fucking sand with all kinds of shit flying. Know what?'

'No.' Magda was despondent, standing there knowing the hoover was silent and if Sister Raphael set up one of her shouts she would be for it. She hated these know-whats, because it meant the old man knew she was still there even though he was almost blind.

'However bad it got in the army, even in prison camp, nothing was as bad as Ranter, that school right here in Eire. They killed another Irish lad's brother in our unit. He got transferred to the Gunners, twenty-five pounders. Survived. I met him afterwards. He liked the army too, same reasons as me. We were safe there. Latree Industrial School was Christian Brothers too.'

'I've to go now, Mr Gorragher.'

'There should be a kind of court, but I wouldn't go if there was. Would you?'

This was the point in the chat when Mr Gorragher would turn his head as if he could see properly again, and raise his chin like he was looking. Magda hated the trick. He only did it to keep her there when she wanted to go.

'I don't know, Mr Gorragher.'

'You mean no.' His chin sank then. She wanted to ask if it was disappointment that made his chin sink like that, but that would prolong the conversation and she'd catch it from Sister Raphael. 'You mean no.'

'See you, Mr Gorragher.'

'See you.' And as she carried the vacuum cleaner from the alcove, 'Here, Father.'

'Yes?' she said. Talking to him tired her out more than work.

'Would you like a spot of the old poteen? Good stuff, got from them Scotch, not local. Yes?'

'Not just now, thank you.'

'You sure?'

And, grotesquely, the old features would wrinkle even more and the old man would give a monstrous wink, moisture running down his face almost like tears, but only one eye.

'Thank you, but not today.'

'I've some right here.'

And the old man would pat his bedside locker and wink. Then Magda would leave. She had seen Father Doran pause, return just as he was about to leave, and reach into the locker for a flat bottle of brown liquid. And he would take one swig and sometimes another. The old man would cackle then, as if complicit in some crime.

Magda left, sickened by the recurring story, wondering if everybody her age or older had been slain inside by events at some horrible place they could never escape from. Prisoner-of-war camp better than school? War safer than the Church's care?

On the way home, though, she remembered laying the tray for Father Doran, and the order of the things. Crockery just so, the Dundee cake exactly positioned, the small knives with their decorated blue handles and the cake plates with borders of flowers.

That evening she walked slowly down the Borro to the residence of the outdoor girl workers, and in her small room she tried to make one of the stolen white tablets dissolve in water, then tried to press it in a chewed piece of bread. It wouldn't melt or even go away. Whatever she did to it, it looked like a thick little wart of white stuck there, easily seen. Daring, she pressed it into her mouth. She felt it there, to her horror. Father Doran would spit it out and say, 'What on earth is this, Sister?' and they would send for Magda and then for the Garda Siobhana.

She washed her mouth out after washing the test tablet down the sink, and sat on the bed staring at the wall. The thing was, the bottle of fluid that Mr Gorragher had concealed in his locker, or somewhere near, might do. She resolved to test the tablet next day when she could get hold of some of that fluid, whisky or whatever the Scotch Protestant heathens brewed in their old bogs over The Water. She knew gin wasn't coloured, whereas the tea-coloured fluid Mr Gorragher sometimes showed her was dark brown, or variations between coffee-coloured and a light tan.

That might be it. She abandoned the idea of feeding Father Doran poisoned cake, and settled for good and all on Mr Gorragher's dark brown Scotch, if the tablets could be made to melt in a test drink.

One thing more worried her. Leaving Mr Gorrhager that day, she saw Sister Francesca standing by one of the other alcoves along the corridor. Just standing, and not doing a thing. Hearing Magda coming, she instantly moved away. Surely Sister Francesca couldn't have been listening, could she? Other people eavesdropped, but never nuns.

Whatever had made Sister Francesca stay like that, so quiet for no reason, Magda knew that glimpse to be a special warning. She had to be careful of everybody, even if they were supposed to be on God's side.

Chapter Ten

Father Doran's appointment with Bishop MacGrath still stood, in spite of the press conference the bishop had arranged for three o'clock that afternoon. The prelate was affable to an industrial degree, creating the impression of posing during the interviews he conducted regularly during the day – two in the morning, two in the afternoon, one sometime round sevenish. Well known among his colleagues was his wish that the evening meeting would take place in some restaurant where the friend would pick up the tab. At such, his lordship would chuckle amiably and, tilting that giant head of bright silvery hair, say with twinkling benignity, 'I pray my chiselling tactics will keep debtors from the diocesan door!'

'Influence, Father Doran,' he sighed, welcoming the priest and gesturing to an armchair. 'The Church has lost influence, I fear. Look at the recent publicity.'

'Indeed, m'lord.'

'It is not as if we don't try.'

'I can't imagine anyone trying harder, m'lord.'

'Tea in a moment.' The bishop gazed across his study at some distant vista before going on. 'The problem is, the university has asked for a debate. Title: Family Issues versus Church Doctrine.'

'Soon?' Father Doran asked, sharper than he intended.

'Two weeks.'

'Do they really mean versus?'

'Without doubt.'

'Inviting the diocese?'

'Me in particular.'

'Any particular department?'

'Guess,' the bishop said dryly.

'Sociology?'

'You have it.' The bishop waited as a housekeeper entered and served the tea. Both clerics watched her fingers, the biscuits, the milk, teaspoons, and thanked her as she withdrew. 'You can imagine such an encounter. It will be planned as a ritual very like the one Mrs Mahoney has just enacted. A service.'

'Indeed. A sermon attended by a congregation of aficionados.'

'That would have been so, once. No longer.'

Father Doran began to fear he was being sent to the firing line. The last thing he wanted was to invite publicity that might prove adverse. Times were changing. There would be no opportunity to withdraw if any scent of scandal rose. He had spoken only twice at such gatherings, and had had an uncomfortable passage at each. Foreign students, of course, were the unpleasant catalysts.

'Modernists abound, James.'

'Indeed, m'lord.'

That use of his Christian name disturbed the priest. Something unpleasant this way comes, he thought unhappily. Was this the bishop's hint he would instead send some up-and-coming younger man, who might prove more theologically nimble to the student body in Dublin?

'I suppose it is the Catholic…?'

'Yes. Though Trinity College has its moments.' The prelate's irony was not lost on the priest. Trinity College was the non-Catholic element in Dublin.

'That is half a hurdle, then.'

'I may suppose so.'

The bishop clinked his teacup. He had lately abandoned sugar, to his personal grief, some Lenten tactic that still oppressed. He did have some revisionary views about doctrine, elements of ordinary life. Taste was one such, for instance. He decided to move things on, because this Doran man was too cunning to commit many errors. Advancement into the diplomatic sphere of Church activities often came to mind after conversations with this priest.

'As it happens, James, I am too busy on that date, so I am stymied. I simply can't suggest an alternative date.'

'Publicity, though, m'lord,' Doran said unhappily, trying to give the bishop a way out. He saw he would have to deputise. It would prove a cauldron, considering the adverse media lately put about. 'It might be embarrassing if no Church representative attended the debate. I suppose it is a debate, not a lecture?'

'Debate.' The bishop detected Doran's reluctance. It amused him to keep the idea going a little longer. 'How would one approach the topic?'

'Modernists, m'lord.'

'Modernists?' Bishop MacGrath was surprised by the alacrity of the reply.

'I should begin my argument – stability of society, proper detailed assessments of what happens in one age and another, changing worlds – by stating how great modernists have managed in the past.'

'Thinking particularly…?'

'Tyrell, of course, as you already guess, m'lord.' Father Doran allowed himself the liberty of a small challenge to the prelate's sense of propriety, though meek as could be. 'Parallels could be drawn between present circumstances, once one had gone over the modernist case.'

'And add his tribulations. You could make out a case for our present situation being a possible instance of Tyrell's problems.'

'It would take some doing, m'lord.'

'But with adequate planning?'

'The Church could come out scented like roses.'

They thought, hesitating over biscuits. Bishop MacGrath did not move when a distant telephone rang.

George Tyrell was a famed, if not notorious, modernist in the Church during the nineteenth century. An undoubted intellectual, the Dubliner [sic] started life in 1861, a Protestant educated in the Church of Ireland who went as a young man to England and there became a Roman Catholic Jesuit. The then Pope Pius the Tenth published his inflexible doctrines on the priesthood in the encyclical *Pieni l'anima*. Subjected, however, to the new scientific forces represented by Charles Darwin, Huxley and the hectic advances in the Victorian era, Tyrell wrote his modernistic views under pen-names – AR Waller, and Dr Ernest Engels among them – but was inevitably discovered. He was dismissed from the Jesuits, to become something of a still greater rebel, and likened papal restrictions to those of the restrictive Czar of all the Russias. He refused to recant, and died shunned by the Church, in an English village on the South Downs.

'He was not the first,' MacGrath said mildly.

'The point is, one could make a good case suggesting that modernistic revisionism was allowed by the Church despite the social and economic tenor of those times. Not that the Church devised the scenarios, just saw they had to be handled differently as times evolved into something sociologically new.'

'Good. Yes, James. If it could be got over to a disaffected crowd of students in that fashion.'

'With acting and apparent analytical thought, m'lord.'

'We are becoming flippant, James. Stop it.'

They smiled. James Doran thought he was coming out of this threatened duty rather well. He could claim he had discussed the topic of the debate in some detail with the bishop before appearing at the Dublin society, and that he was merely recounting the history of thought. He could argue afterwards that media people always misrepresented his views. That would call for an enthusiastic but detailed reply to dissent. The way things were in Rome, not to mention Dublin, such a rejoinder would add to his reputation as a stern orthodoxian rather than some loose canon rolling dangerously about the Church's deck.

He hated the idea of going, though. But duty done rather than duty shirked always found praise. It was settling for less. He was resigning himself to this notion when the bishop spoke, raising his hopes.

'Please give me your frank opinion of Father Kilmain, James.'

The request startled the priest. He wondered what he was being asked for. Hope rose. A deputy for the debate at University College among all those students?

'Father Kilmain? Agreeable, friendly. I find it hard to imagine Father Kilmain in any kind of bind whatsoever, m'lord.'

'And in a wider sense?'

James Doran knew Father Kilmain for a rival, in line for the monsignorship. Dangerous, however, to run Kilmain down, so nothing but praise.

'I would think he was the – what do they say in an American curriculum vitae? – the Man Most Likely To. Unless,' he added with mock haste, making humour where none was to be found, 'your lordship thinks otherwise.'

A natural talent, the prelate registered, and easy with it, when Doran must be apprehensive at doing battle with a crowd of students.

'One problem, James, is the nature of the student body these days. They are so varied. We know how sentiment operates among the African, the Caribbean, the South American churches. Dissent seems to be the norm. No papal conclavical goings-on can ameliorate the problems.'

'No, m'lord.'

'So I thought of inviting Father Kilmain to deputise for me.'

James Doran knew to stay mute for a few moments. He tipped his fingers together a while, then quickly shoved his hands away in case the gesture annoyed. It was his best act.

'Father Kilmain would cope well.'

'He played rugby or something.'

'Yes, m'lord. Hurling too. Not quite international level, but almost getting there when he was ordained.'

'I shall send him.'

'His report will be exemplary.'

The priest deliberately injected a little envy into the comment, merely sowing seeds of malignity, for a report of any dispute always created concern within. That might retard

the promotion of Father Kilmain, and do little harm to the
cause of, say, a possible rival contender for advancement such
as himself.

'Not jealous, Father?' the bishop joked ponderously.

'Invariably. More tea, m'lord?'

They leant forward, smiling.

Magda woke and washed. No shower, and the girls were to
use bath or the communal shower once every second day, no
more.

She started the test with the whisky fluid stolen from old Mr
Gorragher. The tablet shrank until it left only a kind of slushy
white grainy sludge at the bottom of the glass. The label on
the flat brown bottle had a picture of a London gent walking
along with his monocle and grand boots and walking stick,
who could have fed all Ireland if he'd only been moved by
Christian charity to give it to the poor in Dublin. But no, there
he stayed, strolling along on his bottle, grinning like an ape.
She had been terrified that somebody would catch her – Sister
Bernice was the likeliest snooper, or maybe one of the others.
Magda was lucky, and got away with an old tablet bottleful. It
was dark brown with some old label on, and had a water-tight
lid that screwed on. Mr Gorragher's friends from the Sheriff
Street bar brought him a tipple every week. Fine.

She had put the bit of whisky in, screwed the lid tight down,
and hid it in her pinny before escaping outside and breathing
calmly there as she walked away from the scene of her theft.
There'd been plenty still there in the bottle for the old man to
give a glug to Father Doran.

Magda almost weakened, but remembered how he had
been there and what he had done. Father Doran had seen Lucy

before she fell to her death, to keep on falling for ever. Magda was failing in her Christian duty if she backed out now.

The tablet – she sloshed it round and round – was surely smaller? She emptied what she could of the fluid, terrible smell it was and all, a miracle indeed that men would drink the stuff and seemingly get such merriment from it. It sent them mad as March hares sometimes, fighting all over the city. She gazed at the powder drying slowly on the piece of newspaper on the Baby Belling cooker.

Dry, the paper started to curl at the edges and looked stiff and crinkly. She felt it and tried shifting that old greyish – greyish? Why greyish now just because it had gone dry? – powder about. Sure as God it was hardly there at all. No sign of there being enough white stuff left to make a decent tablet of it now.

Therefore God was helping her. He had decided to make the white tablet so it could wash into the whisky the old man drank of a night, so secret was he, without being detected. That meant only one thing. All the drug's power, that kept the old folks' hearts working, would be taken up in the whisky. She had heard that's what they were for, heart working. The old ladies all called them heart tablets. The men called them pills.

She was ready for her murder. The day after tomorrow, Father Doran would come again, and, praise the Lord, would stop to chat to the old man Mr Gorragher and take an illicit snifter with the old man.

The thought occurred only then to Magda that, with the poisoned whisky there large as life, large as death, if she poured it into Mr Gorragher's secret whisky bottle with the smiling frock-coated London gent strolling along with his fine monocle, then what if the old soldier took a drink of the poison before the priest took his swig?

Jesus, Mary and Joseph, she would kill Mr Gorragher too.

She felt so shaky at the notion she had to sit down. The danger was, postponing her murder of the priest would be intolerable, for hadn't she made the devout promise to Lucy every single morning of her life since the nuns had carried the lifeless body of the poor mite away to be buried without a marked grave? Magda had sworn to rescue her, from keeping having to fall, and herself from never sleeping at all ever until the end of time.

No. No question of postponement. Magda knew she must do it.

She would go to Mass early in the morning and pray to be given Divine Guidance, for God Himself had shown her the way by making the chemists melt them old tablets into the whisky without trace. She felt sure God wouldn't get a thing like this wrong. He knew what He was doing. Hadn't he created the world, tablets and all?

Lucy had fallen quite enough, thank you, to her sojourn in Hellfire. God would help in the rescue. He would show Magda a way, what to do to stop the poison from killing Mr Gorragher and his hopeless arm and the wrecked head from the army gunfire in foreign wars, him and his daft old song about leaving Derry.

Plenty of hymns said it often enough: with God's help who can fail, that kind of thing, over and over. Wasn't the Heart of Jesus the fount of love and mercy?

I'm coming, Lucy, she said inwardly, throwing the paper with the remnants of the undissolved white heart tablet into the loo. I'll rescue you, love, don't you worry. We'll kill Father Doran. God knew for Himself what kind of a man Father Doran was. Magda would set Lucy free from falling every time Magda closed her eyes.

One problem: in the evening she must meet the ginger-headed lad who stood astride the motorcycle and had said definite to meet him by the end of the Borro. Maybe he hadn't been crying at all, being one of the Garda Siobhana, from his belt badge and the badge emblem on his stinking old bike. She hadn't done anything wrong yet, so it would be safe to go. And she could honestly tell him she'd looked out for his grampa, Mr Liam MacIlwam.

She racked her brains before the terrible thought struck. Had the lad learnt in some terrible secret stealthy manner that she had been stealing the tablets? She now had almost a handful, and with luck might get more tomorrow.

No. For hadn't he asked if she nursed Mr Liam MacIlwam, and told her his name was MacIlwam too? Now, she never stole tablets from Mr MacIlwam – or had she? She became confused, and stopped herself thinking. The little radio was on, some comedy talking they were sending out from London or maybe Liverpool, far funnier than those from Dublin because they were more careless and had more laughing. She couldn't say she understood much of what they were on about, and in any case some of them were foreign-sounding, like they came from India or maybe Africa or the West Indies. She knew there were plenty of them over there in wicked old England, though so few here they stood out plain as day.

She never slept much, to save Lucy from falling. Only when she found herself dozing and her head nodding enough to roll off and away did she see Lucy start to fall, her cardigan with the bad mending receding before her into the giant space that was the stairwell. Magda's eyes would, even in her sleeping, start to fill and it would wake her, and in her dream she be running again back to the cold dormitory and staying huddled there under her one blanket, praying and praying to God for forgiveness and saying, please, God, please Baby Jesus and Mary Mother of God, please don't hurt Lucy any more from now on, and forgive me for what I did.

She never really slept at all, just went about in a daze of exhaustion from morning to night and beyond into the next day. Mrs Shaughnessy, who took rent from her every Friday, had given her a small television set that plugged in. It showed old fillums the livelong night through, and was a godsend. Old period pictures were Magda's favourites, ladies in crinolines with fans, gentlemen on horses, and everybody so lovely and safe and polite. Magda liked those most because they kept her awake longest, and saved Lucy that fall to her death all over again.

Magda knew all about crying. The Garda man MacIlwam had been weeping all right. Magda knew all about that. She had begun it properly, true decent weeping for things done and never to be recalled and made right, over Lucy. Magda knew herself guilty for it. Until that flash of vision in Holy Mass when Father Doran had turned from the altar to give the blessing to the congregation, and she had finally known it was him. Father Doran, it was. And he started coming to the St Cosmo. The chance of rescuing Lucy herself from Hellfire had finally come, exactly as she had prayed for every night.

Yes, Magda knew all about weeping. What had the lad's name been? Kevin MacIlwam. She'd better call him 'Sergeant', please him so he'd not blame her if he'd found out something terrible about her. Dear God, she thought, he surely couldn't have found out about Lucy, could he? And was coming to arrest her like they did on the pictures, take her away in the Gardai car with its squares like a chessboard, to be hanged in some prison?

No. She would simply ask him when they met.

Chapter Eleven

The old man was talking.

The lights were out, except for the one at the end of the ward that cost, the nuns said, only two pennies an hour, but even that had to be paid for or the light would go out. That's why it was red, which cost less, instead of the usual yellow. This was after Mrs McCaddon complained there should be a brighter light so she could see if she tried to get up in the night.

'My brother was Bonham, that's what I always called him,' the man said.

The other man across the alcove – two in each if you were stuck with being so old you couldn't move or if you had tubes in – said, 'You knew him, then?'

'Sure I knew him.'

'Bonham's what we used to call the new-born piglets, in St Joseph's.'

'Which St Joseph's?'

'Nigl. Industrial School, St Joseph's. I was Nine-Four. That was my name. I ate the swill. Some of it was grand. I was on watch during the night to see if any of the bonhams got borned during the night.'

'Your brother still alive, is he?'

'No, God rest him.'

'Amen to that.'

The first old man let out an almighty fart and relaxed with a sigh. 'Pardon me, George.'

'Better out than your eye, Ted.'

'Did you all go by numbers?'

'Sure we did.'

'So did we.' Another fart, then, 'We've got to change the beer, this old place.'

The old men cackled. One said, 'That old feller-me-lad, Mr Gorragher. Has a tin plate in his head from getting shot. Know he was the best marksman with that old three-oh-three Lee Enfield as ever trod land?'

'Him? Sings a lot in the night? That one?'

'The same. They said he did it listening to the wind. You can get him talking about it, if you ever take a walk down that lane.'

They cackled and laughed, because both were now bedridden, no chance of taking a walk anywhere.

'Wasn't he a gunner? Royal Artillery or something, in the war?'

'Got hisself transferred. Don't know why. He never says anything about it.'

'Never heard of a marksman getting hissel' transferred to the Gunners before.'

'Must have been good if he was champion marksman. I once saw one from the Buffs put a hole in a bell tower somewhere in the Ardennes. There was a sniper in the bell tower of this church, see. Our marksman takes a shot after kneeling for six hours looking with some mirror thing he'd made, still as a heron hunting. All of one whole day, then he takes a shot and his sergeant sez, 'Missed, you pillock,' but the marksman just says nothing and picks up the spent casing to put in his BD pocket.'

'Picked up a spent bullet casing? What for? I never heerd of anybody doing that.'

'Well he did. Every time, every shot. Carried them about until the night came, then buried them like he was a poacher leaving no trace.'

'What about the bell tower?'

'Come morning, we wakes up and he's still there in the rubble, wide awake and still. The lads all got muttering and complaining because he'd pissed himself just staying there, same position. Come ten o'clock of that morning he takes one shot. And gets the sniper. The sergeant sez, 'Jesus, Paddy, you shot him through the hole you made yesterday!' Nobody in the whole unit had ever seen anything like that. He just took up the casing, put it in his pocket, and went to have a crap and a piss.'

'Jesus Christ.'

'Ever since then, the lads called him Holer. Know why? 'Cos he shot through the hole he'd already made, see? He didn't mind. The English lads said he was the best in the world, and they had some shooters among them, a couple or three from Lincolnshire who'd been poachers, great shooters, they. Our company corporal wanted to put Holer in for some competition when we went on leave, but Holer wouldn't have it. Know why?'

'No. Why?'

'He tellt his missus and them at home he was a truck driver. Would you imagine that?'

'Why'd he say that?'

'I reckon marksmen isn't natural. Something in them, to wait that long to do it, pretend he drove a truck all through the fucking war. Know what else?'

'No?'

'He couldn't drive, either. I often wonder how he got on after the war, coming home like having driven a three-tonner all the war then not being able to drive a pram, let alone a Dublin bus.'

'Where was he from?'

'He was schooled at Ranter.'

'Jesus. Ranter, you say?'

'I don't remember him, but there were so many of us, d'you see?'

Somebody in an alcove further down complained about their talk. They simply responded by staying mute a while then resuming. When they did this, their voices started low then grew as the sentences came and their old ideas took shape again until finally they were talking as if it was broad daylight.

'Ted?'

'Aye?'

'Some of that auld swill had bits of meat in it.' A sigh. 'I swear to God it tasted better than any meat I've had since.'

'Spuds,' Ted said. He waited a bit then said again, like he was disappointed at not having elicited a response, 'Spuds.'

'You had spuds?'

'I thought they were from Heaven itself, spuds. Get one cooked just right, it's still like Paradise. I could go on eating them all my life, and that's a fact.'

'Why did Holer do it, then?'

'Holer? The marksman? Did you know him too?'

'No. You just tellt me. The bell tower, the sergeant saying Jesus Christ because he'd shot the sniper through the hole he'd made the previous night.'

'One of the poacher lads from Dorset, I think it was from Dorset, said he wasn't shooting the enemies in the trees, the canals – Christ, but Holer loved shooting anywhere near water. I could tell you some tales. The canals was his favourite. Never smoked in the four years in our unit. Never let hisself get promoted.'

'What did the Dorset lad say?'

'He was a poacher. He said Holer wasn't shooting enemy at all. He was shooting people he knew.'

'Who?'

'I dunno, do I? How do I know?'

'Didn't you ask the Dorset lad?'

With amazement, 'Did you know Jendy from Poole too? I thought you wus in the Dirty Dukes, the Wellingtons.'

'No. You tellt me. You said the Dorset lad told you Holer was shooting people he knew.'

'That's right. Jendy said it was always the way, always like that. Snipers who got lurk-happy, had to keep stiller than in real life because they weren't killing enemy soldiers they'd never met at all. No.'

'Who, then?'

'They were killing somebody else, over and over. The same folk they'd started out killing from anywhere before they took their bonds for a soldier.'

'Who, then?'

They were silent at some distant complaint down the corridor before they resumed in a whisper.

'Maybe from Ranter?'

They paused without being grumbled at from the lane of alcoves leading to the red pilot light. It was quite three or four minutes before they started their whispering again.

Sometimes, the nun thought, standing listening in the shadow by the alcove curtains, they could start their talking again quite as if their minds were young and vigorous and unhindered by old age. Other times, she listened to their mumbled chat as it became incoherent. Though of course, she knew they spoke of a life, and lives, worlds away in time and distance, in eras rather than mere moments.

'Maybe from Ranter, and the same one over and over.'

'Did the Dorset lad – Jendy, you called him? – ever tell you who it was that Holer kept on killing?'

'No. Somebody else from Brummy, Birmingham, asked Jendy that, not wanting to ask Holer outright, because them sort of things is personal.'

'There is that, sure, right. Personal.'

'And Jendy just said, "Oh, that'd be something to do with being a little lad."'

'Ah, then sure it's only the one he was a-killing over and over every time. Did the Brummy mate ask Jendy why Holer would keep on collecting up them auld cartridge cases like that?'

'Once, Holer had twenty-three spent cartridge cases, just emptied them into a hole he'd dug in some floor of a church. Somewhere in North Germany. You remember how it was, you never knew where the fuck you were one minute to the next.'

'Sure, I never did. Once, I asked our sergeant why everybody'd started talking French. Know what he said?'

'No. What did he say?'

'He said, "You stupid git. It's Italian. We're in fucking Italy, you burke." I didn't get laughed at, because the rest of the lads was as surprised as me.'

'Well, you would be. I never knew, either.'

'It was the weather, see? One of the lads was a fell walker. That's moorlands. He collected lost sheep for a living.'

'That's a grand job.'

'Made a good living out of it. Couldn't talk English proper even though he was English, but like he was from out of some olden times and suddenly found hissel' here in this fucking war with shit flying and putting wounds in your old head. I hated grenades. The fucking plug always comes back at the thrower, no matter how you hold it. Did that happen to you?'

'All the fucking time. I got so I wouldn't chuck them. Gave them to my mate.'

'They ever put you on a charge for not lobbing when you were ordered?'

'No. They knew every squaddie had his foibles.'

'This fellwalker. They called him Tarn, from like the lakes they have over there. Well, he come from an old fell-walking family. Whatever weather forecast the officers got, whatever country we were supposed to be in, when we got orders to push on or fall back, they'd send for Tarn.'

'What for?'

'He knew weather, see?'

'The officers asked him about the weather? Jesus.'

'Twice the staff officers talked to him. He'd stand outside, maybe half an hour just looking at the ground – this could be night or day, rain or snow, gale or sun – and then he'd come in and tell them.'

'Was he right?'

'Every single fucking time. At first, the officers would ask him was he sure, how did he know and had he some machine or seaweed, how did he do it? He could hardly talk the King's proper, so they gave up trying to understand what he said. He come from them Pennine moorlands, see? Talked Old English. Except one officer, a young chap who played cricket somewhere, lived up there and could tell what he was saying, this Tarn, and just said to our major, "Sir? He says he listens to the air that's moving." And one colonel says but there isn't any wind. And the young snooks says, "Well, that's what he says he does, sir." And ever after nobody asked, just trusted what Tarn said.'

'Things are different wherever you come from, and that's the truth.'

'That's true as today.'

They remained silent while they both belched and grumbled, then Ted spoke in a low mutter the nun had to strive to hear.

'Who would you kill, George?'

'Kill? Me? Have to think about that, Ted, 'less you mean the bastards who run the hurling team from Leinster.'

They laughed so much at that they choked from wheezing and gasped quite a time before being able to talk again.

'It's them bastards from Dublin. They own the racehorse stables and want Manchester United.'

'Jesus, what bastards. Don't they own a shipping line somewhere?'

'It's airlines, silly bugger, airlines nowadays. They don't have shipping lines any more.'

'I'd kill them Christian Brothers.'

'Here, mate.' A pause for effect, then, full of meaning, 'You could do worse!'

More laughter and folk calling down the lane of alcoves and somebody ringing the night bell, but the nun paid it no heed and stayed still where she was to listen.

'My brother, the one they called Bonham. He couldn't stop eating, him. Jayzuss, but he was a grand eater. I knew him later once I was out. He comes up to me, this feller, and says to me right there on Inns Quay, me being about to cross the auld Liffey, "I'm Bonham, your brother" and you could have knocked me down with a feather.'

'You didn't know him?'

'No. He'd got himself wed, great fat feller that he was.'

'Does he come here to see you?'

'No. He died young, didn't even reach fifty.'

'God rest him.'

'Amen.'

The silent nun mouthed the word, Amen.

'Couldn't stop eating, couldn't Bonham. It was like once he had sight of his dinner he couldn't stop. Went out to the kitchen. His wife said he was a terrible eater. She said he'd have anything that stood still long enough, eat it right down.'

'I like gravy on thick bread.'

'He'd have everybody else's fat right off their plates.'

'Poured right on. The bread needn't be buttered or marged, just thick. Soda bread fritters in your hands, doesn't it? I'd rather have it in one piece.'

'He took ill and died. You know that place near Ha'Penny Bridge? Well, in there. He was supposed to be on his way to work, a clerk in the Pensions Office – he did well for himself did our Bonham – when he keeled over. The doctor said it was his heart.'

'I like a fry-up. Best thing is them bacon things in fried bread.'

'I cried over Bonham. See, if he'd had any decent things to eat when he was little, he'd have been all right with food. Put him in sight of it and he was like, there's a word for it, when you're driven to do something and you know it's daft and you keep on all the same, a word. I heard it on telly.'

Compulsion? The nun did not say the word, just thought.

'They used to call me Baldy,' Ted's voice said. 'At the school.'

'I got the head-shave the same. They did it to me as a routine.'

'I only got it when I bled on my shirt after the Freezer gave me a right old whacking.'

'Freezer? Did I know Freezer?'

'No, you auld daftie. You were in a different school.'

'I forget. Where were you, then?'

'Freezer used to freeze his leather belt in some fridge. The boys called him that because he used to freeze his leather belt in some fridge, see? The Christian Brothers wore this...you'll know that anyway. Did you have a Brother who did that to whack you?'

'Freezed his belt? No. We had one used a hurley and the sliothar, stand you against the wall then fire it at you. If you dodged he got mad and would come right up and whack you with the hurley and make you promise to stay still, then back he'd go and fire his sliothar at you.'

'They always did that.'

'This Brother used to let out a right roar of a cheer if he caught you. I got the staggers. That's what we called it when we got to falling around the place after a whacking. I still can't bend my elbow from falling that way.'

After a pause, 'You know what?'

'No? What?'

'I reckon Holer had his elbow bent like that from a breaking of it.'

'How'd it get broken, then?'

'One Brother had a leather hoop he put your arm through on the wall to stop you ducking. You had to face the wall anyway, so you'd try to stare back over your shoulder, kind of, see the old thing coming, like a rocket it was. The loop stopped you twisting out of its way, see? I broke my elbow doing that. Got mysel' whacked for it.'

'You knew Holer from before, then?'

'No. I tellt you, no. But I reckon he knew. Jaysus, a fine marksman he was. I reckon the Army should send him a turkey at Christmas for what Holer did.'

'Seen him since, have you?'

'No. I heard somebody say he might have gone to work the ships in Cork somewhere. Has a wife and two grand children. Somebody said they'd seen him walking along to the park of a Sunday. Stands watching the games. Never speaks to anybody, just stood watching them two children of his, turned out like new pins. He just watches.'

'Watches them, does he?'

'Somebody went right up to him and asked if he was Holer. He just stared straight ahead and said, eyes on them two grand little children of his, "Never heard of anybody by that name, friend" and turned away. Odd, that.'

'That's not odd.'

'No. I didn't think it was.'

'I hated the well.'

'I heard they filled it in.'

'It's a housing estate now.'

'Some lad drowned. Nobody knew why.'

'They make a lot of money from the housings.'

'That's how they can buy them auld racehorses.'

Grumblings of laughter at the thought of owning racehorses, and some recollections of which they would bet on next time they went to Leopardstown, made them laugh and chuckle and set the calls to shut up from along the ward corridor. The silent nun thought they themselves were quite like a sort of weather, and reflected how strange men were, so different from women. She almost started wondering how it was that they could speak to each other from those frail minds of theirs and their even more fragile memories, and why God had made everyone so different in the genders.

'I'd burn down Daingean,' Ted said simply, after a long gap.

'I got beaten for peeing my bed, started when I was four.'

'I heard I had a cousin somewhere in St Joseph's. He got whacked terrible for bed-wetting. I was scared to ask anybody if I really did have a cousin or not in case they started on me for having a cousin who peed his bed.'

'I got whacked in the night.'

'I don't like nights, not even now.'

'Nor me.'

'That'll be why old Mr Gorragher sings all the night through, to stop it being night.'

'I have to have everything in the house laid out in order. That's what you had to do not to get whacked.'

'I've a tube in my dick, save me peeing my bed now I've got the dribbles. I was so happy the doctor said that and the nurse stuck it in.'

'So you'd not pee the bed?'

'Course. That's what that bottle's for underneath.'

'I tellt my daughter, anything in the house, don't throw that away. I keep on saying it, and she says, "Dad, it's only yesterday's, and what do you want with an auld newspaper anyway?" I don't let her.'

'Saves me peeing the bed, my tube.'

'She clears them out while I'm down the boreen having a drink. She thinks I'm so gaga I don't notice, but I do. Sometimes I take them right out of the dustbin and put them in order on the table. She goes mad.'

'I'd burn that old Ranter school down to the ground, if I could get away with it.'

'The Australians were as bad.'

'Were they?'

'Christian Brothers do it to the little ones. They're called abusers nowadays. I seed it on the television.'

'Even over there?'

'They showed it.'

'There was that great page, pages of it, in the newspapers.'

'There was this great spread, double, saying the Church had gone sorry over what they did.'

'No good now.'

'It's to save the Church money.'

'It's unnatural.'

'The trouble is when you get through the day.'

'I like to think of the war instead of times I was small.'

'That's God's truth. Wars are best.'

'And horse racing.'

'I don't like to watch the hurling.'

'Nor me. Horse racing's better. Football, maybe too.'

'And the war. I had a pal went into the RAF. He liked being not spoken to, in the bombing. Bomber Command, him. He did bomb-aiming. He said it was so quiet, just his old bomber humming away.'

'Was he in the Industrial School with you?'

'No. I think he was from Encrelge in County Wicklow somebody said.'

'Bomb-aimer, eh? Clever, he must have been.'

'They had pencils and maps to work out where they were.'

'Clever lad. They picked them out special, I heard.'

'Said it was so quiet and peaceful. He made up hymns from the airplane.'

'What hymns?'

'One particular. I forget what it was.'

'I'll bet I know.'

'Bet you don't.'

'Bet I do.'

'Go on, then. Guess.'

'If I guess right you'll say I'm wrong so's you win the bet.'

'I won't.'

'You will.'

'Bet you a punt.'

'Who'll decide who's right?'

'Me.'

'What's the point of that?'

Calls began from down the corridor, complaints of George and Ted talking. Sister Francesca gathered her skirts and silently moved away.

Chapter Twelve

Magda was late, from instinct more than accident. She deliberately took her time walking along the Borro, bold as brass, about to meet her young man.

Over and over she said it to herself, meeting *her* young man. Greatly daring, meeting her young *man*. Then meeting her young man. It made her breathless, though the whole day she'd done nothing but forget everything she decided to do. Twice she started the hoovering without plugging the thing in at all. And once Mrs MacLehose, with the five children (with her still saying, wicked old ironing woman that she was, 'and no more of that malarkey, I can tell you now'), had to reprimand Magda for daydreaming, who was secretly saying over to herself about meeting her young man. 'Sure to God it'll be some young feller-me-lad she thinks is going to be her bonny for ever and a day like in them fairy stories, that's it, sure as Sunday.'

Magda thought Mrs MacLehose dreadful sometimes, but Oonagh laughed at her and even egged the old ironing woman on with, 'Tell 'em, old un,' causing Mrs MacLehose to erupt with a mouthful. This only started Oonagh off laughing all the more.

Oonagh it was who told Magda about lipstick. Magda said it was the tool of the devil himself, because they'd kept reading out bits from St Jerome's letters, and he was a saint sitting up there at God's right hand. Oonagh said no, St Jerome hated women being beautiful because he knew girls were always up to something, but as long as you kept your hand on your ha'penny you'd be all right. She lent Magda a lipstick and gave her her first lesson about cosmetics.

'It doesn't mean you're hanging out of the windows in Babylon, Magda, just because you dab a bit of stuff round your eyes and use scent and colour on your mouth.'

'It's wrong, Oonagh.'

'Stuff that old nonsense, girl. Watch.'

And Oonagh got on with it right there and then, standing in front of the mirror by the bathroom door in the St Cosmo with her lips all pursed up like she was going to kiss the mirror. Magda exclaimed in alarm, remembering that if you looked too long into the mirror the devil himself would stare right back at you.

'Now you do it.'

'I don't know how.'

'Let me.'

And Oonagh ran the lipstick over Magda's lips slowly, making her stretch her mouth tight. Magda felt really strange. Her face looked so different.

'See?'

'I look funny. Not like me at all.'

'You'd be nice if you had any colour. Jesus, but you're a pale girl.'

'I'm the same as I always was.'

Magda didn't know if this was true, because she'd never really had a mirror inspection before, except when the Inspectors came to the Magdalenes. Strange, but she felt something of disloyalty to the Magdalenes right now, seeing herself changing before that old mirror. Hadn't she ought to have done this before, her getting on to her twentieth birthday this coming Twenty-Second of July next time round?

'Magda Finnan, you never are. You can't be.'

'What? Why?'

Magda didn't know what she meant. She was becoming flustered, what with Oonagh busying herself about her little handbag she had right there with a scent bottle, a funny shape and blue as blue, a powder compact like the Whore of Babylon and a blackish pencil for her eyes.

'Stay still and I'll do your face.'

'I'd feel horrid.'

'No, girl. You look horrid as you are, white as an old sheet straight from Mrs MacLehose's iron and a sight less interesting, sure y'are.'

'Does everybody do this?'

'Sure we do. The whole world. Keep still.'

'Won't people notice?'

'That's the idea.'

'It's not...'

'Who's to say the Virgin Mary herself didn't run a bit of lippie round her own gob the instant she knew she was going to have Baby Jesus?'

'Oonagh, that's terrible.'

'Shush. Keep still or I'll poke your eye out. You can really look and make your mind up. If you think you've gone over the top you can get it off in half a sec then do it again, until you look like a million.'

'Will they tell me off?'

'Old Sister Stephanie will, sure as God, but that's only par for the course. Go easy at first, seeing you're new to it all. You know they keep marks on us?'

'On who?'

'On us workers here. They have a tally sheet, like them old dockers used in England to keep score of how many sacks they load on them old Liverpool ships.'

'Tally sheet?' Magda sprang away from the cosmetic lesson.

'Mrs MacLehose tellt me. She stows her ironed sheets in the nuns' quarters, them being too busy being holy to carry much. She's seen it, a table like the old men are forever talking about in the football league in the morning papers.'

'Is my name on it?'

'Course it is.' Oonagh was amused at Magda's alarm.

'What's it for?'

Magda thought she was done with all that now she was in a place of her own. Well, nearly her own, in a block where all the other releasees lived among real other people who were getting on a bit, like the old lady along the landing she had to be wary of when Bernard her Garda man came calling to do his sad thing to Magda.

'To keep count of us, what we do.'

'To report us, take us in charge?'

'No, silly. They can't do that. Look, Magda.' Oonagh shoved her down on the edge of the bath. 'What would you do if they said they were going to send you back anywhere?'

'I don't know.'

Oonagh could be impatient sometimes, and made a swipe at Magda in a pretend temper. 'Work it out, for God's sake.'

'I don't know.' Then, timidly worrying about it, 'What would I do?'

'You'd collect your things from here, see, girl? Then you'd catch the DART to Dun Laoghaire and get off there, and buy a ferryboat ticket to England. That's what you'd do.'

'And then what?' Magda stared at Oonagh, aghast.

'Sail to England and go wherever you wanted. God sakes, Magda, you're not stupid, are you, girl?'

'Yes,' Magda said, because she couldn't read or write, and what on earth would she do when she got to England? And Oonagh was so snappy Magda was afraid to speak anything except tell the truth.

'You'd never look back, Magda.' Oonagh spoke slowly, looking straight at her. 'What we do now is up to us, see?'

'Up to us?'

'Lipstick and all.'

'Then what's their tally book for?'

She was frightened to ask, but had to because it was bad enough not sleeping from seeing Lucy falling into the stairwell all night long without having another nightmare to haunt her.

'It's for them, see?'

Magda didn't see at all. 'No.'

'It's because they can't stop making tallies, like somebody can't keep on counting things because they're sick inside their old heads, see? Like these old men as can't help storing up bits.'

'Like old Mr Niall?'

Old Mr Niall had no second name, having come from an Industrial School in St Joseph's in Latree where he was simply Seven. He was a right one for collecting bits of broken things – pens were a favourite, because he was able to snaffle them and keep them under his pullover until he could carry them out to the old shed where he helped with planting and cleaning the gardening tools. He had a sack, rescued from the dustbins and cobbled together with ordinary string from tying some trailing roses. The roses fell and looked weary once old Mr Niall stole their string, but at least he had it to mend his old sack from the dustbins. He collected useless things like paper clips, safety pins, and papers with pins in rows. If anything went missing, like old ladies' knitting needles and bookmarks from the lounge where the oldies read of an afternoon, you could bet it was old Mr Niall away with it in his pullover. He always looked guilty, like he was going to get punished for stealing, but Magda let him say he hadn't got whatever was lost. Once he stole Mrs Borru's size nine knitting needle, length fifteen inches and thick as a pipe, that she had to have to make cardigans for the children in Thailand or somewhere.

'That's it.'

'How can the nuns be like them old men, then?'

'It's the way they've been made to think.'

'God made nuns, Oonagh,' Magda said, full of reproach.

'God made us any old how, Magda. Don't ever forget that. How you get on is up to you.'

'That's a terrible thing to say.'

'It's true. The nuns can't help it. They're a waste of time. I think they know it deep down, because of all the fuss there's been since the papers and the old telly got hold of them and started on the old Church. They got a right rollicking.'

'About them tallies?'

Oonagh sighed and pulled Magda to her feet.

'No, Magda. Just let's finish making you gorgeous. Forget what I've been saying. It just doesn't matter any more.'

But Magda thought over every word Oonagh had said, and ran it over and over in her head hours at a time, endless. This is how she learnt things. She was marvellous with words heard and moved mouths, but hopeless with things read or signed or shown. She might have been clever. That's what Bernard said when he did his thing to her, and she didn't really mind even if it made him sad.

The evening she was to meet Kev MacIlwam, she did her face with a lipstick she had bought, and it cost a fortune. She felt so aggrieved at the price she almost fainted in the shop. It was outrageous, worse even than a loaf. And she didn't know what to ask for or she'd have gone wild and bought one of them blue-black stick pencils to rub round her eyes. She was scared it would never rub off or that Kevin MacIlwam would laugh when he saw her, then she'd be so ashamed she would run away.

Except she did look truly pale, but Oonagh hadn't got any further in that lesson. Magda hadn't gone on experimenting, just did what bit she'd learnt with the lipstick. The one she'd got was not so red as Oonagh's. Another thing was, even though she had paid a king's ransom for the lipstick – so it must be made of stuff that was priceless anyway – the colour on her mouth seemed not quite what the colour was on the wrapping. In fact, Magda looked doubtfully at the colour of the stick itself as it came screwing its way out of the shiny gold tube.

It was a risk. Would she look like a harlot of Sodom and Gomorrah? She wondered if she should take it back, but that was hopeless because she was due to meet this Kevin and here she was dolling herself up like one of the scarlet women who had tempted pilgrims on their way to Rome.

She blotted the lipstick almost off, and thought she looked maybe a little better, safer, but how could you tell? She had the idea everybody would be looking at her all the way down the street outside from the St Cosmo Care Home to go meeting her young man.

Except maybe he was married and had seventeen children and was going to arrest her for stealing those white tablets from Mrs Borru and pinching some of old Mr Gorragher's whisky and mixing them up to poison Father Doran, which she was due to do on the stroke of four o'clock the following afternoon.

She had to be brave. That was what girls were, wasn't it? They had to be brave. Get through this meeting with her young man, and she would be free to stick to her plan.

And Lucy, God save her dear friend, would stop falling, and Magda would sleep soundly for the rest of her life. It was her duty to rescue Lucy, Magda's primary task, nothing to do with herself, no. Lucy came first, God rest her dear soul.

Kev wore a tie, at which Magda was astonished. He went into a café with her. He simply tilted his head the way men did, and they went into the small place at the end of the Borro, where the buses turned left into the street you had to call the shopping mall now, with its grand hair salons and multiple stores – better than Powerscourt Centre, so locals held.

'Tea, is it?'

'Yes, please.' She sat, embarrassed to be served by him. She scanned the prices on the board behind where the ladies served as if she could read, and decided to make out she was scandalised at the prices they'd be charging. She tried to hear what Kevin, in his grand tie and clean shirt, was having to pay, but couldn't hear for the working men talking away. This was really free and adult, here she was a common old girl who was just a Magdalene, being treated to tea in a genuine café. It was like a dream.

Kevin came back.

'There's sugar on the table.'

'Thank you.'

She didn't know whether to offer him money for her tea but
didn't know how much it was anyway. She saw a man and a
woman talking and looking at a bus timetable – she recognised it
from the one hung on a string in the St Cosmo vestibule. Visitors
were forever asking if she could get a new one and she had to
keep pretending she'd go straight away and bring the latest one,
but she only hid because she couldn't read the dates on them.

'Magda, is it?' He knew she was Magda.

'Yes,' she said, looking about. People would notice if she got
arrested in a minute.

'I'm Kevin MacIlwam. I'm a garage man for the Gardai.'

'Yes.'

'Mr MacIlwam's one of them you looks after, is that right?'

'Yes. Not on my own.' Hadn't she told him this? 'There's
others. There's nurses come, they have uniforms. Then there's
the nuns.'

'The nuns.'

'Yes. Sister Stephanie is in charge. I'm only a domestic.
That's like me and Oonagh and the others who do the cleaning
and washing.'

'Is that right.'

'We don't do the cooking.'

'No, right.'

She wanted desperately to keep the conversation going. It
must be hard for him, wondering when he was going to have
to arrest her, if that's what he was going to do.

'There's kitchen staff to do that. They cook for the nuns
as well.'

'I visited Grampa.' Magda stared at Kevin when he said this because he seemed to go longer in the face and his eyes didn't want to look at her. He went on, avoiding her gaze, 'I don't usually want to come to him because…well.' He shrugged.

'You don't?'

'No. Well, because…'

'Because what?' Magda leant forward across the table, ignoring the puddles of old tea spilt on the Formica. 'It's a terrible waste, that is.'

'What is?'

'Having a grampa all your own, a relative, a real relative belonging to just you out of the rest of the world, all your own, and never coming to see him because…' Why did he not want to come and see Mr MacIlwam? 'Why not?'

'He's old.'

'I know.' She felt somehow lame. She wondered what he had brought her here for, in her scarlet lipstick that cost a mint. 'Some of them have tubes in.'

'Tubes?'

'Bottles under the bed. They have to be drained off. The nurses do that.'

'Oh.'

It wasn't the right thing to talk about, when you were meeting your young man, even if he was from the Garda Siobhana and was going to arrest you for being a poisoner, but what could she do? Kevin had started it, on about his grampa he couldn't be bothered to come and see.

'Last time I went – when I waited for you – I talked to him.'

'About being arrested?'

Kevin seemed surprised at that and stared at her. 'Arrested? Who's been arrested?'

'Nobody.'

'No, nothing about anybody getting arrested. He talked about going.'

'Going?' Magda said dully.

She knew it all along. This was his warning, maybe, to tell her she was under suspicion, like on late night television where somebody knew somebody was going to rob a bank and they started up with the music thumping away and the guns came out and you knew the girl wasn't going to get away with it and her boyfriend was going to get shot.

'They keep wondering who it is who's asked to go.'

Perhaps it wasn't her after all, this going? Magda was lost. She kept her eyes on her tea now, wanting to be out of this. It wasn't at all pretty or romantic or interesting, just frightening, with Kevin of the police here wanting to know things she shouldn't even be talking about.

'I want your help, Magda.'

'Help? Of course. I'll try.'

'Thanks. I knew I could depend on you.'

She nearly screamed out in excitement, 'You *did*?' but managed to keep quiet. 'Well, if I can,' she finished lamely.

'It's Grampa. He says somebody's stealing medicines.'

'They're what?' She felt her cheeks prickle and knew she'd gone ashen. Kevin was staring at her.

'Somebody is taking the medicines they give to the old folk. They all talk about it. Grampa told me about it. The old folk are all scared.'

'Scared of what?'

'Of being poisoned. By whoever's taking the medicines.'

'Who is?'

'They don't know. Grampa said it was from one or two of

the older people. Never the same twice, but the medicines and tablets keep on going.'

'How do they know?'

This was horrible news, crucial, definitely the major risk she had to avoid. Clearly a warning from her patron saint, who was St Mary Magdalene and who had engineered this meeting with her young man to give her the warning that the Gardai were on her tail. Maybe they were sent from the Dail Eireann to spy on her?

'The old ones talk about it. One said it was somebody on the staff who was going to put paid to the old ones who had written to the Ministry.'

'Who are they? Wrote to which Ministry?'

Kevin looked evasive, and spoke with his eyes on the door, like expecting sadness to enter itself and sit right down.

'I can't say. Grampa was clear in his old head the day I went. He said they'd asked him to talk to me, me being of na Gardai.'

'What do they want you to do?'

'To find out who's stealing the medicines to kill the ones who have written to the Ministry.'

'Why should anybody do that? Kill anyone, I mean?'

She felt rather than heard God go ho-ho-ho, like a Father Christmas on the pictures, ringing his bell in the street outside snowy shops in New York. She had to keep up the deception, because what else could a poisoner do except keep on pretending she wasn't going to do anyone harm?

'To keep them quiet.'

'From the Ministry?' Magda had no real notion of what this Ministry was. She'd thought it part of the Church, but here was Kevin talking as if it was something to do with the Dail in Dublin.

'Yes. They said they've seen it before.'

'That's impossible.'

'It isn't, Magda.'

She loved the way he used her name, like he'd known her such a long time. She liked him and found herself, full of sin this thought that jumped into her mind, wondering what it would be like bestriding him instead of Bernard to come and do his puffing and sweating and breathing into her neck.

'Isn't it?'

'No. They remember now they're old, how it was when they were small children. It's always the ones from the Industrial Schools and the Magdalenes that worry most.'

'Is it? I was a Magdalene.'

'That's why you are safe, Magda. Why I can trust you.'

'What happened?' she asked, with a feeling of dread.

'When they were small? Complaints always got punished. Sometimes they were so evil it isn't right to tell. Except I believe you have to, like that Holocaust thing they keep on about, them old gypsies and Jews and homosexuals and that.'

'Jews crucified Christ.' It was the only thing she knew for certain. Gypsies now, and homosexuals?

'Magda, they are long since gone. The ones around today did nothing wrong. They're just knocking about, like you and me.'

'Yes,' she cried anxiously, to keep there being no row between them except for this old business about some old Ministry. Who cared about things like that? Writing wasn't probably much anyway, if you really went into it. 'You're right, Kevin.'

There. She had said his name right out, just like he said hers. She'd heard a word 'proprietorial', and couldn't find out what it meant and didn't like to ask, but in the fillum they'd said it meant you owned a house all of your own. She felt proprietorial.

'Now they're old, they wrote complaints about them old schools and convents, from when they were children.'

'They did?'

'Four of them. They got up a letter and have been signing it all round the St Cosmo Care Home. It had twenty-one signatures. They sent it off. Nobody's answered yet, but now they're worrying lest somebody's stealing their medicines intending...'

'To kill them for it?'

'Yes, Magda. That's where you come in.'

'Where I come where?'

Her voice went into a strange high whimper. She did not want to do this terrible thing he was going to ask her. It was exactly like the night Lucy called to her – after the priest went away – in the darkness, and said she was bleeding and asked Magda to save her by doing that terrible, really horrible thing that she would go to Hell for all eternity for.

Magda had gone and done it that night.

And here was Kevin, that she thought was maybe going to be somebody she could pretend was her very own young man, Kevin sitting across from her in this café at the wet Formica table, saying he wanted Magda to do something really sinful, so sinful it would set maybe the whole wide world falling like Lucy. How could you ever get rid of that? It must be just like Christ felt.

'I want you to do some detective work for me.'

'What's that?'

She only knew of detective work like George Raft or James Cagney in them old reruns late at night when she couldn't sleep and she stayed up awake.

'Find something out.'

'What? Where?'

'In the St Cosmo Home.'

'Find out what?'

'Who is stealing the medicines. Grampa said he had got it down to maybe five or six.'

'Who?'

'On the staff of the St Cosmo. He and the others have worked it out. It can only be a few people.'

'People stealing? You'd get told off something terrible for that.'

'I know. They're doing it secret.'

'How does Mr MacIlwam know?'

'The old ones talk when everybody's gone to sleep. They stay awake more than young people. They last longer. Maybe they keep watch. I don't know. But they have worked it out.'

Magda felt herself go even more pale. Had they put her name down too? Old Mrs Borru knew for sure because she'd asked Magda outright – was it her who stole tablets? – and Magda had said no, she maybe dropped one or two. And that had been that.

'Who are they?'

'I just can't have Grampa MacIlwam getting killed by somebody mad on the staff doing it. You read of cases like that, don't you?'

'Yes,' Magda lied, not being able to read.

'Some old nurses got done in America, and one in England, for killing old folk in care homes, didn't they?'

'I read of it,' Magda lied, second time, same lie. Wondering as she spoke if some old cockerel was working up to crowing on the third time, thinking here goes again. 'Who does Mr MacIlwam say it is?'

'I don't know.'

'Didn't you ask?'

'I was going to, but Sister Stephanie came in just then and he couldn't say. He can't write any more, so he can't tell me who. Mrs Borru – d'you nurse her too? – knows who three of them might be, and old Mr Gorragher and his mate in the opposite alcove know of two more. There's a sixth but they were unsure of her.'

'Her?' Magda bleated.

'It's one of the domestics.'

'I'm a domestic,' Magda said, escaping that old cockrel's crow by a whisker.

'Is that right?'

'Yes. Yes.' Truth, truth.

'You have to find out fast, because the letter might get replied to any day, see?' He meant the letter the old folk had sent to the Ministry.

'Yes,' she said, though she didn't.

'Better move fast instead of slow, eh?'

'Yes.'

'I was really upset, Magda, I don't mind telling you. I haven't told Mam or Dad or my sisters.'

He has no wife, then, Magda registered. Only sisters and a mam and dad. Maybe that was less complicated? She wasn't sure, because women could have mortal scunners against anybody they wanted to all of a moment, and unasked too. But would he have mentioned a wife? She might be a harridan with talons and fangs and Magda would never be allowed to be his friend.

'Will you meet me soon?'

'Again? Here?'

'Maybe, yes. Here.'

'Yes.'

'How long before you find something out?'

'Maybe at the weekend?'

'Do you work Saturdays?'

'This one, yes.'

'Then here, about this time, Saturday? Be careful, in case they get suspicious.'

'I promise, Kevin.' She went red as she said it, and was glad of that because Oonagh said she was white as a sheet at the best of times. She felt better now she was the detective for the Gardai and not the suspect.

Anyhow, she had to kill that old Father Doran tomorrow teatime, so the whole problem of Kevin's grampa and the others worrying themselves sick about writing to the Ministry would be over and done with. And she could sleep the sleep of the just, and Lucy, rescued, would float away up to Heaven and stop having to fall anywhere at all for ever and ever.

Chapter Thirteen

That evening, coming off duty, Bernard knocked on Magda's door, giving a greeting to Mrs Shaughnessy. Magda made him a tea though she had none for herself. He was downhearted, there being trouble in the station.

'I hate domestics,' he told Magda.

She sat opposite. 'Domestics? I'm a domestic.'

'Don't joke.'

She hadn't been joking, though smiling came natural now she knew the ins and outs of this stout and rather florid policeman in his fine uniform. She had learnt confidence from, with, because of him and his getting on so matter-of-fact with her when she'd given him his tea.

Today, though, he declined anything except a bit of the cake she had left. More as an after-thought than anything, Bernard ate it through, sipped tea to down it, and kept speaking about trouble in some flats near Connolly Station where a woman and a man shrieked their heads off and two children cowered in a corner.

'What happened?' Magda was so frightened by the story of

the cowering children and the screaming adults that she almost asked him to stop telling her these things.

'Sent for the social services.'

'The children, though?'

'That's it, Magda.' He seemed more tubby than smart this evening. Maybe it was the image of Kevin that was doing it, or maybe he was just tired out having to listen to all that yelling and abuse and seeing those poor mites trembling in fear. 'It's the children.'

'Were they the parents, then?'

'Yes. Married, but to different people. They took up with each other a year or two before.'

'Where were their families?'

'The children's grandparents? I never found out.'

'What will happen?'

Please don't say it, Magda prayed inwardly, Jesus, Mary and Joseph, please don't let them get taken into care, please, please.

'They're taken into care.'

'Them old Sisters of Mercy?'

'The Church representative was Father Doran, and one of the Sisters of Mercy.'

Magda almost exclaimed in horror. She said nothing until, 'The barns have done nothing bad.'

'I know, Magda.'

'Can you go and see to them, see they're not hurt?'

'Not me.'

'Your wife, then? I know you have a wife, and barns.'

'I don't know.'

'How old are they?'

'One seemed about five, the other six.'

They sat in silence, then Bernard reached for her. She let him open her blouse as usual, and she helped him by taking off her top so her breasts showed while he held them and nuzzled. She could scent the sweat on his head, the Garda cap tang still there though the cap was on the table.

He put the contraceptive sheath on, casting the small envelope into the fireplace, and drew her astride him, just like he was the motorbike and she the rider. She grunted slightly as he entered. He took only a short time, shuddering abruptly, and she felt a doubt come into her mind that maybe he hadn't really wanted to do it at all tonight.

Still he behaved as usual after, and she sat comfortably on him, him still giving them old last jerks and sweating like a pig in his clothes. She wondered why he never undressed. Still, truth to tell, she didn't either, not all the way, just there with her skirt lifted and her knickers on the floor, though not at all carelessly, just beneath the chair on which Bernard sat, for the sake of decency, out of sight.

'See, Magda, it's the children.'

'It is the children,' she said.

They remained with their arms round each other, she for support so she didn't fall backwards, him because he was that shape and his arms naturally came round her. It was designed like that, she supposed, then grew a little horrified because what on earth God was up to?

'I did wrong so many times.'

'You?'

She drew back to stare into him, and found his face so sad and fractured with grief, disturbingly close. He was softening inside her and she could feel him starting to slide out. She always liked to keep him in just that little bit longer, and was trying to learn to do it by adroit working of herself to make things tighter. Usually he smiled at those attempts, and she often smiled back like in a secret joke – though what could be secret between a man and a woman when he had just spilt so?

'You knew them before?'

'No.'

'How doing wrong, then?'

'Children I've sent into the care.'

'When?'

'In the past, cases that I had to take in charge and hand to the courts.'

'Who were they?'

Magda kept looking into him. He looked beyond her, at the wall by the fireplace as she remembered the man he'd passed in the street he'd told her about the previous time.

'Children around Dublin. Everywhere.'

'Where did they go?'

'From the courts? Sent to the Industrial Schools, and the Magdalenes.'

'I was a Magdalene.'

'I know, Magda. They hadn't done anything wrong. I was sent to be liaison because I was new in those days. One lad…'

He began to talk slowly, reflective, not really giving an account so much as a list of children who had had to be taken to be handed over. Children orphaned, disowned, of broken homes.

Twice he shivered, this bulky man with the shock of black hair and the grand uniform gaping at his middle where she sat astride. It had seemed a year before, what they had done today, how they moved, lepping like fish tied in the one invisible net together until climax took them shuddering to silence and stillness.

Now this.

He talked on. He told her nothing new. She knew orphans like herself. And the lads, to hear the old men and the punishments they had endured, in an even worse plight, if that could be.

'It's like that thing in the war the old people talk of but nobody listens or cares this side of the Pond.'

'What thing?' She thought, Dear God, not another set of miseries. She couldn't cope with the last set. Look what had happened the one night she tried to do something good for some poor girl, her friend. She was still trying to mend Lucy's fate that she had made so much worse.

'Holocaust.'

Magda remembered that word, from grainy old pictures that were on the TV screen sometimes, arms and legs flying and thin people walking towards the camera, gaunt and full of sores with their heads shaved.

'Holocaust.' She knew it was some kind of thing to do with Jacob – was that right? – or maybe them old prophets whose names came so thick and fast they made your head spin in the Old Testament.

'It's like a children's holocaust, only for them, with all the rest of us adults staying out of it while it goes on and on. And me sending more in, again and again.'

She was the one who withdrew. He continued talking. She went into the little loo and cleaned herself, listening to his droning. When she emerged she could hear the contraceptive sizzling on the fire and Bernard was standing reaching for his uniform cap. He was still speaking, so flat and even as if this was a court room itself, that Magda could only stand and look at the man.

'It's only four years since the Dail said its sorries to all the children of Eire. Do you think the poor barns are not still tortured and abused? I handed over boys who got sentenced just for throwing a stone at a canal. Whose parents had died. Who were separated for nothing from their siblings.'

'Yes, all of them,' was what Magda wanted to say, but not a single sound came from her head.

'Sent to roam round the streets of the Maltebior Fishing School like lepers begging food…'

Magda watched the man's mouth move. She could only think of being astride this man while he finished his rummaging and then, smiling, take his leave of her until next time. She even thought to herself, for what was this, for what all that? It was incomprehensible – a man doing that to a woman, and a woman doing things for the man, even if it was designed by God, His wonders to perform. She was sticky.

There was one question, and she would get round to it soon, about what a priest should do if he felt something like this man felt when coming to call on her. It was what the whole business was, but she would work that out later when she got a moment's peace.

This children's holocaust thing, though. It meant she would close the door on Bernard in his grand Garda Siobhana uniform right now and never let him in again. He was the one who still – still, after all these years of handing poor little mites over to the Holy Mother Church to be tortured and worse – was still throwing the poor mites to… She said goodbye and was alone, with God's work to do. She and Bernard never kissed.

Yet punishment was left in the hands of God, while you prayed for sinners and hoped God would get it right in the Hereafter. Who could prevent the holocaust of children?

For the whilst, though, she would kill Father Doran in the morning, even if they caught and hanged her or whatever they did. Her poison might save one whole child. And if her whisky didn't work, and by some miracle, or God's kind intervention, she got away, she would try again maybe with some old gun or maybe some hammer, anything that might work. She was determined now, and would not give up. Holocaust.

On the other hand, she might be lucky in the morning, and set them a-yirding Father Doran in the cemetery out beyond Parnell Square, which would be great. She had time before she went to bed to make sure her plan was exactly right.

One of the bottles from out of the bins in the backyards of the Borro was the right shape and size, and had that English frock-coated gentleman smiling away in his great round hat and monocle and shiny boots, and it smelt just like old Mr Gorragher's horrid fluid. In fact, there was still a trace of the stuff at the bottom when she got it home to her little flat, and she washed it carefully and wiped it clean so no fingerprints showed, because that's what detectives searched for. You couldn't see fingerprints unless you'd dusted them with a special brush, but you couldn't be too careful.

She rinsed it out one last time and poured in her tablets. Into the bottle she poured the golden fluid she had taken from Mr Gorragher's bottle while he was being taken to the bathroom by the nurses. It was simple. In fact, so shocked was she by her success that she knelt right down while the tablets started to dissolve and immediately said a mystery of the Rosary, praying for forgiveness. She would have used St Anthony, but he was Patron Saint of Lost Causes and that would never do. He might get her arrested, and she would become the Lost Cause and there she'd be in gaol among the lunatics and have to be thanking St Anthony for her hanging when really she'd just got hold of the wrong saint.

She stuck to the Virgin Mary, who'd be on her side, please God.

Before going to bed she worried whether to decant the fluid or simply leave the traces of tablet powder like greyish sand in the bottom of the bottle, and decided yes, leave it there. She would pour it out into a clean jar, wash the greyish residue away, dry it as best she could, then pour the poisoned whisky back into the bottle. Father Doran – she'd seen him take his illicit swig before – took a fair old blooter at Mr Gorragher's secret whisky, that he did, so maybe it would all be down before he tasted something wrong. Or might there be no change in the taste at all? If God was on her side…

Kneeling, she did her prayers for Lucy, then the children left behind in the Magdalenes, all the little boys still in the clutches of the Christian Brothers, and asked the Almighty to give the other seven Orders of persecutors a good old seeing to, if it was His holy wish, and went to bed.

She wished she could read because then she could sit up with a cup of tea like ladies did in them late night fillums in posh hotels, but she couldn't, so that was that. Instead, she switched her old TV set on, saw the sound was well down, and put the light out. She kept her eyes on the screen, saw it was about some old football, the lads moving so smoothly and with such grace, and tried not to see anybody who looked as though they might fall down.

Chapter Fourteen

Father Doran enjoyed, actually enjoyed, the talks with the nuns. Of course, if they were Sisters of Mercy there was a kind of constitutional difference. Not all Orders were the same. Sisters of the Sacred Heart were different from the Mercy, and the nuns up at Rosmonorc must be vastly removed from the Irish Sisters of Charity.

He had quite a time to reflect on his position. Father Kilmain, possibly the one rival in the diocesan monsignor stakes, was a formidable individual, of course, with his grand BSc in Sociology, but what was that when matched against experience of the life in an inner city? And what of his grand articles on *Restitution for Past Wrongs* he was forever sending out to every member of the nursing and teaching orders round Dublin, including (God, the nerve and arrogance of the man) to Bishop MacGrath himself? Presumptuous.

Father Doran reflected, as he waited for the nuns to assemble for his talk today, on the habits and customs of Holy Mother Church. Look at celibacy, the edict of a routine, not of faith. Morals, it sometimes seemed, were a custom, not faith transmitted in the Church. He sighed, waiting. Pity they didn't send through some tea and a few eatables, even a small plate of pandy, one of his secret though fattening tastes, before his lecture rather than after. He might mention it to Sister Stephanie.

Had there been a mirror he would have inspected his form. Stouter, and no longer slim. Lack of physical exercise did that to a man, though he tried to keep active by sometimes cycling slowly down the boreen, where he would receive smiling deference of doffed hats and bobs from all and sundry.

He reflected, too, on the religious figures round the room. The picture of the Sacred Heart, the Virgin Mary, and the Crucifixion. He wondered whether they were 'good' paintings originally, and what they might score on some critic's league. The one Protestant friend he had, a sour youth called Jerry – champion runner at school, and whose father was something in the diplomatic corps – had become a well-known art critic for an English newspaper. Even as a youth Jerry was outspoken. They last met when Father Doran visited Liverpool one day, and there was Jerry staring all disbelieving across the train at him. They chatted, Jerry baffled that anybody could enter the Church.

'Christ, man, have you not noticed the fucking date?' was his opener. Father Doran felt really uncomfortable, though nobody among the passengers as much as batted an eye. There'd have been astonishment in Dublin.

They talked of celibacy, Jerry not bothering to keep his voice down. That accidental meeting was, Father Doran knew, a test sent by his own patron saint, showing the brash comments he would have to face as he advanced in the Faith. He became distant in response to Jerry's attempted affability, and stoic at Jerry's gentle leg-pulling.

Fine, Father Doran acknowledged to himself, to be tempered in the fire of opprobrium. Doesn't steel become harder when tempered by the flame of indignity? He could have predicted Jerry's, 'Why be holier than the pope?' and didn't even give it the benefit of a reply.

Yes, he thought, saying goodbye to his erstwhile friend, several popes and many cardinals had strayed. Some trod notorious glades of evil. Were they not human, like himself come to that? He drew his mind away from past transgressions and concentrated on what Jerry said about art.

'There must really be something in your religion,' Jerry told him with a nudge as the train slowed and a noisy crowd of football supporters got on. 'Otherwise, how could anybody explain the Church's survival when floating on a leaky lifeboat of bad art?'

It had been humour of the gentle needling kind Father Doran remembered. It was Jerry's manner to seek irony. He had even delivered some cracks in class with a priest teaching, Jerry's expression of rue and dismay disarming the clerics.

'The only alternative to religion', Jerry said, rising to leave the train, 'is art. There's no other route.'

'Marketing your wares, Jerry?' Father Doran remembered giving back to the now famous art critic, once his friend.

'Hardly,' Jerry said. 'Trying to throw you a life-belt.'

Bad art? Father Doran never wanted to see Jerry again. He had sometimes, in moments of weakness, wondered whether to write, perhaps ask him to dinner if ever he visited Dublin. Another time he had gone to an art and sculpture exhibition in Temple Bar, frankly keeping an eye out for Jerry. He must have missed his old friend. Though he had given him his address – the first time he had used his new personal cards – no letter or invitation to meet had come. Jerry had not even offered a phone number.

Regret? For what?

Father Doran felt more than a little irritation waiting for the nuns to assemble today, kicking his heels while the recollections of his old friend came densely to mind. A priest should not be delayed without adequate explanation. There should be inflexible priorities in any organisation. If unexplained tardiness happened in banks, for instance, where would their profits be?

That girl's face also entered his mind. What was she called? Magda, the one he asked about. Sister St Jude had said she was a Magdalene girl. The Magdalenes had suffered from the gutter press lately. Perhaps there was a similarity to another girl? Familial links were common among children taken into care. He was still thinking when he was invited to come through to the meeting room, the nuns having assembled at last.

He entered with a light quip, '*Finalamente!*' smiling, his poor command of Italian signifying acceptance of the day's onerous duties. The senior nun, Sister Stephanie, smiled. He was rewarded by one or two meek smiles from the rest.

Had there been words exchanged among them? Father Doran thought to maybe rush into questions-and-answers. Restraint held him back. There was the wise advice from a veteran Hollywood scriptwriter to his new young colleague at his first meeting with producers, 'Keep it shut, pal.' And on leaving, after the neophyte had remained silent, 'You did swell, pal!' It had served Father Doran well on many such occasions. The reefs ahead were always clearly visible before his personal ship risked any voyage.

They started with a prayer, dutifully saying the Hail Mary. He then said a Latin Collect, with the seemingly reflexive reminder, 'This is from the Second Sunday after Pentecost, and is at once a warning that our love must remain constant as the love of Christ, whoever we are and whatever we do in our various walks of life.

'*Sancti nominis tui, Domine, timorem pariter et amorem fac nos habere perpetuum: quia...*'

He liked the Amens from the nuns, such melodious interchanges with his more gravelly voice. How lovely to use a truly dark low timbre, if he'd had a thick bass. Instead, his feeble alto never got him anywhere.

'I wish to speak today about differences in the Church.' He went straight into it. 'We must feel the many influences that exist out there. We could be forgiven for seeing the changes only from within.'

He enlarged on this aspect of normal daily life, and several times introduced quips, of a light and simple kind as befitted a duteous and hard-working community such as the St Cosmo. His favourite was to interrupt himself with a casual aside, such as, 'I often say that if some of our precursors had been Italian instead of Irish, they would already have been beatified!' and himself led the laughter. He also digressed on the thoughts that would be aroused when television soap operas included some priest in a story. 'Not always to the Church's benefit,' he added dryly, 'though sometimes to the advantage of infidels who notice the absence of horns on the cleric's head!'

It was a satisfactory session. The questions arising from his talk proved the usual kind, always meticulously judged by Sister Stephanie as appropriate. The first, from Sister Francesca, concerned scruples: 'When does one become unduly scrupulous concerning the duty to bring matters around the Home to the attention of the Order?' and suchlike old chestnuts. He fielded them with one hand behind his back. There were others, about the necessity for confession when one's sins were merely venial; was the imposition of self-discipline not in fact a prideful eagerness to show an excessive zeal? and so on.

All elementary. He wondered, as he ended his explanation, whether it would prove timely for a pamphlet, written with Imprimatur of Bishop MacGrath, of course, about the routine of self-examination in everyday work. It would bring favourable attention. The notion prompted him to lead the closing prayer with the Oblation from the Spiritual Exercises of St Ignatius of Loyola. He had the wisdom and humility – working well today – to omit any reference to the Indulgence that was given to anyone saying the small admonition. Remission in Purgatory was no less than three whole years! Criticism had lately been levelled at the practice of Indulgences. Any reference to them was best left to another day.

'Take, O Lord, into Thy hands my entire liberty, my memory, my understanding and my will…'

He left with Sister Stephanie. Together they went into her office. The nuns separated to their tea. Father Doran sank with a sigh of relief into his usual armchair after Sister Stephanie had seated herself opposite. She signalled for a girl to bring the tea tray. It was the Magda girl, and he smiled in recognition. She looked as if she had hoped to escape his attention.

'Thank you,' he said, and for one fleeting instant he saw a different emotion in her eyes.

Until now, whenever his glance met those of the girls, they showed a smiling shyness, perhaps a meek assurance that they were gaining merit and were rather proud of a duty done well. This Magda had shown the same, yet with a kind of sorrow he could not help noticing. In fact, it was that glint of sadness

– had it been genuine sadness, though? – that had prompted his alert question previously.

Now, today, though, there was only an inflexibility. He wondered what on earth these girls thought of, so meek and silent about the place. She placed the tray with her usual care and begged Sister Stephanie's permission to leave.

He saw with pleasure it was the Dundee cake. Sometimes, the kitchen ladies in the St Cosmo excelled themselves. Was it Mrs Malahide? If ever he had the opportunity, he would tell them so.

'We are a little later than usual, Sister Stephanie,' he observed.

'A little, Father Doran.'

'Did I go on too long?'

'Not at all. We were delayed by a discussion. I failed to notice how quickly time was flying.'

'Nothing serious, I hope?'

'Nothing that could not be coped with, but it needed addressing.'

'Anything I can do?'

'How kind.' She poured the tea and served him a piece of the Dundee. She was proud of the small confectionery knives she was able to offer, a gift from grateful relatives of an inmate lately deceased. 'Perhaps I should mention the topic?'

'If you think so, Sister.'

'As long as you don't find it an imposition on your time.'

They settled down. She watched her visitor with real pleasure. No false behaviour with this priest, not like some. He was straightforward, plain and honest, and always ready to stand by whatever decisions a nun in charge might take in the interests of the Order. It was loyalty of the highest degree.

An unspoken communication existed between herself and this priest. It had come to her notice more than once, that he always sought her eye when in the St Cosmo, to check no doubt that all was well.

One instance was the extensions she worked out as necessary for the St Cosmo. This would offer several more places for inmates, and earn financial reward to the Order and to the establishment. Those two could, of course, be considered separately, but was that wise? She did not believe so, for several convents had been forced to close because of falling recruitment.

Opportunities in the Order doubled when the number of newcomers fell. Attrition was always a factor, and expenses rose inexorably. Her own position was clear: advancement in the Order was related to efficiency. Improvement in income lessened the risk of insolvency, and would do herself no harm at all. She had already been mentioned as a promotion candidate. The bishop himself looked favourably on her financial reports, and last year's fiscal summaries had earned special praise.

'You are so considerate.' He sampled the Dundee with a relish so obvious it made her smile.

'You ought to enter those competitions the Sorority has for culinary arts!'

'With you as judge, Father Doran?'

'No, Sister, please not. I'd resort to bribery and not survive the testing sessions!'

They shared the humour a moment, then the nun spoke quietly.

'It came to my attention that one of our number has shown signs of discontent. Not,' she was quick to add, 'to be construed as disobedient.'

'How?'

'Merely a kind of depression, Father.'

'A vocational crisis?'

'In part, Father.'

'Something external or internal?'

'To the St Cosmo? Internal.'

The priest breathed a sigh of relief. 'As long as the issue can be handled within the establishment, Sister.'

She awarded the problem a slight hesitation, just enough to suggest it might not go away as fast as one might wish.

'I had wondered why one particular nun was so willing to spend her free time of an evening attending to the inmates. I thought it a voluntary excess of zeal.'

'Scrupulous, then?'

'Perhaps. You noticed, I think, the question I made sure would be introduced in your lecture?'

'I guessed, Sister.' Father Doran was pleased he could say this with a clear conscience, for it had struck him at the time.

'I spoke to Sister Francesca about her excessive devotion to mundanities. She gave me quite a reasonable reply, her work motivated by the plights of the inmates.'

'Reasonable, Sister?'

Sister Stephanie was pleased he had caught her inflexion.

'Sister Francesca does seem a particularly caring nun, Father, moved by the stories of the elderly. I once reprimanded her over one small matter on the ward. She was forever listening to their ramblings when they were quite comfortable and not even asking for any service.'

'A major rebuke, Sister?'

'Not at all. A small correction.'

'Nothing on record?'

'Nothing. It was not that serious. I merely hoped to nip a tendency in the bud before it became a self-indulgent waste of spiritual resource.'

'Then you did absolutely the right thing.'

'I am so relieved.'

'Some old folk dwell unnecessarily on past trivia, and not only tire the nuns but exhaust the priest into the bargain!'

They chuckled in synchrony. Father Doran reflected on how pleasant it was to enjoy the company of some in the Orders, and how unpleasant when encountering others.

He left the office after another fifteen minutes' chat, all equally innocent, and made his way to Mr Gorragher. On the way, he almost bumped into the girl called Magda. She seemed to be waiting in the corridor for something, and said quickly, 'Just taking away the tea things, Father.'

'Good,' he said amiably, and went on past.

Chapter Fifteen

The visit to the St Cosmo was ending. He felt quite exhausted, though he had done little to earn his weariness except deliver his talk, with such eloquence today, then have that illuminating chat with Sister Stephanie about problems of moral waywardness. Nothing sinister, so easily handled. The troubled nun was possibly youngish. They always were. Scruples went with the young. The more a woman matured, the firmer her feet were planted when she coped with changes in the savage weather of ethical dilemma. He couldn't quite call Sister Francesca to mind.

A gripe came on as he went for his coat. It always hung in the hallway. The mirror had been excised from the hall stand, to conform with the natural reserve of the Order. He found difficulty putting it on. He thrust his arm into the armsate – Sister Stephanie, of course, standing away – and felt the pain grow. He wondered about the Dundee. There had been savouries this time, a simple vol-au-vent and a disc of salmon and lemon something-or-other. Very tasty.

The thought of taste bubbled bile into his throat and he halted, having a hard time inhaling.

'Father Doran?' Sister Stephanie said.

'I am fine, Sister Stephanie. Just a momentary feeling...'

He was sweating. The realisation astonished him. Sure, he was a bit thicker round the waist than he had once been, but it was far too early in life for this gripping pain? It extended round his chest as if a giant hand clutched him. It wasn't a gripe. Colic was not serious, and quickly gone.

The coat half on, he froze, dripping with sweat. It ran down his temples onto his chin. The pain waved through him, then held. It grew worse.

'I don't feel very well, Sister.'

'Sit down, Father.'

A chair stood in the hallway, its reflection slightly fuzzy on the polished linoleum. A girl, polishing away in the far corner, was staring, her polishing rag in her hand and the polish lid inverted on the linoleum.

'It will pass any moment.'

'Sure it will, Father.' Sister Stephanie got the priest seated, his coat trailing.

As the girl was sent to find one of the nurses, the priest tried a quiet prayer. It did not soothe. He felt testy, Sister Stephanie doing nothing more than peer at him in alarm. She could have done something to help. Only moments before she had been authoritative and firm. Now, she conveyed a querulous puzzlement and – what? – a kind of fear lest a priest be taken ill in her grand little St Cosmo Care Home for the Elderly.

'I shall feel fine soon.'

'Of course you will, Father!'

Heartiness was misplaced in holy orders, James Doran thought with anger. Look at the stupid woman, dithering when she should...

The pain gripped, suffocating. He lost consciousness and slipped onto the polished linoleum.

'It's not a mild attack.'

'Doctor, we think in the circumstances—'

'I have to see to a delivery in the next road. I'll leave you my mobile number.'

'One of the nurses can stay only another hour, Doctor.'

'Keep her as long as you can.'

'What do we do after that? My only nun who is a registered nurse is away in Cork at the retreat.'

'I shall give you the number of an agency.'

In tones of shock Sister Stephanie said, 'But we might get anybody!'

'They're all trained nurses, Sister.'

'But from where, Doctor? They could be from anywhere.'

'I'm interested only in keeping him among us.'

The two voices used the muted half-whisper Father Doran himself had taught, for moments when somebody had passed away among a poor family stunned by the calamity.

'Doctor, with great respect—'

A heavy sigh. 'No, Sister. Father Doran cannot be moved. Later, perhaps, I shall let him go to the hospital. Not now.'

'Yes, Doctor.'

'I am only two or three streets away.'

'Yes, Doctor. What if there is a change for the worse?'

'You have my number. Nurse Tully knows what to do.'

Father Doran opened his eyes. He was in bed in a spartan room, light and airy, with a curtained window through which weak sunlight came. The pain had not left, though it was easier. He could hear their conversation quite clearly, though each word took a few moments to sink in.

'Doctor?'

Dr Strathan's features swam into view and stayed looking down.

'You've had a cardiac event, Father Doran. I decided not to have you shifted to hospital – all that roaring in ambulances does nobody a power of good. For the moment you'll stay here in the St Cosmo. The nurse can call me any time. I shall be nearby.'

'The pain, Doctor.'

'I've given you all the drug I can for the whilst. I'll be back in forty-five minutes. Got that?'

'Yes.'

'Have you had previous heart trouble? I mean anything you might have thought was indigestion that wouldn't go away when you took antacids?'

'No. Never.'

'Breathless any time lately?'

'No.'

'Nothing like unexplained banging in the chest, or any sudden giddiness?'

'Nothing like that.'

'And you're a fairly agile man, Father?'

'Yes. I've always thought so.'

The doctor went over the priest's past history. Apart from one injury as a student and a few stitches from a fall from a bicycle years before, there was nothing. Heart disease did not run in the family.

'Is it serious, Doctor?'

Dr Strathan's face relaxed in a smile. 'I was always taught, Father Doran, that when some patient started asking if his illness was serious, he was on the way to recovery.'

'Is it, though?'

'Nothing we can't handle. What you really mean, Father, is how soon can you get back to normal.'

'Well...'

'The answer is, when I say so. I'll leave you to it for a while.'

At the door Strathan paused. 'I daresay you're wondering if it lowers the odds if you stay here instead of going to hospital. All evidence is that first attacks like this show an almost exactly equal survival rate no matter whether we pull out all the stops or treat a patient at home. So don't worry on that account.'

'Right, Doctor. Thank you.'

Dr Strathan gave the nun a card and left, Sister Stephanie gliding along behind. A dumpy nurse perched on a chair.

'I'm Nurse Tully, Father.'

'Hello.' He waited, dozing as the pain seemed to move and hold. This time it slid down his left arm and caused it to flex of its own accord, almost as if movement would lessen the pain somehow. 'Is this bad?'

'It's what the doctor said it was, Father.'

'Have you seen other patients this bad?'

'Yes. Lots.'

'They recovered?'

A slight pause before she answered, 'All of them. You.'

A double affirmation meant at least doubt, at worst a lie. That tip had been given him by his tutor at the seminary.

'Is it a heart attack or just, what do they call it, a spasm?'

'I think it's a bad spasm, Father.' This time Nurse Tully spoke more firmly, getting in the swing of deception. 'Dr Strathan said he will make a definitive diagnosis when the tests come through.'

'Tests?'

'Doctor took blood tests from your arm, and set up the monitors. That's what I must record. The blood tests are already off at the hospital laboratory.'

'How long have I been here?'

'Hours, Father. You went down an almighty wallop on the hall lino.'

'I can't remember.'

'It took three of us to lift you. We had to bring the gardener in.'

'Can I have something more for the pain?'

'Not until Dr Strathan says. He'll be ringing on his mobile every ten minutes. He's a stickler for details.'

As if the conversation was a reminder, she took up her clipboard and made a note from the monitor.

He could see the reflection of two small screens above and behind the bed. The wavy lines, shadowy green traces crossing the glass, shone back from the tortured Face of the Christ in agony on the far wall. Father Doran wondered about the selection of the image. Not for the first time he thought of the curious choices of devotional pictures made for the bedrooms of nuns. The casual meeting with his old friend in the train during his Liverpool visit came to mind, those comments about bad art. How different from the Russian Orthodox faith, where an icon itself became sacred by the spiritual recognition of its subject. Was that the secret, but oft-denied, process at the heart of the Catholic addiction to shrines and votive objects, statues and the like? For the first time he realised how his old friend must have viewed religious belief. It was profoundly disturbing, especially now.

'It is worsening, Nurse.'

'I'll give him a ring.'

'Please. If you would.'

She moved from the bedroom, taking her mobile phone. The door closed. He could hear her speaking in the corridor, presumably to some nun, in low tones. That sepulchral voice was a giveaway. Had he been as transparent when attending some sick bed, or asking after the progress of a patient in hospital?

The pain was worse. He groaned as the spasm felt as if it were stripping skin from his left arm, which flexed across his body at the elbow, pressing into his left side. The sense of being crushed made consciousness fade.

He woke slowly, the room in a kind of gloaming. Nurse Tully with her fat knees and bulky form had gone, and a nun sat in her place.

'Father Doran?'

'Yes, Sister.'

'I must call Dr Strathan as soon as you awoke, so I shall be away a moment. How do you feel?'

'Giddy.'

'Are you in pain?'

'Nothing like as much as I was, no.'

'You can have a drink, but only small sips. Dr Strathan said it could be weak tea if you wished, but that is all.'

'Right.'

'The doctor has been in three times to check your progress, Father. He's due back fairly soon.'

'Tell him thanks.'

'I'll call him now.'

He could hear the regular bleeping of the monitors. The reflections of those traces were still eeling over the agonised

Face of Christ. What did they do with patients, he thought, before these gadgets came into being? Hadn't Dr Strathan said something about the survival rates being equal, no matter how you treated the first heart attack? Certainly the doctor had seemed assured.

The door opened, and in came one of the lay workers in the Home. He recognised Magda. She brought tea, laid the small tray by the bed.

'Magda, is it?'

'Yes, Father.'

'I doubt I'll be able to reach that. Sister Francesca says she will be back presently.'

'Yes, Father.'

He smiled. 'Don't be afraid, Magda. These things happen. Sent to try us, don't they say?'

'Yes, Father.'

She looked pale and frightened. Perhaps she had never seen serious illness before, not close to.

'Must I bring anything else, Father?'

'No, thank you. I think that's all I am allowed.'

'Sister Francesca said I am to wait here until she returns.'

'Sit down if you wish.'

'Thank you, Father.'

The girl took the chair as far as possible from the bed. He had difficulty seeing her face, not able to raise his head enough. He was afraid to risk extertion in case that crushing chest pain recurred.

'Where are you from, Magda?'

'I was an orphan, Father.'

'You don't know?'

'No, Father.'

'Were you in any of the schools?'

'Yes, Father.'

'Whereabouts?'

'Sandyhills. Then,' she added quickly, 'I went as an outworker in the paper packing. Me and a girl called Emily.'

'Did you do well there?'

'Yes, Father.'

Father Doran sighed. Like struggling through water dragging a log. We are too remote, he remembered the preceptor at the seminary teaching, too distant from the laity. Unless we become more approachable, the Church will become an anachronism in a generation. So far the girl had said only yes, Father, no, Father.

'Was Emily your friend?'

'Yes, Father.'

'Was she from your Sandyhills convent too?'

'No, Father. We were on the same conveyor assembly.'

'I see.'

No, he didn't see. All priestly conversation seemed to be catch phrases, mere acknowledgements of remarks uttered to mollify, the aim being to keep the clergyman at that terrible distance, remote in his cocoon.

'Were you happy at Sandyhills?'

'Yes, Father.'

'I used to go to Sandyhills sometimes to say Holy Mass.'

'Yes, Father.'

'Did you hear Mass when I said it there?'

'Yes, Father.'

He decided to try jocularity, crack the ice. 'You weren't one of those naughty girls who nodded off during the Creed, were you, Magda?'

'No, Father.' And after an extended pause, 'Once, yes, Father.'

He went for a smile. 'I'm sure you don't doze in Holy Mass now, do you, Magda?'

'No, Father.'

'That's a good girl.'

The door opened and the girl jumped up. 'Father Doran said I was to sit down, Sister.'

'That's all right, Magda.' Sister Francesca crossed to the priest. 'I have spoken to Dr Strathan. He will be here in a few minutes.'

'Tell him thanks.'

'I shall. And Bishop MacGrath rang. He intends to come this evening.'

'How kind. There is really no need.'

'He spoke with Dr Strathan and insists.'

'Very well.' He smiled. 'I hope I am worth all this trouble, Sister Francesca.'

'Let us be the judge of that, Father. I must go down and wait for the doctor. Magda? Please stay. If Father Doran says, send for me. I told you about the bell-pull.'

'Yes, Sister.'

The nun swished away.

'So many dignitaries,' Father Doran said, back in his old position, unable to see Magda as she sat.

'They are grand people.'

He repeated her sentence mentally. Was it quite as straightforward as it sounded? Just for one moment he might have imagined there was something rather dry in her words, as if she understood far more than she was saying. That glance suddenly returned to mind. This was the same girl. He wondered if he had seen her before, closer than he could now remember.

'Aren't they just.'

'So caring, Father,' she volunteered.

'Yes, the essence of charity.'

'Especially when someone is poorly.'

'Especially then, Magda.' The conversation had finally got going.

'I wished I could have done more, Father.'

'More? Helped people more, is that what you mean?'

A pause, then, 'One person.'

'One of the old folk here?'

'No. Back then.'

'Back...?'

He felt uneasy. He heard Magda rise and go to the door and pause a moment before coming back. He heard her movements, sitting down in that chair. The bed could raise. He could have been half-seated instead of lying recumbent, but he did not know how to work the controls. Should he ask her to do it? Except she was an ignorant girl and might not know. He wondered how much longer the nun would be.

'Back when I was in the Magdalenes.'

'Who? Was she too sick, Magda?'

'Yes.'

'Who was she?'

He remembered visiting the Magdalenes. He had been the confessor there for the best part of a year. The nuns had been in his pastoral care. It had been so worthwhile.

'Nobody you would remember, Father.'

Her tone was neutral now. He wondered at the thoughts of these young people. He could not recall any particular spurts of anger when he was young. Being unsettled, yes. And once when passed over for candidacy to the Roman College, where he could have really achieved and made something of a career. Instead, it had been that half-breed man from Armagh, half a Protestant and only half a Catholic. What an obscenity. It had distressed him so much he had almost considered going abroad. Maybe he should have cut his losses and showed the diocese the mistake they had made passing him over like that.

'My friend was at Sandyhills,' she offered unexpectedly.

'Oh? Is she here with you?'

'No.'

'Did you get your examinations at Sandyhills?' Silence. 'Some girls did well in their exams.'

'I did no exams.'

'That's bad luck.'

'Only the laundry and domestic.'

'Oh, I'm sorry about that. Still, there's plenty of time left for a willing girl.'

'Those of us who came out, Father.'

That unease returned. He remembered her glance when serving him that time. Was it only yesterday, or a whole week ago? She had given the impression of doing something quite new and utterly alien. Yet she had served tea several times before, though always trembling with anxiety. But that was only natural, for he was the priest after all. Nuns could be punitive if she made any kind of mistake.

'Who came out?'

'Yes.'

'Where is your friend?' he asked, trying for pleasantry. His manner had always contributed to his success. He was briefly amused at the notion of sending a jocular self-deprecating memorandum to the diocese, suggesting that affability be included as a seminary topic. Education under guise of humour, always a winner.

'She died, Father.'

'Died? I am so sorry.' He quickly adjusted.

'Thank you.'

He wondered at her tone. It had changed. The innocence was still there, perhaps now with a little asperity. However, the laity often failed to come to terms with the problem of God's love, and the inevitable fate that faces us all. It was hard for anyone to comprehend. Nothing more natural than a simple girl like Magda there finding it hard to rationalise the death of a friend.

'When did she die?'

'Years back.'

'In school, was it?' And into her silence, 'It must have been in school, I suppose?'

'Yes.'

'Poorly, was she?'

'Yes.'

He sighed, and felt most unreal. His chest was tighter again. He wished Sister Francesca would come back. He had forgotten where she'd said she was going. Something about the bishop arriving, or the doctor, or both?

'How sad. I'm so sorry.'

'Thank you.'

With a hint of something more disturbing now?

'She died of a fall.'

The words came out in a rush, as if Magda suddenly decided to tell him.

'A fall you say?'

'She fell.'

'Poor girl. Where?'

'Sandyhills.'

He had served the community in Sandyhills. Had he mentioned this to her a few moments ago, or not? It was there that he…His chest tightened. Angina meant, he recalled from his Latin, crushing. This was no gentle reminding squeeze of a heart under stress, no. He had had a true heart attack. He now really truly wanted the nun to return, bringing Dr Strathan.

'God rest her soul.'

'She fell in the stairwell.'

'How terrible.'

'One night.'

'In the night? Poor girl.'

'Poor girl,' she repeated.

'God rest her poor soul.'

'He doesn't.'

He thought he had misheard. She could never have said that, not to herself nor to a priest. He wanted to see Magda's face, to find in it the usual servile anxiety. The expression he saw daily among the faithful. It was the recognition that he, for God's sake, *deserved* as a man of the cloth, compliance to which he was entitled. For the first time he felt impatience with the girl.

'He doesn't? What do you mean, child?'

'She was called Lucy.'

'Lucy. There was a saint called Lucy. Did they teach you that in, ah, Sandyhills?'

'No, Father.'

'Well, there was.'

'I know.'

'That's good, Magda.'

'Virgin and martyr, Lucy was,' she said.

'How did you know, if they did not teach you that?'

'Lucy tellt me. St Lucy was killed for spurning a suitor.'

'Very good, Magda.'

'St Lucy stops you going blind, if you pray.'

'Well done.' He waited, now exhausted by the strain of speaking to this intense yet clearly simple-minded girl. 'Could you please see if Sister Stephanie is coming?'

'Yes, Father.'

He heard her go to the door and a little way down the corridor. For a moment he thought he heard her say something about someone still sleeping, then she was back.

'They will be a few minutes more, Father.'

'Are you sure, Magda?'

'Yes, Father.'

He wondered if he should try to shout, but the nun had said he was to lie quietly until the doctor returned.

'I saw her fall, Father.'

'Who?' He struggled to recover the subject.

'Lucy. I saw her fall.'

'Fall? You saw Lucy fall?'

'Yes, Father.'

'How?'

'In the stairwell. I saw her fall down into it.'

'You did?' He thought, can a girl evidently so docile and obedient be actually mad?

'Yes. I can see her now.'

'Did you raise the alarm?'

'She went like one of them rag dolls they gave us at Christmas.'

'A shame. Poor girl.'

'The nuns gave us presents on Christmas Day.'

'That was kind. Would you ask after Sister Stephanie, please? Ask her to tell Dr Strathan to hurry, please?'

'They took them off of us after Christmas Day.'

'They did?'

'Lucy said they sold them.'

'Who?'

'The nuns sold them. The toys. The people from the Church had a whip-round at Christmas for presents for us.'

'That was a shame.'

'The nuns kept the money. Lucy said that.'

'The nuns possibly sent them to Africa, to children who had nothing to eat.'

'Was that stealing, Father?'

'Of course not. Magda, would you please ask anyone you can find if the doctor is here yet? I am aching rather badly.'

'She talked to me before she fell.'

'She? Lucy, you mean?'

'Yes, Father.'

This was a dilemma. He could neither move nor send for help. He tried fumbling for the button-clicker Sister Stephanie had said would be right there by his left hand. He only had to press the button and the signal would be heard and they would come running. That was her term, 'We'll all come running to straighten you out,' her exact words. He couldn't find the clicker.

'What a good friend you must have been.'

'I wasn't, Father.'

'Oh, I'm sure you were.'

'She said I was, and that she would pray for me in Heaven every single day.'

'She did? She must have been a remarkable soul.'

'She was my friend.'

He could hear someone on the stairs. 'I'm sure she is in Heaven now, Magda.'

'Are you?'

'Of course. I'm sure she was a good girl, so she will be in Heaven.'

'Are you?'

'Of course. God is good.'

'I'm frightened Lucy isn't there at all.'

'Trust in God's mercy, child.'

'You said that before.'

Had he? He could not remember saying it, unless she had heard him speak on the subject from the pulpit.

'Did I?'

'Can you go to Heaven if you know you are going to die anyway?'

'Of course you can. Look at...'

There were voices in the corridor outside. He almost called out, but his voice hadn't strength enough. He wondered if the girl were deranged. These orphans were simple, the sins of the parents passed down as a mark on their illegitimate children.

'Virgins and martyrs, Father? Like Lucy?'

The door opened, and in came Sister Stephanie and Dr Strathan. They came over to the bedside, the nun giving a gesture of dismissal in the direction of the far side of the room, presumably to where Magda was stationed.

'Had Father Doran needed anything, Magda?'

'No, Sister. He talked a bit, that's all.'

'You can go.'

'Thank you, Sister.'

The girl left. She crossed the room in clear view of the recumbent priest. She left without giving him a glance. The doctor came to the right-hand side of the bed.

'Let's see how you are getting along, shall we, Father Doran? Slept most of the time, I hear.'

'I'm glad to see you,' the patient managed, trying the affability for which he knew himself renowned.

During the examination, he asked Sister Stephanie to provide a nurse from the nursing agency, or perhaps from one of the state-registered nurses on the staff. It would incur extra expense, but only until he could be moved to the hospital. Sister Stephanie and Dr Strathan talked it over and agreed.

Bishop MacGrath would arrive within the hour. Father Doran was relieved. He shut his mind to simpletons, wanting to be in the hands of professionals.

Chapter Sixteen

'Can he hear us here, Sister?'

'No, Doctor.'

'He is worsening, I'm afraid.'

'He isn't in serious danger, though?'

'I don't like his appearance. Some measures ought to be mending by now. They've shown no sign.'

'Do you think we...?'

'Move him, Sister? No. I don't think he would stand it.'

Sister Stephanie was paler than before. They stood on the second landing. The sick room was at the end on the right, directly above the chapel.

'The bishop will be here presently, Doctor.'

He knew what she was hinting, that the bishop could overrule the doctor's ruling.

'Father Doran must stay until he recovers sufficiently, Sister, or I shall take no responsibility.'

'Very well.'

'I also want a state registered nurse brought in for round-the-clock nursing care, unless you are able to bring in one of the Order who is SRN?'

'I'm afraid we haven't the resources, Doctor.'

'Very well. Tell me, has Father Doran had any kind of medication I haven't been told of? Like, do you know if he was under any other doctor for treatment of – what? – high blood pressure, or on a weight reduction diet, that kind of thing?'

'We never spoke of anything except pastoral matters.'

'He never complained of any symptoms?'

'None, Doctor.'

'It's a rum business. I have seen one or two patients go so suddenly, of course. But the response has always been according to plan.'

'What must we do, Doctor?'

'I shall stay until you bring in a bank nurse. You have the address? I should ring them now, quick as may be.'

'Very well, Doctor.'

'I should like to have a talk with her and lay down the requirements for the priest.' He delayed her as she turned aside. 'Oh, Sister. Was he under any personal stress? In his personal life?'

'I do not know, Doctor.'

'Would you be present while I open his briefcase and see if it contains any medication? It's a small chance I'm missing something, but as I always say, Sister, why take it?'

He gave her a reassuring smile. They went to collect the priest's case and, as Sister Stephanie telephoned for an agency nurse, Dr Strathan inspected the contents.

'No medicines of any kind.' Strathan straightened. 'I must be getting suspicious in my old age. Too many obscure sociology programmes on television, Sister.'

'I have put Sister Francesca on duty with Father Doran, Doctor.'

'Will she be there now?'

'Yes.'

'I'll pay him a brief call.'

'Very well.'

They found Sister Francesca sitting opposite the priest's bed. He seemed to be sleeping. The monitors were in place. Dr Strathan took a quick look and frowned.

'I shall ask the cardiac consultant from the teaching hospital to make a domiciliary, Sister Stephanie.'

'To come here?'

'Yes, as a matter of urgency. Now, in fact. I'll wait for him.'

'Is it that...?'

'Please stay.'

Distantly the doorbell rang. Magda was on the staircase when Dr Strathan went along to the main office.

'Doctor? May I go off duty now, please?'

'Eh? Oh, are you due to leave?'

'Yes, Doctor. I was afraid to go until I got permission.'

'Good girl. Yes, I daresay you can go.'

'Thank you, Doctor.'

He watched her go. She must have been waiting all this time, he thought, on the staircase, already in her shabby coat. Devotion to duty. It's a pity there isn't more of that in this modern world, he thought. It gave him a sense of comfort. Could the priest be any better looked after in Dublin's finest hospitals? Dr Strathan didn't think so.

Kev met Magda after she'd been home to take off her working clothes. She was not allowed a locker at the St Cosmo.

The bar was across the road from where he said he'd be waiting. He was with a girl a little older than Magda. The presence of the other girl made her hang back.

'It's OK,' Kev told her. 'It's only my sister Jean.'

'Only?' The girl gave him a mild clout with the back of her hand, making Magda gasp at such effrontery.

'She's always doing that,' Kev said. 'She's beyond control. Take no notice.'

'I'm Magda.'

'I know. I heard all about you, Magda. Come on. I'm desperate for a drink.'

Magda looked round, but the café was in the opposite direction. Jean paused, waiting for Magda.

'What's up?'

'Where to?'

'The bar.'

Magda stared. There was a bar, true, but what was she suggesting?

'In there?'

Jean laughed. 'Where else? Have you never been in bar before?'

'No.'

'No? Time you learnt, Magda.'

Jean linked her arm through Magda's and guided her across the road to the bar entrance, Kev following.

'Jesus, Magda, we're not going to ravish them, just have a drink while we chat.'

'Are we allowed?'

'Haven't you heard?' Now Jean was laughing without pause at Magda's reluctance. 'It's compulsory in Dublin! In we go.'

'No football supporters here,' Kev said.

He was not quite as amused as his sister, but Magda knew it was something of a joke so she tried to smile. She kept looking at his sister – sister, a real one, from an actual family, not just a word. Magda felt so proud to be with a sister, and a brother who was genuine too, living shared lives because they had, presumably, the same mother and father. It was a miracle when you thought of it, beyond anything, and here she was meeting them in actual life.

And in a bar and all.

'What will you have?'

'Nothing, thank you.'

'Nothing? That won't do. Give her the same as me, Kev.'

'Right.'

He went to the bar. Jean drew Magda to a seat at a small table away from the bar counter. Nobody was smoking like they did in the pictures Magda watched all night long to keep awake and help Lucy.

'You work at the St Cosmo, Magda, Kev said.'

'Yes. I'm a skivvy.'

'General help. That's what you say. If you say skivvy, you're running yourself down.'

'Am I?'

'Sure. It's what they all want.'

'Who?'

'Everybody. They're all at it. People who pay you. How much d'you get?'

'Stop it, Jeannie,' Kev said, returning. 'Orange juice for you, Magda, because you're a drinker in training.'

'A drinker!' Magda cried out. People looked round.

'Pay him no heed, Magda. He only means it's your first time in a bar. He talks more than he has sense for.'

'Are they depraved?'

Jean stared. 'Are they what?'

'I thought it would be all smoking and gambling fights, like on TV.'

'Fights? Sometimes but not often. Drunk now and then. That's the most we can manage this end of old Short-Change City.'

'What...?'

'Visitors call Dublin that. You never get the right change, see?' Jean waited to let Magda get the meaning. 'That's what businessmen say about Dublin, everybody gives them the wrong change, see?'

'Do they?' Magda felt impressed, not only from being with Jean and Kev but learning all these things in one go.

'Who knows? People will, I suppose, if you let them get away with it.'

'Did you find out?' Kev asked.

Magda tried a sip of the orange juice. She had had some before, from a rectangular cardboard carton from the corner shop, greatly daring. It did not taste as she expected. She didn't like it. Men all around were drinking beer. Many were young, even some her own age. It was astonishing. Not one Garda there, in all these people. It wasn't at all like on Fifth Avenue.

'Find out?'

Jean and Kev exchanged glances. He cleared his throat.

'The medicines somebody was stealing at the St Cosmo.'

'I tried. Three of the old folk said they had things lost. An old lady, Mrs Borru, told me she lost several tablets and thinks somebody took them. She doesn't know why. She even asked me if I was doing it, and I told her no. I asked her who she thought it was.'

'And?'

'She didn't know.'

'Anybody else?'

'Yes. An old man who was a soldier, Mr Gorragher. He wanders in the things he says. He even drifts off sometimes while he's talking to you. Other times he sings songs.'

'Thing is,' Jean said, 'is it real, or is it just made up? Old folk forget.'

'Oh, they're forgetting all the time. Some go to confession and then ask what time the priest's coming. They've already forgotten he's been, see?'

'And the third? You said there were three.'

'Mr Liam MacIlwam.'

'That's Grampa.'

'He's usually quite clear in his mind,' Kev said slowly. 'He wouldn't make a mistake.'

'He could forget, though.'

'Sometimes the pill bottles roll under the bed, and other times they put them on the table in the main lounge room where they play cards and that. Some of them take each other's bottles.'

'By mistake?'

'Yes. Why would they want each other's tablets?'

'Do you get them back?'

'We're forever looking for them old things.'

'You haven't seen anybody actually stealing them, then?'

'No. I looked, like you told me to.'

'Do they keep a record book?'

'The nuns do. The nurses do. They have a drugs book. It's kept locked.'

'Who fills in the prescriptions?'

'Dr Strathan comes and sees to the old folks, though some of them have their own doctors coming in and out.'

'Is he the resident doctor?'

'He sees to the nuns, though today he's hardly left the place. In most of the day, him, since the priest took bad.'

'Priest?'

Magda told them of the priest falling ill and how he was in the sick room upstairs over the chapel on the second floor, with a nurse specially fetched to see to him and stay all the time. She told them all she had overheard standing on the staircase by the landing, though she didn't tell them she had only pretended to be waiting for permission to go home.

'Is he badly?'

'Yes. He wants to go to hospital. Sister Stephanie tried to make the doctor send him straight off, but he said the priest was too poorly.'

'Did he say what was the matter with him?'

'A heart attack. He has machines all round his bed now.'

'Which priest?' Kev asked.

'Father Doran. Do you know Father Doran?'

'I saw him once when I went to see Grampa. Tubby? Forty years old, maybe more?'

'That's him. Well, he's on some of Dr Strathan's machines that have, like, TV sets to them. He has medicines dripping in a tube. Sister Stephanie didn't want the doctor to bring in a hired nurse, but Dr Strathan made her send for one straight away.'

'Is he dying?' Jean looked at Kev, who gave her a sharp glance. 'Well, Kev, people die from heart attacks. You hear of it all the time.'

'I don't know if it's that,' Magda said reasonably, playing the role she had picked out for herself, the ignorant girl who knew nothing but who could listen real good if people talked slow. 'The doctor kept asking the same question over and over.'

'What question?'

'Stop being a Garda, Kev,' Jean reprimanded sharply, making Magda almost goggle with awe at a sister rebuking her older brother straight out like that, and in company too. There seemed more to families than she ever imagined, not quite the stepwise order she was led to believe. 'He only means did you hear them say anything that might help us find out who's pinching Grampa's tablets.'

'Dr Strathan kept at Sister Stephanie, asking, was Father Doran taking any medication. He said that, medication, like he couldn't understand why the priest was so poorly of a sudden.'

'And had he?'

'Father Doran? No.'

'Was Sister Stephanie sure, Magda?'

'Yes.'

'There,' Jean said, triumphant. 'That means the priest was given something.'

'How do you know?' her brother asked. He had a glass of pale beer, the first Magda had seen really close to in a genuine bar, though some of the old men had a bottle sometimes if it was brought in by relatives.

'Or he was taking it himself and got it wrong,' Jean said, firm as ever. She seemed determined at whatever she was saying, never wanting to give in. Magda was impressed by this, and tried to remember the girl's gestures so she could practice them in front of her mirror.

'What would he do that for?'

'Old folk sometimes forget they've taken their tablets or had their spoon of medicine. They're terrors.'

'See?' Kev said. 'It's maybe just Grampa forgetting.'

'I tried to keep a check on him,' Magda said, and she had so it was really true, 'but I'm always off doing things somewhere else. You can't sit and talk. You're not allowed.'

'Do you do nights?'

'Only when they're short of somebody to do a special watch on an oldie who's really ill. There's three of them always sick. They need injections, but a nurse-nun or a real nurse has to do those. Domestics like me aren't allowed.'

'Where do you live, Magda?' Jean had lost interest.

Magda explained, and told Jean how she had been in the Magdalenes and with Faith's help got a job at the St Cosmo after working in the paper packers.

'You should come and have your dinner with us,' Jean said, putting the heart across Magda who had never had an invitation before.

'Dinner?' she said, blank. Did Jean mean in the bar?

'Come this Sunday. To us. It'll be all right.'

The thought of having dinner with a family made her giddy. She didn't say anything, because it seemed unreal. And another thing. Would Father Doran be properly killed by Sunday, or not? She wondered what more she could do. Criminals in them old black-and-whiters never seemed to have this difficulty. She felt close to tears. She was trying so hard to do the right thing by everyone.

'Thank you,' she told Jean politely. 'I accept.'

Jean chuckled. 'I like her,' she told her brother, quite as if Magda was elsewhere. 'She's unreal. You could do hell of a sight worse, the slappers that are about.'

Chapter Seventeen

Bishop MacGrath was less of a friend than he seemed. His great wish was to have inherited a different name than the one he possessed. Wrong, he was certain, to hate one's heritage, but wearing a name identifying a person with this or that stamp was particularly onerous. He had felt this right from being small, when his wealthy family had directed him to the priesthood. From his earliest schooldays he could remember nothing but the destiny that waited for him. The Church invited.

He sometimes wondered if his response to situations like this at the St Cosmo – priest taken ill, a doctor with dark hints on the telephone, nuns in residence wanting everything made different than the situation seemed to dictate – was nothing more than that of a bureaucrat confronted with tiresome in-tray documents brought by some irritating mail clerk. Should there not be more than this?

He alighted from his car, thinking he really ought to get the tyres seen to. And the inevitable draught at the left side of his chin while driving seemed beyond the wit of motor engineers

the world over. Several times he had taken it in for checking.
And now here was this new Fiat, just the same, causing him a
crick in the neck. He pretended to admire the gardens at the
St Cosmo Care Home for the Elderly. So much deception, so
much play-acting. A bishop must seem healthy, full of wit and
vigour, in charge. More political analogy? He smiled with rue
and went in, the door opening immediately.

'M'lord.'

'Good evening, Sister. Peace upon the house.'

'Father Doran is in the sick room. Dr Strathan is on the
telephone presently, speaking to the hospital consultant.'

'Can I see him?'

'Please.'

Bishop MacGrath made a brief pause in the second-floor
corridor to hear Sister Stephanie's impression of the patient's
progress, then spoke with Dr Strathan in private.

'It is serious,' Strathan began immediately. 'I had the cardiac
consultant here half an hour since. He is gloomy, not to say as
puzzled as I.'

'Is there any doubt about the diagnosis, Doctor? Heart
attack?'

'Of some sort. We are unsure as to the cause.'

'Are they not spontaneous?'

'His history gives no clue. The patient's response gives
no clue. If I were less suspicious, I would say he had taken
cardiac medication, but I have spoken to his usual doctor, a
GP I trained with, actually. He passed Father Doran fit a sixmonth since.'

'His chances?'

'Looking less with every passing hour.'

'Can he be sent to hospital?'

'Admitted? I desperately want him in, but don't want to risk shifting the man at this stage. The consultant advises we keep him until morning.'

'Will you transfer him then?'

'If he's able. I've provisionally already arranged it for nine o'clock. Sister Stephanie will bring in two SRNs for round-the-clock nursing.'

'Can I see him?'

'Yes. He wants you to.'

The bishop entered the sick room, his apprehensions worsened by the array of medical instrumentation. The priest seemed to have shrunk. Bishop MacGrath had no recollection of Father Doran being so small, almost a cartoon reproduction of a figure he once knew.

Doran was awake, and asked if he could speak in private. The nurse withdrew. The doctor also went, after suggesting the stay be not more than a few minutes.

Bishop MacGrath drew the one chair up to the bedside.

'Father Doran? I am so sorry to find you like this.'

'It came so suddenly.'

'I've spoken to Dr Strathan.'

'I think I am worse than I was when it came on.'

'He says you may be transferred to the hospital in the morning.'

'If I am spared, m'lord.'

'You shall be, James. The whole diocese is praying for your recovery.'

'I wish you to hear my confession.'

'Certainly. Do you wish to compose yourself first?'

'No. I am afraid I might withdraw from the sacrament.'

Bishop MacGrath was surprised and he hesitated. 'Do you

wish to make a general confession, James, or—?'

'I wish to confess.'

'Do you want to speak to Dr Strathan first? I mean, if you think it might prove…'

'More drugs, to ease the spirit?'

The prelate was disturbed by the priest's wan smile. He took his stole from his case.

'Ready, my son.'

'Yes, Father.'

The bishop intoned, '*Veni, Sancte Spiritus, repletuorum corda fidelium, et tui amoris in eis ignem accenda.*'

He waited. The patient was still, his face turned away from the confessor. The prelate continued with the *Oremus*.

'Your confession, James.'

'Father, forgive me, for I have sinned. While in a position of trust, I abused a girl child in one of the Church's establishments.'

'Was this recently?'

'It aroused suspicion.'

'Did it concern this diocese?'

'Yes, Father.'

'It was reported to me?'

'I do not know. I only know you spoke to me about it.'

'I remember.'

'And I was then moved to my present post.'

'Yes.'

Bishop MacGrath sat in silence. The memory was as fresh in his mind as on the day it was brought to his attention. Father Doran, it was rumoured, had been noticed in circumstances verging on the improper, in some of the homes operated directly by the Church. One incident in particular had resulted

– perhaps culminated was a more apt term – somehow in the death of a girl, who happened to be seriously ill from some form of protracted chest complaint. She had died suddenly.

'Do you wish to detail the events, James?'

'She was close to death.'

'The girl?' Bishop MacGrath hated this.

'Yes. She had been under the doctor for some time, but medical calls proved too expensive.'

The prelate bit back his reflexive justification.

'She was in a dormitory with one girl in a bed opposite.'

'Yes?'

'I went in the night to see her.' Doran's face was still turned away. 'I was not sure what I was there for. I gave her some explanation.'

'Explanation?' MacGrath floundered. He actually felt irritated at the sick man.

'Of a particular need a person sometimes had.'

'And then?'

'I used her.'

'With her agreement?'

'She stayed silent.'

'And the other girl, the one in the other bed?'

'Stayed silent. I thought asleep.'

'And afterwards?'

'I left.'

'Was anything said, or a complaint made?'

'She died next morning. She had fallen down the stairwell.'

'Who found her?'

'The nuns heard something, or they were roused, perhaps by noise. I don't know what time.'

'Did they call the Gardai?'

'No. I believe, I don't know, the nuns returned her to her bed. They took her away next morning.'

'She was certified dead by a doctor-on-call, if I remember the report.'

'Yes.'

'Where were you?'

'I had left early. I do not know why, or where to.'

'You never reported this to me, or to Monsignor O'Brien?'

'No, Father.'

'Did you put in for transfer to the Rosimians, in Upton, County Cork?'

'No, Father.'

'Was that discussed with you in this diocese by anyone, or elsewhere?'

'No, Father.'

'What was the outcome?'

James Doran moved his head to see the confessor. 'I feel interrogated, Father, instead of confessing.'

'My apologies, James.' The prelate was silent a few moments. His fault had been to conflate his administrative and his confessorial duties. 'Did you know the, ah, extent of the girl's injuries or the outcome, before you made your next confession?'

'Yes, Father.'

'Did you commit the sin of presumption?' And into the priest's silence he said, 'You know that despair and presumption are the two most heinous sins against God, James. They confer a character on the soul. Consider, and examine your spirit.'

'I made a general act of contrition, Father. I fear I presumed.'

'Have you anything further to say?'

'No, Father. Except…'

'Except?'

'I wonder if the girl who was supposed to be monitoring the sick girl, stationed in the bed opposite for the night, truly was asleep.'

'What makes you think so?'

'I'm uncertain. She remained motionless, I'm almost sure, during my…transgression.'

'Then what changes your mind?'

'I wonder if I recognise a face, Father.'

'Recently?'

'Yes.'

'Someone here? In this diocese?'

'Perhaps. Maybe I am wandering on account of the medication I've received.'

'Have you any reason to think the matter will be raised again?'

'I do not know, Father.'

'Your confession is completed, James?'

'Yes, Father.'

'Then make a sincere act of contrition, remembering that it is a ready sorrow for all our sins, because by them we have offended so good a God, together with a firm purpose of amendment.'

The priest began his prayer almost in silence, head back on the pillow. The prelate spoke with him, '*Domine noster Jesus…*' and then to the '*Deinde ego te absolvo…*' of absolution. 'Go in peace, my son.'

'Thank you, Father.'

The bishop rose and replaced his stole in the case. He returned to sit by the priest, whose face had taken on an ashen complexion. He pressed the button and the nurse entered almost instantly.

'I shall stay a while, if that's all right, Nurse?'

'Of course.'

'Could you let Sister Stephanie know?'

'Certainly. I'll be a minute.'

The bishop sat. Prayer seemed somehow superfluous. There had not been many instances of this sensation in his life, when the raising of the mind and heart to God became a fantasy, a monstrous irrelevance. He examined the recumbent form of the man on the bed, hearing the faint bleeps of the monitors. Who knew what those traces signified?

One of the great enigmas of his own seminary days had been a study of the Ogdens' *The Meaning of Meaning*, published so long ago now. It had proved a difficulty, directly forcing the reader into a competitive debate with himself about names given to objects, events, activities. It had been a major impediment to his faith for a while. Confrontations with his own seminary tutor had been traumatic. The sensation had just recurred while hearing James Doran's confession, for he, bishop of the diocese, had taken the decision to transfer Father Doran to a safer position – safer being one where his errors were unknown. Whole governments had been party to this trick, and even in the Dail itself a government had wobbled because of similar deceptions worked to conceal the evils in the Church.

It was difficult. To allow the Church to be vilified by the ungodly accusers was tantamount to surrendering to the forces of evil. To do nothing was to perpetuate the sins being worked on the children in the Church's care. To transfer the priest was justifiable, he reasoned anxiously, because it protected the

Church from unjust accusers, and allowed her excellent work to continue.

Excellent, though? Justifiable, though? Unjust, though?

There had been the fire at the St Joseph's – so many St Joseph's Industrial Schools – where many children died in a terrible conflagration there, plus, said the laconic report, 'one old woman.' The Church had survived, of course.

The prelate saw the nurse re-enter. He relinquished his place to her, and she went to make a printout of the patient's indices.

He stood by the doorway another moment, then left. He wished he could go incognito into some bar and just sit a while not speaking, and maybe watch the racing results come through from Leopardstown or Fairyhouse in County Meath. Others of his ecclesiastical rank went, so why not he?

It was seriously dark outside now. He admonished himself for impropriety. It was the duty of the confessor to erase all judgement from his mind on conclusion of the sacrament, eliminate the memory, even, of the penitent's narrative.

He collected his coat, declined the offered tea with Sister Stephanie, and left without discussing Father Doran.

Chapter Eighteen

Magda was truly frightened by morning. All night long she tried explaining to Lucy how she wanted the priest to die immediately, then God would have the problem. Being God, she told Lucy, He would know what to do with the priest before His celestial throne. There Father Doran would stand to say what he'd done that night, and would have to tell the truth. There was no way round it, for God knew anyway who tried fibbing that, no, God, it wasn't quite like that, let me finish, you've got it all wrong. God would know straight off they were lying.

By dawn, she was in doubt. Did God give you a chance to put your case? Or He could say, 'I know everything you did, you did this, you did that, don't try getting out of it, so here's what's going to happen, Hellfire for you, or maybe just Purgatory for a few venial sins.' That's the way she had been told it would be.

Lucy was already up there, Magda told herself. She kept feeling sad that Lucy couldn't tell her what went on, give her some guidance. It would have been so useful.

Arriving in terror at work, she said good morning to the other cleaners. Mrs O'Hare was in early. She had three children, all, by her frank accounts, destined for trouble in later life. They were nine, eleven and fourteen, and already causing trouble. The fourteen-year-old had been caught smoking at school, and was given some penalty points, the meaning of which Magda found difficult to understand.

'Penalty points?'

She thought it was some kind of football thing, but girls at the convent couldn't be doing that, could they? She asked Mrs O'Hare.

'They give the class a bad mark, silly. Don't you know anything at all?'

'No,' Magda admitted, because she had already made a terrible mistake over the priest, who wasn't even dead from the way the St Cosmo Care Home for the Elderly was behaving this morning. She felt so hopeless. Mrs O'Hare talked over the most intimate matters – not in the nuns' hearing, of course, but never mind who else was listening as long as it wasn't a man – with the domestics. She was particularly frank with the two laundry women who only did mornings on account of their bad feet and being as old, almost, as some of the Elderly in the place.

'Then the whole class gets told off.'

'Told off?' Magda dwelt on that a moment, getting her pail and her cleaning bottles ready and placing her two mops second after Mrs O'Hare's mops in the rack by the sluice sink.

'Shouted at, daftie.'

'Who whacks them, though?'

'Nobody.' Mrs O'Hare stared at the girl and laughed. 'They had to stop that after the fuss about the Magdalenes and the Christian Brothers. Don't you even read the newspapers?'

'No.'

'Time you started, girl. What d'you think children would do if they started that old game again? They'd be up in arms and give as good as they got. You know what?'

'No?'

Mrs O'Hare checked with a few glances here and there. 'Millie – that's my eldest – says the class lost points because two of the youngsters were necking at the back of the class in Drama. Nothing to do with the subject.'

'That can't be true.'

'True as I stand here, Magda. Kids do what they want these days. You've seen them down Great George Street and Crane Lane.'

'No.'

'Well, then. Here.' Mrs O'Hare got her mops ready, tutting at a missing spare head for the smaller one. 'You heard what went on last night?'

'No?'

Magda felt her heart go thump. This was it, the priest dying or telling on her and the Gardai coming once she got out of the sluice.

'Bishop MacGrath himself came in the dark hours.'

'The bishop?' The very word frightened Magda.

'He heard Father Doran's confession.'

'Jesus, Mary and Joseph,' Magda moaned. He would tell on her.

'Don't take on, Magda. There's precious little we can do about the poor man's plight.'

'What did the bishop say?'

'How do I know? I was doing a week's washing at home by then, wasn't I?'

'I suppose so.'

'Wait until you get married, girl. You'll know what hard work really is.'

'What will happen, Mrs O'Hare?'

'To the priest? If he gets well enough the doctor will send him to the hospital.'

'He will?'

Magda felt faint. If Father Doran had said his confession, he might have told the bishop anything at all, including things she had come out with while minding the priest. This was her penalty for ignorance, though she knew enough to understand that ignorance, however deep and constant, was not stupidity. Since leaving the Magdalenes, she had come round to think that her lack of understanding, even of things to do with her own self, was due mostly to poor learning, not to being thick.

'What happens in hospital, Mrs O'Hare?'

'They make you better. They'll have him back on his feet in no time.'

'Then will he come back?'

'Right as rain, trust me.'

A third cleaner came in then, so the whole thing had to be told over again to her. Mrs Connery was a middle-aged woman who fancied herself – so current opinion ran – and who spent too much time dolling herself up. She was often reproached for being too heavily scented. The trouble was, she was a good cleaner. Unable to get as splendid a shine on the linoleum as Magda, for nobody could manage that, she devoted herself to the chapel and the furniture, and was an acknowledged class act. She said that herself, the 'class act' of the St Cosmo Care Home.

'Some of them hospitals are good,' she agreed, joining in once she had caught up, 'but you have to be fit when you go in or your chances go down. My Jim says it's always odds-on.'

'What does that mean, Mrs Connery?'

'Like a bet on the horses.'

Magda left it there because it was her turn at the sink with her mops. She always gave hers the best rinsing before starting work.

Her duties today were on the ground floor, the vestibule and the porches, front and back, then the kitchen entrance and then the nuns' separate doorway, which was still called, for no reason she could understand, the postern door. About mid-morning, she would have to do the top floor corridor. That was the one running over the chapel – the chapel was two storeys high, its ceiling the floor of the sick-room corridor.

She set to, thinking what might happen when the priest got better and told the Gardai what she'd said in that old sick room. She would be taken away. What if they were the same magistrates that sent her to the Magdalenes in the first place for being an orphan? She would rather die than go back in the Magdalenes, even though things had changed so much now that children necked in the classrooms right in front of the teachers and didn't get their legs black and blue for it.

Magda had always caught it on her knuckles and her bottom. That was bad enough, but nothing as painful as the thick round rulers that caught her them dreadful whacks across her thighs. They lasted for days, the bruises never seen. That was for the inspectors. She wondered about the inspectors now. What if they came into the class and found the pupils necking at the back when they were supposed to be learning their old drama like Mrs O'Hare's daughter said?

She set to. The morning's work was on a rota. She had to pretend she kept forgetting her glasses, though Sister Francesca, the meekest of the nuns, if there could be such a thing, usually read the rota out. Not being able to write a word had made Magda remember everything she heard, so she was always where she had been told.

The work went fine. By quarter-to-eleven she had had her places checked by Sister Rita, head of the domestics turn and turn about with two other nuns, and was free to start the top corridor. She carried her mopping things back to the sluice and left them ready, then went for her polishing stuff. The cleaners always fought for the best of those, because Mrs Connery was a right one for taking the best. She was not above actually stealing from the polish tins, which were marked with colours for different cleaning staff. Everybody said Mrs Connery was light of finger.

Magda did not pause for a break, but was hard at it when she heard what she had been listening for ever since the cleaners separated for the day's work.

One of the lay nurses, a state registered nurse who wore two badges on her uniform, one from the Rotunda, one from somewhere Magda did not recognise, was speaking on the phone. Magda assumed it was Dr Strathan. She gave a load of numbers and mentioned something about the traces.

'He seems more rested,' the SRN said. 'I think he may have stabilised.'

Pause. The nurse answered.

'About two-thirty? Will they come to the front, then?'

Pause.

'Yes, yes, sir. One thing. Must he be accompanied?' A prolonged pause, then, 'Very well, sir. I'll have everything ready. The transfer will happen about two? Unless you ring back on my mobile, it's to go ahead? Transfer definite before three o'clock, then? Yes. Very well.'

The phone went down with a click. Magda got busy, so as not to delay.

About two hours later she helped to give a blanket bath to one of the patients, doing the heavier work because Mrs Borru had a tube in her nose that a nurse had to keep control of.

Magda had to hold the old lady sideways on while the nurse went for another tube. Magda was always fascinated by the way the new tube slid right into the old lady's nose. It was like magic, such a length of it going in and in and even further in. It set you wondering why on earth God had designed us all like that, such a distance to get inside an old nose. Who'd imagine?

When time for her dinner break came, she had her sandwich from the machine in the ground floor corridor (coins were easy, the slot being the right size for only one sort) and was immediately back at her post on the top floor. She was there polishing when the time came.

Father Doran felt better, except for a serious cramp in his chest, and had asked if he could have his tea before leaving the St Cosmo.

'You can starve for all I care, Father,' the nurse called out cheerfully, swishing in and out and not caring how loud she was at doing anything at all. Magda admired her. The thought even crossed Magda's mind that the nurse, with her strange badge, might even have come from a Protestant hospital, so casual was she talking to the priest.

He seemed to like her because Magda thought she heard his small bark of a laugh.

'Not even a bite of anything?'

'You mean one for the road? I know you lot.'

'Don't be hard, Nurse.'

'It's you being hard, Father, playing on our heart-strings crying hunger. Look at the belly on you! Gob less at dinnertime and you'd not be dying away like y'are.'

Magda gasped at the nurse's effrontery, speaking like that.

'That's the spirit, Nurse.'

'Be sarcastic all you want, you'll not get me to shift.'

'Where's your charity?'

Both enjoyed the banter. Magda thought it all vaguely immoral, the nurse so encouraging and him a priest and all.

'My charity ends with what Dr Strathan orders. He says nothing by mouth except a plain old drink without milk, until they're sticking tubes into you at the hospital. That's what I'll do, so shut your noise.'

Just listen to the woman, Magda thought, aghast, losing her chances of going to Heaven in a few breaths, all for the sake of showing off with a cheeky word. She must have necked at the back of the drama class, for sure.

'Who will be with me?'

'In the ambulance? One of the nurses.'

'Are you sure?'

'Are you going on about that again? There's nobody else to mind you except me or Sister Eugenia, and she's away with the fairies in Wicklow.'

'Promise?'

'Hand on my heart. I'll travel with you every inch of the way – make sure I get rid of you.'

He did that relieved half-laugh. Magda had heard enough, and went to shake the few tablets she had taken urgently from Mrs

Borru's small brown bottle of white tablets into water. She had a discarded pill bottle from the men's alcoves, and had washed it out with great care while watching the singing competition from London, drying it in the Baby Belling oven, turned down after heating some soup. Tomato was the sweetest soup. That and bread with margarine. A cheap meal of an evening, but it had been the first meal she had ever bought herself once released from the Magdalenes, so it was her favourite.

She was on hand when the priest was being got ready for his transfer.

Father Doran was concerned about the tubes.

'Do they have to stay in?' he asked anxiously

'The one in your nose, yes. I plug it for the journey.'

'And these wire things?'

'Can't you see I'm taking them off?'

'Will they know to put them back in the hospital?'

'Of course they will, softie.'

'In the same order?'

'Where d'you think I was trained?'

'Will they do that artery thing to me this afternoon?'

'I wish I'd not told you, only Dr Strathan told me to.'

'I wanted to know.'

'You're an old softie.'

'Just so I'll know.'

'Just to worry yourself into another attack, you mean.'

'No, just asking.'

'Men are worse patients than women any day of the week.' The priest tried for jocularity. 'I've been a model patient. You have to agree with that.'

'You've been a babe-in-arms. Pest.'

'What did I do wrong?'

Magda listened to the bickering, feeling sick at heart. He should have died by now, not be cheerily joshing the nurse and almost teasing, with her responding almost like a harlot with her simpering.

'A woman would be easy and ready for the journey, no questions, just accepting.'

'What's going to happen?'

'A short ambulance ride, for God's sake. You don't even have to walk downstairs yourself. The ambulance men will do it for you. Now you just lie back and try to sleep a short while. Ten minutes, and you'll be off. I don't want you worn out before you leave.'

Magda was there half an hour later when the nurse emerged and went across to the office. She smiled, deliberately getting in the nurse's way, but only a little.

The nurse swept on by. Magda hurried away to the other end of the corridor as the nurse spoke to Sister Stephanie, to promise she would have the patient ready soon. The ambulance men could be brought in. They spoke of the priest's condition. The nurse was frank about his prognosis.

'Dr Strathan will be there when he arrives at the hospital, Sister. I must say he's concerned about Father Doran's lack of improvement.'

'I got the same impression. Has he given different instructions?'

'Dr Strathan? No. Just the one small drink of plain tea before he goes.'

'Is he ready now?'

'Any minute.'

'Then he can leave. I'll come.'

In the sick room, Magda took the drink to the priest. He was flushed, lying back on the pillows, dozing. He did not open his eyes.

Magda had only a few moments, but that was all it took. She had twice seen the nurse administer the fluids through the tube, and had the small syringe in her pinafore pocket. He stayed somnolent throughout. She replaced the spigot in the tube and slipped the syringe into her pocket, and was out and down the corridor making a show of domestic industry when Sister Stephanie and the nurse crossed to the sick room.

Magda went downstairs to the sluice where she was checked out by Sister Hilda.

'Did you finish off up there, Magda?'

'Yes, Sister Hilda.'

'All of it?'

'Yes, Sister.'

'Did they tell you anything about Father Doran leaving?'

'No, Sister.'

'Very well.' The nun went to enquire while the domestic staff talked.

'Is he very poorly?' Magda asked. She felt amazingly calm, as if she had passed one of those examinations other girls were always doing.

'The priest? Of course he is. Heart attacks are dreadful. I had an uncle once died of one.'

'Poor man, God rest his soul.'

'Does the soul know if it's going to die?'

'That's a funny question, Magda. What makes you ask that?'

'I was just wondering.'

She did not say, but thought the priest's eyes had flickered for just one instant as she had inserted the nozzle of the syringe into the gastric tube. Except he would have raised Cain if he had sensed that someone was actually there, giving fluid into him without making a single sound, wouldn't he? You don't just lie there and let folk come in and do anything they want, do you? She had heard him being cheery with the nurse only half an hour before.

'He's coming down.'

They heard the heavy footfalls of the ambulance men on the stairs, and listened in something like awe to the shuffling and the grunts of the men as they lifted the priest downstairs on a stretcher.

'There ought to be a lift here, a building like this,' Mrs O'Hare said. 'I keep telling them that.'

'Shall I go out and see if there's any way I can help?' Mrs Connery asked, but Mrs O'Hare rebelled immediately.

'You stay put, m'lady,' she said rudely. 'I know what you're up to, seeing if your stinking dabs round your earholes work on them ambulance men. No, stay here.'

'You've a terrible mouth on you, O'Hare.'

'You've an ugly face on you, Connery.'

'Please,' Magda said, distressed. 'Don't fight. Heaven alone knows what's happening to the poor priest out there being carried away to his ambulance.'

'There!' Mrs O'Hare said angrily to Mrs Connery. 'See what you've done? Upsetting the poor simple girl.'

'It wasn't me,' Mrs Connery shot back. 'It was you, mouthing off like that.'

'Please.'

'There, girl,' Mrs O'Hare soothed. 'Don't take on. We're only pretending, really. We'll all pray for the poor priest.'

Even Mrs Connery was touched by the girl's tears. 'He'll get better, just you see, Magda.'

'Sure he will, girl. He'll be right as rain once they get him in that old hospital.'

'All them doctors. They say it's the best hospital in the world. Isn't that right?'

'Yes. That's true enough. Everybody knows that.'

The three listened as the main door closed and the ambulance started up and drew away.

Chapter Nineteen

The two old women talked. For nursing convenience their beds were pushed into the one alcove. Normally it was Mrs Borru's, but when night came she sometimes drew the short straw – her husband's old phrase for luck unwelcome but not disastrous. By this she meant Mrs Duffanan, who was from Temple Lane South, near Wellington Quay, lying auld bitch that she was. Mrs Borru knew deep down Mrs Duffanan was all fur coat and no knickers, so said her crude old, now dead and God rest the poor restless bugger, husband Fergus. And no prizes for guessing how his firm conviction was found out. Fergus had been all hands, a randy old sod.

Not difficult to tell, when readying oneself to die as gradually as the St Cosmo Care Home usually managed. Wheeled into a shared alcove for a night's long impatience, waiting for one dawn after another, you had time to reflect what kind of girl an old crow like the wizened Mrs Duffanan would have been. Mrs Borru kept herself to herself and never revealed anything, no. Sure to God, enough would be called out right in front of all them angels and Seraphims and things once she shuffled off the mortal coil, so gossip could wait until then.

About one-thirty of that night, Mrs Duffanan began to talk. For a daft old bat, her voice was surprising, quite mellow and gentle. Maybe that's what sleep did, somehow annealed thoughts to make them presentable for anyone who chose to listen. Normally the beds were rolled by the domestics into alcoves that were deliberately alternated – Mrs Borru would sometimes draw the affable, perennially dozing Mrs Cafferty, who never was awake long enough to put on airs like Mrs Duffanan.

'I wish I wasn't so old,' Mrs Duffanan said into the air. Only minutes since, she'd been snoring like an old carthorse. This was her usual beginning.

'You always wish that,' Mrs Borru said back, also as usual.

'You don't.' Mrs Duffanan, ever ready for any old argument, even in her doze. 'When you're small, you want to be older so's you can decide things for yourself. It's when you're older you want to be young.'

'I don't.'

'Don't what?'

This was as it usually started, quite a litany. Mrs Borru loved the sequences. She even loved the sacred Litany against the Jews, though nobody seemed to do that nowadays in the Church services. Too many changes. This liberal thinking did it. The Litany against the Jews really went with a swing. It was the only bit of Church she had enjoyed when a child in the Magdalenes. Nobody went to sleep in that, all the children bawling the responses with gusto, approval glowing from the nuns.

'Don't want to be back there.'

'You were a Magdalene?'

'Course I was. Everybody was.'

'Everybody wasn't.'

'They were.'

'They weren't.'

'They were.'

And so on, quicker and quicker, keeping it quiet but going ever faster until they gave up exhausted and lay in silence, staring up at the ceiling that was hardly visible in the red-stained darkness. Mrs Borru hated the red pilot light further down the lane of alcoves. Why put it there? It ought to be switched out, or shared about the place. Fine, it would need a workman to make another plug, but that's what your workman is for.

Mrs Duffanan knew what Mrs Borru thought of her. Well, she hadn't the benefit of a rascally bit of harlotry that Mary Duffanan had made for herself round Ha'Penny Bridge and the fine old bars that grew up all over Dublin in them days. One was a grand place for a riot. They called it Ha'Penny Bridge Inn, like some grand Elizabethan tavern from some wicked old English novel, when it was only the old roaring place where she'd learnt to give a decent wank to some randy boy for as many coppers as you could squeeze out of him. It was only later she began to regret not having used her time better, got on and made something of herself. She heard the sneers in the old bitches' voices when she got talking of a night, never fear. The joke was on them, for how many of their loyal husbands had she sucked off in the dark along the towpath of the Grand Canal, and them glad to pay for the privilege?

She gave a cackle at the image. Them fine husbands walking in to Holy Mass of a Sunday, arm-in-arm with their proud spouses, when they were still glowing inside from the ecstasy of some night shoving into a busy girl's cunt. It was a laugh.

'What's the joke, Mary?'

Mrs Duffanan was surprised Mrs Borru remembered her first name, though it was only one she'd made up for herself once she'd got out of the Magdalenes. She decided it for herself that day, and she stole some girl's name off a notice in a shop window, all expensive frocks and dresses of the oddest colours, in Winetavern Street. An advert, a glossy card leaning on a window-dressing plaster model wearing outlandish clothes that surely nobody in their right mind would ever buy, announced *Just right for Mary!!!*

She had always been good at her letters, and slowly translated it into words until somebody came out from the shop and moved her on, angrily demanding to know what she was doing standing there gaping. Well, the joke was on her, the miserable old bitch, because that name Mary had been stolen from under her nose, for that was how Mary became Mary Duffanan. The Magdalenes had changed her name from whatever it had been, and she'd been Two-One all her time in their evil buildings. She hadn't even known her name when she decided to leave of her own accord, and had simply not turned up at work, just gone.

'I was so surprised they didn't come after me.'

'When? Who?'

'The whole Saorstat Eireann with them sirens wailing.'

'Then you were old enough to be forgot.'

'That's what a friend said.'

'What friend?'

'Somebody I met.'

A navvy still with the street dust on him from his digging at some old paving near the old Cattle Market, where they were making a new place for folk to eat and drink, could you imagine? Mary was more interested in what he was going to build than getting him milked dry and herself with enough to get some new shoes if he paid up.

He'd told her, 'They won't come after you, not from them old Magdalenes, not if you've been out more than two months. They give up, think you're on the boat to England.'

She was really proud of that. People really imagining she'd had enough to catch the boat to Liverpool and be free to wander, even if it was among all them heathens and pagans or whatever they had over there.

'What number were you, Mary? I was Four.'

'Is that all?' Mary exclaimed it with glee, for Two-One was obviously better than miserable old Four.

'I hated being just a number.'

'Me too.'

'Know what I hated worse even than the pail lock-up?'

'No. What?'

'Knowing I'd go to Hellfire for all eternity from being jealous.'

'Jealous? Who were you jealous of?'

'Monica. She was the mother of St Augustine.' Silence, as the other realised the misunderstanding and rushed to explain. 'No. I didn't know the saint, God, no, just the girl Monica. She had this grand name. It sounded to me like a raspberry toffee in a wrapper, so I always wanted to be called Monica.'

'Why did they leave her with that posh name, then?'

'Being a saint, see? And you could never tell. Maybe the girl was really going to be come for, and saved out of the place.'

'I saw that happen once.'

'Did you? In the Magdalenes?'

'It was early one Sunday. A gentleman came. There was wild talk among the girls, whispering all along the pews about something going on.'

'Somebody had been come for?'

'Yes. It was a small girl who was always crying, not tough, see? She was seven or maybe eight. I never worked out how old we were from our sizes, though some already came in knowing their age.'

'What happened?' with real excitement in the old croaky voice, because a rescue was a remarkable thing, whoever it happened to. Even now it still had a wondrous allure.

'This gentleman came with another who, the girls were talking wild like you do, seemed to be some kind of servant, because he kept bringing out papers from a leather case when the gentleman said.'

'Where?'

'In the Mother Superior's office.'

'Who was he?'

'He was a real relative.'

'A *real* relative!'

'That he was. He mentioned his dead sister, who was the small girl's mother.'

'What did the Mother Superior say?'

'She asked to see the court papers.'

'And did they have any?'

'They had sheaves of the things. The Mother Superior signed, and then the man, and the servant man said something about concluding and the court would be satisfied.'

'And that was it?'

'That was it.'

'And the girl got carried out in a grand carriage!'

'No. She was left outside in the corridor, frightened out of her wits.'

'Which corridor?' as if they knew, though they had been in places miles and miles apart.

'The one outside the Mother Superior's office.'

'Get on with the rescue.'

'I'm telling you, I'm telling you. They called her in and the gentleman stood up and smiled and said to her he was her uncle and had come to fetch her. And an auntie, a genuine real auntie, was outside in the Austin motor waiting to take her home.'

'Home!'

'Home. We all whispered "home" like it was Paradise, all that day and all the next. Imagine.'

'Having a home, just like...' But there the sentence ended, because home was the place you'd been taken from, and wasn't too good to recall even if you could reach that far back.

'She went out just as she was. The man smiled – Six-Three heard him say the very words – and said to the girl he was rescuing, "No, Beatrice, no need to bring anything with you. You shall have new. My two children, your cousins, will take you shopping later. They are all waiting downstairs for us." And they went.'

'Beatrice!'

'She was called Beatrice, evidently.'

'All the time she was called Beatrice?'

'She didn't know, or maybe she knew and made sure she forgot in case she got the old whacks for remembering.'

'But he knew her name.'

'He did for sure. He asked if she wanted to say goodbye to any of her friends and she just cried. He didn't know what to do. He kept saying, "Here's a thing, here's a thing." Then he just said, trying I suppose to be kindly, "Oh, well, you can always come back for a visit to see your little friends if you want to, eh, Beatrice?" Then they went to the main exit, Mother Superior and all.'

'Did Six-Three see them in that Austin motor?'

'No. She got whacked for listening in the corridor when she should have been washing the steps.'

'Well, yes. That was fair.'

'She never came back that we saw.'

'Well, would you have?'

'Even now I listen out for somebody called Beatrice. I'd like to tell her how she was the talk of the place, her getting out like that. It was like them stories where the airmen and soldiers were kept in prison during the war and made a tunnel to get out.'

The two old ones were silent, then one said, 'I think somebody's taking the medicines again.'

'Who?'

'Somebody clever, like one of them prisoners.'

'Did you see them do it?'

'No. It'll be Mrs Wheelan.'

'It's time she got over it, taking everything the way she does.'

'She hasn't. Nobody ever can, you know that.'

'We don't steal things, though.'

'We do things just the same, like we can't get rid of habits they put in you when you're little.'

'That's true.'

'Mrs Wheelan always steals things. There was that newspaper, wasn't there? That visitor to the men's wards laid his newspaper there with that little plant thing, a poppy, I think, and Mrs Wheelan couldn't get out of bed for her bad arm, but sure as Jesus she had that old newspaper with its flower away quick as wink.'

'Mind you, I know a man who collects old bus tickets from the floor, right there in the Busaras in Store Street. Can't get enough of them.'

'They never got it back, that flower.'

'With Mrs Wheelan, I'm not surprised. They'd never have kept her in prison, not them. She'd steal the cross off a donkey.'

'What does he do with them?'

'The ticket man? Puts them in a shopping bag, he does, takes them to where he lives.'

'Where's that?'

'How do I know?'

And after a silence, 'There's a lot of us like that.'

'Who is taking the medicines?'

'I heard Mr MacIlwam saying something. I think the men might know.'

'It won't be Mrs Wheelan, or the men would already have found out.'

'That's true. Men think different. All them engines, I suppose. My husband couldn't get enough of them old engines.'

'They talk boring, men, I always think.'

'Me too. You've to be polite to them though.'

A prolonged silence, so extended the nun listening in the curtained shadows of the corridor thought they must have nodded off. She had so far made no sound, and was all the more certain for it.

'What was your pail lock-up?'

'That place at the top of the cellar steps? You got locked in for being bad.'

'How long?'

'One girl was in for a whole day. Wetting the bed, see?'

'For wetting the bed they stood us outside by the class doors. You had to stand against the wall where everybody could see you. If you wet your bed, out you went with your wet mattress and had to stand with it on your head, but so they could see your face. You'd to do it sideways. They give you the old whacks too, your bum, and your back or the inspectors would see.'

'Did you ever see inspectors?'

'One. A lady who had spectacles. I thought they were grand things, all shiny. I prayed to Jesus to get me some spectacles. It was no good.'

'Did anybody say anything?'

'Glory be to God, no! How daft do you think we were?'

'I wet the bed. We had plastic sheets under. You had to stand there with the wet sheet wrapped round our head. I had to do it when it was raining. Once when it snowed. I went blue.'

'When I was about seven or eight I got it too.'

The listening nun wanted to see their faces as they spoke, though she knew well enough who they were. It would have been more right to see how they looked when they talked, but she had never been caught yet. She did not know quite what she would do if ever they called, 'Come out, Sister, come out. We know you're there listening away!' It would be so shaming.

'What did you have for a lock-up?'

'A tin bath. It was on the steps outside.'

'You had to get in?'

'No. You got put under it. It was put upside down on the ground, see? You had to be invisible, and the girls coming past on the way to dinner or prayers had to hit it. It made you get sick. I was sick all over myself more than once, I can tell you, that banging. Like being in a drum.'

'How long were you kept in that old bath?'

'Half a day. For bed-wetting, see?'

'Oh, well, there is that.'

'I always got the whacks as well. There was a leather belt thing the nuns wore round their middles, some part of their habit, I suppose. This one nun would take hers off when it was time for me to come out, and that was me up for the belting.'

'I prayed a nun would die.'

'Was she poorly?'

'She started going pale, but much we girls knew about being pale. She had to lie in her bed of a day at the finish, and we older girls – I must have been fourteen, maybe, because I think I'd started my periods – had to take turns watching over her.'

'They always did that.'

'It was the white spit.'

'We called it the bloody spit.'

'It was the cough I hated. That nun coughed her old lungs out.'

'The nuns always went to sleep in the night. It was me always got the spit watch.'

'I prayed for this one to die, and die she did.'

'You didn't...?'

'No. How could I? I was nothing but a barn myself.'

'I used to try to filch the food, if there was any left.'

'From the dying nun?'

'This one didn't die. She seemed asleep when I started to nick her slice of egg-and-butter in a sandwich. I had a night light to see by, how she was getting on. And she said, as my hand went out, "I can see what you're doing," and that was the end of my watching. I got the whacks.'

'Was your place as bad as St Kyran's?'

'Darmuth? How should I know? That was the Sisters of Mercy, only for boys, wasn't it? County Wicklow?'

'One of the men – I think he was the one who went to England and won a bright silver chalice for bowling – went to St Kyran's.'

'Then he deserves all the silver things he earned, poor lad.'

'Did any of them old nuns…y'know?'

'No, thanks be to God. I heard of lots.'

'You can never tell, though, can you?'

'Not now. Only those of us who were there.'

The pause almost set the nun thinking of moving from the shadows into the corridor and stealing away, when one old lady said, 'Them things. The one the person's nicking. Is it tablets or medicines?'

'Tablets, I think. I've forgotten. My mind's not what it was.'

'The wrong things stay in your mind, don't they? I find that. I went to England, stayed with some cousin who'd turned up and had a fine little house on the outskirts of a town called Oldham. She was frightened because I kept waking up from my sleep and her children got scared. I was twenty-two, or so I thought.'

'What did you do?'

'My cousin took me to see a doctor, right there in that Oldham. He was worried, and sent me to see a psychiatrist. He made sure it was a lady, because then I'd not be frightened.'

'Did she make you better?'

'No. She said just to pretend nothing bad ever happened back when I was little.'

'It doesn't work.'

'She said forgetting's the best. She didn't seem to have heard of any schools like we lived in, and wrote what I said down, but I got scared, because what if the old Gardai came after me for telling on everybody? She asked me to come back again and she'd see me a few more times, but I couldn't stay with Glenda, my cousin, after that and came back to Eire.'

'When's the next meeting?' the nun was startled to hear one of the old ladies say in a matter-of-fact voice. There were no meetings in the St Cosmo, except among the nuns.

'Two days or so.'

'Who is telling us?'

'I think that old Liam. It was Mr Gorragher last time.'

'Will it be when they put us out by the pond where the fishes are?'

'How on earth do I know?'

Sometimes, the nun thought, the old ones who had to stay most of the time in bed got wheeled out in chairs or their trolley beds to sit under cover where they could see the goldfish in the pond. One or two were allowed to feed the fish, but you had to watch them do it because they'd empty every packet of fish food, like they were doing something surreptitious. The fish food cost a fortune, but the old folk seemed to think everybody and every living thing, flesh, fish or fowl, was secretly starving and had to be fed with anything to hand. It was the old folks' sickness.

'They'll tell us.'

'Did you ever find out who's pinching the medicines?'

'You've forgot. We didn't know.'

'Maybe it's that old Mrs Wheelan.'

A sigh. 'Go to sleep.'

'Did you hear about when she pinched the newspaper with that plant in it? I think it was a poppy.'

'Yes, I heard. Go to sleep.'

'I wonder where she puts all them things she steals? She's a terror, that Mrs Wheelan.'

'Know what?'

'What?'

'When I go, I don't want them to bury me just as that old number. I've a name.'

'Names are best.'

'They always bury you by your name, don't they? Not some old number.'

'Always a name. That's the truth.'

'Mrs Wheelan's a terror.'

'You're right. She is that.'

Sister Francesca stole silently away. The old ladies slept.

Chapter Twenty

There had once been, Father Doran remembered, floating as free as if he flew on some power-free glider, a place dedicated to the care of children, in the tender mercies of Holy Mother Church.

Who burnt them to death.

This was in living memory. The nuns had protected the little girls so well that death by burning was almost inevitable. It was not the only incident. He tried not to think about the terrible fire, but it kept coming into his almost absent, drifting mind.

He floated, mildly uncaring of his being moved from one place to another. Beautiful, this airy sensation. He heard one of the ambulance men – was that accent Galway? – say to his mate, 'Down that end a bit,' and on he glided into the ambulance.

So many strange things had happened. Not many minutes since, there he was, doing as he was told by Nurse Duggan, SRN, with her, 'Go to sleep and rest, then you can go jogging, ha ha.'

First was that he had realised he was going to recover after all his terrible imaginings. Being struck down, and with calamitous results to this ticking heart of his with its frequent wobbles on those traces across the screens – now four of them, for Heaven's sake – would scare anybody, even the most religious and well-balanced personality. He was no exception. He truly had been really frightened. Now, though, it would be smooth sailing. 'Once we have the wrinkles ironed out, Father Doran,' Dr Strathan had said only this early morning in his pre-dawn visit, 'you'll be into hospital then you're off my hands, thank the Lord.' The doctor's usual quip, provoking the right sense of confidence in the patient. Was it all a mannered front? Father Doran did not care. It sufficed.

Then, lying there while the nurse went out to check the departure details with Sister Stephanie, he had sensed, dozing, rather than seen, a presence of somebody who smelt of Mansion Polish, that familiar tin of waxy orangey polish women used to clean church furniture. Mam had used that, so he knew he must be imagining it. He'd concentrated on obeying the nurse, and in truth he did feel sleepy. She must have given him something for the journey, to keep him calm.

'Father Doran?'

The whisper had almost made him open his eyes, but he was nearly away and could hardly flicker his eyelids. The voice reminded him of another. A woman's, sure, but whose? Did it matter? Not really. If it had been Nurse Duggan he would have recognised it.

He felt his tube being moved, and heard the slight plop of the spigot. Then she was gone, and with her the aroma of Mansion Polish. Only when he was woken by the return of the bustling nurse did he recall the voice. It had sounded very like the woman who had stood in for the nun that time, when Sister Francesca had gone for Dr Strathan. She had spoken of Sandyhills, where she and a friend had been Magdalene girls.

A girl died there. She fell one night in the stairwell. The cleaning woman was called Magda. She had been the falling girl's friend.

He had said his confession the previous day to Bishop MacGrath, of the girl who had died. Realising how close the cleaning woman must have come to him, he became momentarily anxious, then calm. In fact, it felt quite like resignation. Whatever happened would happen. Yet had the cleaning woman adjusted one of these wires, flexes, tubes? How had she dared, her with no nursing training whatsoever?

But why would she? Perhaps she had come in merely to say goodbye, to perhaps express forgiveness or ask for a blessing. That happened all the time. A priest, after all. He considered asking Nurse Duggan what the woman had been sent in for, then decided not to. He had no idea why he started thinking of that horrendous fire. The 'death toll', as the media always logged the dead at any calamity. Thirty five children, and one elderly woman. Why did he remember that?

He felt the stretcher sliding then a slight shudder as it clicked into place. A door slammed shut.

'Is that it?' a man asked.

'Don't they come out and see he's OK?'

'Nobody said anything. Sister?'

Sister Stephanie's voice: 'Nurse Duggan will accompany the patient.'

'In with him?'

The door opening shuddered the whole vehicle, Nurse Duggan, it must be.

'Dozing away as usual. It's working.'

'Ready now?'

'Yes.'

The men's footfalls crunched the gravel. He heard Sister Stephanie's goodbye and thanks to the ambulance men. The vehicle started. He felt movement. He was safe!

'Father Doran?' the nurse said.

He did not reply. Odd how voices became similar in odd circumstances, but then he'd been given some drug or other. There was no telling what drugs did to you. Certainly he had been managed well enough at the St Cosmo. Good that Dr Strathan had been so unsparing of his time.

The Cavan fire had been the subject of so much discussion at the seminary. Of course there was blame. Criticism that was still going on, and why not? For Heaven's sake, so many little girls dying in a fire. And not in some great tower block. It was in Cavan Town, in 1943, where the Order of the Poor Clares ran the St Joseph's Industrial School for Girls.

There was no blame attached, the Poor Clares being a closed Order. That was a given, in the way of some religious things. Nothing more or less than logic, not to examine history with a blaming hindsight. Otherwise you could level accusations at Wellington for not finishing Waterloo hours earlier, for not using tanks. Ridiculous. No, the Poor Clares were a closed Order, and so constituted. The townsfolk who came to try to rescue the children from the burning building were not allowed entry.

Intrepid souls from the locality somehow gained access but could not find light switches to see who was there in the smoke and the flames. They did not know where the staircases were, even. They had no idea how many children lived in the place or where the dormitories lay. Disorder was total, would-be rescuers hunting for dormitories where the children were dying.

The Inquiry said so. That too was a given. A fire escape door could have been got open somehow, had hopeful rescuers worked it out. It was kept closed. The nuns wasted valuable time, insisting that the little girls be completely dressed so they should not be seen in a state of partial undress by outsiders.

The final Report exonerated the nuns, all of them saved. The Inquiry praised the Sisters, of course, for they had the responsibility of coping with survivors. No lawsuits. The thirty-five children were reported by their assigned numbers, none by name. And were buried in a mass grave by number. Unknown soldiers?

In one sense, it was a beautiful instance of worthiness, the way society in Erin responded to tragedy. The dead children of Cavan were frequently invited   he had conducted such prayers himself – to 'pray for us here on earth'. What was more of a testimony to the Church's enduring character than that? In the very best sense, it was proof of holiness.

A true deep slumber came. He almost smiled as he felt the nurse's hands on him, tucking him. Very like being a child again, after a bad fall, something like that. Cosy. His mind glided among clouds.

The girl was called Lucy. He had been given the account of the ailing child's progress, at Sandyhills.

The nun – what on earth was her name? – had primly given him the doctor's verdict.

'The white phthisis has her, Father,' she'd said.

'TB?'

'Yes. Tuberculosis. Lucy's always been a frail child.'

'It is getting worse?'

'The cost of treatment is so expensive. We don't know what to do for the best.'

'I'm sure you have done everything.'

The nun sighed. 'We certainly have. She has been allowed all kinds of special favours, but has wanted to work. She would have felt left out if she were left in idleness. Life,' the nun said with arched primness, 'is instruction, Father, with these young girls.'

'I agree.'

'Without it, there is nothing but a mad void.'

'Indeed.'

'And into that void Communism can rush like an invasion. Children are at such risk.'

'More now than ever.'

'I blame the loosening of family ties.'

'Yes. And some of these children are the product of that laxity.'

He thought of Lucy, so waif-like and sinking fast.

'Is the girl in the sick room?'

'No, Father. That is reserved for the nuns.' She averted her eyes, quite coyly he thought. 'We have a rule that wherever possible the girls should be kept together. We foster their sense of community, of belonging to the Church's society, in a way that will work in their interests when it is time for them to go out into the world.'

'She hasn't responded to treatment?'

'Nothing like the way she should.'

'Unfortunate. The poor child.'

'It will be a merciful relief when she finally goes.'

Startled, he exclaimed, 'Is it that close?'

'Yes. The doctor himself said that last week. We try to have him up to see the sick girls once a month, sometimes sooner if we can afford it. You know only too well our lack of funding.'

It was his turn to sigh. 'Yes indeed, Sister. Always too little, always so much to do.'

That had been the start of his thoughts of Lucy. She was vulnerable, not merely to any passing germ, but to any moral onslaught. She was too weak to resist. The thought was a kind of affliction. The notion kept coming back. Seriously troubled by the image of the poor pale girl so weakened as to be hopelessly defenceless, he found he could not push her from his mind. Images, of people averting eyes, of the pale girl, at the mercy of anyone and anything, recurred.

Three times in the next month he made a point of asking after the poor girl. He was given details. Yes, she was an orphan, a product of a sinful mother. The children of such casual encounters never amounted to anything. They were doomed in life. Thanks only to the Church, they got a semblance of life. They inherited wrongdoing, sins of the mothers. It was their fate. What good could they do in a world where they were marked for failure?

'Are you feeling all right, Father?' somebody said. It was a woman's voice. He felt so tired now, probably the ambulance journey taking it out of him. Remember, he told himself, he had been stuck in a bed for quite some time now, to be put on the road to recovery.

'Yes, thank you.'

'Father Doran?'

That squeezing on his chest had come back. Probably nothing more than the effects of the vehicle juddering. They were turning right now, probably onto the road into Dublin proper. The hospital would be getting his bed ready, and the doctors well warned he was on his way in.

* * *

Lucy had been so docile, as if her complicity stemmed from the certainty of her impending death. Poor girl. He had been so solicitous, and explained it all to her with great sympathy. He had almost wept, back there in her dark dormitory.

Life, he had gently told her, gave her a chance to do some good, so her record as she ascended to Heaven was unsullied. He was sure she was always helpful. He told her that. He remembered it quite clearly, his words precise and compassionate.

This was her chance, he'd said, perhaps even her final chance, to do some good, create happiness and love that would be appreciated by God. It was not given to everybody to be so kind and loving. It was an opportunity she should take.

None of us could ever know when the last moments would come, but to some it was given as a friend, by someone like himself who really could guide her, and truly did care. The chance was too good to miss, to administer love in the only way left to someone who was ill and near to her end. And in that love, freely given and freely taken, she would bestow a kind of sacrament on the other person. It was the most beautiful thought, and the happiest way for a girl to leave the Church Militant and enter the Kingdom of Heaven.

He spoke her name in his mind, 'Lucy, Lucy.'

Hers was a melody, a tuneful statement of love and generosity that would remain with him for ever. There was something here magical, quite mystical. The thought was certainly not blasphemous, though some with less perceptiveness than he would be unable to recognise a gift so holy that it would be a lasting treasure for the person left behind. God-given, through Lucy herself. It would guarantee for the giver a constancy of prayers and devotion from the one receiving her gift. It would be exactly like those Crusader knights of old who, inspired by God in motive and spiritual ecstasy, took up the Cross and abandoned all to help the great cause of the Faith. In doing that, they rescued their souls from peril and achieved immortality. They entered the Kingdom of Heaven right here on earth.

They were even now receiving their reward in Heaven, and were sitting at the right hand of God the Father Almighty.

He whispered his promises of lasting devotion to her in the darkness even as he reached that enormous ecstasy in consummation with Lucy. It was beautiful, more a raising of the heart and mind to God than any prayer he had ever uttered. Of course she had to suffer a little, but she was in no doubt or she would have protested. It was worthy of her, and supreme to him. It was everything a sacrament should be.

Her last sacrament, in a mystical way. It was the most glorious gift he had ever received. He was blessed because of her. In giving, she received the benefit of his eternal devotion. He had prayed for her ever since, and would continue to do so. This was the reason God spared him from the inquiry, when somehow news and rumour spread from somebody in Sandyhills. Who started that rumour he was unsure. He had tried to discover that. The girl Magda could not read or write, he knew that, but there was always somebody who was disaffected, malicious, or inspired by Satan to assault Holy Mother Church with wicked lies and scandal, spreading tales of perversion and abuse and injury. It was all so unfair.

That was the reason, he was sure, he was now so devoted to the clerical life. The Church was everything. He had endured the transfers, got his letter of obedience from the bishop to report to a personal board who would judge his progress. Fair enough. He had fallen in line, and obeyed. Now the matter was entirely over. Done. The girl was still there in his mind, and an object of, almost, worship in his dark hours.

Love was of so many special kinds. He knew where his love lay. It was with the Church and all her wonders.

The voice came nearer.

'Father Doran?'

He tried to reply but the pain gripped. It was more severe than before. It came again with renewed force and he felt sick, almost unable to move.

'Father Doran?'

The pain took hold of his chest, his heart, and finally his mind, and he relaxed, surrendering to its majestic power. It recurred, bringing with it a sense of peace.

Chapter Twenty-One

'They can go out in the yard today, Magda.'

'Yes, Sister.'

'You're to go with them.'

'Me, Sister?' Magda was taken aback. This was new. She was always straight onto cleaning duty.

'Nine-thirty. Old Mr Gorragher will need wheeling out in his bed. Two others can help, and Mr Cronin can lend a hand from the garden. He will be at the chapel end.'

'But I'm to clean the sluice this morning.'

'You get them out. Sit with them. Who's to go, they've done themselves.'

'They have decided?'

Magda felt uneasy. Too many new things disturbed even the worst lives, as Lucy had ever since disturbed hers. Only this morning she said her prayers, asking Lucy's forgiveness for failing in the murder of Father Doran. The previous night had brought the clearest recollection, the worst re-enactment, of Lucy's fall to her death that Magda – meaning Lucy, of course – had ever experienced. She even remembered Lucy talking about dying and then having tea in a garden in Heaven, with white cups and saucers with grapes drawn round the edge. Magda had woken up weeping worse than almost ever, even when she'd been frightened by that Damien rubbing his old thing round her front bottom and spilling his seed like in the Old Testament and scaring her to death until her month came round.

'They are allowed, today. Get on, girl.'

'Yes, Sister. Who will clean the sluice?'

'You shall do it this afternoon. They will be in by then.'

'Yes, Sister Francesca.'

Magda went to make her peace with the other cleaners. Magda saw Sister Stephanie put the list of which inmates were to be taken out in the little yard where they could talk and daydream within sight of Mr Cronin's flowers and them old yawning goldfish. Truth to tell, the blooms weren't up to much, but he'd worked in a nursery garden in England so knew a thing or two about blossoms. He was always on about vegetables. Hear him talk, they were all mankind should eat.

'That poor priest,' Mrs O'Hare was saying when she arrived to put her mops in the queue for the sluice sink.

'What's happened?'

'He was taken bad in that old ambulance on the way to the hospital. Sister Stephanie was phoned as I came.'

'Is he all right?'

'Don't take on so, Magda.' Mrs O'Hare could be kind sometimes, for all her bad mouthing. 'He's in the very best hands.'

'No use crying over a priest. They're halfway to Heaven anyway.'

'Amen.'

The cleaning women chattered, and Magda explained about the oldies being wheeled out early today into the yard. They already knew, and were critical. It would disrupt the whole rota. It was unfair. Magda said she'd been told plain as day what to do, and did what work she could until somebody said it was half-nine.

They put Mr Gorragher out first because he said it was his turn, otherwise that Mrs Borru, who could go today in a wheelchair, would take the corner spot where the sunshine started its climb – like there might actually be some in gloomy old Dublin, Short-Change City. Only one day in the week there hadn't been rain.

Mrs Borru, of course, created and said she would complain to Sister Stephanie, but Magda was taking no grumbling today. She had suffered the previous night. It was all right for all these old folks, who had nothing to do but sleep all day and all the night too if they'd a mind.

She returned for Ted, who was surprised to be included, or so he told Magda, because he had never been part of the team talkers. And then Mrs Duffanan, who arrived complaining the air in the city was terrible.

'I'm more used to Temple Lane South,' she was already whimpering. 'Down along Wellington Quay was never this cold. We was a better breed of person there. We knew how things should be. Now it's all these supermarkets.'

'Daft auld bat,' Mrs Borru said, comfortably ensconced in her wheelchair with the lock on so she didn't rock about. 'You wus nivver down Wellington Quay except for the wrong reasons.'

'Here we go,' Mrs Duffanan said, happy now the rows had started as Mr Cronin and Magda positioned her recliner.

'Jealousy. That's what's made us worse than we are.'

'How d'you reckon that?' Ted asked.

'It's made us worse.'

'You can't be worse than you are. Stands to reason.'

'Jealous of what?' demanded Mrs Borru, stung.

'Jealousy's made Eire a bad lot.'

'Jealous of what?'

'Everything else.'

'How d'you reckon that?' Ted asked a second time, wondering how women kept things straight in their heads. 'I knew a sniper once who did everything by order, but they were orders he gave himself, not from officers or sergeants, no. He was the best marksman ever trod land.'

'Shut up, you and your auld wars,' Mrs Borru said, truly annoyed now with Mrs Duffanan for starting the old men off. Once they got reminiscing about killing there'd be no stopping them, and it wasn't yet drinks time. Drinks were ten-to-eleven, and there was still the rest of the day to get through.

'Jealous,' Mrs Duffanan said, comfortable the day was decently begun. 'All Dublin's jealous of everything everybody else has. That's why Dublin is hated all over Eire.'

'Is it?'

Ted felt he was asking for two, because George arrived already dozing. He'd had a bad night, talking from one in the morning. George would have wanted this thing about Dubliners being jealous explained, if he'd been awake. With any luck he'd not rouse until drinks time, and maybe the women's row would be all over and done by then so it wouldn't matter. Ted felt he'd get the blame from George if the silly old sod missed a good explanation. Nothing George liked more than some longwinded gripe that meant nothing.

'Course it is. Hated. Hated from jealousy.'

'Is it?'

'I'm telling you. That's why Mrs Borru here's got it all wrong.'

'I've not. It's you that always starts things off by saying something daft.'

'I got a plate in my head,' Mr Gorragher said. 'Did I tell you?'

'Can I have this wheelchair moved, Magda?'

'No, Mrs Borru. We've to bring one more yet.'

'There isn't room here for six!'

'Sister Stephanie said bring out Mr Liam MacIlwam.'

'There isn't room!'

'There is that.'

'Bring Sister Stephanie and make her tell us where Mr Liam MacIlwam's to go, then.'

'No,' Magda said reasonably as she could. 'It's what Sister Stephanie said.'

'There's no room. You'll see.'

'Look, Magda,' Ted said, as usual trying for peace. 'There's never been more than five of us here.'

'Never,' George said, eyes closed, which astonished Ted who thought he'd been asleep all the time. That's a comeuppance, he thought, worried how many explanations old George had missed and would now think he was entitled to ask for. 'Ted's right.'

'There wus four once or twice,' Mrs Borru said.

'That's never been the case,' said Mrs Duffanan. 'Down the St Simon and Jude's Care Home at Wellington Quay there's a rule, you can't have more than three in one place. But they're a cut above the rest of Dublin's old dumps.'

'Don't go on about Dublin.'

'I'm not. I'm just saying.'

'Here he comes.'

Magda and Mr Cronin wheeled in old Liam MacIlwam, and had difficulty manoeuvring him round to get him between Mrs Borru's wheelchair and Ted's spot.

'There's hardly room for six,' Mr Cronin the gardener said.

'There!'

'There what?' the gardener said, surprised.

'Complain to that Sister Stephanie and tell her straight out.'

'That's not my place, missus.'

Mrs Duffanan waited until Mr Cronin was through the gate of the walled yard then yelled, loud as she could, 'Your chrysanthemums aren't half as good as them they sell cheap at Barlow's!'

'Mrs Duffanan!' cried Mrs Borru, scandalised. 'That's terrible.'

'It's true. His don't last.'

'They do!'

'He won a prize at the great flower show once.'

'Yes,' cried Mrs Duffanan, adding in a loud yell for Mr Cronin's benefit, 'And I'll bet they wus bought from Jersey.'

'Stop it,' Mr Liam MacIlwam said, conversational. 'You'll be at each other's throats.'

'Aren't you going?' Mrs Borru asked Magda.

'No. I've to stay.'

'Why?' Two oldies said it together, full of mistrust.

'Sister Stephanie said so.'

'What for, though?' Ted asked quite amiably, smiling. 'Think we'll get up to no good?'

'Stop that, Ted,' George ordered. 'It's him and his wicked ways. He was stationed in France, see?'

'I knew this woman in France,' Ted said. 'She had false hair on her head, great big wig.'

'Why?' Mrs Borru asked, interested. 'Was she bald?'

'You can go bald from being ill,' Mrs Duffanan told them all. 'I had a cousin like that. It only happens to the better class of persons.'

'Why, Magda?' Mr Liam MacIlwam asked.

'I don't know.'

'We don't need any extra tablets or medicines, do we?'

'Not that I've been told, no. Anyhow, that's the nurses say that, not me.'

'Today isn't a nurse's day. It's tomorrow.'

'Magda,' Mr Liam MacIlwam said. 'Can you see if Sister Stephanie or one of the other nuns is there?'

Magda went to look. 'What do you want her for, Mr MacIlwam?'

'Nothing. Just wondering.'

'No. You want me to give her a message?'

'No. Just in case.'

Magda did not know what they meant. They went silent, looking at each other.

'In case of what?'

'In case she hears something she shouldn't.'

'Like what?'

They were worrying Magda. They seemed less sleepy now than before. Old George was definitely awake, and Mr Gorragher's old tin plate in his head was having no effect at all.

'Like what we might talk about.'

'You want me to go?' Magda asked, in doubt now because Sister Francesca had definitely said she was to stay.

'Not if you'll get in trouble.'

'It's the tablets, see? We want to know.'

'Know what?'

'If anybody has worked out who took the tablets.'

'Whose tablets?' Magda said in a shocked whisper. Old Mrs Borru had asked her that once. Then Kev. And here it was again.

'Well, mine for one.' Mrs Duffanan said, 'I laid a trap for whoever it was. I put one tablet near the glass of water on my bedside table, and it went.'

'You took it yourself,' Mrs Borru said with disgust. 'I told you at the time. I said you'd woken up in the night and taken it.'

'I didn't.'

'You must have.'

'Father Doran was took bad in the ambulance,' Mr Liam MacIlwam said. 'That's the point.'

'What point?'

Mr MacIlwam looked at Magda and answered, 'Our question. We wonder if somebody was stealing the tablets for old Mr O'Mucherty.'

'I did it once, for Mrs O'Dowd.'

'Shhhh, Mrs Borru. You're not to talk like that.'

'Why not? It was a kindness.'

'It was nothing of the sort. It was a misunderstanding. We decided.'

'It was.' Mrs Borru went into a sulk. Magda knew it would be half an hour before she came out of it now. That was her way, stubborn old crow.

'What did Mrs O'Dowd want them for?'

'Misunderstanding,' Mr Liam MacIlwam said sharply, altogether different from the way he normally spoke. It made

Magda feel quite queasy, and she was tired enough without that.

'It was kind. I did most of it anyway.'

'Now stop it.'

'I didn't start it, Mr MacIlwam. She starts it, every time.'

'What does Mr O'Mucherty want other people's tablets for?' Magda asked.

'It's medicine, not tablets.'

'Tablets,' Mrs Borru explained, 'make him gag. He can't get them down. If he manages to get one swallowed, up it comes after a retching.'

'We don't steal tablets or medicines at all,' Mr Liam MacIlwam said. 'Nobody does, do they?'

Silence fell at that. Their glances missed Magda out. She began to feel she was somewhere else.

'Do you know, dear?' Mrs Borru asked Magda sweetly.

'Know what?'

'If anybody mislays any of the medicines, or tablets?'

'No.'

'No,' Mrs Borru was triumphant. 'See? I told you.'

'Somebody does.' Mrs Duffanan looked from one to the other. They were almost in a semicircle, so could see each other. 'Did I tell you I left one by my glass of water that time?'

'Yes.'

'And it was gone when I woke up in the morning?'

'Yes.'

'Then that proves it. Somebody is filching.'

'Magda wouldn't know what to do with them, would you dear?'

'No, Mrs Borru.'

'There! Told you.'

'People who filch medicines and that don't always tell up. They say they don't when they do.'

'What would anybody take tablets for and give them to Mr O'Mucherty? He's got his own.'

'That's the point,' George said. 'In the war we didn't see a doctor from one campaign to the next.'

'Unless you got shot or wounded in some way,' Ted put in comfortably. 'It depended on how badly you got hurt. If you wus really bad, then you got left behind. There wasn't much else you could do.'

'Were you in the Eighth?' George asked him.

'We had a bloke called Holer. I ever tellt you about Holer?'

'You talk about nothing else, you daft auld sod.'

'Really?' Ted was astonished. 'I thought I'd respected his confidence and said nothing. He was my oppo for a time. Taught me to be a marksman. I lay down on my back, the only good way I managed the Lee-Enfield Three-O-Three. Holer, though, he'd stay in one position hour after hour.'

'Stop it, you two,' Mrs Duffanan protested. 'Tell them to shut up, Magda.'

'If they want to, they can, can't they?' Magda felt embarrassed appealing to everybody. They took no notice.

'That Mr Cronin's chrysanthemums is rubbish,' Mrs Duffanan told them. 'I'll say it to his face. Says he won a silver cup in some English garden championship, but where is it? Tell me that!'

'Once I saw Holer – a furlong away he was, in a cess pit. Know what he did? Stays like a statue. Unless you knew he was there to start with, you wouldn't know there was anybody alive there at all.'

'Give it a rest,' Mr MacIlwam said in a tired voice.

'Know what I asked him when he shot the Jerry and came crawling back? I sez, "Here, Holer. What happens if you want a piss?" Know what he said?'

'Mr Cronin orders them flowers from Jersey in the Channel Islands. It's cheating.'

'Holer said, "I piss in my pants." So I sez, "And what if you want a shit?" Know what he said? He said, "I did." And he had, shat right there in his keks.'

'Please.'

'Nothing stopped him.'

'Listen,' Magda said, desperate to stop all this. 'If there's anything I can get you, just say. Do you want the telly on? I can ask Sister Stephanie. There's one in the lounge. I think I can move it.'

'It won't work out here.'

'Won't it?'

'We want to decide,' Mr Liam MacIlwam said. 'No more talk of shooting and flowers.'

'Tablets.'

'Did you go with Father Doran in the ambulance, Magda?'

'Course not. I was here when he went.'

'Were you?'

'Yes.'

Magda felt desperate. It was as if nobody believed her. She remembered one time when Faith, her friend at the paper packing and who told her all about men and women being so different, had said how she'd not stolen any clothes brush from any of the nuns when one went missing. And how Faith had said she'd actually prayed to God to let her die in the night so she'd not be blamed for stealing the brush. It was a silly old clothes brush for the nuns' long habits. And, remember, she had been to a different convent and actually had a last name and everything. She was marvellous and knew everything.

The end of that story was, the brush was found under the wardrobe in the vestry by one of the cleaning girls the second day after Faith had got the lock-in in the pail cupboard and she was taken out and was the subject of a stern telling-off by the nuns. They'd told her class that punishments had to be accepted by all because it was love made manifest. God wanted it that way. And, if accepted in the spirit in which punishment was administered, it was full of merit. That was God's ineffable design, for us to be meek and bear His yoke.

Faith said it was a load of old crap, because there she was praying for God to rescue her from getting whacked and stuck for two days in that dark old pail cupboard. And when she came out and couldn't read her lessons, it was all because some nun had been fucking stupid.

That was what Faith actually said, words right out while they were packing that old paper in the paper packing, 'It was that nun's fault, stupid old cunt. She should go to Hell for making me say bad words.'

And Magda was amazed Faith wasn't struck down where she stood for saying things like that. Well, these questions from these daft oldies were making Magda feel like that.

'You saw him upstairs, didn't you, Magda?'

'In the sick room? The priest? Yes.'

'Did he say anything?'

'No.'

'You sure?'

'Yes.'

'Not a thing?'

'He was asleep most of the time. I was only there for a few minutes.'

'You usually do the top corridor?' Mrs Borru asked, sly old thing.

'Yes. The polish.'

'Why did they ask you?'

'I was there. Sister Francesca had to go to the phone. Or, no, this was it – Dr Strathan whispered with her about the priest in the office.'

'Did you give him his tea, then?'

'No. You weren't allowed. Only the sisters and the nurses were allowed to give him anything.'

'That was the day a last lot of tablets went missing. I lost three. I'm sure it was three more than I'd taken. I counted them.'

'Did you?' Magda couldn't count, let alone read, so that seemed a strange beauty, this old lady who wasn't long for this world, counting away and able to read.

'Yes, after you went with my tea. It couldn't have been long after four.'

'I don't remember.'

This denial seemed the most brilliant thing Magda had ever thought of, a true deception, but Mrs Borru wasn't convinced. She simply snorted and said, 'You nicked them, Magda.'

'Did you?' from Mr Liam MacIlwam.

'No!'

Magda was frightened of Mr Liam MacIlwam, because she associated him in her mind with Kevin MacIlwam, his grandson the Garda, and Kev could come any time and arrest her.

Like the seventeen prisoners who were marched in to that old prison and seventeen thousand heroes marched out, which is what they all said these days, but Magda knew it was more a sarcasm than a truth. Like Christ's tale of the Good Samaritan who had found that old soul battered on the highway, and who got taken for his last penny. Magda reckoned – though was this Emily's version, one of her old slants on the Gospels – it was simply Christ saying don't you lot be so daft as to get taken in. It would be a lot better all round if they used Emily's version than the Church's, though you went to Hell for saying things like that.

'The thing is, Magda,' Mr Liam MacIlwam said, 'did you give Father Doran anything?'

'No.'

'No tablets that went missing?'

'No. I wouldn't know how to.'

'That's true,' Mrs Duffanan said. 'She's an orphan, and they're all degenerate runts.'

'That's not true,' Mrs Borru said.

'The sins of the mothers and fathers shall be visited on the infants,' Mrs Duffanan intoned.

'You made that up.'

'I didn't. It's in the Good Book.'

'Prove it.'

'It is. Everybody knows that.'

'Where does it say that?'

'Everywhere.'

'Ignore her, Magda. Daft auld cow.'

'I'm going to tell Sister Stephanie. Magda, ring for Sister Stephanie. I want to make a complaint.'

'Don't, Magda.'

'She'll have forgotten what she wanted Sister Stephanie for by the time she comes anyways.'

'Listen,' Ted said. 'Who has them if Magda hasn't?'

'They say Father Doran is going under the knife today.'

'They'll give him a new heart, will they?'

'I don't know.'

'They'll give him new blood vessels. They get them from people's legs.'

'God help him.'

'Amen.'

Magda said nothing. She had caused the most terrible things to happen, and sat stricken. How did these old folk know so many things? She'd thought she was so clever, all unnoticed. The question was, if these old people saw so much, did the nuns notice?

'Do you talk like this when you're here on your own?' She was amazed at herself for asking it outright.

'When?'

'About getting tablets and medicines for Mrs O'Dowd and Mr O'Mucherty?'

'Yes.'

'Does anybody hear?'

They fell silent, and one or two cleared their throats as if to start talking, but deferred to Mr Liam MacIlwam.

'We actually thought in the night that somebody was listening when we spoke. We thought it was you. It must have been one of the nuns.'

'That's why we wanted you to make sure nobody was there.'

'Just now?'

'Yes.'

Magda thought, and went to see if anyone was inside the door to the lounge. Nobody. She returned and told the oldies.

'The door at the end is open, but nobody could be out of there before I saw them, no.'

'That's all right, then.'

'You're a load of old dafties,' Magda chided, wanting things to be back where they should be, these old folk daft in the mind and herself in charge. 'I can get the radio?'

'No, thank you, Magda.'

'You didn't give him anything, then, Magda?'

'Father Doran? How could I? I wouldn't know what to give.'

'He was moved after some things happened.'

'Moved?' Magda placed a hand on her throat. Mrs Duffanan gave one of her sharp glances at Mrs Borru, as if that proved anything at all.

'From wherever. Dingean, Nigl, or somewheres?'

'I don't know.'

The oldies talked among themselves, though none said Sandyhills like she would have done.

'That Bishop MacGrath was the worst, I think.'

'Worst for what?' Magda asked.

'There's that abuse. The children.'

'Is there?'

The silence hung as if it was something living and looking down into the yard. Magda had only ever felt this kind of imagined being, quite like a cloud or huge leaf that would not fall of its own volition, a few times before, and they were when she was waiting for the worst things to happen. One, quite the worst ever, was the night Lucy fell. The others were less, but frightening all the same. Like when she was going to get punished. Why God never answered her prayers to let her die instead of having to face punishments, she never quite worked out.

'Shall we tell her?' Mrs Borru said.

The others were silent. They avoided looking at Magda, except slyly when they thought she was not aware.

'It's that some of us get tired, Magda,' Mr Liam MacIlwam said. 'Like old Mrs O'Dowd.'

'She was so desperate,' Mrs Duffanan said. 'I'd want you to do the same for me.'

'Mrs O'Dowd isn't here any more.'

'No, Magda. She passed away.'

'Weeks since.'

'Yes, Magda. Weeks.'

'We went to her...' Magda could not say the word. She had been sick in the churchyard at Lucy's. She'd had to go out of the church in the middle of *Sweet Heart Of Jesus*, the hymn she would always hate now because Lucy said it was all only show.

'Funeral's the word you want,' Mrs Duffanan said, getting a hard look from Ted and Mrs Borru.

Magda thought. How strange that they were talking about extra medicines for somebody who was already passed on to her eternal reward, and somebody like poor old Mr O'Mucherty, who was still alive but very ailing, when the doctor saw to his treatment anyway and nurses did the injections on the drugs rounds.

'Why do you want extra medicines for Mr O'Mucherty?'

'We don't. He does.'

'Why? The doctor comes every...'

Words seemed harder in the yard among these oldies. Normally, the rare times she'd had to sit with them, perching on the cold wall so her bottom almost froze like today in the weak watery sun, she'd either doze or imagine stories to pretend everything was all right. Or, even, the truly superb fairytale, that somebody came in to the Magdalenes with a motor car and a dog called Spalpeen, and said, like in them old fillums, 'Hey, there, child. You wouldn't be Magdalene, would you? Birthday on the Twenty-second of July?' And Magda would say, 'Yes, sir.' And the gentleman (he would be a gentleman with a hat and everything and shiny shoes) would say, 'Then you are my brother's daughter, and they are all waiting at home for you in a lovely warm house and the kettle's on and there'll be ham and biscuits, so go and get in the motor car where your auntie is waiting at the entrance.' And he would go and sign some papers and the nuns would not be able to do a single thing, and if they came to the gate snarling and threatening the gentleman with the pail cupboard or the leather belts, he would just give a gay cavalier laugh and flourish his walking stick (he would have everything, including monocle and leather gloves) and say, 'Do your worst, nuns. The Gardai are outside on their special motorbikes and will ensure our safe departure.'

And she would be taken away to meet her very own father and mother and she would have two sisters and three brothers, the eldest a lawyer and equal to any trick them old nuns and priests might try just to get Magda back, and the other two would be Gardai on motorbikes like Kev. So many like Kev in her new dreaming, and none like Bernard.

'Sister is coming.' Magda said it in a harsh whisper, quite as if they had all been guilty of something bad and would get punished if they were found out.

'Shhh,' George said, waking up quickly and smiling to pretend he'd been enjoying the air.

It was only Sister Francesca, not Sister Stephanie or one of the nurses.

'Hello. Everybody all right out here?'

'Yes, Sister.'

'Magda not bullying you, is she?'

'Fine, Sister.'

Sister Francesca smiled, but more tightly than usual.

'We have some serious news about poor Father Doran. They will operate on him this afternoon.'

'Will he be all right, Sister Francesca?'

'That is in God's hands.'

'Will they make him better?'

'Don't take on, Magda. We have every hope. They are very hopeful. This afternoon we shall lead prayers for his recovery.'

'What time, Sister?'

'Three o'clock. Magda, it will soon be time for their drinks. Could you attend to that, please? I'll stay with these miscreants and chat until you come back.'

'Yes, Sister.'

Magda went quickly, thinking, if somebody at the St Cosmo was to put a good foot under her, she might get somewhere – a Dublin hospital, say – before the operation began. That would be a kindness, wouldn't it? Or, if she was not allowed to go, and she wasn't, then she could always ask how long these operations took. She could leave here and get there before the hospital ended its work. Or, maybe, get there as he woke up and tell him what she'd done, so he could tell the doctors, even if it meant they'd then tell the Gardai and they'd come and hang her.

What was best? She went to make drinks for the oldies, and came out carrying their tray with her decision made. She would hurry to the hospital the minute she finished work, and tell Father Doran what she had done to him.

That would rescue him. Even if Lucy kept falling all Magda's life long so Magda never got a wink of sleep from the horror, then it would be some reparation for the wrong she, Magda, had committed on the poor man.

Tomorrow was the day she was to go and meet Kev's family. She was frightened now all round the clock. It was a terrible way to be. For once she was glad she couldn't tell the time.

Chapter Twenty-Two

No more news reached the St Cosmo that afternoon, and Magda was out of the place like a cork from a bottle. Kev was waiting by the gate. He did not have his motorbike. He was dressed in casual clothes, no leathers. He insisted on travelling with her, two buses and then a hurry along the road to the hospital. She told him about Father Doran's calamity, breathless at all this distress.

'Is he badly, then?'

'Serious. They'll cut his heart.' The thought staggered her. 'His *heart*!'

'Why the hurry?' Kev was laconic, wanting to stroll rather than dash, but that might be the way men were. They had so many things on their mind, as she knew.

'Father Doran's maybe dying in there.'

'You can't stop it, Magda.'

'I know. I must see him.'

'Have you a message for the man?'

'No.'

'Then what?'

She slowed. Maybe she should tell Kev because he was, after all, Gardai and would find out soon. She had a notion of the speed of time because it figured so largely, having a measurement all of its own.

'I did something.'

'You did what?'

'Something serious.'

Did this feel like confession, she wondered, without the priest but like in maybe some kind of court? Kev was a Garda, though, and would instantly dash off for his old handcuffs and chain her to the railings. That would stop her from going in to confess to the priest, and that would delay telling the doctors what she'd done. It was a desperate choice for sure.

'What did you do?'

'I think I gave him something he shouldn't have had.'

'What something?'

'Nothing.'

He hauled her round to face him there on the pavement.

'You gave him the wrong things in the St Cosmo?'

She said nothing, feeling tears on her cheeks. She couldn't wail like some women did, giving out satisfying bellows of weeping to encourage everybody all around to start up just the same.

No. She could only do it dead quiet in case some nun would come and thrash her and have her standing in the cold waiting for more.

'Let me go, Kev. I have to tell them.'

The hospital was now a mile away, that was all. She knew the way to go. A cross was up there among the street signs plain as day. There was no time to stand and talk, not even to Kev. The terrible thought came that, once she had confessed to him, he would walk away like on them old pictures she watched all night long. He would sneer and never look back and that would be the end of meeting his family and seeing his real if cavalier sister Jean who didn't care what went on anywhere but who came along to help her brother ask to help their grandad.

'I can save him, see?'

'Save who?' Kev wondered what on earth she was talking about.

'Father Doran. I've to tell the doctors what I did.'

Kev stayed her. 'Look, Magda. They are doctors, surgeons, saving his life by an operation.'

'But they might be doing the wrong thing, see?'

'No.' He stood between her and the hospital in her path. No way round. 'Look, Magda. They know what they're doing. You think they haven't done all the right tests? You think they haven't made sure of everything he's had and eaten and drunk since he was taken ill? Course they have!'

'Have they?'

'Yes, Magda. You can't have done anything they don't already know about.'

She looked at him through her tears, still trickling down.

'Is that right?'

'True as you're standing here.'

'Will he be all right?'

'Course he will. They make everybody better in them old places.'

She felt safer, though the consequences for her and poor Lucy would be serious. Sometimes she faced the future with despair, almost, and interminable nights full of darkness and Lucy falling, with exhaustion tomorrow at work. Work, in fact, was the only brightness in the world. That, and Kev. His arrival occupied her mind more than it should. Bernard was almost forgotten, whatever he was getting up to now long in the past. Two days previous she had kept her door closed when he had knocked. The day following he had returned. She had not opened to him then, either. He had gone away.

It had been a wrench, and she had stayed white-faced behind her door, glad for once that Mrs Shaughnessy along the landing would be listening and, eventually, coming out to peer. Magda had heard the exchange: Where is she? Oh, she's in, right enough, Sergeant. Why doesn't she answer? I don't know, it may be she's sleeping. And then the clumping boots on the stairs, then the knock and Magda opening to the old lady and telling her no, she would not be in to Sergeant Bernard again because the Garda work was finished thank you very much and the old lady going away satisfied.

Magda didn't know how she would manage after those two episodes, him getting spurned, but that was the way things were. It was only thinking this that she realised Kev's coming had changed things more than she understood. Was it morality, in a hidden way the Church always taught? The Jews had invented Original Sin to keep Christians under. Was that it?

Lucy always said, and Emily too believed, most of what they taught you in the Holy Catechism was crap. This didn't mean it wasn't to be believed, did it? She had no means of telling Kev these thoughts out loud, because how could you speak words like cunt and prick and genitalia and penis to a man? Even womb was hard. She always went red when Holy Writ went on about it. Lucy was much more critical, telling Magda off for even bothering.

'We'll be lucky if we ever find out what it's about, girl,' Lucy would say between coughing the blood-specked phlegm onto her mouth, chin, lips.

'Will we?'

'Sure as God made apples, Magda. Or,' and here Lucy would laugh, sometimes setting herself off with that red cough, 'unlucky, truth be known.'

And that was frantically desperate to Magda, for then Lucy would laugh herself into one of them dreadful coughing fits. Magda would bang her back to stop her coughing because the sisters – especially Sister Annuncion, who kept on about all the girls being hard-line sinners – would clout Magda for setting Lucy off. She always insisted that Magda told her word for word what she had told Lucy to make her laugh. Then the round rulers would come out and the leather belt and Magda would be slapped across the backs of the calves. Coughing was dangerous to everybody in the Magdalenes, and twice she had her skirt raised and her thighs thrashed black and blue to the admiration of all in their dormitory because it was the worst ever they could remember, and God knows they had plenty to recall right enough.

The thoughts rushed through her mind, standing there in the rainy street staring at Kev, him in his casual clothes saying, 'What's the matter? You've gone white as a sheet.'

Magda came slowly back from wherever she had got to. 'I think I must have given him the wrong medicine.'

'Did you?'

'I don't know.'

'What medicine did the nuns tell you to give him?'

'None.'

'Then how can you have given him wrong?'

'I don't know.'

'Know what I think, Magda?'

'No.'

Kev started walking again, and this time he let go of her arm and thrust his hand casually through her arm so they walked along arms linked – that's *linked* – together and it felt so odd she wondered if she ought to stop in case people saw.

'I think you dream what goes on in your head.'

'Dream?'

'Like, imagine.'

'But I did...'

'You did what?' Kev was so sure of everything he said. She began to believe he must see inside her. That was truly terrible, for all kinds of thoughts were in her head and her body. God, even that word, body, was enough to cause trouble, think of it that way.

'See?' he said with a kind of triumph. 'See? You can't even think what you're supposed to have done wrong. Or right. My sister Jean says it's the wrong road them old nuns took you on, berating you for fuck all and then sending you out wrong.'

Magda's head was spinning, Kev using words like that and the world still going along on its old axis or whatever it did. She didn't want him struck by lightning just when...just when what? He walked with her, his arm through hers, not pressing it, nor breathing funny like that Damien did so many years ago behind those sheds, or Sergeant Bernard as he spilt under her or into a contraceptive he sheathed on himself before starting. That was all over now. She had rescued herself, this time without Faith's help. She was free of encumbrances (the word learnt from a Victorian story about a squire's goings-on, some old black-and-whiter. She liked their voices).

'I try not to think wrong, Kev.'

'Good for you. It's something everybody has to learn for themselves, once they're out from under the Church. It's run by a lorry-load of miseries, that it is.'

'What is?' she asked, startled.

'The Church. Nobody believes them any more, unless they've been forced into it when they were little. Me and the family don't. Unless...'

He eyed her, and she knew he was speculating on whether he was giving offence, her having been a Magdalene girl and all.

A right lorry-load of miseries was something Lucy might have said, and Emily without a doubt. Magda admired him for risking all sorts of Heavenly punishments, here in the open street where anybody could hear him and take action. Maybe because he was a Garda it was something he could get out of?

'The hospital, now. That's another thing.'

'What must I do, Kev?'

This made her feel grown-up, at the hospital gates with those notices full of words and coloured letters telling folk where they were to go. It was a whirlwind of people, cars in the car park and a bus, people coming in a drove and bringing flowers. Flowers!

She had some money in her purse. A proper handbag seemed a terrible waste of money, once she learnt how much handbags cost. What, she was to pay a king's ransom for a bag in which to hold another bag, just because one was called a purse and the other a handbag? It seemed ridiculous.

'Must I take flowers?' she asked Kev, timid now. She had never visited a hospital before, though she knew what you had to do from hearing the other cleaners.

'Who to? Father Doran? Why?'

'Well, it's him I'm going about.'

'He won't be able to have them for days. They take hours over that kind of operation, then there's recovery.'

'Isn't it the right thing?'

'Doubt it.'

'I can leave them at the desk.' She had heard of people leaving flowers at desks for newly born babies.

'I shouldn't. What will you say?'

'I'll tell the doctors I think I might have given him the wrong thing when I was minding him at the St Cosmo.'

'They'll laugh in your face.' He shook his head slowly, just as she imagined him at a traffic accident before he took out his notebook and started writing it all down.

'What do I do, then?' This was even worse. Now she was lost.

'Look, Magda. The best thing you can do is leave a note at the Reception, and then come away.'

'A note.'

'They'll lend you a pen and a note-pad. They have them. God knows I've been in that old place often enough.'

'Leave a note?'

'Ask which ward he'll be in, leave a note addressed to him, then I'll see you home.'

'No!' She wanted to conceal the shabby place she lived in. 'I'll do that, then visit the chapel a minute. I'll see you Sunday.'

'If you're sure.'

'It seems proper.'

'My folks are looking forward to seeing you Sunday. Is twelve o'clock all right? They said to ask.'

'Yes, thank you. Twelve.'

This was the sort of invitation they wrote yet more notes for, from a reticule with a silver pencil that unwound itself, while a footman waited obediently to do the lady's bidding. She, being Magda, was at a casement window looking wistfully out onto extensive gardens laid out by her great-grandfather before the family's fortunes fell prey to the wiles of a wicked neighbouring squire who had designs on the maidens of Magda's once-exalted family.

'You don't want me to wait? It shouldn't take more than a minute.'

'No, thank you.' No lengthy note with this offer. 'I'll get on, and speak to the desk, ah, lady.'

'Fine. See you then, Magda.'

'See you, Kev.'

She waited until he waved. He made for the bus, caught it with a bound. She was relieved but saddened. He was lovely to be with, though troubling. What did he want, coming all this road to the hospital he had no intention of visiting?

A sense of growing choice, such a rare word to her, came on her as she went slowly into the hospital grounds. She felt afraid of it. Before now, choice was beyond her, as if it was a colour she could never see or even guess at. It was out of reach and too far for sight. It was unknowable. Now? Now, choice was somehow here and blocking her path. She simply did not know what it was. The distress within made her feel ill. She'd had no idea it had such intensity. It was so gentle and gay in those grainy old pictures, a sort of game. Was this how – what was her name, in that story they kept re-making in London and showing on late TV, Miss Bennet? – felt? Magda had reservations about her, though, for wasn't she just a gold-digger? Or was she the tender innocent she made herself out to be? Magda distrusted her for chiselling.

Magda judged the hospital. Choice was here again, in front of her face.

In the Magdalenes, she was punished for being an orphan. She deserved it. She was a lesser person, without real certainty. Whatever the world of nuns, older girls, the Church, the cosmos of her Magdalenish existence and priests, said was so, had to be so. If some element seemed, just for a fleeting instant, not to be quite so – like the dog, the vegetable man, the girls who fainted, being whacked and thrust into the pail locker, whatever – was forced into the mould. The world was made to comply. Everything was forced to come into and be an orthodox part of the world as the Church defined it. The world was the Magdalenes. She was an orphan. God decided that for her, for Lucy, for everybody.

Now, she seemed able to do things without reference to anybody else. Uncertainty was a new and dreadful thing. She could go into the hospital and ask after Father Doran. She had phrases all ready, from being awake in the night worrying what to say. Or she need not go in at all. She could go home and have her meal – egg and oven chips tonight, red sauce and bread-and-marge to make butties, then settle down to watching them old black-and-whiters rerunning the livelong night, to save Lucy her frightening fall again. Or she could stay here a bit, watch folk going in or out. But rest was sinful. 'Do nothing, you sin,' Sister St Paul the provisions monitor of the kitchen at the Magdalenes, explained as she leathered Magda's thighs for dozing behind the scullery when she should have been hard at the newly scrubbed pans. The litany was always three questions fired at her, all the girls in earshot responding.

'Whose work is idleness?'

Satan's work, Sister.

'Why is it evil?'

Because it offends against so good a God, Sister.

'What is your resolution?'

To never more do Satan's work, but to act in true and faithful obedience to our holy Mother Church, Sister.

Magda decided to make a choice of her own. Nervous about it, she went to the damp bench outside the entrance and sat, looking round guiltily. She kept turning, to deceive anybody who might think she was just there being idle, maybe even on the way to falling asleep and earning punishment in Purgatory.

It didn't work. In a minute, she was up and into the hospital. She asked the woman at the desk how Father Doran was.

'He is poorly with his heart,' she said, following her rehearsed speech. 'He is under the knife today.'

'Father Doran?' The lady seemed disinterested, clicking on some computer thing and not even glancing at Magda.

'Yes. He's…'

'Yes. Cardiothoracic. Take the lift to…'

Magda heard little of the speech, but went in the direction indicated, mystified by the signs, following a woman who was having difficulty marshalling her three small children. Maybe they were going to see some father, husband, brother, under the knife too?

The choices seemed to be several, Magda thought in dismay, too many. The Church was no choice, sure, being there by God's orders anyway. Everybody did as the Church said, except for Lucy, and just look what happened to her. And except Emily, who did whatever she wanted anyway. It was controlled and had to be obeyed.

Then there was this strange entity that was Kev. In the background was Sergeant Bernard, or did he not count now? And Damien. In it too was her own behaviour, so inept when Kev talked to her, and not knowing what to say to his sister Jean in that bar. This strange world of reality was all of a piece. In it too was her poisoning Father Doran to kill him dead, and the listening hard she did so much of. The lay cleaning women lived more in this radical reality-driven world than ever they did in the holy ritualistic Church.

Then there was a pretence world, which was the dangerous world of imagination. This was the no-work world of idleness the nuns condemned in God's name. It was wrong, discipline was essential, or the world would come to grief. All history, Magda had learnt, was there to prove that calamity followed where immorality led, and civilisations tumbled.

She followed the stout lady and the three children. At the lifts, she asked the lady where the Cardiac Unit was. The lady saw her bafflement, and went with her up to the third floor in the lift, pressing the buttons as if she was familiar with everything.

Magda stepped out into mayhem.

A bench with a table, some magazines, and two armchairs, seemed safe enough. She took up her stance of waiting for someone, and stayed seated there while everybody moved by. Frightening, it was, disturbing the mental order Magda was trying so hard to construct. The problem was *how* to decide things. If she had practice, she might have been able to make up her mind. The choice was the threat, not the decisions she might make. Guess wrong, people out here in this reality just said, oh, well, and started a different thing entirely. How on earth did they have the nerve?

She sat there. The visitors stopped coming. The nurses seemed to change duty – Magda recognised the signs, some coming on and wanting to know what about this, about that, and signing things. Doctors went by. A patient was wheeled by, bottles and tubes and shuffling gowned staff leaning on the trolley, their hands about the patient's face. It could have been anyone, so wrapped up. Surely, she thought, they'd be too hot under all that? For an instant the patient's eyes opened, gazed in her direction with a flat kind of opacity. She believed it might be a man. The eyes seemed vaguely familiar, but by now Father Doran would be sitting up in bed having his no-poison tea and reading his old breviary. Then the figure was glided off on them quiet wheels, all them boots squeaking away.

By now she was desperate to go to the loo, but didn't know if she would be allowed. She didn't know how to get back to the outside.

A nurse came to her. 'Are you waiting for someone?'

'Yes. To see Father Doran.'

'Father Doran? He went to theatre. He's long back.'

'Is he...?'

'Are you a relative?'

'No. I'm...'

'He's not to have visitors just yet. Do you want to leave anything?'

'No.' It came out sharper than Magda had wanted, and she said it again but softer, 'No. I wanted to say something about...'

'Can I have your name? You could leave a message.'

'No. I'll come back.'

The nurse pointed the way to the lifts. Magda went in the right direction, hoping to see that little black mark that meant

the women's loos were through the signed door. Then she felt
bold. Had she come all this way, dithering like an imbecile, to
leave without at least telling how she'd done wrong and was
sorry? Yet she had worried herself sick, thinking all that about
how there were three lives she was trying to live all at once.
You had to keep trying, even with one life at a time. That was
what God said, she was almost sure.

Returning, she said to the nurse, 'Could I leave a message
for Father Doran please?'

'Certainly. Do you want to write it?'

'No.' Magda took the plunge and said out loud, right to the
nurse's face, the nurse in her grand uniform with its badges and
everything, 'I can't write. I'm sorry.'

She could have made up her usual tale about needing
spectacles. Her favourite was, 'I dropped them under the sofa,'
which didn't sound too bad because she hadn't a sofa either so
it was a complete falsehood.

'That's all right.' The nurse found some paper, a whole
notepad, and a ballpoint. 'What do you want to say?'

'Could you please say, Dear Father Doran, I'm sorry for that
wrong stuff.'

The nurse wrote, repeating the message. 'Is that it?'

'Yes, thank you.'

'No name? He'll want to know who it was from.'

'Oh.' Magda knew the nurse must watch that old telly on
duty of a night. Well, no time for speculation. She couldn't
say the full details, not even to this friendly nurse. The nurse
must want a decent ending, like in them old stories in country
houses.

'A name?'

'Yes. Unless he'll know who it's from.'

This was a dilemma. To give the nurse the whole tale would get the priest arrested when he was poorly. You had to visit the sick, like honouring thy father and thy mother, if you ever learnt who they were.

'Say, *Yours sincerely, Lucy*.'

That was a brainwave, signing it Lucy. He would know straight away it was to do with Magda's friend. That would ease his mind, telling him he was forgiven. Then maybe they'd meet like under that tall tree in that great park where Mr Darcy comes walking up to the lady seated in a bower, where flowers grew and everything and they became all friends again. It was such a peaceful arrangement, nobody got whacked and their legs made black and blue where the inspectors could never see.

'Yours sincerely, Lucy,' the nurse repeated. 'That it?'

'Yes, thank you.'

Magda waited a moment, then turned and walked away towards the lifts. As she went past one of the rooms full of machinery, with nurses and them tubes all round a patient, the desk nurse called, 'Oh, Lucy.'

Magda turned in fear. 'Yes?'

'No address?'

'He will know,' she said, and left.

Luckily, two doctors got in a lift and asked where she wanted to go. She told them the outside.

'Car park?' one said, smiling just like Mr Darcy. 'You were lucky to get space. Never seen it so crowded.'

'True,' Magda said, thinking she was being brilliant, like that Sherlock Holmes when he got the Spider Woman, and that old police Inspector Lestrade in his daft bowler hat went off grinning with the Spider Woman on his arm.

She went outside. On the way, greatly daring, she entered the door with the sign and went to the loo, washing her hands afterwards with the most beautifully scented soap ever. It was a pity to waste it in old water just to wash, but she didn't need telling what was right and what was wrong, no.

Chapter Twenty-Three

Sunday dawned with Magda frantic. The thing was, she had two things to wear. Choice was a terrible thing.

This became more terrible today. She thought of praying, and went to church full of devout pleas to Jesus to help, because he was sort of neutral. Then the Virgin Mary, then St Veronica. She was never quite sure of St Veronica, who did all that cloth business and ought to know a thing or two about material. She came away none the wiser, and went home to do baked beans on toast in the most ineffectual grill in County Dublin, her Baby Belling on full.

She had one nearly black dress, her best. It troubled her because it needed cleaning and the dry cleaner's at the corner of Crown Alley was extortionate. Worse, it picked up every dust fleck, every hair, every fragment of lawn blowing from the silly displays at the Dublin Woollen Mills, to nobody's benefit but the dry cleaners of the world. She wanted a string of pearls, as worn by – who, Jean Kent? Patricia Roc? – the previous night in *Wicked Lady* when out riding on her horse, in her crinoline or whatever, singing that lovely song about love

stealing your heart, so pretty. Luckily, James Mason got shot.
He always frightened Magda so she had to turn the sound off
when he was talking in case his words started coming through
when Lucy started falling as Magda dozed off, as the outside
darkness slowly became its usual morning grey.

Well, like that set of pearls, but Magda had none.

Her other dress was a flowery thing one of the cleaning
ladies had passed on to her, handed on from her daughter, who
was more or less Magda's age. It didn't really fit, but was the
one she usually wore all the time. Magda rattled on about it.
She knew it had some signs on the label behind the neck, but
since she couldn't read she had to have it cleaned.

She had started a savings account, putting her wage money
in. She listened to the saving place people as they explained the
ins and outs, and said she had hurt her hand so she couldn't
sign her name at all. They gave her a plastic card. This was
even more trouble but in a new way, since she had to hand the
card over when she took her wage to them at the end of the
week. She asked for what she thought she'd need, guessing on
their say-so, and they kept the rest.

They got to know her, and she deliberately crooked her right
hand as if it were twisted from birth like Mrs MacConnigal's,
who cried every night from terrible things that had happened,
poor lady. She had been taken away to a mental hospital at
the finish, and she had no family to speak of so it was hard.
Magda often wondered where Mrs MacConnigal had got to,
and thought how nice it would be to go and see the old lady,
maybe to telephone her and just ask.

Magda's entertainment was listening to the people telephoning
on the concourse of the railway station. 'Take it easy!' blared
some Tannoy all the time for a whole month or two once, when

Magda first started going there. It sounded demented and put the heart across you, but there was no stopping it. They'd given the slogan up now, thanks be to God.

She made a habit of standing there as if waiting for some train, or perhaps meeting some gentleman in his natty trilby, like Trevor Howard, who'd take some train dust from her eye, and then start up a romance at the snack bar, nothing carnal that would call for confession or anything. It was only the listening to the old telephones that she did.

Every single life she overheard at them old telephones was worth it. Sometimes there were rows, though these happened in the very best circles, she knew from her informal education at the TV screen of a night. Usually they talked pleasant. Some were disappointments, just a barked instruction to do this or that or meet somewhere. Those didn't repay all the effort Magda went to, positioning herself just to hear what was being said. Other times there was a serious talk, some relatives might be poorly or, once, in a breathtaking chat of sorrowfully brief duration, about whether the man talking and the lady at the other end should go ahead and buy some house. It was exhilarating. Sometimes Magda walked away as if floating on air, delirious with pleasure at the images raised in her mind, better than any old fillum, that was for sure.

The trouble was that nobody she would ever come to know by all this watching and listening ever revealed how it was they came to some decision. Worse, there was a terrible final realisation. However well she eavesdropped at the telly and heeded what the lords and ladies said on their galloping steeds, Magda never would know the outcome of their decisions. Did that smiley lady with the pearls and getting the love of that lord as they sang riding on the moors ever think back and tell herself, 'Goodness gracious, how exciting to hold up some London coach with the cry "Stand and deliver!" then ride off laughing with the wind in your hair'?

That's the bit she needed to learn about. If she'd got her age right, she must be knocking twenty, the twenty-second of July, to be about as precise as guessing allowed.

Maybe this was an opportunity? Kev was probably checking his family was getting on with it as they came back from Holy Mass. She felt scared, like she was going to get clouted by Mrs Rooney and Sister St Paul as they set about her in so much anger they shook with rage over her slow carrying them frosty vegetables in. Worst had been the time Lucy had coughed so bad Magda had had to carry them in on her own and hadn't been strong enough to do them as fast as she should. Lucy, poor sainted thing, coughed under the lintel of the kitchen door, and Sister St Paul had berated Lucy for setting herself choking on something she'd stolen from the vegetables and walloped her hard. Then they gave Magda a leathering for concealing Lucy's theft of vegetables. It wasn't true at all. Magda found herself weeping at the pain, but was it right to cry when Lucy too got a whacking when she'd done no wrong?

Magda looked into her cracked mirror. She looked a fright, and her hair was a ghastly mess. She did her own hair with a brush and comb, and washed it in the sink along the landing. She would have liked to have done it at the St Cosmo but that wasn't allowed. You were stealing time from God Almighty, and stealing the St Cosmo water supply and heating.

She combed her hair. It wouldn't stay straight, curling in a troublesome manner. She gave up and let it get on with it. The hairdresser two shops down from where Dame Court did that sudden end into Exchequer Street looked pleasant. They showed you a list of things they could do to your fright of hair, but how could she read it? They showed you lists of dinners in bars too, that Kev had coped with so magnificently, checking with a casual glance the wall list. He was elegant, so much in command. This was the difference that God surely intended when He designed the world.

She chose the black dress, too long but how could she shorten it? The nuns made the older Magdalene girls shorten or lengthen their habits. The oldest girls, nimble with their fingers and counting and working lengths out, made the nuns' underskirts. You could always tell which girls knew spelling and counting, because their hands were always thick in the palms and their fingers often bled. They were paler and squintier than the other girls. And you could always tell the serving and washing girls by the sudden end to the hard chapped skin just short of the elbow, where the arms didn't need to dip any further into the washing.

The rest of her time she spent brushing the dress. She worried about her bottom, and spent a long time trying to position the mirror piece so she could see there was nothing going wrong back there so people would notice her stupid shape and be mortified by the sight.

With trepidation she left, going back several times to make sure of nothing in particular, and caught the Sunday bus.

Kev met her off the bus and they walked together, no arms linked today. She had a terror of railways, not knowing why except she didn't know how to work the tickets and you'd have to ask and know counting.

'It's easier to come right up Ballybough Road,' Kev said. He had a clean shirt on and jeans. Magda thought him debonair.

'If you've a motor bicycle,' Magda said, defending her secret ignorance. She smiled, to make a joke of it.

He nodded, not smiling back. 'There's a bus from the Busaras goes straight to Tolka Park. Get off at Fairview.'

'I'll do that, then.' She caught herself thinking, Jesus Mary and Joseph, would he now be dismayed that here's this stupid girl with the effrontery to assume she was coming out here to every Sunday dinner just because he'd mentioned some old buses?

'You're right, Magda. I think everybody's on a bike.'

'I always imagined...' being on a motorbike, was her next unthought tragedy that had to be extinguished before it got out properly into talk. She only meant *Easy Rider*, where they rode their old bikes across wild and free America and were so happy and cavalier, not caring. She didn't mean she kept imagining him steering with one hand while he held her on the bike and they drove off into the sunset, no, nothing like that. 'How hard it must be,' she made up quickly, 'to drive a motor bike. Do they show you in the Gardai?'

'Yes. I learnt there.'

'I can't read,' she said suddenly, thinking it had to be said straight out. 'So I'd never learn.'

'Not at all?'

'Not a word.' She smiled, trying to lessen the shame of it, and made things worse. 'I'm hopeless with numbers and all. I never learnt, you see.'

'There's lots like that.'

'Not as bad as me.'

'I'm colour blind,' he said with candour. 'So you're lucky.'

'Are you?'

She was astonished. The world was so queer. Once, everything was simpler, back when wrong was her fault because of Adam and Eve in the Garden of Eden. Now, here was this hero, in the Gardai for Heaven's sake, with a deformity. She knew some girls in the Magdalenes got punished for stubbornness when they got colours wrong, but that was just usual. One question, what colour was the priest's vestments on a Feria day, which of course was a green chasuble, a girl said red as if it was a martyr's Sunday like St Peter. The class went silent as the girl was called out and whaled. This was the first Magda had heard of words for it, colour blindness.

'I'd have got on further if I wasn't,' he said, seeming not to care either way about it, which was superb.

Magda always thought that all females – nuns, girls, the rest – were merely men who hadn't quite come off, so to speak. It was right and just to know you were wrong all the time, because that's what life was. Yet if God had made a lovely man like Kev then left something out like this colour blindness thing, what was God up to? It suddenly seemed like God was playing about, letting some have nothing at all wrong, and making others with a club foot that proved your mother or father, or both, had got up to no good, so serve you right. To be limited, as herself, was only right, deserving a bad start because of your mother's sins, but Kev? With his authentic genuine family?

Suddenly she slowed. Kev asked her what was wrong.

'We're nearly here,' he said. 'Just there, fifth along.'

'I got a bit worried.'

'What of?' He laughed and she thought it was so marvellous laughing like that and not caring. 'Us? We're boring, and that's the truth. You'll see.'

Boring? A real family in the image of the Holy Family? Her mind span, and she decided she must see this through. She walked on with resolve. This was a decision, an almost firm one, to carry something through.

'Is it all right me coming?'

'Why?' He seemed surprised.

'Because...the Magdalenes.'

'What about them?'

'I'm an orphan, see? Do they know I'm a Magdalene girl?'

He said with a frown, 'I can't remember if I said or not. Why?'

Why? She wondered for an instant if he was deranged, not seeing things as they actually were. How could she explain to him, who failed to see the truth of things, when he was already pausing at this house, going up the steps to a grand door where a woman was coming out?

She was smiling and wiping her hands on her pinafore and two girls were saying hello and taking her arm and saying to come on in.

'I'm sorry if I'm late,' she blurted, because she'd heard it said on TV, a gentleman caller at a house in Berkeley Square, where coaches trundled and a sinister doctor was killing Victorian girls in gas-lit old Whitechapel, a typical piece of London immorality.

'Oh, think nothing of it,' a girl said, pulling her up the steps.

'Sure, how could you get here if you've had to learn the way?' the woman said. 'I'm this spoilt brat's mother, and everything he's tellt you is wrong.'

'Mam means me,' Kev confided, not even minding, which shocked Magda.

'We'll put you straight,' one girl said. 'I'm Marla and I'm fifteen. Isn't being a teenager rotten luck?'

'Yes.' Magda agreed without thinking, then asked herself, is it? She had never thought this.

'I'm Beth,' the taller girl told her. By now they were at the top of the steps and into a hallway with flock wallpaper of a strange reddish hue. 'I design things. I'm eighteen. It'll be marvellous to have somebody sensible to talk to. Kev's hopeless, start to finish.'

'Pay them no heed, Magda,' Kev said.

'Hello, Magda,' Jean's voice called. 'Down in a sec.'

Magda's head was going round. Was this a family? All pretending to be at each other's throats? She was taken into a room where a man was putting something into a small steam engine thing. His frown disappeared and he smiled, ruefully grimacing at his hands. They were covered in oil. Bits of metal scattered all over on a board.

'I'm Dad,' he said. 'Anything wrong here, Magda, I'm responsible for, but blame Mam. That's what she's for. God knows, none of this brood's good for anything except telling off.'

Magda was gripped by fear. What had they done wrong, and why didn't they even care when Father was cross? He grinned and said chiding to Mrs MacIlwam, 'Give the poor girl a cup of tea, Ness, she looks done for.'

'I'm not!' Magda said, desperate to set things right.

Silence came. The girls looked at each other.

'OK,' Marla said. 'But I'm desperate for a drink, so you'll have to have one too. And this old Dad of ours grumbles if he doesn't get his rotten old tea, so we all have to suffer.'

'That's right. Isn't he in a terrible mess?' Mrs MacIlwam led Magda away. 'Dad never finishes them heaps of rubbish. Would you believe he's been working on the one wretched thing for a year now? Costs him the earth and he won't give up.'

'Dad's a railway fanatic,' Kev told Magda. He came with them. 'Don't let this rabble get you down. They're trouble enough without a visitor. Heaven knows what they'll be like now we have one for the first time in our history.'

Magda almost went giddy with delight. A visitor! Like when that cleric arrived at the Bennet house and Mr Bennet had to receive him in his study! Just for one moment she thought, this is really happening to me!

Jean came flying in and said hello. Her hair was different. 'Come and see what we have ready.'

They went into the kitchen, Dad calling after them that Magda would be more interested in hearing about his engine than any old women's chatterboxing, but they just laughed. At their father! Magda felt nothing but amazement and doubt.

As Mrs MacIlwam brewed tea and poured for Magda, she explained about Kev's dad working on the trains. He used to travel a deal, but now nothing like so much. He worked in some engine centre, easier on his time.

'Even when he comes home he's fiddling with that toy,' Jean said.

From the front room came a shout, 'Don't say toy! It's a model.'

'It's an old toy engine,' Marla agreed without a care. 'Child's game.'

'I can hear you!'

'Shhh,' Magda said, desperate.

They only laughed. 'Ignore him,' Beth said. 'Marla's right. A grown man, too!'

'Do you cook at home, Magda?' Mrs MacIlwam asked. 'We're doing lamb and roasted potatoes.'

'I have a Baby Belling thing,' Magda admitted. 'There's only me, see?'

'Haven't you brothers and sisters?'

'No. I was an orphan.' She said it outright, bold as brass, readying herself to be asked to leave because she was the product of a sinful liaison.

'What a shame!' Marla said. 'That's awful.'

'You poor thing,' Beth said. 'Well, never mind. You can share us for the whilst.'

'I was a Magdalene girl.'

Even this did not faze them. Marla nodded. 'Kev told Dad that. Dad said you're to have the top brick off the chimney for braving that lot.'

Magda stared round the kitchen. It was plain, with just a sink, an old-fashioned kitchen range with a fire, and an iron oven of the sort she had seen illustrated in one of the Charles Dickens TV serials. This looked authentic, but the family's words were extraordinary. So much disrespect around, or was it just casual and quite uncaring and even, she risked the thought, friendly?

'Was it bad?' Beth asked, anxious.

'Stop all that,' Mrs MacIlwam commanded. 'You know what I told you. No cross-examinations, the lot of you.'

'I only want to know.'

'So do I, Marla,' Beth said. 'Grampa's always on about the Industrial School and them Christian Brothers and the Rosimians—'

'That will do,' Mam said. 'Enough questions. Magda will be driven demented.'

'You know Grampa, Magda, don't you?'

'Yes. Except I'm only a cleaner. I don't do anything with his treatments, just clean and help in the kitchen sometimes.'

'Well, it's a job.'

'Magda worked in a paper packers, out of the Magdalenes,' Jean said.

Kev came in and took a mug of tea. Magda filled with admiration; him so full of confidence simply picking up a cup without even asking and putting his feet up on the chair's stretchers, braving all kinds of rebukes and abuse. Transgression was Sister St Paul's favourite sin.

'Was it hard?'

'Just ordinary.'

The question puzzled Magda. Hard? What sort of a question was that? As if your thoughts of it mattered. Like asking if life was all right or not. How could you answer?

Mrs MacIlwam talked of how she'd done the lamb, and how her mother had insisted on timing the cooking and getting the oven just right. Father came in wiping his hands on a rag and plonked himself down on a chair, feet up on anybody else's chair's stretchers and was given a mug of tea by his wife.

'I'm glad you're here, Magda,' he said.

'Thank you, Mr MacIlwam,' she said formally.

'Is Grampa much trouble?'

She took her time adjusting to the notion of Mr Liam MacIlwam being Grampa, perhaps even once having lived here in this very house.

'No trouble at all.'

'He says you are the kindest there.'

She felt her cheeks grow hot and Mrs MacIlwam exclaimed he was embarrassing the poor girl and to stop right there.

'What Dad means,' Jean translated without a blush, 'is that Grampa says you aren't cruel as them nuns.'

'Now, then.'

'It's true, Mam, isn't it?' Marla was indignant. 'Grampa says they're treated like prisoners.'

'It's the Church,' Beth said quite casually. She was buttering bread. 'We don't eat vegetables enough in Eire, do we? I have a friend who's gone veggie.'

'Vegetarian?' Kev was interested. 'Don't you get anaemic?'

'No, silly. They live longer, that's all.'

'Do they?' Marla asked. 'Do they, Mam?'

'Nobody knows whether they do or not.'

'It is the Church,' Beth said. 'Grampa says so. And he knew.'

'I escaped by the skin of my teeth,' Dad said. He was sent to clean his hands ready for the meal, and took his wife's order without demur, just telling Magda he'd be back and to watch his tea so that nobody else would drink from it.

The whole concourse of opinions and instructions, ignored or rebutted, confused Magda. She felt like crying because it was all too different.

'Escaped?' Magda wanted to know as he left.

'Tell you in a minute,' he said over his shoulder.

She kept an anxious eye on his mug of tea, almost reaching out to keep it safe when Marla took some bread and butter without asking.

'Make sure you eat the crust, Marla,' Mam said. 'It'll make your hair curl.'

'Do you have to curl yours, Magda?'

'No. It does it on its own.'

'Where do you go?'

'I do it myself.'

She explained how she didn't know how to go into a hairdresser's, and not being able to read or write properly.

Marla and Beth were fascinated.

'Oooh, Beth!' Marla cried. 'We can take her! Show you the ropes, Magda. There's a decent one near Little Mary Street that charges the earth, but they've started an offshoot that's half price on Wednesdays. We'll go there.'

'Stop it,' Mam ordered. 'You're bewildering the girl. Let her decide what to do in her own good time.'

'Grampa is very nice,' Magda put in, hoping to avert the looming war.

Kev cut in. 'He was raised in an Industrial School, Magda. He suffered a lot. He got away into a ship from the Maltebior School one day, just didn't go back when him and two other lads were out scrounging for things to eat.'

'Sailed away,' Marla said, proud.

'And stayed a ship's boy until he worked in England. He came back and got married. They had Dad.'

'Who,' Dad said, returning and waggling his clean fingers at his wife, who shook a fist in mock anger, smiling, 'was told never to trust a word of them old holy folk. He sent me to a school, me and my three sisters, where there was no religious teaching.'

'And Dad turned out the better for it.'

Magda looked about, aghast. No crucifix, no pictures of Christ in agony on the walls. None of the girls wore a cross. She felt as if she had emerged into a Wonderland with no Alice to guide her.

'That'll do about religion,' Mam said firmly. 'Come to the table everybody. Fingers.'

'Mam means wash our hands.'

'Inspection in one minute.'

Marla and Beth showed Magda to the bathroom and she diligently washed her hands. For some reason she felt close to tears. The family seemed so contented, for all their pretence of squabbling that wasn't squabbling at all. Was this how all families were, behind their doors and blind windows?

Magda was going to hold out her hands for inspection but Mam seemed to have forgotten her order. She was given a chair by Marla, who kept asking her about the Magdalenes until Dad said, 'That'll do, Marla', and she pulled a face at him and went unpunished. Marla was allowed to sit for the meal as if she had not shown the slightest defiance.

Grace Before Meals never came, though Magda waited. They started their dinner straight off. Kev saw Magda's hesitation and gave her a slight wink. She went red.

'We're not holy here, Magda,' he said with a grin.

'Kevin,' Mam said, serving, 'Magda will start believing you, and then what?'

'We'll be the better for it,' Dad said. 'Are they nice people in them rooms, Magda? Where you live?'

'I don't know many, Mr MacIlwam. There's one old lady, Mrs Shaughnessy, along the landing. The rent collector comes every Friday. There's somebody on the ground floor who plays a lot of music. I think they're two music students from Trinity College. One writer sings sometimes, they say he writes books but I've never seen him. On the ground floor. Then two women who work in a bank, and one who is a caterer. I don't know any of them to speak to.'

'Is that it? Who're your friends?'

'Nobody.'

Magda almost started to say she had a friend called Emily who worked sometimes at the St Cosmo, but now didn't even bother to come to work most days because she was going over the water to England to train as a veterinary nurse with animals. Faced with this family, though, it didn't seem much of a friendship.

'Well, there's plenty of time,' Mam said comfortably. 'There's plenty more, Magda, so start.'

Magda looked at the plated meal. It was gigantic. She'd never seen so much food on one plate. The lamb was in great slices, and four roasted potatoes, gravy and green cabbage pressed dry, and carrots. She was offered some vinegary liquid with leaves chopped up floating in it. Kev took it from Beth and spooned out some to drip it onto his own meat.

'I can't get enough of this mint,' he said. 'Oh, sorry, Magda. I grabbed it first.'

'Manners, Kev.'

'He was always a rude lad,' Dad said. 'No hope for some people.'

'Oh, he's very…'

Magda halted and Mam said quickly, 'Grampa is worried because somebody keeps losing some medicines, Magda. That's not the reason I was glad when Kev said he'd asked you here.'

'Thank you.'

'It's just that Grampa was a sniper during the war,' Kev said. 'So he notices things. Even when you think he's dozing, he's really awake in a bit of himself.'

'They called him Holer,' Mrs MacIlwam said. 'Didn't they, Dad?'

And Dad said, 'Yes. I believe he was very famous. I only learnt that from somebody who came up to him in the park while I was at the lads' football one Saturday.'

'He's got medals.'

'Doesn't like to talk about it. He told this chap, "No, you're mistaken. I was never in the wars." It's not true. Just he doesn't like talking about it.'

'Thanks for looking out for Grampa, Magda,' Kev said. 'I feel you're an ally in that old place.'

Magda was stunned. An ally and a visitor all in one day.

'I'm always frightened,' she said.

'Frightened?'

They were interested in that. Marla even stopped eating. Magda noticed how, despite their proximity to each other, none of them had need to guard their dinners from the rest. That was family, she supposed, or maybe that Mam and Dad were there to see it didn't happen.

'What of?'

'The nuns telling you off. They look after the old people.'

'Why are you scared, though?' Jean was indignant. 'They've no right.'

'If you get told off and it's not your fault, you just tell them to stuff their silly old job and walk out.' Beth glared round the table.

Mr MacIlwam said in a bland voice, 'Easy for us to say. Difficult for many.'

'I can't see why.'

'That'll do, Marla.' Mam made Marla keep quiet a second time and Marla became even more outraged, then started on about the prices they charged in supermarkets for meat these days, and how the costs were going up, Euros or not.

From there Kev started on the routes to get into Dublin, best on a Sunday for bus and train services. Marla grumbled about the buses she had to take to school. Beth said it was all the same to her because she was going to work in a video shop selling videos, and then would be promoted and make TV films. Magda admired their bravery and said so. Beth said it wasn't bravery, it was taking opportunities.

Marla asked how Magda managed, not being able to read, and kept on despite the warning signals from her mother. Magda told her of her many tricks, such as pretending she'd hurt her hand for a signature, then the business with the bank card and her wages, and then about telephones she didn't know how to use. Marla thought it lovely, really sweet. Beth and Jean decided Magda was clever. Magda had never told these things before, not to anyone.

Dad blamed them nuns, and said the only way out of the Pit of Despond, which Magda had of course heard about, was for Eire to go socialist and get rid of the Church altogether. Kev grinned at that and said, sorry, it was one of Dad's soap boxes, and that when Eire did vote for a socialist Dail everybody would have to do model engineering for a hobby. Everybody laughed at that, even Dad, just when Magda was waiting for his explosion of anger.

'Ignore them, Magda,' Dad said. 'Have some more or you'll starve to death in this house.'

'Toy trains will be compulsory in school,' Kev said.

'You can laugh, son.' And the father confided to Magda, 'My ambition is to make a scale model of the *Great Eastern*, Isambard Kingdom Brunel's wonder of the world. I'd start with a scale model outlined in wood before tackling the metal components...'

'Hello,' Kev said. 'That's torn it. Off we go.'

His family groaned as one.

Beth said, 'We've had it now. He'll not stop his old yakking now until it's dark.'

The family meal frittered itself in mild squabbles until it was time to leave. Magda was shown back to the bathroom by Beth, and when she came down, worried she hadn't been polite by using the loo when Kev was waiting to take her to the bus stop, nobody seemed to think it was anything out of the ordinary. It was an astonishment.

Magda said her goodbyes as well as she could without going on too much. Mrs MacIlwam said it had been a pleasure to welcome her and she hoped she would see Magda again soon.

Kev took her to the bus stop and waited with her, telling her about his sisters and how they came to be living in that house and everything. She got the bus after a lovely wait, and that was the end of her visit to a real live family and a Dad who didn't fight or hit her and a Mam who didn't shriek or hit her and their children who weren't being taken away to prison and who talked about doing her hair and making models from tin.

She thought it was the most marvellous experience in the world, and she their ally and visitor all at one go.

Chapter Twenty-Four

Waking was a double thing, unreality first, followed by a sense of wonderment. Father Doran could not think for a moment. The five senses kicked in, the distinctions of sight, sound, touch first, then he knew taste, and finally smell with the overpowering anonymity of hospital scents. And at last the senses cobbled him together.

With a sombre awareness of something not quite right, he took in the room, the window looking into the hospital corridor, the green sheen on the ceiling where monitors showed they were still supervising away, beyond the mere few senses God had started *Homo sapiens* off with. They were in charge, technology sneering at the Almighty, You did whatever You could, with paltry tools and the minuscule imagination of the neophyte, but now, Friend, You are superfluous. You might think You have a place in all this technology, but You are done for, God.

It could go on, this computerised world of know-how that religion had to eschew, unite with, or condemn. No means of redress, if you thought yourself hard done by. Nothing you could argue would benefit you more, because it wouldn't, it can't and it won't. The harsh world will see to that. The technical computer world was controlling this defective organism made in God's own image. Society now refuses to acknowledge that He made it, and people refuse to give thanks on their knees to God.

That might be it, for all the sense it made to Father Doran lying there staring about. He was afraid to move. The last time he had been in this position – waking in territory unknown, in a state of dependence and impotence – was in the sick room at the St Cosmo Care Home, with that idiot girl seated across from him and himself unable even to see her.

He remembered with sickening directness how she moved and talked...about what? Something about a girl. Or something even vaguer, with him lying there baffled and becoming really rather frightened. Then, blessed moment of relief, the nun had walked in, come into his arc of view. He had been so relieved. The girl had gone.

The girl had brought him a drink, her with her strange glance. How curious that her look should be the very first memory coming into his mind. For he knew that he was in hospital. He could recapture, if he wanted, being seen off in the ambulance, the two paramedics – is that what they were called? – and the nun's voice, and somebody promising they would do a Novena for his certain recovery, so trusting.

The operation. He could remember nothing, he thought with relief. There were these tales, weren't there, of people waking up and actually hearing and even feeling surgeons talking and pulling and cutting...Dear God, what a horror. But was it real, with all this super technology busy flicking and bleeping and calling everybody's attention to the fact that the staff out there were actually superfluous to requirements? The miniaturised world of technocracy ruled. Whose requirements? Why, the computer's, for what the technology wanted was essential, and all else a monstrous irrelevance.

'Father Doran?'

His heart skipped a beat – well, perhaps not; it beat steadily under the iron control of gadgets, the centre of whose attention he was. No, no extrasystoles, just a twinge of anxiety.

A nurse in some kind of overall, her hair strapped to her head and globular spectacles and flex clamped to her chin.

'You've done well, Father Doran.'

'I have?'

But he had done nothing except lie supine while they slit and tinkered with his heart then handed him over to these machines.

'And you're going to do better.'

'Thank you for all you've done, Nurse.'

'Moira,' she said. 'It's all first names now.'

'Me included?'

She laughed, checking the arrangement of some tube thing and several wires, dabbing her fingers at a console behind his head.

'Not those connected to the Almighty, Father, no. We're not that pushy.'

'Yet,' he said, an attempt at humour that merely got a nod.

'Heard about the robot surgeons? They have them in London and the USA. The surgeon just sits in a glass bowl and watches the robot do the business. It'll come, Father, it'll come.'

'Then what?'

'Then we can all go on holiday with the boyfriend.'

'Can I have a drink of something?'

'Maybe in an hour. I'll be right here. None of this in-and-out business like it used to be.' She laughed again, adding, 'Make sure we get you well enough to get shut of you.'

It was evidently her standard joke, and he smiled. He was surprised to find he had a tube in his nose, and another in his mouth making a hissing noise.

'There've been messages for you. Bishop MacGrath called from the diocese. The people at the St Cosmo, a Sister Stephanie, and others. They are on the locker there.'

'Thank you.'

'Masses being said for you.'

'So kind.' He began to feel a little dreamy. This was always a dangerous state, meaning risky for morality, not health.

'The doctor says you can have fluid by mouth in an hour, so we'll drag you up from your pit there and set you going.'

'Going?'

'None of this lying about for days at a time after surgery, Father. Don't think it's going to be easy. You're up and about almost as soon as you're awake these days.'

'You mean today?'

She laughed again. He liked Moira.

'Certainly. No exceptions, Father. You'll start today, no mistake.'

'Thank you.'

He dozed and went through a few daydreams until she came back. He could not believe it was a whole hour. The fluid was bland, tasted like nothing more than water and seemed far too much, but he drank obediently and was lifted by two nurses into a semi-recumbent position. He could see through the long window into the hospital corridor, people passing, nurses pausing, banks of monitors on the walls.

'Your notices of banns and births.' Moira, joking as usual, pointing to the bedside locker. 'Keep up your fluids, or we'll catch it from the surgeons. They're doing their rounds thirty minutes from now.'

'Am I getting on all right?'

'You're fine, Father. No worries, our Australian registrar's always saying. Like we're worried sick until he says his old catch-phrase.'

'I'm grateful.'

'Don't say it. We nurses pull the wool over the doctors' eyes pretending we've done everything they told us to.'

Another of her jokes. He moved and grimaced. His chest was starting to hurt. She caught it and said he'd have that for quite a few days.

'Once the physiotherapists get in, that'll be the end of you.'

'Today?' he asked, alarmed.

'Tomorrow you'll end this idleness and abandon. In your state, you might never make it. They're formidable people, them old physios.'

He found her jokes somewhat wearing but smiled gamely along.

'Thanks for all you do, Moira.'

She indicated the sheaf of messages on the locker and left, promising to be no further than the window. He watched her go through and perch at the counter to deal with a keyboard. Everything was keyboards and monitor screens.

It was a relief to get to handwritten messages.

He opened the first and read. So kind of people to think of him. Soon to be out and back in circulation? Strange how those waking thoughts had deceived him into imagining all sorts. He recalled his five senses, trying to collect his thoughts about the order in which they governed awareness. Were we nothing more than an organism somehow developed, presumably by this evolution mechanism of survival of the fittest, into a being with philosophy, memory, the ability to comprehend the workings of the mind and to understand the soul? Odd that one should revert so. Presumably God had left this tendency there as a reminder of mortality. Human beings were always vulnerable and, being so, could not hope for any further advancement unless God Himself entered into the scheme of things.

He said a short prayer, choosing the humble prayer from the Compline, *Salva nos, Domine, vigilantes*...asking to be saved while awake and to be guarded while asleep.

He had difficulty managing the cards and notes off the locker, with the wires trailing from his chest. Avoiding looking at his dressings in case they made him queasy, he decided to read through them all later. He felt better, but it was right to re-commence his duties, as a small thanks to the Almighty for making him well again.

Magda woke in her bed-sitter. The day filled her full of new resolutions. She would somehow learn to read and write, though the terror of doing such a thing brought all her fears back. Fear of the classroom, of nuns, of punishments, of the way she had been so often left out because she was thick and stupid and never going to amount to anything, being an orphan.

On duty today, because somebody was going somewhere and they were a nurse short. She and Mrs Brady from the polishing were due to do floor work.

Glad to be told she was on time arriving at the St Cosmo, Magda started working out, while she took the mop (no queuing rows to get mops in first on Sundays), how she knew it was time to be at work. The buses tended to come along at regular intervals. Another clue was what people said to each other, 'Ooh, I'm nearly late this morning, what with our Jamie's leg,' that kind of thing. Then teams, going out to Mass already carrying football kits so they could go straight to the pitch and start their hooting and hollering after some stupid ball. And she could ask the time, if she had a clue what the numbers meant. Half-past something was her great favourite, because it always meant she was maybe in time for work. The rule was, she started work on the hour sharp, and half-past something meant early or late. She had once arrived in tears and terrified because her half-past had let her down something awful, being late. She got less money that week, and Mrs O'Hare had explained to her, maybe guessing she hadn't a notion in her head, that it only meant you were not punished in any other way.

And Mrs O'Hare had said afterwards, thinking Magda out of hearing, 'Poor girl thinks everybody's out to give her a thrashing. Let anybody try it on me, they'd get a seeing to. My daft auld husband'd be at them with both fists and elbows out, sure to God.' And Mrs Doherty from the kitchen said, 'I blame them Magdalenes.' They agreed it was the nuns' fault, yet still they went to Mass, which proved things should stay as they were. You had to agree with the whole world.

Armed with these clues, Magda decided on vigilance as a means of learning. She would look at the clock, this time staring at the clock and trying to keep the numbers in her mind. They seemed odd, the first time she tried it this morning, because they were all straight lines. Those on Mr Liam MacIlwam's clock were curled, except for some. It was strange. She wondered if they told different times.

She couldn't feel the same towards Mr Liam MacIlwam since she had been a visitor at his house and met by his grandson Kev from off the bus. And just knowing that his son, Kev's father, made tin toys on an oil soaked board while his grandchildren pulled their father's leg without mercy. The family only pretended to get cross when they were really amused by the whole thing. That experience, so new, made Magda proud – though pride was a sin so you had to watch it. Did she now have friends? The image of friendship caused her to almost keel over with pride, which had to be curtailed. Realising you had pride meant you had to end thinking in that fashion.

'One, two, three,' she knew, from hearing them said, but which was which? Was it the straight numbers she was saying, or the bent ones?

She gave up, for the moment. She had to make her friends think she wasn't just giving in. Dad MacIlwam back there with his tin toys – no, models – didn't give in when everybody laughed because he was a grown man. No, he got on with it. Sooner or later he'd set to, making that *Great Eastern* thing, and Magda knew the world would be a better place for it. Also, there was this strange conviction: if there was half a chance, even, of Dad MacIlwam's daughters Beth and Marla and Jean helping their father to make that thing, even though they pulled faces, Magda knew they would all try their very best. The fact that he'd be delighted must make it, to them, worthwhile. And Kev too.

And if she wanted any more proof, you'd only to look at the way they called after her on the doorsteps, 'Thanks for looking after Grampa,' which set her eyes leaking wet down her face just like Kev's that day.

Who knew? If she learnt to write and read lettering on a page so she could say it out loud quick as talking at a bus stop, she might be able to help Dad MacIlwam to make that model thing on his oily board, and make the world a better place. It would make her feel so grand.

'Here on Sunday, Magda?'

That was Mr Liam MacIlwam, talking with his eyes shut and making her jump. She'd been sweeping under his bed so quietly nobody could possibly hear. Except she now knew, from being in his house as Kev's guest at dinner, that he was Holer who always was a bit awake from shooting enemy people even when everybody else was fast asleep.

'Yes, Mr MacIlwam. Sorry I woke you.'

'It's only half-eleven. Is tea there?'

He knew it wasn't, but now she knew he knew. She instantly worried he might know she had been the one stealing the tablets, and that she was the one who had almost killed Father Doran and put him into hospital with the surgeons' knives hacking away at him. And worse to relate was this: poor Lucy had fallen again last night just as she had ever since Magda and Lucy had been together in the Sandyhills Magdalenes.

'Not yet. I was going to bring yours the minute I finish round here.'

'Thank you for looking after me.'

'Not at all, Mr MacIlwam,' she said formally. 'Anything I can do, please ask.'

It was straight out of, what, *The Barchester Chronicles*? She wasn't sure, because without lettering them stories all blended in. She wondered if somebody from Mr Liam MacIlwam's family had spoken to him earlier, because they were allowed to telephone sometimes.

'Have you heard how Father Doran is, Magda?'

'No!'

'I heard he's improving.'

'I know.'

Mr Liam MacIlwam opened his eyes. He seemed almost amused.

'Did you ask after him at the hospital?'

'Yes.'

'He was doing all right, eh?'

'Yes.'

'I'm gasping for a cuppa.'

'I'll get it now.'

'Have Ted and George already had theirs?'

'Yes. I gave it them earlier.'

'You're a good girl, Magda,' Mr Liam MacIlwam said comfortably. 'Don't let anybody tell you different.'

'Thank you, Mr MacIlwam.'

'Anything you want?'

She could have sworn he was being roguish, this wicked old man who pretended he wasn't somebody everybody who'd been a war soldier knew about. He was somebody famous for doing the oddest things, like crouching among rubble to kill somebody else and pooing his pants. It didn't seem rational, when there was freedom out there, for a start.

'Yes, Mr MacIlwam.'

'What is it?' He grinned, closing his eyes for comfort. 'Not that I've got much.'

Magda had noticed that people going to tell the truth closed their eyes, like, here goes and I'm hiding from your face when the words hit.

'I want to read.'

'Read what?'

'Lettering. Books. Numbers on a clock.' She knew she sounded miserable. 'Anything, really.'

'Easy as pie. There are folk who do nothing but how to teach people that stuff. It's free, too. Any evening class'll do it for you.'

'I'm old.'

His eyes opened and he laughed, really laughed so he set himself coughing and she had to bang his back. 'You're a titch, Magda, that's what you are. Barely out of the egg, and you're old? This is old.'

He made a comical face, drawing his neck down like a chicken so she had to laugh, looking round with guilt in case somebody heard her and she got told off.

'Where do I go, then?' she asked, right out, bold as brass.

'Ask anybody, they'll tell you.'

Thrilled by knowledge – for that's what this gem was, pure knowledge – she thanked him and went to put her things away and wash her hands and fetch his tea.

The nuns were coming from the chapel as she came back with it. She could hear their footfalls on the polished corridor. She guessed the clock would strike soon, bongs with long intervals between. There always seemed more bongs in the middle of the day than any other time. She wondered if one was half-past anything. Pretty soon she might know that, and even the numbers round the clock faces. Some, though, wouldn't you just know it, had faces with no numbers at all, just dots the clock's fingers pointed at.

Prayers would be said for Father Doran at three-thirty, Sister Stephanie told Magda a moment later. Everybody on the staff would attend. Magda said 'Yes, Sister,' and so the day was ordered. All society needed order, and continuity gave the world peace. It could not be upset without grave consequences. Magda knew that was so. God had made society in His own image of Heaven, if only we behaved as He intended. It was a long job, sure enough, but once she was in the learning school she'd help to straighten her bit of disorder, and make the rest of the world all right.

Chapter Twenty-Five

They prayed for Father Doran, the intercom scratching out the prayer for the sick.

'It's all a waste of time,' Mrs O'Hare said under her breath to Magda as they stood in the utilities sluice, saying the words with Sister Stephanie's voice.

'What is?'

'He's going to get better, isn't he?'

'Is he?'

Magda fervently hoped so. She had done her best to make reparation for her terrible sin of poisoning him, but it was still a horror that, oddly, did not replace Lucy's ghastly fall each night. Magda found that strange. You'd think that a real sin, such as murdering a priest, a man of the cloth, just to help a ghost that was in difficulties, would take precedence over what...over (Magda steeled herself), over what had happened that night. You couldn't even think about it in the daytime, but in the lantern hours it became so truly awful it stopped you doing anything else except watch.

'Course. He is a priest, isn't he?'

'Do they always get better?'

'No,' said Mrs Mulready, sent in for special work on the movable posh furniture because the bishop might come the following week. This was her special job, and she was seen as an interloper from the cabinet maker's shop down Temple Bar. Mrs Mulready considered herself a cut above the rest of humanity. The resident ones grumbled that Mrs Mulready didn't do anything the other cleaners couldn't do. It was putting them down, bringing in this snotty nosed cow. Magda didn't mind, because the lady must know an enormous range of things about furniture, such as, did furnishings need special polish or didn't they? That sort of thing you saw on antiques shows on early evening TV.

'Don't they?' Magda was in doubt. God would be bound to take a priest to Heaven, so it was all right.

'No,' said Mrs O'Donahue. She was unhappy at having been brought in to do the ordinary clearning work before Mrs Mulready did her stuff, for Mrs Mulready hated having to actually move furniture before she started her special polishing. 'Look at Father Kilfoyle.'

'Who?' Magda asked, not knowing any Father Kilfoyle.

'He came in here to be an oldie,' Mrs O'Donahue said, ignoring the looks darted at her by other cleaners.

'Well, that's all over,' Mrs O'Hare said.

'It's over for Father Kilfoyle all right.'

'What happened to Father Kilfoyle?' Magda asked.

The prayers were continuing over the loudspeaker for Father Doran but the women had stopped saying them, more interested in the argument being worked up in the sluice room.

'He died of a sudden, in that side ward where they do the flowers.'

'When?'

'Some time since.'

'What of?'

'Magda,' Mrs O'Hare said sharply. 'That will do. We ought to be praying for the poor Father Doran.'

'He died so sudden the Gardai came,' Mrs O'Donahue said. She was one of those women who secretly liked a good row, and would pick at something until it unravelled into open conflict.

'Did they?' Magda asked, wide of eye and wondering if one was Sergeant Bernard or even Kev.

'They did. Asked us all what went on.'

Mrs O'Donahue grinned, tossing her head, like she was saying them Gardai should mind their own business.

'Like they had a right to know every little thing.'

'They do,' Magda said. She had never heard people say anything like this before. It was just as strange as visiting Kev's house for dinner, everything the wrong way round, but this time queer instead of nice.

'They just think they do,' Mrs O'Donahue said sharply. 'They ask too many questions.'

Magda shut up at that because criticism was always aimed at her.

'It's best forgot,' Mrs O'Hare said.

'As long as it was all above board,' said Mrs Mulready.

She was inspecting her cloths and special polishes that she brought in a box with a curved wooden handle, but Magda knew she was only pretending. Magda wanted to know what had happened to Father Kilfoyle.

'I think we should pray for Father Doran,' Magda offered nervously, for peace.

'I think we should, too.'

'Father Kilfoyle came here to be in a place where he got respect,' Mrs O'Hare told them just as Mrs Cussen came in, singing the hymn *Now With The Fast-Departing Light, Maker Of All!* that was just starting with Sister Francesca on the piano in the chapel.

'Respect? Father Kilfoyle is it?'

Mrs Cussen had a son who played football for some team in England far away, so she couldn't be touched whatever she said or even did. Magda really admired Mrs Cussen because she sometimes swore, which was really terrible and would incur unimaginable penalties when she died, but she said when anybody pointed this out – as Magda once had, trying to save her from Purgatory – 'Like I should care, with my back?' And she'd go on about her bad back for hours if you let her, and from there to her varicose veins, to which she was a martyr. Mrs Cussen went to Wales where she stayed with her son's girlfriend, a Welsh virago who was often drunk and whose photograph got into the papers for it, but you daren't tell Mrs Cussen it was improper behaviour or she went mad.

'Well he did,' Mrs O'Donahue said. 'Father Kilfoyle told me that himself.'

'Didn't get his old respect, then,' Mrs Cussen said with a wink at Magda. Magda was shocked by that, because it suggested something had gone wrong with poor Father Kilfoyle, subject of an investigation by the Gardai. 'Only in here.'

'That'll do, Millie,' Mrs O'Hare said in a warning voice.

'I've got to get on.' Mrs Mulready gathered up her box and left the sluice, taking her list of furniture with her. She was uneasy, Magda knew, and alarmed at the turn the conversation was taking. 'See you later.'

'Not waiting for the end of the service?' Mrs O'Donahue said quietly after her, knowing she spoke too softly to be heard by the departing polisher. Then she laughed to herself, getting her mops in line for a double wash and rinse after the grime was squirted out. Magda had copied her method when coming here first because it worked best. Rinsing alone didn't do half as well. You could learn a lot from the older women.

'You can't blame him,' Mrs Cussen said. 'Not really.'

'Who?'

'Whoever made the mistake.'

'Nobody would, in their right mind.'

'Are the prayers for Father Kilfoyle too?'

'Best if you don't mention Father Kilfoyle, Magda.'

'Was he very sad at the finish?'

Mrs O'Donahue barked a laugh. 'He didn't know when the finish was, girl. It come far too sudden, and that's the truth.'

'I mean the mistake,' Magda said, not wanting to pry if it was too sad to remember.

'Look, Magda,' Mrs Cussen said, as if she'd suddenly lost patience. 'You being a simple girl, you've got to realise not everything is as it seems. You Magdalenes know to keep your mouth shut.'

It began to frighten Magda, like when her first period came and she was petrified because another girl in her class who it happened to had been beaten something terrible for having blood down her legs and on her clothes when she couldn't do anything about it. It was there, coming up ahead like maybe tomorrow and nobody to ask or tell you what to do, and knowing you'd get blamed for being dirty and the girls all white and frightened too because they remembered their first time or it was to come. Magda had prayed to Mary to tell Jesus she should like to die, please, before it all happened, but Jesus had spared her for a life after the Magdalenes, out here among the strangest things.

Magda would have said she didn't understand, if she'd been talking to Kev or maybe the old lady along the landing, or even maybe Mr Liam MacIlwam with his tendency to smile when he was supposed to sleep.

'About Father Kilfoyle?'

'That's your man.'

'Was it before I come here?'

'Sure it was, girl. Nothing to do with you.' She banged a pail across the sluice sink and started the tap running. Mrs O'Hare tutted in annoyance because the prayers for Father Doran were still going on the loudspeaker. They were all supposed to be praying along.

'I'm sorry.'

'Don't be sorry.' Mrs O'Donahue gave that muted cackle and slowed the tap down to make the sound quieter. 'Nobody else was, except them old Gardai.'

'They went on for days,' Mrs O'Hare put in.

'It was a mistake, see? Anybody asks you, Magda, you know nothing except you heard maybe somebody made a mistake.'

Like I pretended to make that same mistake? Magda wanted to ask it out loud.

'Yes, Mrs O'Donahue,' she said.

'It was somebody pulled the tube out of his throat, see? Or it fell out. Or somebody forgot to leave the red emergency button within reach.'

'And did Father Kilfoyle...?'

'About seven in the morning when the day shift started in.'

'Was he worse?'

'He was dead, girl. Sister Stephanie was pale as death herself. Everybody was lined up like in them fillums where they identify the murderer.'

Magda's hand crept to her throat. She would rather be singing hymns than listening to this.

'They said somebody might have done it deliberately.'

'And had they?' *Like me?*

'Nobody knows.'

'It couldn't have been,' Mrs Cussen said with a hard look at Mrs O'Donahue, 'could it? Who on earth would be so cruel, to hurt a poor old man in a care home?'

'No,' Magda said fervently. 'Course not.'

'Then there you go.'

'You mustn't be so frightened,' Mrs O'Donahue told Magda. 'You can talk yourself into being so scared you're too worried to do anything. It's no way to be.'

'The word was,' Mrs Cussen said, 'that somebody in the St Cosmo had—'

'Now, then,' Mrs O'Hare said.

'The word was,' Mrs Cussen said in defiance, 'that somebody had known Father Kilfoyle when he was the priest in Winterhills.'

'And they didn't forget things that happened there.'

'It was for girls.'

'Sisters of Mercy ran it.' Mrs Cussen stopped everything and stared into space. 'It seems unreal, things the old ladies tell me about that place. Some outside girls went to the same school as the orphans. What must they have thought, being taught along of all them little scarecrows?'

'They got punished a lot, Magda. That's what Mrs Cussen means.'

'And worked to death. It wouldn't happen except with religion.'

'Mrs O'Donahue!'

'It's true.'

'That's enough, now.'

Magda tried to think where Father Kilfoyle must have been, in what alcove and what corridor.

'Did people reproach him?' she asked, picturing it in her mind, an old priest in bed, really sick with candles all round the panelled bedroom with relatives in their crinolines and gentlemen in their fine frock coats and lace ruffles at the throat like poetry. And Father Kilfoyle, feeling his hair stiffening on his head, like in the prayer for when you started to die, as it forebode your approaching end, would summon them round his death-bed and beg their forgiveness. And the most beautiful lady, who was some relative (couldn't be his long-lost daughter who was going to marry Mr Darcy or whoever in this grand house called Mandalay) would say tenderly, looking quite like Margaret Lockwood in *Madonna of the Seven Moons*, though she got up to no good with a raggle-taggle gypsy, 'Yes, Father Kilfoyle, I forgive you. Please do not suffer.' And the priest would know everything was all right now and peacefully die with images of his mother and father, such decent and hard-working folk, floating about and he would smile up at them and his soul would wing its way to Heaven.

'They didn't need to, Magda.'

'He was told about it the day before.'

'Told about what?'

'That more than one person in here – I don't mean nuns, of course – remembered him only too well.'

But forgiveness, Magda almost cried out, and the floating images, and the ladies and gentlemen being really smiling and forgiving all round his sick bed, what about them? She said nothing.

'No good grieving, girl. It can linger.'

'In some,' Mrs O'Hare said, 'not all.'

'Them as were there, it can.'

'So we've heard tell,' Mrs O'Hare said with determination, 'but don't go on about it.'

'Some of the men knew Father Kilfoyle from before, too.'

'It makes you wonder what goes on that nobody hears about.'

'I still don't agree, whoever it was did it. I mean, they could have reported him.'

'Like that would have done any good. They'd have sent him somewheres else. They always have, always will.'

The prayers ended then with the Glory be to the Father, and that was the end of the conversation. Magda wanted to know more about Father Kilfoyle, the visits of the Gardai, and knew she would never ask. What she had heard distressed her, though she didn't understand. Something bad had happened in the past, maybe someone on the staff here, or maybe the oldies. Shocking, that Father Kilfoyle arrived to become one of these same oldies, thinking he was entitled to respect only to get died.

It was touching, the notion of a safe harbour at the end of a long and serene life serving the Lord. Magda filled up. Mrs Cussen misunderstood and put her arm round Magda.

'Look, girl. Memories are long in Eire. Things happened when people were small, and you don't tend to forget. Ask anybody. Don't get upset.'

'I'm not, Mrs Cussen.'

'That's good, Magda. If somebody here pulled that wicked old bastard's tubes out so he choked to death, well, serve him right for what he'd done to them children. That's what I say. If the law doesn't do what it should, then people will.'

'People?' Magda asked, thinking, what is Mrs Cussen saying?

'Children grow up, and if they take it into their heads to take revenge, then there's no power on earth'll stop them if they've a mind. And who's to stop them anyway? It's maybe the only right thing. That's the way to see it, Magda.'

'The only right thing?'

'There, now. Talk over. Them old prayers have shut up, thanks be to God. Time we got on ourselves, or we'll be for it from them old black bats.'

In a daze, Magda went to put her floor things away and collect her polishing stuff. She was so bemused she had to go back twice for the Mansion Polish and felt a fool. Mrs O'Hare laughed at her and said she'd forget her head next if it wasn't stuck on.

Chapter Twenty-Six

'Father Doran?' Nurse Gaffney woke him with a quiet smile in her voice.

He came to. He felt warm. Had he often felt snug? He did not think so. In a way, it was almost shameful to realise that it was this heart attack that had brought him to understand what folk called comforts. Perhaps it was something from his past, when as an infant he must have been wrapped in his blanket for parading out in his pram. They had done that at Killiney. He could just about remember the tap of the sea dotting his cheek as he looked at the waves there. A long strand, now so fashionable he believed, property developers hard at work.

'Not more fluids.' He pretended a groan. 'I'm waterlogged.'

'No. Visitors.'

He supposed it was the bishop, but saw the two standing there looking in through the picture window.

One was a plain woman with dark hair, not smartly dressed but definitely no casual passer-by. The man standing with her seemed not quite as tall as she, stocky, maybe even portly. Wavy hair, a little short of middle-aged, businesslike, intent on duty.

A passing doctor talking to a nurse who walked alongside did not even attract a glance. He felt a faint foreboding.

'Who are they?'

'Gardai.'

'I wasn't even in my car last night.'

She smiled at his joke. 'I think it's routine.'

'The surgeon hasn't left an instrument in me, has he?'

'They just want to ask you a few questions, Father. They won't take more than a few minutes.'

'Now?'

'The doctor says they can.'

'Very well.'

He was also curious. Often parishioners got up to all sorts of tricks that sometimes had to involve him. One of his regulars at weekday Mass had given an alibi – a robbery, supposedly armed – as presence at the service on a particular day. Mercifully, or perhaps not, Doran could not remember. The police accepted his word somewhat doubtfully, though it was honestly given. There had been other instances, several including shop-lifting by women, no men oddly enough, a statistic he learnt was commonplace.

He recognised neither of the two Gardai.

The nurse admitted them and gave them chairs, carefully positioned a distance away. Father Doran was propped up. He was able to sit up fairly well, though with discomfort. His chest had started to pull across, the pain stretching from armpit to armpit. It had alarmed him at first, but he was assured it was quite the regular thing.

'Morning, Father Doran. Hope this doesn't trouble you too much.'

'Good morning. Not at all. Anything I can do to help.'

'Good of you to see us.'

The woman spoke first, affability itself as she gestured to herself and her colleague.

'I'm Maria Finty. This is my senior, Joe Murragh. We've got to show you our ID. They're quite clean and not likely to contaminate your injury.'

'We're threatened with all kinds of punishment if we do,' Joe Murragh said, earning a mock grimace from the nurse as she left.

The two Gardai sat looking round at the array of gadgetry.

'How are you, Father?'

'As well as can be expected.' He made a slight joke of the response, glancing at his strapping on his exposed chest. 'I'd thought I was going to be cocooned in plastic, but they had me up the very first day after the operation.'

'Marvellous,' Maria Finty said. She looked the more gingerish of the two, as if it was her first visit to a hospital where serious work was done.

'Look, Father,' Joe Murragh began. 'The minute you get to feeling tired, you just say and we'll duck out.'

'We don't want to outstay our welcome.'

'The nurse won't let you,' Father Doran said lightly, now concerned.

'I'm sure.' Joe Murragh glanced at Maria and nodded.

She pulled out a notebook and consulted the first page she flipped open.

'We won't need to record this, Father, so feel free to say whatever.'

'Sounds very serious.' His bantering tone caused no appreciable slackening of their crouched attitude.

'The matter under consideration is the way you were suddenly taken ill, in so serious a manner that you needed rapid medical attention and care, and then transfer to hospital and heart surgery.'

'Well, quite. Out of the blue.'

'You never experienced any heart difficulty before of any kind?'

'No. I told the doctors all that. Dr Strathan was surprised, but managed me very well.'

'We have also spoken to the doctors here, Father,' Maria Finty said. She seemed the less worried of the two, Joe Murragh appearing uncomfortable at having to question a priest. 'They said we can ask for any kind of medical details, if you wish to divulge them.'

'Heavens, I'm not concealing anything. Nurse will bring you the data, if you can understand them.'

'Thank you.'

'Ask the doctors for my records. Feel free.'

Still no slackening of the tension in the two Gardai.

'When you were taken ill, was anyone on hand to help you?'

'Yes.' Doran was taken aback. It might have been the kind of thing detectives asked at the scene of a crime. He was almost amused. 'The sisters, the staff of St Cosmo Care Centre.'

'Nobody immediately there?'

'What *is* this?' He let his amusement show. 'It is an old folks' home, remember.'

'Yes, Father.'

Joe Murragh smiled at that, and nodded to Maria Finty to take up the thread. Doran felt it was something of an act, the sort when two detectives cross-questioned a suspect. But suspected of having done what, fallen ill?

'Who was first to help you?'

'I have little recollection. Ah, I believe it was Sister Stephanie. She is the senior nun at the St Cosmo.'

'What happened then?'

'I can't exactly recall. Is it important?'

'Anything you might be able to remember could be significant, Father.' Her notebook, that worrying implement, now came into play. Something in it made her brow clear. 'What is the last event that stays in your mind before you felt unable to move?'

'I think I had just come from one of the wards.'

'You remember which?'

'Yes. I spoke with several old folk. One was the second alcove, two old gentlemen there. The next one was a slightly larger area with two ladies. Then one old man on his own.'

'You had had tea with Sister Stephanie?'

'Yes.'

'What did you have?'

'Goodness.' He pondered. 'Tea, with milk. I try to keep away from sugar, but occasionally…' He would have shrugged to show an innocent failing, but did not dare for fear of pain. 'Piece of cake. Then I went to see the old folks.'

'You took nothing with them?'

'No.'

'Absolutely nothing?'

'They'd already had their tea.'

'The point is, Father,' Joe Murragh stirred with impatience, 'we spoke with one of the consultant physicians, the cardiac man, who was somewhat puzzled by the sudden onset of your symptoms. And the severity.'

'Well, heart attack.'

'Sure, but they commented, as Dr Strathan did, on the similarity of the symptoms to some kind of toxic substance.'

'Toxic? What does that mean?'

'Apparently the heart responded differently to various drugs.'

'*Drugs?*'

'Yes. Could it be possible that you unwittingly took something that might have brought on this attack?'

'I can't even begin to imagine.'

'You had nothing besides the tea Sister Stephanie gave you?'

'Nothing. Oh.' He smiled, self-indulgence. 'I had a drop from Mr Gorragher. He has a small bottle on occasion, and it's his fancy to provide me with a nip. He is so proud of it, and delights in my staying to talk a little of innocent memories. Against the cold, you understand.'

They relaxed somewhat as if they had reached the end of an approaching run.

'Mr Gorragher?'

Father Doran knew they had no need to write the name down.

'A very old gentleman. It seems unlikely that he will ever leave the Home.'

'We heard.'

'Did you notice anything unusual about the taste?'

'No. You surely can't think…? That's impossible.'

'Of course. We're just eliminating possibilities.'

'And,' Maria Finty put in, 'once we've done we can all go home and delete the file.'

'File?' Now Doran was startled. A file on his illness. Why, for Heaven's sake? 'Is there some possibility that there may have been some contaminant in somebody's drink?'

'It's remote, but Dr Strathan did make that comment when he first saw you.'

'He said nothing about it to me.'

'Well, of course he wouldn't. You were not in a condition to chat much.'

'I suppose not.'

'You were taken ill as you left the St Cosmo?'

'Yes. I felt a griping pain, as if I had eaten something that disagreed. Colic. I believe,' he offered helpfully, 'that suggests heart pain at first, particularly when it comes out of the blue.'

'And then?'

'I was taken to the sick room. I'm unclear about the actual details. A Nurse Tully was called to sit with me.'

'And the nuns, of course. Anyone else?'

'Oh, there was one girl, a trusted girl called Magda, one of the Magdalenes who now works in our establishments. She sat with me for a short time.'

Father Doran felt that same sense of misgiving he had when Magda spoke about her friend, some friend who had possibly not been treated well – could this memory be actually false? He could think back over how slightly shocked he had been when, possibly mistaking what the girl said, she had spoken of God maybe not playing fair with her friend who had died so sadly at some establishment. His memory of the conversation was fuzzy.

'Magda. Anybody else?'

They were compiling a list, Doran knew now. They were going to take this further, exploring the past. Had people, including the Gardai, nothing better to do?

'Not that I can recall, no.'

'Father.' Joe Murragh crossed his legs, sighing at the effort it seemed to cause him, or maybe his loss of concentration in a difficult moment. 'Look. Have you ever heard of any other event at the St Cosmo?'

'Event?' The twinge of apprehension recurred. Did he need a lawyer now? 'What event?'

'There was some business a while back. We investigated.'

'Could you remind me?'

'A very elderly priest was admitted there. He was ill, but the doctors cleared him to go to a final care home where he would have good nursing. Support systems, drugs and the like.'

'Ah, I do remember hearing about it, yes.'

'Father Kilfoyle, it was.'

'Didn't he die?'

'That was it.'

'He died,' Maria Finty said, the lightness having gone from her voice, 'when some obstruction happened. It was put down as an accident.'

'At first,' Joe Murragh added.

'Then it seemed the obstruction to Father Kilfoyle's airway was only part of the problem. Some fluid was misdirected into his vein.'

'It was almost as if the tube had been moved.'

'Deliberately?'

'We're not making that allegation, Father. We're commenting on the first notes Dr Strathan made at the time, and that he reported to the coroner when Father Kilfoyle was found dead.'

'Dr Strathan reported something odd about my heart attack?'

'Not really. He submitted his extensive notes to the cardiac unit when you were admitted here.'

'It's what usually happens.'

'Dr Strathan made no suggestions about foul play.'

From an innocent greeting of hello, to foul play and serious allegations all in a few minutes? Father Doran found events racing through his mind, but they were not quite in sequence as they ought to have been. Something kept intruding, as if a cinema reel was shaken up and the frames patterned out into kaleidoscopic images.

'Thank goodness for that.'

'Nor have the doctors here, Father.'

'That's a relief.'

He ignored the vision of a face, a glance, a darkness with another face, possibly asleep, across a room where there was only night's gloaming.

'Can you not be more specific?'

'I wish we could, Father. We have little to go on.'

'What are you implying?'

'We're trying hard not to imply anything at all, just examine events as they occurred. That is, the ones we know the sisters and the inmates of the St Cosmo Care Home can be sure of.'

'Have you ever felt any kind of animosity directed towards you at the home?'

'Certainly not. The people are all kindly.'

'And nobody has shown you the slightest resentment?'

'Nothing like that.'

'Do you know any of them from before you took up your appointment, Father?'

'No. At least, I don't think so.' He frowned, now becoming tired. 'You can never quite be certain. So many people in a parish, you understand, speak to you. You can't be absolutely positive.'

'We understand.'

'One can't always be bothered to try.'

'Try?' Maria Finty picked up.

'Try to recall where this face was seen last, where that person was when we previously spoke, that kind of thing.'

'Of course. We're the same.'

'Has anybody at the St Cosmo ever mentioned Father Kilfoyle to you?'

'No, pretty sure, no.'

'And you get on well with them?'

'Certainly.'

'Father Doran. Please don't mind if I ask this, only it's in the manual, sort of. Is there any event you might remember that could have any bearing on you, your career, your position?'

'What kind of thing?'

'Some criticism, perhaps, a disgruntled parishioner who could have misinterpreted something you once said or did?'

'I'm not at all sure of your meaning, Mr Murragh. Do you mean have I ever been guilty of a felony?'

'Nothing quite so serious.' The detective's eyes twinkled, and Father Doran suddenly realised, *This is a dangerous man; he isn't the placid Maria Finty, who is brought along merely to disarm whoever's being interrogated.* And it was an interrogation, not merely a few questions asked by a couple of people in for a chat about the crops and the weather. Not quite a cross-questioning, for then they would have brought a recording device. 'Only a bit of tidying up to do, then we can report, close the file, and all go off to the racing at Fairyhouse where Maria here loses all her ill-gotten gains.'

'Sad to hear it,' Father Doran said.

'Nothing we can put down in that particular column?' Joe Murragh said with finality.

'Nothing, no.'

'Where were you before here, Father?'

'I had rather a roving commission. I had been wondering exactly what direction my vocation was taking me, so I took a year as interlude. The hierarchy allowed me to take up duties in three different diocese.'

'You met a great many people in different locations?'

'Yes. I can let you have a list of the places, if you wish.'

'That would be fine, Father. Just to dot the i's and cross the t's. No need to hurry at all.'

He already has the list, Father Doran knew instantly. He envisioned a list on A4 paper, with pencilled notes from the scrupulous hand of Maria Finty and a covering letter from Bishop MacGrath, and knew Murragh was fishing away, seemingly idle. Would it be disarming to mention, quite casually, that several incidents had occurred at one or two places that could be open to misinterpretation? Harmless to admit them now, surely, in these cynical times when everything was subjected to appraisal by a press avid for concealed conspiracy. It was a sorry world.

'That was some time ago, was it? Or recently?'

So he knows that too, when and where.

'Oh, four years back, I think. From there I came to my parish here, and I must say I've enjoyed the experience very much. Hard work, of course, and unrelenting. But work done properly is never easy, or it has no merit at all.'

'Well, that's it, Father Doran.' The priest did not detect what signal passed between the two, but they instantly rose as if physically connected. 'We'll say goodbye and wish you well.'

'Do I have anything to worry about?'

Father Doran could have kicked himself, but judged it was not too serious a mistake. Maybe an innocent suffering from a sudden health setback such as his would naturally ask that kind of question, round the chat off.

'Only about doing what your doctors say.' Maria Finty smiled as they moved to the door and waved to the nurse outside.

'Don't let your blood pressure go wrong until we're out of sight, Father.' Joe Murragh did his innocent twinkle. 'Or we'll get blamed.'

'I'll take care.'

'See you do that.'

They said their goodbyes a second time, Father Doran waiting for a sudden parting question in the time-honoured routine of TV detectives, but they amiably passed from view. He noticed they did not head straight for the visitors' lifts, which lay along the corridor to the right, but to the left. He had come to think the doctors' offices and the nursing stations lay in that direction, but wasn't sure.

The nurse came in with complete unconcern, to check he was unruffled. She knew better than ask what they had come for. Church matters were confidential. He sank back, weary from the strain, and wondered about the sequence that he had tried to establish in his mind, the ones that kept intruding, not the ones forming the true pattern of memory. The possible interview between the bishop and the two Gardai was disturbing.

Whatever information they demanded, damaging events in the past were within the seal of the confessional, so he could forget them.

More relevant was the fleeting yet disturbing visual hint of someone's face, in a vast room with only gloaming to see by, and then a suggestion of a voice, familiar though far too recent to be connected with that episode of sombre shade where he had experienced such rapture.

'Still not going to go through all these letters and cards, Father Doran?' a nurse asked.

'Too tired,' he said hazily. 'Sorry.'

'It's a labour of love tidying them every time another load comes in. Do you know you have thirty-six?'

'Have you got nothing better to do than waste your time?'

'I know what the trouble is. You're trying to get out of answering them. Typical man, that's you.'

'That's me.'

He felt so sad, as if this oasis of peace was now ruined. He had never before felt such tranquillity. Except, he remembered now, there was always one episode of, what, a certain emotion that drew him over the dangerous reefs of passion and into the lagoon of sanctuary, but that was never to be spoken or thought of, just remembered as a period of paradisical calm in an ocean of turbulence.

'Getting out of going through them yet again, eh?' Nurse Gaffney's voice said, amused and distant.

'That's it.'

He dozed, but only after a time.

Chapter Twenty-Seven

Sister Stephanie received the Gardai at the front door. It was just twenty-past ten, and the St Cosmo Care home was preparing the morning drinks.

She was all restrained smiles, having been told the reason for their visit, and led them to her office without any casual good-morning talk. They declined a drink, which put her at a disadvantage. Providing authorities with some form of service always put them on the back foot. Some of the oldies in her care still used such phrases, derived from some competitive sport, she presumed, but not far from the actual truth.

'What can we do for you?' was the nearest she could come to disturbing their assertiveness.

'I'm Joe Murragh, and this is Maria Finty,' the man said, thanking her for inviting them to be seated.

He appeared quite at ease, benign even. Sister Stephanie instantly did not trust the woman. What kind of a name was Finty? It had connotations, perhaps, of Flint, the Flintshire county of North Wales, and the Welsh were all shiftless, notably Protestant, and therefore shop-soiled to say the least as well as shifty. She had heard them called worse, believing as they all did that their Lutheran, or worse, singing was the only religious caterwauling to be allowed. Despite the nun's misgivings, the woman seemed to have a genuine Irish accent and intonation when she finally deigned to utter.

'We wish to ask for details of events leading up to Father Doran's illness, Sister Stephanie,' she began.

Was it Kerry, perhaps? Sister Stephanie was a great believer in localities. A region conferred a character on the personality. It was an accurate guide as to how far a visitor would presume, always a source of knowledge about their willingness to compromise. Any form of give and take was, of course, out of the question where Holy Mother Church was concerned. The Church alone held truth. It was for others to adjust their own determinants, and even sacrifice them for the sake of progress. It was the same with punishment, physical and otherwise. Others had to learn, the Church to remain the same and impart guidance by whatever means thought fitting. People were presumptuous.

'Certainly,' Sister Stephanie cooed. 'Anything I can do to help.'

'Thank you,' but said grudgingly. Kerry now without a doubt, and that name was unquestionably one of those North Walean inbreds. 'Can I ask how Father Doran's incapacity first came to your attention?'

Official language was nothing like language, not truly. However, it had been perfectly correct for those English imbeciles who wrote the King James Version of the Bible to apologise for their imperfect use of ordinary speech of their times, considering they lacked the necessary flowery courtly speech their holy subject deserved. So far have we descended, she thought bitterly, that two scruffy clerks from the Gardai are sent to interrogate anyone they suppose might be able 'to assist them with their inquiries' as some illiterate whining woman had pleaded over the phone to herald the arrival of this pair. She noticed that the man's shoes were shabby, and the woman's hair looked unkempt. Was it fashion? Sister Stephanie concealed a sneer.

'He was about to leave, after speaking to the inmates. They always enjoy his company.'

'Is it a regular thing, to stop off, delay his departure, have a chat?'

'Part of his duties, Mr Murragh.'

'Course it is. Why wouldn't it be?'

Sister Stephanie now decided Joe Murragh was a deal too hearty for her liking. She coursed on, pausing frequently to show how intensely reflective she was on these details, getting everything right for them.

'He sits a while with Mr Gorragher?'

'I think so. I'm not exactly certain of the order in which he speaks to the old folk. Some of them have particular concerns they need advice on. You understand.'

'Certainly.' Maria Finty's brisker manner announced that she was here to make sure they got a move on. She might as well have said Sister Stephanie should cut the cackle, or some other vile Americanism. 'At the risk of seeming impatient, could I ask about this girl Magda?'

'A trusted girl, one of the cleaners. She came to us on a recommendation. She has worked well since being here. She is popular, though not terribly bright.' She brought the admission out like a dirty cloth, to be shown then quickly sent to the wash. 'She has no family. Just a charity girl from the Magdalenes.'

'Trusted, then.'

Not even a question, but Sister Stephanie answered as if it were. 'Yes.'

'Did she ever stand in for any of the nurses?'

'Stand in? For a qualified registered trained nurse? She did not. She sat with Father Doran so he wouldn't be left alone. It could only have been a minute or two, and my office is a pace away across the corridor.'

'Is that a usual practice?'

'When a sister of the Order is sick, we usually have one of the sisters watch over her during the late hours. In the circumstances, Father Doran was watched for mere minutes by Magda.'

'And he had his emergency device, I suppose?'

'We were all within earshot. And Magda is trustworthy.'

'No emergency system?'

Inevitably from Maria Finty, the question was levelled, not simply asked. The thought passed through Sister Stephanie's mind that here was a Protestant, even possibly some kind of Welsh Emmanuel Baptist. Her benignity shrank and hardened into anger.

'Yes, we do, of course. It is a simple press-and-release button. It was ready for Father Doran, should he need it.'

'Was it ever used?'

'No.'

'Could we have a list of all available staff?'

'Yes.'

'That's kind of you, Sister Stephanie.' Joe Murragh sensed the growing animosity but was unequal to the problem of preventing it.

'We shall need it immediately, please.'

'I shall get one.'

'That's kind of you.'

'Will there be anything else I can help you with?'

'Yes,' Maria Finty said without embellishment. 'This Magda. Home address and availability, please.'

'Very well.'

'We will want to ask her a few questions.'

'Of course.'

Sister Stephanie left. Joe Murragh said quietly to his colleague, 'Take it easy, Maria. No need to antagonise the sister. She's just upset.'

'She'll sit like a crow while we speak to this Magda girl, just you see. Directing every syllable the girl speaks.'

'Will you tackle the Father Kilfoyle business?'

'Oh, I'll do that all right. You just stand there with your two arms the one length.'

Joe Murragh smiled. He was always amused by Maria's localisms. Standing there with your foot tapping the hours, was another zinger, one of his favourites. Best of all was a phrase he sometimes asked Maria to insert into some report when the issue was particularly silly, to lighten the pedantry: 'So we proceeded in an orderly direction'. It had been used three times, undetected, and each time Maria got a free midday meal at Clancy's Bar. Others he sometimes persuaded her to use was, 'And we accordingly found the child lost...' Plus another winner, 'Arriving there, we asked if we were here.' Joe Murragh thought them hilarious. Maria called him a big child.

Magda heard the Gardai were in the Care Home just when she was about to leave duty.

It was after five, and she had said her prayers for the priest who was suffering because of her. Lucy had still not stopped falling in the night. Magda was going to have Masses said for Lucy's soul. It wasn't the first time she had done this. Now, she was forced into asking the priest at St Michael's to pray just for Lucy, whose soul was presumably fine there on the right hand, etc, and having meat every day except Friday, to stop her falling.

There was no way out now. If she had to divulge the details of what happened that terrible night and it got her sent into the Kilmainham Gaol to be killed stone dead in Inchicore Road, well, that was the will of Almighty God, so she'd have to take the consequence.

She stopped still when they told her.

'You've to talk to the Gardai, Magda.'

'Dear God.'

That was Mrs O'Hagan, who had started doing the evening shift and whose two daughters were a tribulation because of their fecklessness. They stayed out ('west of Grafton Street at their ages, can you imagine?') and got into bad company. They got with boys, told lies and tales. So many options came from way back in Catholic training that you were spoilt for choice. Mrs O'Hagan's two daughters had all these wicked foibles plus several more that couldn't be mentioned in the presence of an unmarried girl like Magda. Straight out of the Magdalenes, Magda would be likely to get in trouble herself if she heard how things were done. The stout blowing lady, always in the same tabard, used every invocation to saints of any stripe, begging them to intercede and put a stop to her girls' behaviour.

'Don't worry, Magda. It'll just be them wanting to know how he started being poorly.'

'That's the trouble.'

'What trouble?' Mrs O'Hagan knew of only one kind of trouble, and that was whatever her daughters were doing west of Grafton Street.

'I might not know,' Magda said feebly, trying for a lie that didn't quite make it.

'Then tell them that.'

Mrs O'Hagan was loading the washing machines and having a hard time. Magda delayed her questions by stopping to help, making sure the washing was all unfolded in the correct way before each item was put into the machines. They had two machines only, not enough for so many inmates, all with problems that had to be catered for. When two or more soiled their bed linen, things got delayed and the machines were on the go all day long. The difficulty was that each machine simply stopped once it overheated, and when stopped could not be made to work for quite an hour at least. Magda knew it was an hour because it was when the tops became cold and you could feel the machines going chilled round the back. They would then start up if you pressed the right knobs.

'What will they do to me?'

'Don't take on, darling.'

Mrs O'Hagan was not without sympathy. She had a special feel for Magda, seeing the girl as somebody without anybody to worry over her in the same way she worried herself sick over her two daughters. It wasn't as if Magda had a mother who was driven to distraction and who lived in terror of going home one evening to find her daughters white from pregnancy and her husband Pat from the DART tracks waiting with blood on his eye going to kill you stone dead because your two feckless daughters had got themselves pregnant against the walls back of Grafton Street or, worse, against the walls of St Audben's

Church, a place of well known harlotry of a night. St Audben's was not of the true Faith, of course, bring Proddy.

'Will you come with me, Mrs O'Hagan?'

'Bless you, child, I'd come like a shot if they let me.'

'No.' Sister Francesca appeared suddenly, something she was prone to do and in silence. Mrs O'Hagan didn't like Sister Francesca for this sinister habit. 'On your own, Magda.'

'Yes, Sister Francesca.'

'Shall I get on with this, then?' Mrs O'Hagan tried bravely.

'Please do. Come with me, Magda.'

'Yes, Sister Francesca.'

'Sister Stephanie will be present throughout, so you've no reason to worry, Magda.'

'Yes, Sister Francesca.'

'I'll be here, Magda,' Mrs O'Hagan called after them, for comfort.

The nun rounded on the washerwoman. 'Magda is going to have a talk with the Gardai over small matters of detail, to help Father Doran in his illness, not to be punished, Mrs O'Hagan. Please do not imply that she is going to be sanctioned.'

'Yes, Sister Francesca.'

They entered the room, only Joe Murragh rising. Maria Finty gave Magda a smile, not even glancing towards the nun.

'We are from the Gardai, but don't take any notice of that, Magda.'

'Please sit down. We'll be hardly any time at all.'

'Magda,' Maria Finty started even before Sister Stephanie had seated herself. 'You helped when Father Doran was taken ill, didn't you?'

Magda glanced at Sister Stephanie, who started to speak but was interrupted by the Finty woman.

'You remember when he was taken ill, don't you?'

'Yes.'

'Where were you when you heard?'

'I'm not sure. I'd just been to take the old folks' drinks, cups and things, away. Father Doran talked to them.'

'Did you stay and hear what they said?'

'No!' She looked at Sister Stephanie. 'I didn't, Sister.'

'It's all right,' Maria Finty said. 'I'm glad you can remember. And when Father Doran was in the sick room upstairs, you sat with him while Sister Francesca went to wait for the doctor?'

'Yes.'

'And any other time?'

'No.'

'What did you do, Magda?'

'Do?'

'You stayed in the sick room while the sister went downstairs?'

'Yes. I just sat there. I hadn't been told to do anything.'

'Nothing? You didn't give him anything?'

'No. I hadn't been told. Father Doran was just lying there.'

'Was he asleep?'

'No. He talked.'

'What about?'

'He asked me things.'

'Can you remember what things he asked about?'

'He asked where I was from, the school, that kind of thing.'

'Anything else?'

'No.'

'What did you tell him about?'

'Where I lived, at school.'

'Where was that, Magda?'

'Sandyhills. The Magdalenes.'

'Father Doran was there once, some time ago. Do you remember him from there?'

'No.'

'Are you sure?'

'I remember he asked if I was one of the girls who fainted in the Credo. Or who fell asleep during the sermon. I think it was that.'

'What did you tell him?'

'I said I sometimes did. He just smiled and said never mind.'

'Anything else, Magda?'

'He told me we should all be obedient and not do bad things.'

'Nothing else?'

'No.'

'And then what happened?'

'The sister came back in. I was sent out.'

'And Father Doran was all right when you left?'

'Yes.'

Joe Murragh stirred. 'Magda, there was a sad thing happened some time ago here in the St Cosmo. It was a priest, Father Kilfoyle. Have you heard anything about that?'

'No, sir.'

'You sure?'

'Yes, sir.'

'Were you working here then?'

'No, sir.'

The two Gardai paused, carefully avoiding exchanging a glance. Sister Stephanie too had caught Magda's error.

'It seems somebody might have accidentally – I do mean accidentally, Magda – have caused Father Kilfoyle to die on account of something going wrong with his breathing tube, or maybe something to do with his medicines. We don't know. Have you heard anything of that?'

'No, sir.'

'Have you heard of anything similar?'

'No, sir.'

'Nothing that might have been a difficulty in what the old people take?'

'The old folk sometimes lose their tablets. And one time a medicine bottle was lost under a bed, and had leaked.'

'Do you remember whose?'

'No. I found it under a lady's bed, but it wasn't hers. It had rolled from someone opposite.'

'Did you not check the label?'

'No, sir.'

'Why not, Magda?'

Here it was, her moment. Magda felt morality, that ineffable thing called goodness, with all its attendant virtues and lovely consequences, was giving her a chance to declare her soul to stand firm on the side of righteousness. But that way had served Lucy nothing but falling every night, time after time, hour after hour. Lucy had to be rescued. That was her promise when she'd done it, and she would stand by Lucy. She prayed a moment to God, looking at her shoes on the Wilton carpet. *Sorry, God, but I have to save Lucy from perdition.* Magda longed to be able to read enough, anything, just to look up words like promise and rescue and saviour, and even perdition.

'Why did you not look at whose name was on the bottle, Magda, when you found it?'

'I found it lost,' she said lamely, trying to postpone the inevitable. The man Garda gave a glance at the woman. Neither spoke.

'But you knew it had to be reported, Magda. Why didn't you simply take it to the person whose name was on it and ask them how it came to be there?'

She took a breath and said softly, 'I haven't the reading, sir.'

'You can't read?' Maria said.

'No.'

Now it would come out, fingerprints and everything. She had disposed of that flat whisky bottle in a waste skip that had been standing at the corner of Ryders Row. She had walked miles to reach some place she was not likely to be seen. Drinkers were about there, she knew. They must have found the glass fragments, though she had heard it smash on rubbish in the skip. She was not tall enough to stand on tiptoe and see inside them old things, but she had cast it well enough and it had gone into smithereens.

'Nor write either?' Joe Murragh was lost. He shrugged at Maria Finty to take over.

'No, sir.'

'Did you know that, Sister Stephanie?' Maria Finty asked directly.

'No.' The nun was almost inaudible.

'Magda, did you tell the sisters that when you came here?'

'No.'

'Why not?'

'Because I might not get the job.'

'Is your sight all right? I mean, can you see everything clearly?'

'Yes.'

'Have you always been able to?'

'Yes.'

'How do you know which inmate is which?'

'I ask them.'

Maria Finty smiled. 'And very sensible too, Magda. Some of us don't have the common sense you do.'

'Did you go to see Father Doran at the hospital, Magda?'

Here it was, the evidence coming up they needed. It had to be the truth.

She vowed to Lucy, *Lucy, I'm so sorry I haven't been able to save you now, or back then, like I should, but I swear on my mother's grave and my father's if I ever learn them and where they lie, that I will rescue you some time, honest to God. Please don't listen now because I have to tell the truth so it won't be the worse for you when I'm put in that old prison and strapped to a chair and shot to death, Amen. Amen.*

'Yes.'

'You did?'

'Yes.'

'Why was that, Magda?'

'I wanted him to get better.'

'Not because you had done anything wrong?'

'No. I wanted to leave a message to him, say we hoped he would get better soon.'

'Magda.' Maria Finty held up a restraining hand when Sister Stephanie wanted to speak. 'How could you leave a message when you couldn't write?'

'I don't know. I asked somebody to write it down for me.'

'And did they?'

'Yes.'

'And did you leave anything else for him? Chocolates? Flowers? Some gift?'

'No.'

'Why not?'

'I haven't the numbers at all. I can't buy things. I only have what's in my purse ever, see. I keep back part of my wage to use, and put the rest into the book they gave me.'

'You have a savings book?'

'Yes. But I can't buy things. They're all numbers, see. I don't know how to pay, if I'll have enough money to pay. If I don't, and I'd have asked for something like flowers, they'd see I hadn't enough money and laugh.'

'I see.'

'That was a very kindly thought, Magda,' Joe Murragh said, 'to visit the hospital. Did you see Father Doran?'

'No.'

'How do you telephone anybody, then?'

'I can't. It's the numbers.'

'I see, Magda.' Maria Finty rose, smiling at Magda and ignoring the nun. 'Thank you. You've been very helpful.'

'That's all. Off you go, miss.'

'Thank you.' Magda stood waiting. Sister Stephanie finally gave a nod. Magda left, closing the door.

Had Kev told them about her visit to the hospital? He had accompanied her there. Or the lady at the desk who wrote her message? Yet why had she been allowed to go and not arrested? It was puzzling. She knew they put a tail on you, to find things out. This was some clever sort of Garda stalking you through the city streets near downtown Manhattan so you would reveal all. Were they going to do that?

She would tell Kev. They were to meet soon, at the corner

of Ha'Penny Bridge, because he wanted to buy some records. He would explain how he had to tell the Gardai that she had visited Father Doran, and say how he asked her to keep a look out for his Grampa on account of somebody stealing medicines to poison people.

Kev would be fair about it, she knew, for he was honest. There was no pride and prejudice about Kev, who was the loveliest man any girl could wish to know. He simply drove a motor bicycle instead of riding a thoroughbred steed, that was the only difference. Freed by them Gardai, she felt on holiday until she remembered their trick of setting a tail to trail you through the gas-lanterny streets of Victorian London to hunt Jack the Ripper. She was glad Mrs O'Hagan would still be there in the sluice and wash room below.

Chapter Twenty-Eight

Kev had his motor bicycle when she got to the corner. She was silent until he took his helmet off and said hello.

She said hello and she had something to tell him, please, if that was all right. He said sure, and they sat on a bench by the edge of the small park. He must have been waiting quite some time, and she worried if he might get in trouble at the Gardai for wasting his hours, but could police suffer in that fashion?

'What is it, Magda?' He laughed. He had a nice laugh, though thinking that was probably a sin, for where did thoughts like that lead?

'The Gardai came today. To the St Cosmo.'

'Did they?' He looked away.

'They wanted to ask me questions.'

'What about?'

She told him, and how she had responded. She did not explain the reasons for some of her answers to Mr Murragh and Miss Finty. He gave curt nods to help her along. She told him they asked about a Father Kilfoyle, and said she told them she hadn't known him or heard anything about the incidents they kept on about.

'I didn't think they would. I wonder who told them.'

'Who told them what? Did they know about you telling me to watch out for Mr Liam MacIlwam?'

'No.' He held her look. 'No, Magda. I said nothing. It's nobody else's business.'

He asked her about this Father Kilfoyle. Magda replied with care.

'He was in the Care Home before I came. He was a priest and passed away when something happened to one of his old tubes, or his medicines. I don't know.'

'Did they say what they were going to do?'

'They made me remember everything I did that day Father Doran took badly. I told them.'

'They'll have been to see Father Doran.'

'Will they?' Magda was shocked. Here it was, the truth coming out and her soon to be taken off in chains. 'Did they tell you so?'

'No.' Kev smiled at her innocence. 'I don't know them, Magda. They're in a different division, department, a whole place away. I've never seen them. I don't want to, either. They just investigate things like, well, sudden deaths or wrong things.'

'Like what?'

'Like that Father Kilfoyle dying sudden, I suppose.'

'Kev.' She felt broken, for it was now the time to confess to him, and to Father Doran. 'I want to telephone Father Doran in the hospital.' She decided this was the only way to make it all right with the priest she'd tried to poison, then she'd tell Kev, and he would drive away and never be seen again. Her message had failed somehow to get her arrested and properly punished, so she'd have to speak up to Father Doran himself.

'What for?'

Definite care needed. 'I did something wrong.'

'Might have, d'you mean? Or might not?'

'Might.' It was as far as she could go for the moment, to him at least. 'Would you help me?'

He stared at her, blank. 'Help?'

'Do the telephone.' She rummaged in her handbag. 'I have money.'

He laughed. 'You can use mine.' He handed her a cell phone no bigger than a box of matches.

She gazed at it in astonishment, having seen these small gadgets but never close to. It was curved at the sides, with buttons sticking out carrying numbers and signs.

'Here. I'll get the hospital for you.'

He stood, stretched and strolled a pace or two while she watched in admiration. How marvellous it must be to be so, what, carefree, casually telling his little phone to get him a number and then tapping it as if in chastisement. He strolled back and handed her the little creature.

'Press that sign there, and you'll reach the hospital.'

'What do I say?' She gaped. It had a screen with numbers in black written all across.

'Tell them who you want to speak to.'

'Then what?' Suddenly it didn't seem a good idea.

'You say, "Please can I speak to Father Doran." Tell them he's in the cardiac unit.'

'Thank you. Now?'

'When you're ready, do it. It'll ring a little, then somebody will answer and you say your piece.'

She waited and he understood he was to move away. He pushed his motor bike a few yards off and sat on it, legs extended and feet crossed. Two women approached with prams, and he moved to let them pass, casually resuming his pose, hands in his pockets. She admired him for thinking nothing of this phoning business, but then he'd been raised in that cavalier household Mr Liam MacIlwam had provided. The dot was surprisingly simple to press. The gadget gave two small thrills then fuzzily spoke in her ear.

'Hello?' she said. 'Can you hear, please?'

Father Doran went through his stack of envelopes. He was able to eat almost normally now, and was up during the day for three spells, walking slowly between physiotherapists. His chest was still sore. Misgivings about the Gardai lingered, with a feeling of foreboding. They contacted him by telephone after their visit, and then another occasion through an intermediary, a uniformed woman with a summary of his remarks to Finty and Murragh. He said, guardedly, that it was a fair approximation and signed her slip of paper.

The nurse had said it might not be long before he could go out to rehabilitation. The bishop himself would be along to see how the hospital was mistreating him, her standard quip. He was sure she enjoyed light-hearted banter, thinking it cheered everybody up. It almost succeeded.

First thing this morning she told him the doctors would assess him the next day, and say when he was to get his skates on.

'You'll leave us in peace, thanks be to God, Father Doran,' she announced. 'Get rid of all the twelve-lead ECG, so you can do it again to all your other arteries and waste our money.'

His remarks were much less jocular, wholly inept, too hearty.

'Be clearing that stack of nonsense, Father.' She indicated the pile of cards and letters. 'You started on them twice. I can see we'll be having to post them after you.'

'I'll do it.'

'See you do. We've enough on our plate without your leavings getting in our way.'

The nurse left him smiling. The staff were marvellous, and there was no residual trace of suspicion once the Gardai left. He was back on course.

He took up the first card. He needed a pencil to open it, with its fancy Euro stamp. He smiled, reading the sentiment. Inevitable that parishioners felt it necessary to be so tortuously formal when addressing a priest. No brief good wishes, except from those with difficulties getting thoughts down.

The next was a small thing written on a piece of hospital notepaper, evidently done at some admissions desk, and was signed Lucy.

He thought, still half-smiling, of the name. It rang a bell. Lucy? He vaguely remembered that name, some...

Memory returned, a wash as if a picture's opaque covering slowly dissolved.

A girl's eyes, glimpsed or possibly not? It had been gloaming somewhere. The girl coughed and coughed. She lay in bed in a long place of beds. During that night, she had died.

The next day, he remembered with sudden clarity, he had definitely been telephoned. Disturbing questions were asked. He was moved, at his own request, and Bishop MacGrath, a man of sound judgement and wholly behind the Church, advised him as a counsellor on readjustment. Changes had become necessary, a switch of duties, for the whilst. It had been beneficial to his career, and would be safer for the Church.

Father Doran felt no guilt. Guilt was something for the confessional, to be told then the sins expiated. He had a vision of faces, the coughing girl's eyes, other eyes moving in darkness, and wondered mildly why this was. Good heavens, he remembered thinking once when he woke up too suddenly, probably from the anaesthetic, his heart banging away like a drum of the Orange Order in July, how strange that these early undeveloped thoughts disconcerted a mind.

A face swam into his mind. He had to think hard, trying to identify the expression, then make an abrupt change so he didn't need to think at all. How disturbing, to reflect on images and sensations that came unbidden and proved so disturbing. He knew that regret could prove a source of dismay, if you let it enter in. But how to control regret for things done?

One of his colleagues at the seminary, now in Rome at the College and doing very well, thank you, progressing up the firm ladder of ecclesiastical promotion, held to the view that it was far easier for a lay person to reach Heaven than a priest. Father Doran tried to follow Edward's logic, stepwise and solid though it was. Definitely provable, yes, but it did not feel right, as if some mathematical proof of a theorem provided the answer so you could see it was correct in every particular, yet you knew by instinct it would not work out in practice. The sheet metal would not fit the designed space, the weight would be short, and the plank's length measure far above the limit you'd wanted to set. Did poets feel this when, their glorious syntax in place and a newly composed sonnet ringing beautifully, the poem's first reading fell flat and holes seemed to appear in the metre and cadence? He imagined a newspaper taking fire in simultaneous patches as it was being read. That felt like his ambition.

He stared at the name. Lucy?

Then he recalled the matter, or something of it.

Lucy. A girl had died. He had celebrated Holy Mass for the repose of Lucy's soul. It had been a Mass for the Dead, before a congregation of nuns and girls. Wordsworth's lines had been said, he remembered, but not at the funeral for the girl. Had he said them alone for her, somewhere in private? He could not quite remember. Were they around still somewhere in his head?

She lived alone, and few would know
When Lucy ceased to be
But now she's in her grave, and oh
The difference to me.

Had he got it right? Lucy was perhaps a mixture of several different people, girls of any age. He could not think. This note was there to be read again. A woman's hand, rounded letters. Or a girl's? But Lucy was dead. He could remember conducting the service, many girls and several nuns forming that congregation. He was absolutely sure. The girl had been spoken of by a number, not name.

Lucy had been Three-Two, only that. No name. He'd learnt her name by asking her in the semi-darkness of that long dormitory.

'Father Doran?'

'Yes, Nurse?'

'There's a call for you. I'll bring in the phone trolley, right?'

He was pleased to be interrupted. Sombre thoughts, and

this seemed to be some ill-remembered gloom from the past that would only prove a source of regret, that terrible indelible traumatic derivative of mind games. Regret was for outside, not inside, hospital. He would deal with it later, if at all.

He smiled as the nurse brought the trolley in and plugged the thing into the wall.

'If it's your bookmaker ringing from Fairyhouse, Father, I'll be the first to tell the bishop what you're up to, unless you give me a share of your winnings.'

'It's a deal.' Another lame rejoinder. The door swished to on its rubberised flaps.

He picked up the handset.

'Hello? This is Father Doran.'

A girl's voice said, muted and diffident, 'Father?'

'Yes? Who is it?'

'I'm sorry, Father.'

'Yes?' He paused, inviting her to go on. Was this a confession over the telephone? It would not be the first he had heard. 'Do you want me to hear your confession?'

'Yes. Sort of.'

'Then please start.'

'Not yet, Father.' The pause lengthened. 'I want to say I'm so sorry.'

'For what? Something you did that was wrong?'

'Yes. For what I did. To you.'

'Did to me?'

'Yes. I thought I'd kill you.'

'You thought...?' Had he heard right?

'Not kill you, just kill you back. For what you did.'

He lay, receiver in his hand, and closed his eyes. 'I don't understand.'

'I decided to kill you.'

'For what I did? Did you say that?'

'Yes. To stop the fall.'

'Fall? What fall?'

He felt sickened. Bile rose in his throat and his chest pained, but nothing like as badly as the first time, more of a warning squeeze, watch out, no more of this or it may lead to trouble.

This conversation would have to be taken in hand immediately, or it would get nowhere, just remain an unpleasant residue that he would have trouble over. This sort of thing, from a defective personality, would become a source of worry night after night, and that would never do. A priest with ambition on his mind had to focus.

'Tell me more plainly what you mean.'

'I decided to kill you. That way I'd stop the falling into the black stairwell every night.'

'Stairwell?'

'It wasn't fair. You had no right to say it would be all right if you did that bad thing. That's why the fall and everything.'

'Because of something I...?'

Wait. He wanted to tell her to wait, there must be some misunderstanding, she had the wrong priest, she could not possibly mean himself.

'Are you sure you've got the right person?'

'Yes. You are Father Doran.'

'Yes.'

'I killt you to stop the falling every night into the stairwell.'

'Who are you?'

A pause. Then, with deliberate care, 'Lucy. You remember Lucy?'

He felt his chest grip, slowly at first then with a seriously steady tightening that caused him to hold his breath, except he had not inhaled and needed the air. The next inhalation proved harder, but he got it going by conscious exertion. The pain stayed, his chest thumping now.

'Lucy?' he asked stupidly.

'Yes. You remember, the night in the dormitory.'

'Lucy?' But Lucy died. She threw herself down the stairwell from her dormitory.

'Yes. I sent a note.'

'I just read it.'

'Well, I'm sorry.'

'Where…?'

He could not speak. Not from dizziness, but shortage of breath. He seemed to have run out, as if a canvas, seeming so wide, and the brush still laden and much more of the painting to convey, had run out of surface. Like a penny rolling across a table and reaching the edge and starting to fall. These were fanciful notions, irrelevant and childish, and would not do. He had to get on with the business of recovery and getting better to perform his duties.

'St Joseph's at Sandyhills.'

'I don't remember, child.'

'The Magdalenes. You remember.'

The name came at him like a physical blow and he gave a quiet grunt of distress.

'I forgive you, Father,' the girl said. 'I wanted to say it to you because it wasn't your fault. It was all my fault. I should not have behaved like I did. I was told to be on watch by Sister Natalia. I didn't obey properly.'

'What are you trying to tell me?'

'I have to confess everything now.'

'Wait.'

He did not know why he was asking the girl to wait, or if she imagined he was someone else.

'No, Father. I have to tell the Gardai everything.'

'No.' He strove to speak, articulating slowly. 'What are you trying to tell me, child?'

'I must confess to Mr Murragh and Miss Finty.'

'No. Please.'

'I should have stopped you and I didn't.'

'I remember now,' he said, not needing any breath for this. He had never forgotten. Lucy was there within him, and always had been. She would stay for ever now, in clear thought.

The receiver fell from his hand on the bed. He did not hear the girl say, 'Hello? Hello?'

The world slewed. He felt himself on some kind of vehicle starting to slide on black ice in the darkness lit by distant glims, some dots of light in chains and some in patches, one or two in flashes. The vehicle took hold of the surface, held firm a moment then started to glide, carouseling on.

'Lucy,' he said.

Lucy had been found dead in bed. This had been told to him the next day. A girl had been discovered dead in bed. She had suffered a long illness, tuberculosis. The night before, he had taken her in the dormitory where she was resting that final night. It was the preliminary to her death, her last night.

Hard to recall at this distance – what had it been now, four years, maybe five? – the words he had said, persuading her not to cry out or shriek for help. Some girl had been lying in the truckle bed opposite. He had seen her in the gloaming.

The stairs were steep, far too steep for a cohort of children, he had thought. He had reached the top floor where Lucy lay, given her the last sacrament that afternoon, and been struck by the extraordinary pallor of her skin. Her features were less stencilled and merged into one lovely form, with those luminous eyes so huge and profound with their awareness of the meaning of suffering. In that instant, giving the last anointing, desire had begun. His hunger to associate himself with that radiance, that profundity of understanding that was in the girl, almost blinded him all the rest of that day. She dazzled. He had to see her again. To unite, even, with that comprehension was surely what God had intended for all mystics to accept, acknowledge and somehow know. So must Blake have sensed his tragical visions. So must great artists discover when, released by their art from morality and its shackles, they soared into the bliss of an ecstasy unknown on earth to themselves and to anyone who was not God.

That instant of revelation became his. He knew it gave him an entitlement to use the girl, to return to the dormitory where she lay, and to have her, join in the most perfect union God designed for mankind. It would be the girl's own release too, for she would confer that brilliance, and by her acceptance lift him to paradisical understanding of the nature of all religion. It would be perfection given by Lucy, to him alone, and he would see glory in its splendour.

She would benefit by being his saviour, for he would always be denied the experience until she offered herself willingly and openly to him.

He would prove it to her. When she heard his explanation she would realise his desperation and pacify him with visions of Heaven.

Across the dark dormitory, he had once glanced around as if sensing someone watching. He had glimpsed twin points of light, or thought he had. They had instantly dowsed. He had gone on. And that next morning she was found dead, from her TB disease, in bed. By then he had gone, to return later to conduct her funeral service.

There was no question about it. He had been truly and deeply affected, and his eyes had become moist, to the nuns' evident satisfaction. They had said nothing specific about the sorrowful events. After all, a girl who had lived in a chronic state of poor health since being a child was going to succumb sooner or later. The local doctor had predicted her death, expected on every grounds. The funeral had all gone off quite as it should. Tragic, of course, but the girl had died after a long and steady decline in her condition despite all that the nuns could do. And there was no more caring body of sisters in Christ. They must have struggled to make the girl well, given her special treatment as good as they could afford.

Only later, maybe one or two years later, had he heard of some rumours originating in a case at Sandyhills. At the time, he had been puzzled as to how something so remote in the past had surfaced. He remembered speculating that maybe some disaffected girl – wasn't there always one? – perhaps motivating herself by imagined wrong, exercised her liberty after leaving the Magdalenes by writing, probably, malicious letters of accusation against the nuns who had cared for her and brought her up and given her a decent education and background in the Faith. The malicious libel was of a girl who had been sexually abused by a visiting priest. She was dying of the White Spit, and immediately after the abuse had killed herself by throwing herself down a stairwell. Desperate to conceal such an event, the nuns had returned the dead girl to her bed, where she was discovered when nuns, dutiful as always, came to check on her, and found her dead. They removed her body to the Sandyhills chapel before the girls awoke to begin the day.

Inevitably, the Church acted to show quite clearly how groundless such falsehoods always were. The Church, always oppressed, always came through by the grace of Almighty God. 'When wicked men blaspheme Thee, we love and bless Thy Name,' the good old hymn sang. How true that was.

Some time after hearing about it, in a kindly well-intended telephone call from a monsignor in the local diocesan office, Father Doran now remembered how he was quite fairly called to a discussion – certainly no investigation or interrogation – with two prelates, on the first occasion. Later, after another month of deliberation in the higher levels of the office of Bishop MacGrath, a second appraising discussion took place. No opprobrium attached itself to his name, and he continued on in the Church, after a move to different localities.

One question remained, and burnt in his throat with the bile taste that wouldn't go. Who was this Lucy? For a girl had died. He had said Mass. She had the same voice he could clearly call to mind, as clearly as if she had…as if she had offered him a tea tray at the St Cosmo Care Home, when he had tea with Sister Stephanie.

And who had been there, evidently waiting, when he had left old Mr Gorragher after they shared an illicit tipple.

And who immediately started clearing up the alcove of the ward where Mr Gorragher's bed was positioned.

And who doubtless could have changed the content of the whisky.

And who had given him that half-caught glance as she served that tray at tea-time.

And who had...

And...whose face he'd seen in the gloaming of the dormitory as he had taken the dying girl in Sandyhills.

And whose face, those same features, he had seen at holy communion when serving her with the Host weeks ago. Whose eyes had flicked open and stared into him, instead of modestly remaining closed, as he had blessed her with *Corpus Domine Nostre Jesu*...

And who was out there making malicious telephone calls, pretending she was Lucy who'd somehow survived that terrible fall.

And who must have seen Lucy tumble to her death in a suicidal act.

And who would now allege he had driven Lucy to suicide.

Who clearly would not give up in her poisonous campaign of vengeance.

Who had told him frankly that she would not give up. That she was going to confess everything in a deposition to the Gardai, leading to his prosecution.

The pain was hard now, firm and unyielding. It was nothing quite like as bad or as evil as the first time, or as disorientating, but it would not leave. Like the memories of the blessed Lucy, or the presence of the hateful pretending one.

Her revelations, in the confession she was on her way to make, would damage the Church. It would spell his own ruin, as it had spelt the ruin of so many priests and nuns before him. As it had led to the bankruptcy of mighty dioceses in the USA and elsewhere. As it had besmirched the holy name of the Church in Australia, in Canada, throughout Eire and elsewhere. Wasn't there even that scandalous series of accusations in Scotland, even? Could the Church take any more?

It called for sacrifice, of the sort martyrs made.

He felt the gripping chest pain turn slowly to a stifling ache, and knew that God was making him an offer. It was an option, to endure, survive and brave the accusations out, when clearly the onslaught would simply go on and on with blame hounding him and the whole Church establishment. He felt aggrieved. The whole thing was unjust, an insult to a man who had dedicated his whole life to the Church. It was so unfair.

Or he could proceed to a quiet act that would leave his place in the Church unsullied.

He lay back, knowing what had to be done.

Chapter Twenty-Nine

That night, Magda dreamt a dream. It was how she murdered her friend Lucy. All she had said and done on the night Lucy began falling lived through her mind exactly as it was.

Truly beautiful, but gorgeous in the evil way you saw in some paintings, with eyes looking and faces that shouldn't have the right to even seem like real faces changed into something that might not be a face at all. She had heard the word 'features' several times. It was one of those words you longed to look into books to find out about, and eliminate problems like, when was a feature them Rocky Mountains in New York, wherever those things might be, and not a feature in some story like in *Star Wars*, or features of a baby you had to smile and say *Awww* at?

She was back in the dormitory in Sandyhills.

Lucy had coughed bad all that day, and been sent to lie in bed with nobody to see to her because she was shrinking all over her face, her body, and coughed blood and was damp of hair and hot.

The other eleven – was it eleven? Some number anyway that sounded like a cerise colour; Magda had lately grown to like numbers because of the colours they imparted, like seven was always a dark umber; eight was, of course, yellow; thirteen, a terrible magenta. No number existed that ever shaded or faded at the edges, no. They were complete and total, all the way across. Well, the other maybe eleven girls in the dormitory were sent somewhere else. That night, the Dormitory Sister, a stout nun called Sister Natalia who wheezed and was said to eat non-stop, a feat the girls in St Joseph's Sandyhills envied, made all eleven move into another dormitory where there had once been a fire and, rumour said, several girls died worse even than Cavan. But none of the girls in Sandyhills knew Cavan, so the rumour stayed where it was.

'You will remain in your bed,' Sister Natalia said sternly, smacking Magda's face with flips of her backhand. That was what she did, backhand your face between things she told you. 'What?'

'I will stay in my bed, Sister Natalia.'

'And pray if anything happens to Lucy in the night.' Flip, flip.

'And pray, Sister Natalia.'

'Lucy is very sick.' Flip, flip.

'Lucy is very sick, Sister Natalia.'

'And Jesus may take her into His bosom.' Flip, flip.

'And Jesus may take her into His bosom, Sister Natalia.'

'If she calls out, you give her a drink of water.' Flip, flip.

'I must give her a drink of water, Sister Natalia.'

'Now resume your duties.' Flip, and a serious smack that almost knocked Magda over.

She straightened, thanked Sister Natalia, the necessary phrase to obtain clearance to leave, and fled.

That night it happened, exactly as it had ever since. Magda found herself watching, hearing, every event in sequence, leading to the terrible final separation when Lucy and she went apart in that slow fall in the gloaming of the stairwell, and Magda knew herself to be a murderess and Lucy the resigned victim of a murder.

They went to bed after praying, Lucy coughing terrible and the pillow covered with a plastic bag that Magda had managed to get over it to save it from getting all bloody when Lucy coughed. They said the words in English because neither had the Latin off.

It was a very special prayer this time, though it was commonly said by everyone at Sandyhills after the supper at five-thirty. This night, when Magda would murder Lucy, the prayer really did seem holy, not just things coughed up as Lucy said all the prayers in Sandyhills were, just pushed out like old spit or grolly. Kneeling at Lucy's bedside, Magda wondered if prayers were any different if they were said elsewhere, like in them big churches that were supposed to be everywhere in Eire because St Patrick made sure of it. She supposed not, because otherwise Lucy, who knew almost everything, would have told her.

'Deliver us, Lord, while we wake, and guard us while we sleep, that we may watch with Christ, and rest in peace.

Amen.'

They both dutifully said *Ayyyy*-men, as good Roman Catholics should, not the less abrupt *Ahhhh*-men of Protestants, who would go to Hell, serve them right.

'Do you want a drink of water, Lucy?' Magda asked.

'No, ta.'

'You sure?'

'Yes. It'll only set me choking.'

'You might feel better.'

Magda desperately wanted Lucy to say yes she'd have a drink of water because then nobody could flip her face, which still stung where Sister Natalia had flipped her when repeating her instructions about watching over Lucy as she died in the night. But if Lucy wouldn't have a drink of water what could she do? There was a tin mug just for the purpose on the floor by Lucy's truckle bed. Magda put water in it, making sure.

'Goodnight, Magda.'

'Night, Lucy.'

'Magda? I might die tonight.'

'No, you won't, Lucy.' Magda was frightened Lucy would die because she might get blamed for letting her, and then what?

'I will. I know I will.'

'Don't say things like that, Lucy. I'll bring you some water.' Magda meant if she took Lucy the water and she drank it, she might not have to die.

'I know I will. I can feel it sort of coming in my chest.'

Magda was drawn to the notion of her one friend feeling something coming so serious and ending everything for her on earth.

'What's it like, Lucy?'

'It's just there. You know it's going to happen.'

Magda began to weep. 'Don't Lucy, please. You'll get better.'

'I'll be better in Heaven. I'll pray for you when I get there, Magda.'

'Lucy, maybe they'll discover something, like some special tablet that will stop the coughing and then you'll be grown up and get out of Sandyhills in the nick of time.'

Magda was a right one for phrases like 'nick of time' and 'with one bound' and 'spur of the moment'. Not having the letters had somehow made her able to remember every passing phrase, whatever it was supposed to mean.

'I'll see inside Heaven, Magda.'

'I'll stop it happening, Lucy. I'll pray all night to stop it.'

'No. You'll go to sleep.'

'I won't.'

'You will.' So resigned, and Magda knew it was true because everybody was always so tired that they slept the instant they were told to. 'Magda?'

'What?'

'I'm sorry I tellt you off so much.'

'You didn't. You never tellt me off, Lucy.'

'I did.'

'No, Lucy, you didn't, honest.'

'Well, I'm sorry if I did.'

'No, you put me straight. I wouldn't know what to do without you.'

'You're my friend, Magda.'

'You're my friend, Lucy.'

The only one I'll ever have, Magda realised in a sudden flash, and she wept some more. She held Lucy's hand. It looked so pale, even in the dark dormitory, as if it had a colour she could see when all was almost darkness. She could make out Lucy's eyes as dots of shinyness there within a yard of her own. This was how they knew sometimes each other was awake in the night, those shiny dots reflecting some minute fragment of light when it was all supposed to be black.

'Goodnight, Magda.'

'Goodnight, Lucy.'

Magda had a perverse wish to ask Lucy to give her a special mention to Jesus up there in the sky, but thought it would be presumption, and that was a sin, wanting to feather your own nest. Lucy had enough to do tonight getting on with her terrible illness, without worrying about how she'd beg Jesus, Oh, there's a friend, would you like look after her until she gets died too and comes up here? No, that would be really awful.

She went to her own cot. It was a few feet away across the other side of the dormitory. The windows were all blacked out because of people maybe wanting to look in, though there was nowhere for anybody to even stand and peer, the dormitory being so high on floors above the main places in Sandyhills.

She had been asleep, with no notion of how long she had slept since saying goodnight, when she woke. She thought instantly of water, and almost sat up to ask if Lucy wanted a drink.

There was somebody opposite. For a moment Magda thought it was a nun, maybe Sister Natalia seeing if Magda was making sure Lucy had some water to drink. Then she heard the bed creak. She heard a whispering voice, and knew it was Father Doran.

She heard him say there was something Lucy could do, make her life a true realisation in the very Name of God and His only Son. Magda knew he had been there some time. The voice whispered on, kept saying how Lucy would not be any the worse for conceding, that good had to come from everyone's life somehow. It was that final goodness that enabled a soul to leave earth and arrive pure and unsullied at the Gates of Heaven.

The voice was insistent. Magda had no idea how long it kept up its whispering. She saw the priest move, just one set of shadows shifting and merging and then moving some more and the truckle bed squeaking as if it was enjoying itself and the bed starting to creak with a regularity she thought strange, so strange, like some jumping exercises the nuns made the girls do in the yard when they had to sing some kind of song about counting. Magda only ever chanted numbers she knew nothing about and could not write on paper, just seeing colours flit by through her mind as she jumped and tried to keep time and failed and the other girls said she was rubbish and never picked her for their teams.

The sound went on and on and during it, she almost went across and asked if they both wanted a drink of water. It came to her that, if she tapped Father Doran on the shoulder while he was doing whatever she could then ask him if he too wanted a drink of water, though she only had Lucy's tin mug to bring it in. Then Father Doran would be proof to Sister Natalia that Magda, the vigilant girl left to look after Lucy in the night, had faithfully done her dutiful obedient service, and Magda would not get whacked in the morning.

She was looking, doing all this wondering about mugs of water, when she saw Lucy's dots of illumination reflecting back that fragment of light at her, and she knew Lucy was awake and looking across in the darkness and knew Magda was awake too and watching during the night for her. And Magda saw Lucy's dots of eyes become blurred, and knew Lucy was crying.

And new sounds began then with a kind of grunting and then a choking sound and then it reached a spurt of sound and Magda covered her ears because it frightened her. Was this dying, was this what it was? She wanted to go over and ask if everything was all right but could not. And she saw both Lucy's eye dots vanish and knew the priest was turning round.

Maybe Magda had inadvertently made some sound that gave her awakened state away. But he was turning to look across at Magda's bed and she closed her eyes in case she too made bright points of light for him to notice.

The sounds resumed and kept on and on and on.

And he gave Lucy a blessing and told her she had done a great and good thing, endured in the cause of the Lord and would be holy now and it would not matter at all, in any way, because she had served God in a way He would know was just, because God had made the world to be as it was. Lucy would find favour with God in Heaven.

He left quietly. Magda had not heard him enter the dormitory. Had she slept, not even bothered to watch an hour with Lucy like St Peter before that sword business?

She waited enough time until she was sure Sister Natalia wasn't going to come shuffling along in her night slippers, or Father Doran come back to do it again. Then she went across to Lucy.

'Lucy?'

'Yes.'

'Are you all right?'

'Magda?'

'What?'

They whispered and held hands. Lucy's looked paler than death. It seemed to have become much smaller since they had said goodnight, and damp with sweat.

'Would you help me?'

'Help you?' Magda said she would and eagerly relinquished Lucy's hand to rush and get her the mug of water, but Lucy grabbed feebly in the air and Magda felt her hand meet hers again.

'Would you shove me?'

'Shove you?'

Magda was lost. So many things seemed to be happening. Did everybody else in the whole world know what dying was except Magda herself? She felt so inadequate. This was what came of not being able to read or write. Maybe once she got the letters in her mind, if that ever happened, she would know everything just like the others.

'You saw, Magda.'

'Yes.' Magda didn't know what she had seen, if she had seen anything.

'Father Doran. He did it to me.'

'Did what?' For one moment she thought of Extreme Unction, that last sacrament, anointing with oils and prayers that made you sacred. Lucy already had had that, in the afternoon.

'I'll have a baby now.'

'A baby? You can't.'

'I will. It'll come.'

'A baby?' Magda felt dizzy. Was that what it was, all that creaking and groaning and gasping and then that sound of a flailing body? 'Who?'

'Me. He did it. Now I'll really go to Hell. I'll be pregnant and cast out into outer darkness for ever.'

Lucy started coughing and Magda whimpered about water some more and this time Lucy, to Magda's gratitude, said she'd have a swig, and Magda tried to sit her up enough to take a swallow from the tin mug Magda had put ready under the truckle. She managed it and Magda breathed prayers of thanks to any saint who might be listening out in the mad night.

Not coughing, Lucy sank back on the bed. The plastic made a crackling sound. Magda remembered it having made the same sound but repeated over and faster and faster as the shadow of Father Doran had merged with Lucy's and eclipsed the dots of Lucy's eyes.

'You'll have to help me, Magda.'

'What do you want me to do?'

'Can you get me to the stairs?'

'What for?'

'I'll show you.'

'You want to go to the lav?'

'No. That's all over.'

All over? The phrase sounded terrible. Lavs were like the weather, always there.

'How?'

'Any way you can, Magda.'

'What if they catch us?'

'It won't matter, Magda. I need you to do this.'

'The stairs?'

'Yes.'

'What for?'

Magda could never make up her mind about anything, just usually did what everybody else told her. Now she was half-standing, thinking how to get Lucy up. You had to be strong to lift somebody, and Lucy had been too weak to walk herself these two days because of her coughing and the blood from it on her mouth and chin.

'Get me up, Magda. Please.'

Magda managed to sit Lucy up. They waited a few moments, Lucy sitting with her legs over the side of the truckle bed just about touching the floor. The pity was there were no lights.

Lights only came on in the morning. No lights upstairs except for some small red thing at one end to show where the door to the lavs was.

'What do I have to do?'

'Get me to the stairs.'

'How?'

'I'll try to walk.'

'What if you start coughing? They'll hear.'

'I'll stuff something in my mouth.'

'It might stop you breathing.'

'It won't matter.'

'Won't it?'

'No. If I start coughing, Magda, you stuff something in my mouth.'

'*Me*? I can't do that.'

'I'll have a good cough before we start off, then I'll get there without doing it.'

Magda knew it wouldn't work because sometimes Lucy had been punished by nuns for coughing and had tried, really tried, so much it broke your heart just seeing her struggling not to cough and failing so she got punished anyway. Lucy coughed, dark patches staining her front and mouth and all down from her chin. Lucy whispered it wouldn't matter when Magda, obsessed with water tonight after how Sister Natalia had warned her, kept on about bringing some water to try to wash it clean.

Lifting Lucy upright was the hard part, because strangely, once she was standing, a mere bag of bones in the gloaming, it became almost easy to move her forward pace by single pace, Magda clutching Lucy to keep her straight up. Standing seemed suddenly good against the cough returning, and they shuffled towards the red dot of the pilot light. As they went, Lucy started to whisper what she wanted Magda to do.

'Shhh,' Magda kept saying, hardly listening, anxious only not to make a noise so the nuns wouldn't come and beat them both.

'It's important, Magda.'

'What is? Shhh.'

'If I jumped and died from it, that would be a sin,' Lucy said.

It was spoken in gasps, one word then a pause then another word then a long pause and the rasping breath as of a door creaking open slowly. Magda felt her friend's chest barely moving, just a skeleton hardly covered at all.

'But if I didn't do it myself, I would go to Heaven, see?'

'Yes,' Magda said, desperate now because they'd reached and were about to pass the red pilot light on the wall by the door showing the way to the lavs at the end of the dormitory.

'Then it will be all right.'

'What will? Shhh.'

'Everything.'

'Shhh.'

The top of the stairs began outside the main dormitory door. The nearby lavs always smelt cold, as if wafting cool air onto the landing. No carpet, nothing to stop you slipping, so it was difficult to get Lucy leaning against the bannister without sliding and falling. The nuns slept further along the corridor, where two other dormitories lay.

They were here now.

'What, Lucy?'

'Magda.' Lucy had her mouth close to Magda's ear, no sound escaping as she whispered, 'Promise you'll do what I ask. It's all right, I promise.'

'Yes, Lucy.'

'Promise? The holiest promise you have.'

'I promise.'

'Promise. On your mother and father.'

Magda had no mother and father, except some nebulous shapes out there who had long since gone never to return. 'I have none.'

'You must have.'

'Must I?'

'Yes. They're somewhere. And you must honour your mother and father.'

'Go on, then. On my mother and father. I promise.'

Magda had never said that before and it felt truly weird. For the first time she wondered if there were such people, perhaps real and talking to each other and maybe with a family by the fireside.

'Really promise?'

'Promise, yes, Lucy.'

'Get me on the bannister.'

'On? But you might fall, Lucy.'

And how to lift her friend to the wooden railing? If you slid down it your bottom would hurt, and if you fell it could be terrible. And the nuns would hear, and that would be the end of everything.

'It's all right. Don't worry, Magda.'

'I can't, Lucy.'

'You promised.'

That was the most truly horrid accusation, to renege on a promise. Magda struggled to lift Lucy up. Lucy started coughing a bit and that set somebody else in the dormitories further along coughing too for a moment. They froze until it subsided then resumed the lifting. Lucy got one leg across the bannister and Magda, holding her friend round the chest to steady her on the rail, managed to raise the other leg over so both Lucy's legs dangled over the void.

'Lucy,' Magda said, now almost paralysed with fear, 'I think we should go back now.'

Lucy had her cardigan on. This was forbidden in bed, but maybe Lucy thought it would not matter any more. Magda remembered Lucy told her she had once had a visit from somebody who was a relative of hers, from before she came into the Magdalenes, and that cardigan was her one special thing. It was mended all over the place, but Lucy tried to do bargains with other girls for extra special bits of cotton or wool even and used them to keep it mended. It was her true special thing. That Lucy had it on now was more of a warning than anything Magda had ever felt, including threats from the nuns.

'Magda?'

'What?' Magda whispered.

'Say a prayer.'

They whispered the goodnight prayer just as they had when about to go to sleep that night.

'Can we go back now, Lucy?'

'Magda. You promised, remember?'

'Yes.'

'When I tell you, push me.'

Magda realised then. Holding her friend upright, balanced on the bannister rail in the dark, she knew what was in Lucy's mind, and it was the most terrible thing she had ever heard.

'Push you? But you'll fall, Lucy.'

'I know.'

'How will you...'

How will you get back so we can both be safe in bed, without any of the nuns hearing and coming up to punish us for doing this bad thing? How can you not go to Hell, for committing suicide? How can...?

'You've got to, Magda. You're my friend.'

And then Lucy coughed, so long and gravelly Magda was afraid she'd waken the dead.

'Shhh, Lucy. They'll hear us.'

'You promised, Magda. It'll save me.'

'Save you?'

'Please, Magda.' And in the faint shaded darkness Magda saw her friend's face turn towards her, those glints of dots that were Lucy's eyes. In them was emotion, a begging for help. 'You promised me, Magda. You're my only friend. You've got to.'

'I can't.'

Magda struggled to keep her there, though Lucy was not trying to jump or do anything at all, just there freezing cold yet damp with sweat, sitting on the wooden rail with her legs hanging over the huge drop into the stairwell. Even if Magda let go, Lucy would stay there and not move, not even fall off. She'd just be found still sitting there the next morning and they'd come and punish her, and Magda too for not having taken her a drink of water and kept her in bed so she could stay there and...and become pregnant and get...what? Get a baby who would be in the Magdalenes to get its little self punished for being a bastard too and them other things. Whatever Lucy told them, and whatever Magda corroborated, they would say Lucy egged Father Doran on because they always warned all the girls that bad things were always looking out for girls, and this must be one of them.

'Magda. I'm dying anyway. You'll see.'

'I'll see what?' Magda whispered, so afraid now she was weeping worse than ever. Strangely, Lucy was dry of eye, exhausted and drooping.

'You can't leave me here like this. I'm dying.'

'I can't.'

'Magda.' Lucy spoke in a strangely powerful, assured voice. 'You promised. You know what we say about promises.'

'No.' Because Magda didn't. If she had known, she had forgotten.

'So you must. Just give me a push when I say. I'm praying now.'

'I can't, Lucy.'

'Please, Magda. I'm praying a minute.'

'Then what have I to do?'

'Then you go back to bed and pretend that nothing's happened.'

'Must I?'

'Yes. Thank you, Magda. You were always my very best friend. I shall tell God that, and ask him to lay off you.'

'Will you?'

'I promise.'

'Can I say it with you?'

'Yes. It'll be our prayer.'

Together, in a whisper, they said,

Deliver us, Lord, while we wake, and guard us while we sleep,
that we may watch with Christ, and rest in peace,
    Amen. Amen. Amen.

'There,' Lucy said, and Magda ever after knew she saw her friend smile, just as though it was bright sunshine and not night, as she closed her eyes and turned to look away.

'When, Lucy?'

'Goodnight, Magda.'

'Goodnight, Lucy.'

A pause, then, 'Now, please.'

Magda pushed.

She saw the material of the jumper, as clear as if it were day, recede. The gloaming seemed almost lit from Lucy falling. Magda stared aghast, saw her friend turn and her arms come from her sides as if to prevent a further fall, but Magda knew that wasn't her intention. It wasn't a wave either. They had done with that.

The twin points of light showed in the dark of the stairwell, then came a thump and simultaneously the two dots vanished. Magda shook, standing there, unable to think. Lucy's instruction came back to her because that too was part of the promise. She stole silently back to bed, hoping the tin mug of water wasn't spilt by Lucy's truckle so that Sister Natalia would know it wasn't for lack of a drink of water that Lucy had wandered off on her own and fallen accidentally.

The appalling sin of murder came to her, and Magda knew herself for a murderess. Murder someone, you went to Hell and got hanged or shot in the prison where they killed people on chairs or made them stand upright. She lay down, her heart banging away like an old drum waiting for morning to come and herself be dragged off screaming by the Gardai.

But that didn't happen. She was wakened by somebody tiptoeing into the dormitory and then somebody carrying something heavy, several pairs of feet treading as softly as it was possible for people to tread, and a lot of whispering in the dark. And then she knew somebody was carrying Lucy's body, several nuns perhaps, back to her truckle bed, and then leaving.

But one nun stayed there, breathing so softly it was as if she was in hiding from Magda, who was supposed to be asleep in her own truckle across from Lucy.

She knew they had come carrying Lucy back to bed. But why were they not helping her, calling the ambulance, taking her to hospital so she'd be mended and got better from her coughing and whatever hurt her when she fell?

And Magda, for the first time in her mind only, but for the second time in reality, saw Lucy, her dearest and best and only friend, turning over in the darkness of the stairwell as she'd fallen. And Magda knew it was the Pit of Despond and that Lucy was in Heaven, or maybe not? And Magda saw herself as a murderess, never more to see her dear friend, not even in Heaven when she too died.

She would have to go to confession and say what happened, and confess her terrible sin.

And in the morning, when the darkened-out windows began to look ash grey, the whispering nuns came and silently carried Lucy away.

Sad, that was the last Magda saw of anything, for the truckle bed and everything was gone next day, and she woke up and was talked to by Sister Natalia, and then by two other sisters and then Sister Natalia again, and that was the end of Lucy at Sandyhills, and the start of Lucy falling every night, and Magda knowing she had done wrong killing her friend by pushing her from the bannister of the top floor so she flew down the stairwell to her death.

Magda was to blame. She knew it. She should have watched over her friend, like St Peter should have watched over Jesus in the Garden of somewhere Magda could never pronounce, and that was the way life would be for ever and ever, without any sleep, in case, when she tried to sleep her friend Lucy fell again, and kept on falling again and again. To protect Lucy, Magda would never sleep.

And Magda woke up in the morning having slept, at first ashamed, then frightened by what she'd done, so she had betrayed Lucy even more than three times. She was worse, and more guilty, than anyone ever.

Chapter Thirty

Magda knew what she must do now. There could be no going back.

If she only knew how to telephone, she would be able to call the St Cosmo Care Home for the Elderly and explain the reason she was unable to come to work today. She could imagine how they would all go on, especially in the sluice and the kitchens, saying, 'Goodness. Who would even think that a simple girl like Magda, such a holy name, called after such holiness, to go and try to poison a priest to death?'

And one or two might say, 'Well, she wouldn't have even tried that on unless there was some sort of reason.'

Or, 'Once a bad lot, always a bad lot. It's always taught in the Magdalenes, that if you're spawned in sin you'll be forever in sin.'

Then the conclusion of them all, sighing together, 'That's true, sure to God.'

She caught the bus into the centre of Dublin. She had bought the usual day ticket, travel anywhere you could with that, all over the DART they said, if you'd all day to go nowhere in. She only had the vaguest notion of where Kev worked, but had heard his family mention some place he had to get to every day. That must be where he did his garaging. He mended motor cars and noisy power bicycles for the Gardai so they could go crazy all over County Dublin like madmen, reckless as they always were. Kev had told her about one special motorbike he admired, talking of it like it was a hero. She'd pretended to agree with him, not knowing a thing he was telling her. Or was there a separate place they mended bicycles? She had no idea if Kev could drive a car.

Getting arrested for confessing this was the right thing. She had promised Father Doran she would confess all, so she must. A promise is a promise. Lucy had told her that, so she had to.

Somehow, it was degrading to be arrested by Gardai who were not Kev. Also – think of it this way – there was a plus. Kev might get promotion for capturing a dangerous killer, and she would have done some good. She felt a faint glow of pride at this last achievement. He might get made sergeant, or was he already that? And while those two in plain clothes who questioned her in the St Cosmo hadn't been bad or cross or anything, really quite pleasant if you took away what they were asking about and why they were there, she was not beholden to them the way she was to Kev. He had invited her into his family, where at one go she was made a visitor and an ally, and shown her how holy and pleasant a family truly could be. Without that glimpse, she would never have known.

All right, she was a little taken aback by the light-hearted manner in which they had joked with their father and pulled his leg over his old toys, but he had seemed to be glad of it. And he had criticised his wife for her cooking, saying visitors starved to death waiting for her to get serving a meal up and hardly anything on the table when she finally got round to it.

And Kev's mother had taken a mock swipe at her husband, calling him an idle good-for-nothing when he said that. But it all seemed so casual, and nobody was angry and it was lovely.

So she would get Kev his promotion, by confessing all to him, and that would be excellent. She would help them Gardai all she could, and be as frank as could be. She would have thought words like, 'make a clean breast of things', but that sounded a little obscene, too blunt anyway.

She asked somebody in the Busaras how to get to the garage place, proudly giving the name of the Gardai garage. She was pointed to a bus. She caught it and asked the driver to tell her when she got there.

This will be my last bus ride, she thought, remembering a fillum about coloured people in the United States of America, who got on a bus they weren't allowed to. And there was such a fuss. People took sides about whether it should be all right or not. Well, she was like that. It was in colour, not black and white like most of the all-nighters. How strange, she thought, that she had not made Lucy suffer during the night again – first time ever – for Lucy had not fallen once even, and Magda had roused with her eyes not grainy, her head clear as a bell.

She had had a good bath this morning, first thing, and had as much food as she could take in without making herself sick, for she knew they starved prisoners in gaol before shooting them, on chairs or standing didn't matter much. And she had her clean knickers on underneath, with her shoes polished and her teeth done. If she'd had the sense, and the knowledge, she'd have gone to that hairdresser saloon where Kev's family said, and made herself look really smart for her arrest, but would that be pride? She had no way of judging, because she had never been arrested and imprisoned before.

The street was called. The driver indicated the garage. It wasn't just a small place, like a small brick shed. It wasn't even like a place where motors went to get petrol. It was more a yard, with buildings. She thought, goodness me, and approached the uniformed man on the gate and asked for Kev.

'I have an important message for Mr Kevin MacIlwam,' she had ready, standing ready, purse in hand.

'Is it a complaint?'

'No. Just a message.'

'Nothing serious that could be handled by somebody else?'

'No.'

She wondered why the man seemed suspicious. Did her guilt show on her face? She supposed it must, to the trained eye.

'What is the nature of your message?' Yet more suspicion.

'I work at the St Cosmo Care Home for the Elderly. Kev's grandfather is one of the inmates.'

She spoke quite proudly, a venial sin but all right, she could work those off in Purgatory with a decent penance after confession. This was, after all, important business for Kev's family.

'Oh, nothing serious, I hope?' His brow cleared.

'It is important.'

'Right.'

He went inside his hut and spoke briefly on a telephone. Magda saw Kev emerging from a long narrow building across the opposite side of the wide yard. He came walking over. She felt so proud. It should be a black-and-whiter, of herself about to get shot and her friend – you couldn't say boyfriend because that meant all sorts of prideful implications, and she would never reach there anyway – and it would make everybody cry real tears when they saw it.

She wanted to go forward and meet him like on the pictures

but the gate guard said no and pointed to a bench a few paces off. That was a pity because it was much prettier the way she had imagined on the road in, but if they were the rules she didn't want anybody getting into trouble just because it would be better on TV.

Kev came up to her, concerned.

'Magda? Is it Grampa?'

'Nothing like that, Kev. I came to confess.'

'Confess?'

He came with her and they sat on the bench facing the road.

She got herself ready, and said, 'I poisoned Father Doran. It was me stealing the medicines, those tablets.'

'You, Magda?'

'Yes. I gave it to him in the poteen stuff, that whisky Mr Gorragher gives him.'

She told how she had hovered, making sure the old inmate didn't drink from the bottle she had poisoned. She explained about the tablets.

'I don't know how many tablets I put in, not having the counting.' It seemed vital to say this and make sure he understood, because it was evidence and lawyers were always trying to trick material witnesses.

'If Mr Gorragher tried to drink first, I'd have come in fast and taken it off him and say to him I'd tell Sister Francesca, and I'd have taken it away.'

'Magda. Are you sure of this?'

She was puzzled by his doubt. 'I could prove it, but I washed the bottle clean. I smashed it in a skip the other side of the Liffey. I did it in the night so nobody could say they'd seen me.'

'Magda. You know what I have to do now, don't you?'

'Yes, Kev.' She tried to look noble, as befitted somebody on the pictures. She wanted to behave her best for him. 'What do I have to do?'

'I must report this. You see that?'

'Yes. I knew you would.'

'Will you come and stay in the gate hut while I telephone, please, Magda?'

'Yes.'

She wished she'd been able to get a new coat, but had put on what best she had. Maybe, she suddenly thought with a pang of regret, she actually did have enough to buy something nice to look smart for her arrest, in her old savings book the bank gave her. It was too late now, and anyway, how could she have asked over the counter at the bank after a new coat?

The gate keeper gave her a chair and Kev spoke to him beyond Magda's hearing. He returned and kept glancing at Magda as she waited but she didn't cry. She wasn't going to gaol with her eyes all red and face all blotched. Kev would be ashamed enough, somebody he knew getting herself arrested for poisoning a priest.

Some time later, after watching cars entering and leaving and Gardai coming through and getting bits of paper signed by the gate man with much consulting of watches and checking duty rosters, she was called in by Kev. He accompanied her to a separate building that looked more of a set of offices than anything belonging to a garage.

In the interview room Maria Finty and Joe Murragh rose to greet her. They did not seem particularly angry, just puzzled. They checked her name, agreed she was Magda whom they had interviewed before. Kev was asked to stay.

They had a desk and pens and paper and everything, with a kind of radio playing silently to itself. Magda noticed the occasional movement of numbers, and a red light shining.

'Could you repeat what you said, Magda?'

She explained that she had tried to kill Father Doran. That's what had put him in the hospital.

'Father Doran died last night, Magda,' Maria Finty said.

'That can't be,' Magda said firmly. 'He's in hospital.'

'When did you see him last?'

'In the Care Home.'

She explained that she had gone to leave a message to wish him well the day of his operation. She looked at Kev, and he said immediately that he had gone with her there.

'Magda looks out for my grandfather, Grampa MacIlwam. He is an inmate at the St Cosmo. That's how Magda and I became acquainted. I was visiting Grampa.'

'You haven't visited Father Doran since?'

'No.'

'Magda, this may be a shock to you. But Father Doran really did die last night.'

'He seems to have taken his own life.' Joe Murragh looked his apologies at Kev. 'At least, that's how it appears. He seems to have taken an overdose of something. How he actually got hold of the drugs is still unclear.'

'He can't have,' Magda said. It was going all wrong.

'Magda, we've just come from there.'

'He distracted the nurse somehow, then misappropriated drugs from the schedule drugs store. The hospital authorities will make a statement later today.'

'I'm sorry, sir. I did it. Not Father Doran.'

'Magda telephoned Father Doran last evening. I was meeting her,' Kev said slowly, looking directly at Magda.

'You telephoned Father Doran?' Murragh asked Magda.

'Yes, sir.'

'Why?' Maria Finty asked.

'To say I was so sorry he was ill, and it was my fault.'

'Anything else?'

'I heard Magda speak to Father Doran,' Kev put in. 'I did the dialing, and it was my mobile phone she used. It can be checked with the hospital switch.'

'I see,' Murragh said, remembering. 'You'd need help with it, somebody to dial the numbers?'

Magda made to speak, but Kev interrupted a second time and said more or less the same thing. Magda thought, does Kev not want me to say anything else about what I told Father Doran? She kept quiet, but as long as they all knew she was confessing, that was the main thing.

'Was that it? You didn't go to the hospital?'

'No. I just went home. I was late. Then I got ready to come in here and confess.'

'Can I explain to the officers, Magda?'

'Explain what?' She saw Kev's determination so she said yes, not knowing what was to come.

'Magda hasn't the letters yet. She is going to learn writing and reading, but she doesn't quite know enough so far as to be able to use a telephone or shop or buy things or count. It will come, because I am going to arrange for her to be taught. I'm going to ask one of my sisters to show her.'

Joe Murragh left the room a few moments. He returned, and spoke to Maria Finty before saying, 'Magda. You were right. You did not attend the hospital yesterday. Father Doran definitely did take his own life. Probably while the balance of his mind was disturbed. He might have become delirious, from his operation, stress, or anything. There will be an inquest, I suppose, but that's as far as we can go at the moment.'

The officers left with Kev, and she heard them speaking in low voices in the corridor but could not get their meaning.

Kev came back alone and took her hand.

'Come on, Magda. There is nothing more to be done. They will take your statement down from the recording device, but that's it. It is as they said, about Father Doran.'

'Am I not to go to prison?'

'No. They say there's no need for that. It looks like the priest was under serious stress from something in the past. They don't know what. That's an end to it, I think.'

'Are they sure?'

'Yes. Absolutely sure. They said so.'

'I don't understand,' she said, but then she never did.

'It's all in hand, Magda.'

They walked to the gate. She was so sure of what she'd done, and knew it was wrong.

'They said things had gone on. The priest did it to himself. They know it was so in the hospital.'

'But I started him off doing it.'

'They don't see how you can be certain. You couldn't work out the dose or anything.'

'I gave him what I had. In the poteen.'

'How can you prove it? How can the Gardai?'

'I don't know.'

'The tablets could have been any old thing, Magda.'

She was worried now that her confession somehow didn't seem to count. She told him so. And now she would be told off for taking time off and not turning up at work when she was supposed to.

'Look, Magda.' He faced her at the bus stop. 'Wait until it's my dinner hour. I'll get permission in the circumstances to come with you to church. You can call there and ask for a Mass to be said for Father Doran.'

'I don't know how much it will cost.'

'I'll come with you. It can be your first lesson in counting. I'll work the money out with you and show you. Like I told the Gardai detectives.'

'That was a lie, Kev. Saying you were teaching me.'

'No. It's true. Your lessons start now.'

'Is it true?' She was getting a headache from not knowing where she was with any old thing.

'First of many, Magda. I'll be about forty minutes. See the clock at the gate?'

'Yes.'

'When the long stick gets to the top, I'll be able to come with you. We'll pay for the Mass, then you can go on to work and tell them you're late because you called to arrange a Mass for Father Doran. OK?'

'Yes. Will it be true?'

'Don't be so worried. From now on, you must learn some things are almost true, and other things so near as makes no difference.'

'Is that my first lesson?' she asked seriously.

'Yes. Magda. The first of many.'

'I'll wait then.'

Wondering which of his sisters would teach her the letters she lacked, she sat down to watch the long stick on the clock slowly start to climb round to point to the top when Kev would come for her.

Author's Note

The brutality towards children in industrial schools, orphanages, convents and reform establishments are well documented. Such abuse shames civilisation. That it was condoned by governments and authoritative bodies is as great a crime.

Those who have relatives who suffered so will need no further study. Others may consult an introduction to the subject, e.g.: *Suffer the Little Children* Rafferty, M, & O'Sullivan, E (1999) Continuum, USA.

Jonathan Gash